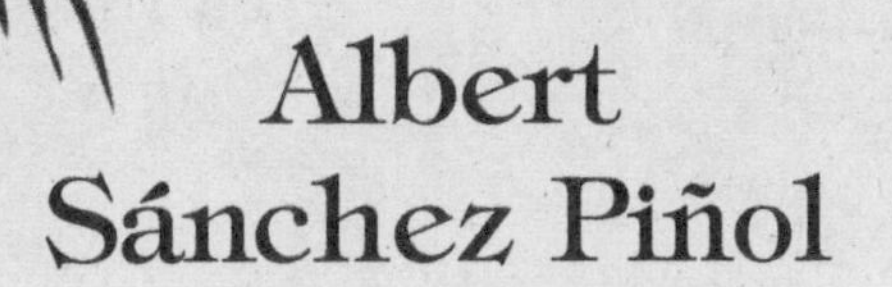

Albert Sánchez Piñol

Pandora in the Congo

Translated from the Catalan by
Mara Faye Lethem

CANONGATE
Edinburgh · London · New York · Melbourne

This paperback edition first published in 2009 by Canongate Books

First published in Great Britain in 2008 by
Canongate Books Ltd, 14 High Street,
Edinburgh EH1 1TE

Originally published in Spain in 2005 as *Pandora al Congo* by
Edicions La Campana, Barcelona

3

This work has been published with a subsidy from the Directorate-General
of Books, Archives and Libraries of the Spanish Ministry of Culture

British Library Cataloguing-in-Publication Data
A catalogue record for this book is available on
request from the British Library

ISBN 978 1 84767 124 0

Typeset in Baskerville MT
by Palimpsest Book Production Ltd, Grangemouth, Stirlingshire
Printed and bound in Great Britain by Clays Ltd, Elcograf S.p.A.

canongate.co.uk

ALBERT SÁNCHEZ PIÑOL was born in Barcelona in 1965 and is an anthropologist and writer. *Cold Skin*, his first novel, won the Ojo Critico de Narrativa prize on its original publication in Catalan in 2003. *Pandora in the Congo* is his second book. Together with *Cold Skin* it will form part of a trilogy.

FURTHER PRAISE FOR *PANDORA IN THE CONGO*

'To a bouillabaisse of H Rider Haggard Piñol adds a dash of Dave Eggers . . . Readers leave this book dizzy, unsure whether this was a tale of Empire's sins or a cunning commentary on authorial deceit. A literary dynamite charge, it's raucous and leaves everything shaken up.'
INDEPENDENT ON SUNDAY

'Here's a wonderful oddity – an adventure yarn that could stand alongside the works of Edgar Rice Burroughs.'
THE TIMES

PRAISE FOR *COLD SKIN*

'Superbly controlled and creepy, akin to *Lord of the Flies* or *Heart of Darkness*.'
INDEPENDENT ON SUNDAY

'Thrillingly vivid . . . It overtook my dreams.'
TOBY LITT

'A philosophical tale wrapped in a gripping plot, a meditation on solitude, violence and what it means to be human, a great, creepy, tender read.'
YANN MARTEL

Also by Albert Sánchez Piñol

Cold Skin

The Congo. Just imagine a surface as large as England, France and Spain put together. Now imagine that entire surface covered with trees between twenty and two hundred feet high. And below the trees, nothing.

ONE

THIS STORY BEGAN WITH three funerals and ended with one broken heart. The summer of 1914 I was nineteen years old and half asthmatic, half pacifist and half writer. Half asthmatic: I coughed half as much as the sick and twice as much as the healthy. Half pacifist: because really I was too soft to be politically active in opposition to wars, I was just against participating in them myself. Half writer: the word 'writer' is too pretentious, and even when I say 'half writer', I'm exaggerating. I wrote books on assignment. Which is to say, I was a ghost writer, what the publishing world calls someone that writes books with other people's names on the cover.

Who remembers Doctor Luther Flag anymore? No one. And he's better off forgotten. But before the Great War he enjoyed a certain popularity. He was one of those pulp writers. All of Doctor Flag's stories –I never knew if he really was a doctor – were set in Africa and were exactly eighty pages long.

There was always the same photo of Doctor Flag on the back cover: a man with a thick mop of white hair and a rectangular beard, whom life had led in a straight line along the path to wisdom. He leaned his body on a table where a large map of the black continent was spread. He pointed to some undiscovered spot with his finger; with the other hand he held a monocle in front of his right eye. His gaze implied all mysteries.

There are few places that offer such a wide window of narrative elements as Black Africa. The Masai, the Zulu, the Boer rebels. The savannah, the jungle. Elephants, crocodiles, hippos and lions, explorers and hunters. All that stuff. With so many suggestive ingredients and a lively imagination it was relatively easy to write a handful of facile stories. But Doctor Flag had become the most prolific author in the English language. He'd been publishing three novels a week for twenty years. And each one had its requisite eighty pages, which meant that every seven days he wrote two hundred and forty pages, an average, if my arithmetic is correct, of 34.2 pages daily. And nobody can write 34.2 pages each day for twenty years in a row. Nobody.

In that period I met a man named Frank Strub. Strub was a ghost writer for Doctor Luther Flag. It was he who offered me the job. Since Doctor Flag paid him by the page, he was interested in writing as many pages as possible a day. Strub was married with three children, and three children are a big incentive to work extra hours. But everything has its limit. After a while working for Doctor Flag, Strub was on the verge of a nervous breakdown.

Even though we hadn't known each other long, Strub was one of those men that are easy to get close to. One day he invited me to lunch in a cheap restaurant in north London filled with noise and blue-collar workers. There were so many people that we held the silverware with our arms glued to our necks, like the wings of hens in a coop. Noise reverberated through the restaurant and, even though we were right in front of each other, we had to shout like town criers to make ourselves understood.

'Look, Tommy,' said Strub after dessert, 'if I keep this up they'll have to put me away in a sanatorium. But old Flag demands a certain number of pages a week. If I don't produce, he'll fire me. That's his strategy. He exploits a ghost writer until he's worn out and then just finds another one. I can't lose the work, Tommy, I've got three children.'

'Oh, Frank,' I said supportively, 'that's terrible.'

'I thought that you could help me. I'll pay you a little bit less than he pays me. I'll make a small commission for the pages you write, it's true, but take into account that I have three children. What's more, you're very young and you have no writing experience. I'm taking a risk.'

I hesitated a bit. He wanted to wrap it up quickly. 'Don't worry, you just have to follow old Flag's outlines. And remember: eighty pages, not one more or less. It's a requirement for the printer. You want your first outline?' he asked me with a wink. 'Course you do, you're dying to write it. Well, here you go.'

And he handed me a couple of typed pages. He was still wiping his lips with the napkin when he stood up. 'Waiter! This boy will get the bill.' And turning towards me, 'You don't mind, do you Tommy? Look at it this way, I've got you a good job. More than a job: a chance to enter Parnassus. Must dash. I haven't finished my pages for today.'

'When do I need to have it written by?' I asked.

Strub laughed. 'When? Yesterday. Get busy.'

Once I got home I read the pages. It looked like Flag was in a rush even writing the outlines. They were a few pages typed quickly and carelessly. The outline was entitled *Pandora in the Congo*. It was my first contact with the literary industry. I guess that's why I kept it. Here it is.

PANDORA IN THE CONGO

CHAPTER 1

– Create a portrait of a Young Anglican Pastor.

– Protagonist is called to accompany some Father Superiors who are returning to their African mission.

(Remember that the protagonist ALWAYS has to be YOUNG and ATTRACTIVE, and in order to describe YOUTH and BEAUTY we need ADJECTIVES. You are completely ignorant of the art of using adjectives, I know. But I'm beginning to think that your extraordinarily limited intelligence is not even familiar with the concepts of YOUTH and BEAUTY.)

SUBTOTAL chapter 1: 5 pages

CHAPTER 2

– Spiritual battle at the Mission, Protagonist notices that his Faith wavers once he is in Africa due to his contact with the wretchedness of paganism. And the black continent can easily turn into a Pandora's Box, from which, once opened, spring forth monsters and ghosts. (Do you understand the title now??)

– Protagonist goes deeper into the Jungle to reflect. A Lion wants to Devour him. Protagonist Tames Lion, whom he Baptises as SIMBA.

– Protagonist and SIMBA (remember, the tamed Lion) continue heading into the forest. They get lost. They discover a Roman Castrum!!!

(Note: 'Castrum' is a Roman military camp. It's not that I doubt your level of general cultural knowledge. I've defined 'castrum' because I doubt your ability to find any word with more than one syllable in the dictionary.)

– The jungle castrum is inhabited by the remains of a Roman legion lost in the first century BEFORE Christ while searching for the source of the Nile. The colony has decreased in number and now there are only two left, two very blond, very military, archetypal legionnaires.

(Obviously we have NO plausible explanation that would justify Roman legionnaires being able to genetically perpetuate themselves in the middle of a forest without the help of any female womb. This is the type of narrative incident where there is no other option except to resort to the SPORE THEORY.)

– The two Roman legionnaires are engaged in a continual ongoing war with the surrounding pygmy tribes, who are extremely bellicose cannibals and tree-dwelling head shrinkers.

SUBTOTAL chapter 2: 25 pages

CHAPTER 3

– Protagonist is unsure if he should spread GOD'S GOOD NEWS to the two legionnaires (they don't know about it because their ancestors left the Roman empire in the first century BEFORE Christ, remember). Since he's unsure if he's lost his faith, he feels it would be a contradiction to evangelise the legionnaires.

(Do you get this spiritual subtlety??????? I hope so.)

SUBTOTAL chapter 3: 5 pages

CHAPTER 4

– Large battle between a horde of cannibal pygmies that attack the castrum and the Roman legionnaires that defend it. Protagonist is an active participant in the defence, as is Simba.
– Protagonist does a scientific experiment with two pygmies captured in the battle. He cuts open their skulls and vivisects them in public, showing that they are NOT human, as opposed to the legionnaires who, as I've already said, are blond and speak Latin.
– I forgot to mention before that the two legionnaires had

given refuge to a Bantu princess who was very pretty but Negro and had also ended up lost at the castrum. The two brothers love her very much, but since they are very chaste they have NEVER touched her. (STRESS THIS.) Our hero also falls in love with her. Important inner battle between lustful cravings and the desire for sainthood.

SUBTOTAL chapter 4: 15 pages

CHAPTER 5

– There is a new attack by the pygmies, this time *en masse*. Millions of pygmies storm the Castrum and the two legionnaires end up dead, although they put up a heroic fight. The pygmies don't kill the protagonist, obviously, because that would end the novel. They merely capture him. Simba is wounded in one paw. Faced with this catastrophe, the Protagonist insists that the lion escape, which loyal Simba resists, refusing to abandon his master. Still, eventually Simba obeys and heads further into the jungle. Before returning to their arboreal city the Pygmies spend the night at the castrum. The Protagonist and the Princess are tied to parallel stakes. The Princess confesses to our man that she is hopelessly in love with him!!!! But the fact that he is tied up keeps our man from succumbing to the passions of the flesh. (If we set up the scene in this skilful way we can avoid having sinful scenes in the story, which are always uncomfortable. Behold my narrative skill! That, sir, has a name that you are unfamiliar with in any of its variants: T-A-L-E-N-T.)

– The pygmies take the Protagonist back with them as a trophy. The Bantu princess stays at the castrum with a small group of pygmy soldiers charged with negotiating her sale to some merchants of Arab slaves. Once the Protagonist gets to the pygmies' arboreal city a big party begins. (They live in cabins built between the tree branches; make them like monkeys with a certain degree of manual dexterity.) Horrific nocturnal scene. The pygmies prepare the cauldron where they will boil the Protagonist. The pygmies drink blood out of the skulls of the legionnaires killed in combat. Orgy: millions of pygmies dancing and fornicating everywhere like a cloud of mosquitoes. (Orgy, indeed, but play down the erotic descriptions. Who knows what to expect from a degenerate like you.)

SUBTOTAL chapter 5: 10 pages

CHAPTER 6

– In the morning the pygmies plan to cook and eat our man. The Protagonist warns them that if they try it 'the Sun will disappear.' (Of course, it's an eclipse predicted by the astronomical calendar.) The horror of the pygmies when the sun is covered. Simba, who has faithfully come looking for his master even though he is wounded, attacks the pygmies ferociously and this adds confusion!
– Protagonist and Simba flee.

SUBTOTAL chapter 6: 15 pages

CHAPTER 7

– Protagonist and Simba annihilate, with humiliating case, the few pygmies that had stayed at the Roman Castrum guarding the prisoner. Spectacular climactic emancipation of the Princess.
– These events have made the Protagonist recover his faith in God. Grave disappointment on the part of the Princess when the Protagonist rejects her offer of marriage. (Give some satisfactory reason, whatever you want, but they DO NOT get married. Nigger girls do not marry British men. And failed love stories sell more books, DON'T EVER FORGET IT.) Bantu princess, Simba and Protagonist return to England. He also brings with him a particularly small pygmy, by which I mean a pygmy with dwarfism, as a scientific specimen.
– Bantu princess is very happy in the convent. Lion Simba is very happy in the zoo. Dwarf pygmy is very happy in the zoo. Protagonist visits them periodically and maintains a friendship with all three that is beyond description.

The Protagonist recalls this whole adventure many, many years later, when he has already become the Archbishop of Canterbury and is very highly respected in the religious world.

SUBTOTAL chapter 7: 5 pages
TOTAL BOOK: 80 pages

THE END OF PANDORA IN THE CONGO

DON'T STRAY FROM THE OUTLINE!
DON'T SCRIMP ON THE ADJECTIVES!
DON'T FORGET THE DEADLINES!

When I remember the days that followed I can't believe my own naïveté. I was very young. And the idea of being published filled me with awe. The fact that my name wouldn't appear on the books, the fact that they were paperbacks, none of that mattered much. If Doctor Flag didn't like the book, it would be Frank Strub and his three children that paid the price. And I didn't want my literary flights of fancy to harm a poor family.

In terms of the plot, I offer no comment. *Pandora in the Congo* was Doctor Flag's typical rubbish. But, as I said, bad or good, we are talking about my first book, and I was prepared to toil away at it. I wanted to do my research conscientiously and I had locked myself away in a public library. After three days of study I had arrived at few conclusions, but they were irrefutable ones:

1. the pygmies were not cannibals;
2. there are no lions in the jungle;
3. what in the hell was the Spore Theory?

In the name of fiction, and with some very flexible literary licence, I could allow the protagonist to tame a lion. Or have an entire Roman legion get lost below the Nile. As far as the pygmies go, I had never questioned that they belonged to the human race. The worst of it was that all the ethnographic evidence agreed they were the most affable and anarchistic society in the world. How could they create an empire? So, Flag's pygmies didn't exist. And without hordes of man-eating pygmies there was no book. But I didn't dare alter an outline by *the* Doctor Luther Flag. So that very same evening I went to visit Frank to explain the problem to him.

It was very late and I already regretted having rung the bell when he opened the door. Frank received me in a vest and long johns, that ridiculous underwear we all wore before the Great War. At first he smiled. But when he found out why I was there his face changed. 'I thought you were coming to give me the novel, finished and polished!' he said from the doorway.

'But there are no lions in the jungle, Frank . . .' I said hesitantly.

'Lions? What lions? Of course there are lions in the jungle! If Doctor Flag says there are lions in the jungle, then there are! And that's it! If a Roman legion can't find its way back, why can't a fucking lion get lost? Or do lions carry compasses?'

'But Frank, pygmies aren't cannibals . . .'

'Who the hell cares if pygmies aren't cannibals!' he cut me off. 'Have you lost your mind, Tommy? You want Flag to string me up? He could take me to court. He could accuse me of anything, if he put his mind to it. Even plagiarism.'

Behind one of the house's windows a light went on. Frank saw it and got even more worked up, 'Now look what you've made me do! The children are awake. Do you want them to have to sleep under a bridge? Is that what you want, Tommy? You want to destroy an entire family?'

'No, Frank, of course not . . .'

'Then go home and write the damn novel! Three days more, Tommy, three days and I want it here, typed and in triplicate. And now get out of here! And use new ribbons or the carbon paper won't make the third copy dark enough.'

Before closing the door he lowered his voice. But even now, more than sixty years later, I can still hear what he said: 'Who do you think you are, Tommy? A scientist? A philosopher? You're a writer now, Tommy, a bloody writer.'

What did I do? I went home and I wrote *Pandora in the Congo* in three days and two nights. Strub hadn't even given me the chance to ask him what the Spore Theory was.

In the beginning I said this story began with three burials, and the deaths are still nowhere to be seen. But that's because this story still hasn't begun. I just explained all that to put my job in its proper place. In other words: if anyone thought that working as a ghost writer had its charm, I hope I have burst that bubble.

After *Pandora in the Congo* there were many similar little novels. They were all as abominable as that one, some more so. I know, it's hard to believe, but yes, there were worse.

The structure was always the same. Deliriously patriotic: the British explorers were glorious; the French, pedantic; the Italians, mannered; the Portuguese, primitive. Biblically militaristic: the vast majority of the protagonists were either missionaries or soldiers, sometimes both at once: army chaplains. And with a level of racism that was reactionary even for its time. All the African characters fitted into one of two categories: noble savages or savage cannibals. The former could aspire to becoming submissive servants, with an intelligence that never went beyond that of an eight-year-old. And as for the others, let's just say I'd rather forget about them.

In terms of my income, I had no complaints. It's true that Frank paid me little, very little. Old Flag shamelessly exploited Frank. And since I was the ghost writer of a ghost writer, I had to accept double exploitation. I didn't argue about Frank taking a part of my hypothetical profits. Otherwise, what would be the point of him hiring me? And besides, I could understand his situation as the father of a large family.

But one day Frank didn't show up for our meeting. We usually got together in a small pub where we exchanged material. I would hand in the novella I had written and he would give me the outline for the next one. It was in both of our best interests to be punctual, so after waiting forty-five minutes I was feeling perplexed. Only a situation of *force majeure* could explain Frank's absence. I thought he must have been ill, or one of his children must have had the chickenpox, or all three of his children at once, so I decided to go to his house.

The woman who opened the door was Negro. I was surprised that Frank was married to a Negro woman. In 1914 mixed-race couples were very rare, but then I thought maybe his fondness for Africa had come from his marriage. The woman was a bundle of nerves, and all she said was, 'You're a friend of Frank's? Please, come in!'

She led me to the bedroom as quickly as she could and pointed to the bed.

The reason why Frank hadn't showed up definitely fell under *force majeure*: he was dead. He had one eye open and the other closed, as if he were winking at eternity. As I said before, Frank wasn't in my circle of close friends, but everyone gets emotional in the face of something like that.

'Oh, Mrs Strub! I'm so sorry!' I exclaimed, and I hugged her like a sister. 'If there's anything I can do to help you or your three children, don't hesitate to ask for anything, anything, really. Poor Frank! The poor bastard!'

But the woman frowned, and I suddenly realised that my words had struck the wrong chord.

'What children?' the Negro woman asked me. 'As far as I know, Frank doesn't have any children. He's single.' And right away she corrected herself, 'He was single.'

I didn't get it at all. I took a step back.

'Single? Then who am I talking to?'

'We had an agreement. On Thursday nights we slept together. Today I woke up and he was dead.' She said all that while avoiding my eyes. Then all of a sudden her tone became more lively. 'I think I've seen you before. Aren't you the young man who knocked on the door one evening? I saw you through the window.'

At that point Luther Flag's literary production was written almost entirely by me. I had perfected the system and I was able to write three novellas a week. In fact, I often started them even before I got the outlines. All Frank did was correct the punctuation (I've never been good with full stops and commas, much less with semicolons), fix those paragraphs where the characters weren't patriotic enough, and censure those where the Negroes were too intelligent.

Disoriented, I sat in a chair with my hat in my hands. I looked at the bed and I thought about a lot of things, or perhaps about nothing at all. I don't remember anymore.

'What a great writer the world is losing!' said the woman, now more contrite.

'Yes, a great writer . . .' I said with a hollow voice.

'Do you know Doctor Flag?' she asked me, more cheerfully. She had a rather fickle personality.

'Yes, I've heard of him,' I said, barely listening to her.

'Do you want to know something? It would appear that

Doctor Flag doesn't write his own books!' She laughed, even more gleefully.

'Really?'

'Yes, and do you know the funniest part?'

'Let me guess. That Frank wrote Doctor Flag's novels?'

'No! That's funny, but just a little bit. The best part is that Doctor Flag thinks that Mr Spencer writes them!'

I flinched. 'And who is Mr Spencer?'

'The man who gives Frank the outlines. Mr Spencer was Doctor Flag's ghost writer until one day he suggested to Frank that he write them, the novels. Ever since then, all Spencer did was pass Doctor Flag's outlines to poor Frank.'

She became melancholy once again. 'Poor Frank. Anyone can write an outline. What really counts is writing the novel, don't you think?' And more indignantly, 'That Spencer had some cheek! I always said that to him, to poor Frank . . .'

I asked her to give me this Spencer's address. I put on my hat; she saw that I was leaving and pointed to the bed.

'And what do I do with Frank now? You said you would help me, didn't you?'

But I was thinking about all the commissions that Frank Strub had pocketed at my expense, when all he was doing was acting as the intermediary between me and this man Spencer, and I said, 'I think, miss, that I've already helped enough.'

The woman held me for a moment by the elbow. Perhaps she had worked out who I was and what I was doing there. In the tone of someone confirming a suspicion she said, 'You're a writer, aren't you?'

I don't know why, but I felt like a criminal caught red-handed.

'Yes, and you, miss, are a prostitute,' I said.

The two accusations balanced each other out and I headed off. To Mr Spencer's house. I was sure that this Spencer would be the first one interested in replacing Frank Strub. Really, when you took a good look at it, all we had to do was make our already existing relationship official. I was expecting, naturally, that once freed from the surcharge added by Strub's mediation, my profits would increase.

There was nobody in. A neighbour leaning on the iron railing separating the two small gardens in front of the houses saw me. He pointed at me with his finger and said, 'Are you here to offer your condolences to the Spencer family? You'd better hurry up! The funeral procession left for the cemetery ten minutes ago.'

Spencer was dead too! The neighbour told me the details: that morning he had been run over by a tram. Its wheels had split his body into two halves, like a motorised guillotine.

What could I do? I went to the cemetery; I had nothing to lose. I was hoping to find someone there who knew about Spencer's business, so I could explain who I was and they would recommend me to Flag. The truth is I wasn't at all sure what I was going there to do. But I went anyway.

I had no trouble locating Spencer's funeral. Among the tombstones that stuck out of the grass, I saw a ring of people congregated around a pastor who read from the Bible and mentioned the deceased. A fat man, with red cheeks and a short neck, was standing amongst the last row of attendees. He was so short that in order to see anything he had to hop up every once in a while, lifting himself above the heads of the mourners in front of him. I approached him.

'What a shame, what a stupid accident,' I whispered as a conversation starter. 'Death always takes the good ones.'

'Spencer? One of the good ones? Spencer was a right bastard. I'm here to collect a debt.'

I was surprised when he started laughing softly. 'They say the embalmers had a lot of problems.'

'Problems?'

'Well, Spencer wasn't the only one killed by the tram. The wheels cut two men in half at the waist, Spencer and some other bloke. Since they had very similar trousers on, now they don't know if they're burying him with his own legs or the other bloke's.'

He had to cover his mouth with his hand to hold back his laughter. I thought aloud, 'What a coincidence . . .'

'Not really. You could say it was an on-the-job accident. Spencer was a writer, and the other man was giving him the instructions to write one of his books.'

'The literary outline?'

'Hmm, yes, whatever it's called. Outline, instructions, guide, who cares? They were distracted for a minute and wham! Well, damn it, that's life.'

'And how do you know all this?'

'Because he told me himself. I lent him some money, on the condition that he return it the next month with interest, when he had been paid for the three books he was writing. Imagine that! He was writing three books at once! But in order to write them he needed an instruction manual.'

'And how do you know so many details about the accident?'

'Because I was there. I had been following him around for weeks trying to collect the debt, I knew everything about his life. Spencer and the other man said goodbye after having exchanged the usual papers. I saw how the tram cut them into two pieces. Four pieces, to be precise.' He wrinkled his brow. 'But I have a debt to collect and as God is my witness I am going to collect it . . .'

I had a revelation. I squeezed the fat man's sleeve so hard that he looked at me as if he was afraid I was going to hurt him.

'Who was the other man who died?' I exclaimed. 'Doctor Flag?'

'Doctor Luther Flag! Please! Obviously not!' said the man. 'Doctor Flag is a great writer. For the love of God! I don't know what the hell Spencer wrote, but if he could write as well as Doctor Flag, he wouldn't be in debt.' He came a bit closer to me, 'Do you know Doctor Flag's work?'

I looked at the clouds and thought out loud, 'So, if the other dead man wasn't Flag, who was he?'

'I have the complete collection of Doctor Flag's work. Everything except for one from April 1899, which has sold out. You wouldn't happen to have it, would you? I'm willing to pay a reasonable price.' And he began, 'A Spanish regiment from Cuba is sent after a boat filled with mutinous slaves. The Negroes have seized the ship and they go back to Africa. But the Spanish regiment perseveres, following them deep into the jungle. There there's a great pitched battle between the tribe of Africans and the Spanish regiment.'

I came to the only possible conclusion: that Spencer was nothing more than another Frank Strub. Spencer just got the outlines, which he quickly turned over to Frank, and then Frank to me. So, above Spencer there was yet another man. A man who got the outlines directly from Flag. And that man was also dead. Beneath the wheels of the same tram as Spencer.

'In the midst of the battle, an English missionary arrives, who tells both sides that Cuba has been freed by the Americans and that slavery has been abolished. The battle is absurd!'

The man was becoming tedious. I couldn't think with all his talk.

'But what regiment are you talking about?' I growled. 'Where does this war between African tribes and Cuban Spaniards come from?'

'It's the plot of the book I'm missing. Do you remember it? If you remember it, it's because you've read it, and if you've read it, you might still have it at home. I'm open to offers. Ten shillings? I'm willing to negotiate.'

There was nothing more I could do there. I left with my head bowed, ruminating. I felt like I had been defeated, even though I didn't really know by whom.

I was just about out of the cemetery when I ran into another burial. Funerals are all alike. A circle of weeping people; a pastor that laments the death and praises the defunct. I didn't want to stop, but I heard the words 'tram' and 'accident'.

It was obviously the other victim. The third and last individual who came between Flag and me. And among those attending the ceremony, in the first row, was a man whose hair was whiter than snow.

In the photograph on the back covers one couldn't make out the red nose furrowed with very, very thin purple veins. Or that he limped with his right foot. But it was him. It was Doctor Luther Flag, indubitably. He had gone to the burial of his ghost writer. The overseer of his ghost writers, to be more precise.

Suddenly I remembered the outlines, or should I say the extra commentary. I have to say that the notes in *Pandora in the Congo* were extremely kind compared to the ones in other outlines. In some outlines he had gone so far as to describe his ghost writer as a literary leper, or an illiterate gypsy, or accuse him of adjectival genocide. I also thought that, even though he didn't know it, the ghost writer to whom he had directed his contempt on the recent outlines was none other than me. I didn't know Flag personally yet, but I was pretty damn sure he would not be going down in history as the Abraham Lincoln of the literary slaves.

I waited for the ceremony to end before approaching him. When the people were already scattered I moved towards him. He was looking at me suspiciously from the very start. I offered him my hand. His rested on a cane with a white knob. He had no intention of shaking my hand. He looked at it, assessing the possibility that I would infect him with some contagious skin disease. All his suspicions were hidden behind a sweet voice that spoke as if we were far away from each other.

'Have I had the honour of meeting you, young man?'

'Indirectly, sir,' I said cheerfully, 'I'm the ghost writer of the ghost writer of the ghost writer of your ghost writer.'

It was a big mistake. Flag didn't realise we had common interests, that I was only offering myself to replace those fallen in combat. There were still other people around. Flag must have thought that perhaps they had heard me and my words brought his honour into question. Or perhaps he was irascible by nature. Or perhaps he wasn't even aware of the whole delegated industry his books had generated, the last link of which was my humble self. But he half-opened his mouth, indecisively. Beneath the man's chin extended a generous double one that inflated like that of a pelican gulping down a tuna. His cheeks turned the colour of a pumpkin, and his nose got even redder. And when his entire face was boiling like a laboratory tube, when the effervescence of colours made me scared his skull would explode, just then he spat out, 'I don't know you, nor do I have the slightest interest in knowing you! And if I were twenty years younger, I would challenge you to a duel!'

He raised his mahogany cane but before it hit me, I grabbed the end. Old Flag momentarily forgot about the noble cause of murdering me. Now we fought for control of the cane, each of us pulling on one end. We looked like two children playing tug-of-war.

'Let go of my cane!' he said. 'Let it go!'

'But you attacked me!' I wanted to calm him down.

'Get out of here! You are an Arab extortionist! A Pharisee! A wingless beetle! Let go of my cane!'

What a pathetic scene. But those insults broke the dam of my tolerance. I was an architect with a chimneysweep's salary. And Flag was to blame for my indigence. He hid behind a name earned by the sweat of countless ghost writers, all as anonymous and poorly paid as I had been. And that apostle of sewer literature was spewing more insults at me than even the wise men of Zion had had to put up with. I retaliated with an even stronger tug.

'And you are an old drunkard, a miserable usurer, a Pharonic impostor!'

'How dare you slander me!' he replied, pulling even harder. 'My work has inspired twenty-five graduating classes of British officers!'

'Maybe that's why the Zulus massacred the English army at Isaldwana! And the Sudanese at Khartoum! And the Boers in South Africa! Now I understand all our disasters abroad!'

'Let go of my cane! It was a personal gift from the Emperor of Munhumutapa! Get out of here, you opportunistic mercenary!'

'Opportunistic mercenary? Me? You are an ambassador of literary bad taste! And a word pimp! Take your bastard cane! You can keep it!'

All I did was open my hands. But because of all the accumulated force, Flag fell on his arse and rolled around on the ground. He looked like a turtle on its back. Hearing our skirmish, the funeral goers, who were already scattered, had gathered to watch us up close. A fan tried to lift him up by the elbow, a woman knelt down and dried his forehead with a handkerchief. Everyone there, it goes without saying, was on Flag's side.

The crowd shouted at me as if I were a criminal stepping up to the gallows. I felt completely out of sorts. I was very young, and youth is when one is most susceptible to discrimination. But what could I do? Everyone hated me and nothing I said would improve matters. I felt my cheeks burning hot, my ears must have been red as peppers. I smoothed my trousers with my hands with as much dignity as I could, picked up my hat, and took my leave.

Sixty years later it makes me want to laugh: Flag, the cemetery, the *opera buffa* it all turned into. And yet, then, as I crossed the cemetery grounds, I didn't find it amusing in the least. I was like some sort of cauldron in which all human indignation boiled. I was no more than twenty paces away when someone said to me, 'Excuse me. This is yours.'

At first I didn't pay any attention to him. He was one of those men who have nothing striking about them, radically bland. He dressed with discreet elegance and might have been born bald; his was a complete baldness, as perfect as a full moon. His facial features, very clean, brought to mind portraits of the young Nietzsche. But that was it. That and a small moustache below his nose, thin as a sideburn.

He must have been following me, because he offered me a pack of papers bound with twine. I didn't even remember that that whole ill-fated day had started because of Flag. I held out my hands, stunned and apathetic, because what I had written didn't mean a thing to me anymore. The man smiled.

'Have you ever been in an automobile? I can take you wherever you like.'

No, I had never been in an automobile before. And the emotions of the day had made me very receptive to any assistance, as unexpected as it might be. I sat next to the driver without saying a word. My throat was parched. The man pulled a small flask of whisky out of the glove compartment, and I took a swig.

Haltingly, I explained it all to him. My dealings with Frank Strub. The ridiculous stories that I wrote. The disgraceful exploitation I endured. The chain of absurd events that culminated with me. With each sip from the flask I broached a new topic. When the cauldron stopped boiling I felt a little more calm. What was I doing there, inside an automobile, relating my life to a perfect stranger?

I noticed the hands that guided the steering wheel. No one can hide the age of their hands. And my good Samaritan was younger than he seemed. He had nails as pink as flamingos that sank deep into his flesh. His baldness and his moustache were deceiving. His clothes, classically cut, were too. His air of respectability added years, perhaps on purpose. I felt uncomfortable. For the first time it occurred to me that he knew everything about me and I knew nothing about him. I begged him to drop me off right there, we were now very close to the centre of the city. He told me that he was in no hurry. The dead man had been a very distant friend. He had gone to the burial out of obligation, so he had the whole morning free. But I insisted. When I got out of the vehicle, he gave me his card. It read: 'EDWARD NORTON. BARRISTER.'

'I'd like to see you again, Mr Thomson,' he said from inside the car. 'It is possible that our interests complement each other. Come to see me tomorrow, please.'

'Do you think I would consider suing Luther Flag? His type always wins cases. And I can't afford a legal bill.'

'You've got it all wrong,' he laughed. 'I want to talk to you about something very different. Come tomorrow at around half past eight. My address is on the card.'

We said goodbye. But I didn't have time to get very far.

'Thomson!' he shouted. 'You've left something. It's the second time you've lost it today.' And once again he gave me the package that contained the novella and the three copies. 'I was very amused by your outburst earlier, with Doctor Flag.' And he added, 'I'm looking for a man with passion. See you tomorrow.'

In London in 1914 there were very few automobiles. As I crossed Trafalgar Square an open-topped Rolls-Royce passed, driven by a man with white gloves. Behind him sat an adorable old man, with both hands on a cane with an ivory knob. The vehicle stopped at the junction to let a carriage pass. I took advantage of the pause to throw the package of pages at Flag's skull while shouting, 'That's yours!'

It struck him right on the nape of the neck, as precisely as if I had thrown a rock. I hope it really hurt.

TWO

AT THAT TIME I was living in a rented room in a modest neighbourhood, a place where humans and mice fought an unresolved war. A century earlier the building had been a well-to-do residence. The baroque ornamentation on the façade and the two staircases, one for the masters of the house and the other for servants, spoke of a splendid past. But the umpteenth expansion of the outskirts of London had absorbed the building. This proud country home was now deep within the urban fabric of the British capital. It was Royal Steel's fault, a company devoted to manufacturing locomotives and railway materials. A factory had been built very close by, and around it had sprung up blocks of cheap housing. The grazing pastures and fields of beets vanished, the land lost value, and the rich moved out. When I arrived there the building stood like a haggard relic, an island amidst a red brick sea.

I explain all that because without knowing the history of the house it would be impossible to understand Mrs Pinkerton's personality. She was the owner and she had been forced to convert it into a boarding house. My God, it all happened a lifetime ago and yet I still get the shivers when I hear the name Pinkerton.

She was a thin, stiff woman, her back always as straight and tight as a pipe. I have never seen a chin so arrogant, always held high, as if pulled by an invisible hook. She had a rabbit's expression, constantly mulling things over and sniffing about but without any real focus. Her clothes repulsed me. Black shoes, black stockings, black shawl, black coats. A coconut-shaped bun, also black. It's not that she was especially pale, but she only wore black clothes and the inevitable contrast made her face resemble an ivory mask. She wasn't in mourning (I think she was only sad the day Queen Victoria died), she wore black because it was the only colour she could stand. I soon grasped that what really irked her was that the rest of humanity wasn't as bitter as she was. And since I couldn't like anything about her, I at least tried to hate her the same way scientists hate viruses: dispassionately. My efforts were not very successful.

I was one of the lodgers who had been there the longest and, to save myself a few pennies, we had an arrangement in which I would take care of little tasks around the house. Call the plumber when the pipes got clogged, distribute the mail to the rooms, pick up the bottles of milk at the door. Things like that. But having a conversation with Pinkerton was like struggling through a forest of cacti. What drove me mad were her dialectical ambushes. Pinkerton never attacked at close range with a bayonet, but rather like naval artillery bombing from miles away. She was unable, for example, to say, 'Mr Thomson, why is the letterbox full?' or 'Mr Thomson, the tap's leaking.' Or 'Mr Thomson, where is the milk?'

I assure you I would have appreciated the direct approach. Instead, she would say, 'Someone's forgetting his weekly obligations.'

My brain circuits then had to make a triple effort, asking: A: Who might that 'someone' be? B: What 'obligation' has been overlooked? C: For the love of God, why can't she speak clearly?

It all sounds petty, but it wasn't. There are very subtle methods of torture. Imagine eyes that only look for faults. Ears that only hear blasphemies. Someone with whom it was impossible to have a trivial, relaxed conversation. Every time she opened her mouth I was forced to be on guard, to sense where she would attack me. I always had to be thinking about what she might be thinking, and it was exhausting. We were like professional chess players, each one trying to predict the other's plan five or six moves in advance.

Another example: it took me months to work out that she hated to be called 'Miss'. She never told me, but I deduced it from the symptoms. Each time she heard the word 'Miss', her chin lifted higher and higher, and her gaze was so high that more than once I wondered if there was a leak in the ceiling. No. It was just that she didn't like being reminded that she didn't have a husband. One day I tested my theory, calling her Mrs Pinkerton instead of Miss, as if there were an imaginary Mr Pinkerton, and the invisible tension around her lessened. At least slightly.

The fact that a coal-black scarecrow like Mrs Pinkerton was unmarried shows that the male of the species is sharper than some women think. Without a man, and therefore without children, she would have liked to be one of those fancy governesses that raise the Kaiser's children. But she wasn't. She was just a landlady in a poor neighbourhood, and her frustration couldn't be measured in rational terms. She confused love with etiquette, and her biggest anxiety in life was the fear of arriving late to her own funeral.

Besides the landlady, the other permanent member of the house was Marie Antoinette. That was her name, just like the decapitated French queen. She belonged to Mrs Pinkerton and she was a turtle, the most perverse and unusual turtle that has ever existed. She was either born without a shell or had survived its loss, I don't know which. I wouldn't be at all surprised if some intolerant lodger had broken it with whacks of his hammer. And that's because Marie Antoinette had a very bad temper. Any pet, even a parakeet, is able to understand some basic commands: 'Lie down', 'Shut up', 'Get out', etcetera. With Marie Antoinette it was just the opposite: she took for granted that humans were the ones who should obey her.

A turtle without a shell is a very strange thing. Even with shells, turtles are very strange things, with their miniature elephant's feet, parrot's beak and ludicrous tail. Marie Antoinette was disgusting to look at, thinner than a sausage. She had nowhere to hide her head, so her haughty reaction was to carry it constantly in the air like a periscope, daring humans to be brave enough to criticise her monstrousness on parade. Because Marie Antoinette never sat still, and when she moved she looked like an epileptic swimmer. It was impossible to get used to a turtle that ran like a beetle, freed from the ballast of her shell. Suddenly you'd notice a fleeting shadow stuck to the wall or coming round a corner. Marie Antoinette hated anyone that looked at her with repulsion. Which is to say: everyone in general and Tommy Thomson in particular.

But enough about Marie Antoinette. What I found truly incomprehensible was the odd relationship that Pinkerton had with Mr

MacMahon. Even though he had a Scottish surname, he was Irish. There are all sorts of prejudices about the Irish being drunks, jokers and shoddy workers, and while I'm aware that a writer has to avoid such stereotyping, that's exactly how MacMahon was. Catholic, the father of seven children (or eight, I don't remember), always joking and whose manners, especially at the table, would have scandalised pirates.

He moved into the boarding house shortly after I did. His biceps were slightly softened by age, but as thick as Canadian logs. His hair was short, a sailor's cut, and dense as a brush. He had come to London, like so many of his fellow countrymen, in search of a more respectable wage. I didn't think he would last a week, that Pinkerton would either have him locked up in jail or sent straight to the madhouse.

He worked from sun-up till sundown at Royal Steel. He came home late at night, dirty and with his face black. You could tell he was home by the trail of soot you could follow through the hallway. I remember Pinkerton's expression the first time she saw it. It was reminiscent of a biologist following the tracks of an unknown species: perhaps some kind of snail that weighed a ton and left slimy tar in its wake. Pinkerton advanced along the corridor with her body bent in an inverted L, unable to believe her eyes, until she came up against the door to MacMahon's room. What a fright! She looked like Martha turned into a statue of salt. Black salt, in her case.

That evening I had to stifle my laughter; she, her tears. The other lodgers had already eaten when MacMahon came to the table. He served himself food while sucking snot back up his nose, coughing, sneezing and clearing his throat as if he had whalebones stuck in it. Mr MacMahon didn't eat, he swallowed potatoes like a crocodile would zebra meat. And he had the distinction of doing it along with five other simultaneous operations: chewing, guzzling, gobbling, talking and singing.

At that time there were few lodgers, two or three, and they were very boring. We hardly spoke because we had little to say to each other. MacMahon interpreted that in his own way.

'Are you sad, maybe?' he said happily. 'I'll sing you an Irish song.'

And he sang us a cheerful Irish song. I don't know that it was very successful, but I can assure you that it did warrant a change in Pinkerton's face, from vanilla white to artichoke green.

On Sunday mornings he liked to stroll through the house barefoot, with trousers and leather braces. And nothing else. You could see him in the small lounge. A place filled with armchairs, bad paintings of Pinkerton forefathers and an old piano that hadn't been played for three decades. MacMahon took the liberty of converting the lounge into some sort of workshop. He repaired any domestic device that had broken or damaged. Sewing machines, locks, bookcases, shoes. He did it willingly and we saved a few shillings, so Pinkerton didn't dare complain. He spent his days off there, singing and working half-naked, scratching his chest and his big round belly that was as hairy as his chest. For Pinkerton that Sunday show was the closest she had ever seen to a Roman orgy.

He was a practical man. He was also very thick-skinned. I think that there must be rocks in the Kalahari desert more sensitive than Mr MacMahon. One day he asked me for one of my Doctor Flag novellas. I lent him a copy, curious as to what criteria he would use to judge it.

'Thanks, Tommy,' he told me three days later when he returned it. 'I fixed the leg of the bed. It was a little wobbly and the Bible was too thick.'

On another occasion he had to go to Ireland to get some papers. He left the telegram that he had sent his wife on a table. It read: 'Next week I'm coming on the ferry STOP take a bath STOP.'

But the worst thing about Mr MacMahon was his farts. They erupted as the evening turned to night, behind his door, and they could be heard throughout the entire floor and half the building.

After living with MacMahon I came to the conclusion that he was the inventor of five types of farts. One of them I baptised Big Ben farts, precisely spaced out, as if marking the hours. *Poom*, pause, *poom*, pause, and on and on until midnight. Another kind were the Vickers farts, which were less loud but had the cadence of a machine-gun. Their main trait was that they had no quantitative limit. They could be ten, twenty or thirty. They all made exactly the same sound, MacMahon controlled the dilation of his sphincter and the dose of gas perfectly. Sometimes, though, MacMahon lost control and his farts sounded like a flock of wild ducks, *quack, quack, quack*. The fourth kind was the Violin fart: thinner, longer, like a kitten that meows because it's lost its mother. Those ones really got on my nerves. The fifth type, well, those were Doctor Flag farts. I gave them that name because of one of Doctor Flag's novellas, in which some sort of widespread flood throughout Africa was meant to redeem the continent from paganism. It began with a large thunderclap; just one, but an omnipotent one.

There was no escaping the surprise attacks of Doctor Flag farts. When a Doctor Flag fart erupted it woke everyone in the house, and there was no way we could get back to sleep. They were like bombs, bombs of a calibre that in 1914 no military engineer had yet dreamed up. An earthquake that made us open our eyes and, bewildered, look up at the ceiling beams in horror. Of all the lodgers I was the only one that was close enough to him to be able to talk to him about the problem, even discreetly. His reply? 'Better out than in.'

Why didn't Mrs Pinkerton kick him out? Good question. What most surprised me was that with him she didn't employ any of her characteristic torture techniques, not by a long shot. She maintained a totally neutral attitude. Pinkerton looked at Mr MacMahon with silent, attentive and resolute eyes. An expression that could say it all or not mean anything. Without getting involved, without expressing an opinion.

He disconcerted her, I think. Somehow she understood that her sophisticated malice would have been useless against MacMahon, who was too crude to comprehend it. As annoying as a mosquito can be, it will never get through an elephant's hide. It is also possible that MacMahon awakened mixed emotions in her. As I mentioned, Pinkerton was a bankrupt middle-class woman. She fled from the working class like typhus. But in MacMahon working-class values and bourgeois urbanity combined in a very strange way.

An example: when one of those horrible Irish swearwords slipped out, he always added a very polite 'Excuse me, Mrs Pinkerton'. And another: on Sundays he went around half-naked, yes, but only after coming back from mass. And no one could question that he took his responsibility as a father seriously: he worked like a mule and sent all of his salary to Ireland.

It's also true that that same man had his thoughtful gestures. After mass, Mr MacMahon always came home with a bouquet of flowers for Mrs Pinkerton.

'You should put soap in the water,' said MacMahon. 'The flowers will last longer.'

'Are you sure? I've been told bicarbonate of soda is more effective.'

'Bicarbonate of soda instead of soap? Hmm . . . let's test it out.'

When they were together they had a unique ability to turn any topic of conversation, even flowers, into a technical question. They sat in front of the vase, staring at it like people waiting to see a tree grow, and they would spend whole hours there discussing whether it was better to add soap or bicarbonate of soda. To someone who didn't know them the scene would have seemed absurd. Pinkerton had the perverse ability to use up all the oxygen in a room. But MacMahon pumped out double, so they established some sort of homeostatic equilibrium.

There was still the farting issue. But, when you think about it, MacMahon only farted in his own room. The right to privacy is one of the great victories of modern culture. Why can't a man fart in his own room? In his own room, a man has the right to fart and the right to cry. At the beginning of the month, when he got paid, he got drunk. It was the only special expense that he allowed himself. We would hear him cry all night long when he drank. He recited the names of his wife and of his seven or eight children, between sobs and whimpers. Once this prompted one of those typically twisted, exasperating dialogues with Mrs Pinkerton. She said to me: 'Mr MacMahon is crying.'

Naturally, Mrs Pinkerton was trying to say something more than just describing an objective fact. She was trying to suggest that 'that' was bothersome, to her and to the other lodgers, and that 'someone' should stop, repress or censure Mr MacMahon's weeping, and that 'someone' was none other than me, Thomas Thomson.

And that's because the height of emotion that Mrs Pinkerton felt was when she received her Christmas card each year: it came from an insurance agency that sent the same card to all its customers who had had their home insurance policy for over twenty years. It was very hard for such a woman to understand something as basic as a man, far from his home and his family, crying with grief. I think that feelings scared her the same way the African jungle scared Doctor Flag's readers. She didn't know what dangers lurked within, she was completely ignorant of them, and therefore any aberration was feasible. And if some feeling dared to express itself, unsuspectingly, she repressed it as if it were a tribe of cannibals on the warpath against the British government.

My response was quite blunt: 'Go on in and speak to him yourself, then.'

Anyway, that dialogue stuck in my mind because it had some very constructive effects: Mrs Pinkerton never mentioned Mr MacMahon's crying again, nor did she ever again ask me to do anything about it at all.

From what I've just explained you might deduce that I was rather unhappy. Quite the contrary. One shouldn't confuse hayfever with the springtime. It was, in fact, the happiest and most carefree period of my life.

My room was in the most isolated part of the house, at the end of a hallway, a safe distance from Pinkerton, MacMahon and the others. From the window, on the horizon, I could see the smokestacks of Royal Steel. Their schedule marked the pace of the neighbourhood. You could count up to eighteen different shades of grey. The grey of the clouds, of the façades, of the houses' roofs, of the street, and of the pavement. When it rained each shade duplicated, adding one more tone. I didn't mind a bit.

My furnishings were as simple, or more so, than those in van Gogh's room. A table, a chair, a bed, a chest of drawers and my most valuable possession: a very modern typewriter.

I had grown up in a state orphanage, where, in contrast with the spirit of the times, I received an acceptable education. In those days the legal age for leaving orphanages was fifteen years old. But I was so comfortable there, and the institution's staff so pleased with me, that through various legal sophistries they were able to keep me there four years longer. During those four extra years I worked mostly in the library. That was the stimulus for my love of books. So much so, that when I decided to leave the orphanage of my own accord, at nineteen, I did so with the firm intention of devoting myself to literature. The day I left, they paid me, with the strict rigour of a bookkeeper, the equivalent of four years' salaried work as a library assistant. It was a generous parting gift that allowed me to live for a while without financial worries, which I spent writing.

In any case, I had arrived at the boarding house with the healthy intention of becoming a writer and I applied myself with spartan discipline. I used Royal Steel's whistle to establish my schedule. First thing in the morning my index finger would be poised to start typing, waiting for the high-pitched squeal. I would write and write, and my day didn't end until the whistle let me know that it was time to stop. I lived, literally, like a labourer in ink.

In those days I was a member of a group of young inexperienced writers that made up in pedantry what they lacked in talent. That was where I met Frank Strub. He came one day, only once. When I go back over this story, I realise that he came to snare someone like me. I met him, he read some of my pages right there and asked me to meet him in that cheap restaurant in north London. You already know the rest of the story. Poor Strub? Poor me.

Edward Norton himself opened the door of his office for me. He was dressed as elegantly as he had been at the cemetery, with a tie, a bright white shirt and a silk waistcoat. The front entrance's hallway led directly to a living room turned into an office. The walls were covered in wood up to eye-height.

The day we had met my defences were low. This time I didn't want Norton to catch me unawares. It was clear that I would have in front of me a professional who exercised his trade inside and outside the courtrooms. A man that measured each of his gestures with a compass. The trouble with barristers, like doctors, is that if they're good, you never know what they're thinking.

He had me sit down facing him and said, 'One moment, please.'

During an entire minute, a long minute, he wrote something, using an expensive fountain pen. I was sure that it was a trick, that he was just scribbling. He was making me wait, which underlined his importance and diminished mine. I had no choice but to sit there looking at his thin moustache and perfectly bald head.

He put down his fountain pen and made a gesture, a gesture that I would see him repeat many times: his fingertips pressed together as if praying, forming a small pyramid, touching the tip of his nose. I wasn't there. A few seconds of meditation and he returned to me.

'Look what I read last night.'

He pointed to a novella by Doctor Flag that rested on one end of the table. Coincidentally it was the same one that had begun my ghostwriting career: *Pandora in the Congo.*

'Did you write it?'

'My name isn't on the cover,' I said apologetically, 'but I did indeed write it.'

'Then you have a lively pen. I've always admired agile writers. I would have tried my luck in the literary world if it weren't for my congenital lack of imagination. Does your dexterity with words come from your family?'

'I never knew my parents,' I said. 'I was raised in an orphanage.'

'I'm sorry. I suppose you had a very rough childhood?'

'I was phenomenally happy.'

My response surprised him. Since he was so sure of himself I felt proud to have disconcerted him a bit. He changed the subject.

'How do you create an entire story out of thin air?'

'I don't. I just follow an outline,' I explained curtly. 'I don't create anything, I just fill in the blanks.'

Norton frowned slightly. 'Perhaps you're right,' he said hesitantly, 'but I still think that you have a lively pen.'

I guess that he couldn't compliment that ridiculous book in any other way. Anyhow, he switched topics. 'What did Doctor Flag pay you for each book?'

'Flag didn't pay me anything,' I said. I was still infuriated and the resentment became evident in my voice. 'Flag paid a man, that man paid Spencer, Spencer paid Strub, and Strub paid me. Each one squeezed a little bit more out of me than the last.'

'Well, I'll pay you three times that. As a compensation for the triple exploitation.'

I didn't say anything. Norton leaned over the table a fraction.

'I'd like you to write me a story, an African story. The person who will explain it to you is named Marcus Garvey and he is in prison.'

'How did he end up there?'

'Awaiting trial. He's accused of murdering two brothers, Richard and William Craver. It's not looking good for him.'

That got my attention. 'The gallows?'

Norton let out a disillusioned sigh, opened up a file and said, 'The evidence points to him. And worst of all, the victims weren't just any two ordinary men. They were the sons of the Duke of Craver.'

I didn't know what he was talking about.

'The Sudan, the Siege of Khartoum . . . remember that?'

'Oh! Of course!' I rejoined. 'Craver, the officer that General Gordon was unable to rescue, besieged at Khartoum. Years later they reinstated him. And they made him Duke.'

'Exactly,' he assented. 'William and Richard were the sons of a patrician. And Marcus is an insignificant stableboy. I don't think they are going to give him many opportunities. Right now I only have one strategy: to present appeals for procedural errors and slow the proceedings down.'

My eyebrows rose like a drawbridge. 'But I don't know anything about the legal world. I've never written juridical documents.'

* * *

'That won't be necessary. I am the barrister, you are the writer. Tell the facts according to Garvey's version, write it as if it were a novel. The plot is worthy of it.' Here Norton adopted a more solemn tone. 'Richard and William Craver went to the Congo in the summer of 1912. Marcus went with them as an assistant. The three men travelled deep into remote areas of the jungle. But only Marcus came back out. He escaped justice until he was caught right here, in London, at the end of last year.'

'And the evidence?'

'Overwhelming. There is the sworn testimony of the British ambassador to the Congo. The crime's motive has also been requisitioned: two giant, priceless diamonds. The public prosecutor's office even has Garvey's confession. Just one of these pieces of evidence would be enough to hang a failure like Marcus Garvey ten times.'

'What good will it do him if I write an extensive narrative of what happened in the Congo?'

'I don't know,' said Norton laconically.

'Why then do you want me to write Garvey's version?'

His next statement was more rhetorical than sincere. 'Because I'm desperate.'

He paused and ruminated at length before speaking.

'I don't have time to take down an exhaustive declaration from him. Perhaps by reading the whole story we can establish some reasonable line of defence.'

I didn't know what to say. He smiled.

'Your novellas have entertained many people. Now you may have the chance to save a life.'

From his perspective they must have been very solid arguments, because he didn't even ask me if I would accept the assignment. It's also true that I didn't object. We tied up a few contractual details and he walked me to the door.

Norton could be very warm and he could be very cold. During our short walk to the door, in the hallway, he said, without looking at me and in a tone somewhere between instructive and recriminating, 'Don't ever again ask a barrister if his clients are guilty. If Jack the Ripper were my client I would defend his interests. But we don't have to mix the job of defending someone with the choice of believing him. That belongs to the private realm. And my most personal conviction is to oppose the death penalty. When the state kills, we stoop to the level of the worst murderer.'

'Are you saying that Marcus deserves the gallows?'

'What I am saying is that you are smart enough to be able to form your own opinion. No one has ever been as close to Marcus Garvey as you'll be.'

He opened the door for me. With his hand still on the knob he smiled shyly.

'Now that I can count you among us, we're three people involved in this case. A man, a noble spirit and a gentleman. I'm not entirely sure which one is which.'

'I don't understand,' I said.

Norton erased his smile.

'What happened in the Congo surpasses human understanding, Thomson. It's one of those stories that makes us doubt everything. Listen to it and write it down. I've never heard anything so extraordinary. Never. And neither will you have.' Norton presented himself to the world as a young ambitious barrister. My intuition told me more: that behind that cold exterior there was a rational steamroller, without friends or enemies; a privileged mind and a stubborn will at the service of basically selfish interests. A man like that couldn't be on Tommy Thomson's side. We should pay more attention to our intuitions.

THREE

MY TASK HIT SERIOUS difficulties from the very beginning. Marcus Garvey had not yet been tried. That situation, as contradictory as it may sound, offered me fewer advantages than disadvantages. He hadn't been sentenced and, therefore, had none of the rights of the long-term prison inmates. Prisoners awaiting trial were only allowed two visiting hours every fifteen days. I would have to use those little blocks of time wisely in order to interview him.

Two warders escorted me inside the prison. We passed through some workshops and I saw that the saws, planes and squares the prisoners used were chained to the walls. It depressed me: even the objects in there were doing time. We finally arrived at a cell, sparsely furnished with two chairs and a large rectangular table. A sergeant with a Serbian-style moustache and a very straight back was waiting for me. His top button and his belt buckle were separated by quite some distance. I reflected that the civil service must have spent extra money on the cloth for that uniform, but the investment had paid off, thanks to the authority that such a long torso projected. This man was whom I would have to deal with during my visits and I gave him the name Sergeant Long Back.

I heard Marcus Garvey before I saw him. From the hall I could hear some rhythmic sounds, like wood or iron moving. He entered the room with his wrists and ankles shackled; on his feet were wooden clogs, which explained the peculiar combination of sounds. He wore the grey uniform that turned the convicts into souls in purgatory. But that sad grey failed to negate Marcus Garvey. He was an exotic-looking man. And the covering of grey created a contrast that made the other colours on his body sparkle even more. The first thing one noticed about Garvey was that Moroccan hair that some women love so much, curly and tight. From his dark complexion, bright like leather soaked in oil, two green eyes shone with the phosphorescence of a summer glow-worm.

It's odd, now that I think about it, but even though he must have been a few years older than me, in our relationship I was always the one in charge. I knew that first impressions leave a lasting mark. A well-dressed, well-coiffed man is a man and a half. So, I prepared myself from tip to toe for my first visit. I wore my hair very short and damp with moisturising lotions. I'm sorry to say that even at nineteen my lovely blond hair was already threatened by violent receding, two estuaries as deep as all the hair I had left pooled in a yellow band at the base of my skull. Each hair was turned toward its respective side, like an army in formation. I couldn't afford expensive clothes, but who ever said that you need a lot of money to dress impeccably, with dignity and even a certain elegance?

Marcus, on the other hand, was at a disadvantage. He was a

prisoner, with all the indignities that that implied. What's more, there was another element: Garvey's physicality, which had an undeniable bastard, gypsy beauty, had some anomalous facet that detracted from it. The two guards who escorted him weren't giants, not by any means, but even so they stood a whole head taller than him. I finally realised that his thigh bones were shorter than normal, excessively short. And his weak knees eliminated all aesthetic merit. When he walked it made one think of some sort of wooden puppet controlled by an inexpert hand.

I was just about to take my place at the table when Sergeant Long Back stopped me. 'No, please, not here.' He ordered the two guards to place the chairs on the short sides of the rectangular table. So our hands were far apart, making any type of contact impossible. We sat down and I felt as if we were one of those rich married couples, more separated than united by their dinner table. Instead of silverware, Marcus had his chains, I had blank sheets of paper and a pencil. (They had confiscated my fountain pen because it was metal and pointy.)

'We'll be watching you,' announced Sergeant Long Back, 'in case there's any problem.'

The way he said it didn't make it clear if the problem was Marcus, me, or the combination. I interviewed Marcus Garvey many, many times. And I have to say that that tall, lanky sergeant didn't miss one minute of our sessions. He was always behind the bars, seated, politely deaf to our words, incredibly attentive to our hands. He was never substituted, he never took a holiday, he was never off sick. He was a perfect human sphinx. I often wondered: does this man never rest? Doesn't he have physical needs, doesn't he have eyelids?

There is a private universe of sounds inside prisons. From unknown corners, we heard echoes of bars opening and closing, and fragments of human sentences so muffled by the layers of cement that they were unintelligible. We sat facing each other with a silent chasm between us. I wasn't at all sure how to begin the conversation. I shuffled paper to buy time. Garvey may have sensed my hesitation. He opened wide those green eyes and said, 'They're going to hang me, aren't they?'

His simple sentence had the virtue of fusing sadness and beauty. I don't know how to describe the candour and deep conviction with which he said those words. They would have soothed Attila.

'You have to have faith in Norton,' I said tersely. 'He sent me to write your story. All of it.'

Marcus looked from one side of the table to the other as if he was searching for something he had lost. In the sessions that followed I would realise that that was his way of expressing uneasiness. Finally he asked me, lifting his eyebrows high, 'And how do we do that?'

I didn't have the slightest idea. I was supposed to be a professional but I had never written a biography. And it could almost be said that I was about to invent a new genre, halfway between a biography and a will.

What is a man's life? What he thinks it was? I didn't want to judge it, that wasn't my job. I had promised myself that I would talk little and listen a lot. I wanted to be an uncritical, cosmic ear. We had a lot of sessions ahead of us, which would by their nature create a certain intimacy, and I didn't want to sympathise with him.

'Let's start from the beginning,' I said.

'I didn't kill William or Richard.'

'No,' I said, 'from the beginning.'

'If I remember correctly we landed in the Congo on . . .'

'No, please,' I interrupted. 'Where and when were you born?'

Marcus Garvey didn't know how old he was or exactly where he was born. He mentioned a small place in Wales, but I could see that the name meant nothing to him. His father came from somewhere in the Balkans, but Garvey wasn't very clear on that subject either. On the other hand, he expressed deep emotions of gratitude and remorse for his mother. He had inherited his father's hair and eyes, and his mother's naïveté.

No one will ever know how, when or why Mirno Sevic came to England. But once there, he met Martha Garvey (there was no wedding, neither in a church nor in a registry office), an orphan without a past who had just come out of the institution where she had been brought up. Martha was very thin. I was surprised that Marcus's first memory wasn't visual, it was tactile. When he nursed, he recalled, his fingers would move above his mother's nipples and brush against ridges covered by skin: Martha's ribs, which cut across her chest.

Martha was very odd. She often talked to fairies that only she could see, beings in the form of lit matches that appeared to her on Tuesdays and Thursdays. She once explained to Marcus that the fairies smoked mashed oak leaves, that they were anti-Catholic and that they hated riding on mosquitoes, which they were obliged to do by the forest God. Martha was a heavy smoker; the orphanage she had grown up in, Catholic; and Mirno, an insatiable lover. We can conclude, then, that the woman projected her phobias onto those imaginary beings.

This woman, disinherited by the world, without fortune or forebears, spoke to her son in French. Perhaps because it was the only positive thing she had learned at the orphanage. Perhaps because it was a way to avoid the tortuous relations with Mirno. During the violent rows between Martha and Mirno, as frequent as the reconciliations, he would end up bellowing in some Balkan language. She screamed in French. Who says that children aren't discerning? At the age of five, Marcus had opted for French, which he spoke as well (or as badly) as he did English. He learned not a single word of his father's savage tongue, that 'language of the forests', as he himself defined it.

Too poor to even rent a room, Mirno purchased a wagon that he converted into the family home. And thanks to a passing acquaintance he bought an old bear that was going to be put down from a circus company. The bear was as thin as Martha and had as few teeth as little Marcus.

And so began the Sevic family's artistic career. Mirno was the tightrope walker. The worst tightrope walker ever, according to Marcus. The man's mishaps, which he survived unscathed even though some of his falls were quite violent, were more popular than his feat of walking on a rope that was nine feet high. Soon it became a comic act. Pepe the bear danced like a drunken goat. They dressed him in a red beret, like the Spanish Carlists, and the Welsh miners accepted the farce. In terms of the bear's ferocity, suffice to say that on summer nights Marcus slept with him under the wagon. Besides making Pepe dance, Marcus acted out fragments of Shakespeare. The miners were moved by the sight of a little boy with such short legs doing *Macbeth*. The men applauded. The women cried.

The overall picture was one of an unfortunate and erratic existence. But that wasn't how Marcus saw it. He explained all the ups and downs of the MMM company (Mirno, Martha, Marcus) with a smile on his lips the entire time. Those were his golden years.

It was as if every sin in the world had passed through him without wounding him, without making him bitter. He spoke of his adversity and he never blamed anyone or anything. I only noticed some resentment when he told the story of a beating he had received from his father.

One day the company set up their camp on the outskirts of a town just like all the others. The wagon sat under a tall oak tree. In his free time Marcus climbed the oak like a monkey. It fascinated him that something so large and so solid could be alive. It would have taken three men to get their arms around the trunk of that tree. After a few shows Mirno and Martha decided to move on. But Marcus refused to leave. Finally Mirno had to thrash him.

'I don't know why I disobeyed my father. It was just a tree,' said Marcus with a slight laugh.

But I knew why. Or I thought I did.

Perhaps Marcus appreciated the roots of the oak tree more than the tree itself. Perhaps that tree had made him want a more settled life. With other friends besides Pepe the bear. With a decent roof above his head.

I said before that a man's life is what he thinks it has been. I should add that men are sovereigns when it comes time to ascribe an order to their lives. I went over my notes later; during a two-hour conversation, Marcus had devoted forty-five minutes to talking about his mother, and thirty minutes to Pepe. The rest of the time was taken up by his father and family events, in that order.

'Sir, time's up.'

It was Sergeant Long Back. He said it as if he were announcing an execution. Garvey stood up. Until that moment I hadn't realised that the prison uniform and the grey of the walls were so indistinguishable. I stood up too.

'I enjoyed it very much, actually,' said Marcus, and he was more animated than he had been at the start of the session. 'I've never told anyone so many things about me before.'

Long Back directed the two guards while they lifted Marcus up, watched over him and took him away peacefully. Long Back didn't have to move. He led Marcus just as he would have led a cow. His cruelty was within the limits set by the penitentiary code. He seemed to me to be a good librarian of men, that was how I read him.

'It's hard to believe that he's accused of killing two men,' I said to the sergeant as Marcus was escorted down the hallway. 'He's so little, and dark . . .'

The sergeant was putting the chairs back in order with mechanical movements. When he heard me he stopped for a second. With his hands on the back of a chair, and without looking at me, he said, 'Yes. Like a tarantula.'

If Garvey or Norton, either one of them, had been a bit stronger or a bit weaker, I would have given up the case that very evening. But neither one was strong enough to proceed without me. And neither one was weak enough for me to have the guts to decide, without a guilty conscience, that their cause was hopeless and I'd be better off washing my hands of the whole affair.

We have a tendency to believe that our decisions are based on perfectly thought out criteria. I believe that we're first moved by our emotions, which act like an invisible crowbar on our reason. 'They're going to hang me, aren't they?' My problem was that once I had listened to Marcus I couldn't escape his influence, which in certain aspects was slight. What a paradox! Marcus Garvey emanated only weakness, but an indestructible weakness. If he had been an arrogant, stubborn man, hellbent on fighting for his life to the last breath, I would have left him to face the challenge himself. Instead, the image that came to me was that of a child struggling against the waves of a typhoon. And you can't ask a shipwrecked man if they're guilty or innocent, you can only offer them your hand.

In terms of Norton, his weakness didn't so much come from his personality as from his position. As he had admitted, he was desperate. The fact that he asked for my help said it all. He didn't want me to write a book, he wanted me to navigate a dark map. He would interpret the charted area with a barrister's eyes. That way, perhaps, important hidden information would come to light that would speak in Garvey's favour.

The write-up of the first session didn't amount to much. I had two whole weeks to transcribe the interview before my next visit. Since I was used to the pace imposed by Flag's outlines, that was nothing. I even rewrote the first chapter five times to improve its style. Without realising, I had stuck to Flag's style in the first draft. I opened my eyes. Flag was history, Doctor Luther Flag no longer existed. I was able to allow myself, with singular satisfaction, to suppress dozens and dozens of adjectives.

Each adjective that I eliminated was a personal revenge. Armed with my red pencil, I remember killing more and more adjectives, and my laughter made its merry way through the entire boarding house.

'Tommy, old boy, what are you doing up there in your room?' MacMahon asked me one day.

'Liberating myself, Mr MacMahon, liberating myself!'

However, my author's joy was inversely proportionate to the hopes the tale offered. If it had any value, if it transmitted any emotion, it was only because I sympathised with the character of Marcus in a very irrational way. What was Norton expecting having such a limp, dull story written up? Did he hope to provoke some easy tears? Beg for society's clemency? If judges were compassionate, prisons would be empty, and they are full to bursting.

When we observe the tragedy that murders cause, we always come up against an irresolvable conflict: that the murderer can defend himself and his victims cannot. I had a wild idea. I couldn't bring William and Richard Craver back to life, but I could let someone who was very close to the victims have his say. What was stopping me from paying a visit to the Duke of Craver?

Getting an audience with the Duke was easier than I expected. I arranged an appointment over the telephone, and a week later I was in front of the entrance gate.

The residence of the Duke of Craver was a stately home, twenty miles north of London. Too crammed with objects for today's tastes, perhaps, but the visitor had a sense that behind those ornate walls endless generations of Cravers had lived secluded in an ecstatic tranquillity, immune to the shocks and mutations of the outside world. Once inside, the butler took me to a small waiting room. He assured me that I would be seen right away. By whom? The

Duke in person, of course. I would never have thought that it would be so easy to gain access to nobility.

He was a man as broad as an atlas, immensely vital. His corpulence bound together body and soul well. He sported scars and mutilations, half an ear snatched by a bullet from an Arab musket, for example. But the Duke was some sort of Roman coliseum, where the ravages of history, more than damaging him, actually defined his profile. He emanated natural authority. When Charles Craver walked in I had the impression that the furniture sat up straight and the tiles wanted him to step on them. I even had the reflex to stand to attention.

'Well,' he greeted me with affable irony, 'another book about General Gordon and the Sudan. When are they going to get tired of it? Clearly, never. First came the journalists, then the biographers. I suppose you must belong to the historian's guild . . .'

He spoke as he walked towards me. When he stopped a palm's length in front of me, I opened my mouth.

'It's not Gordon that brought me here.'

He looked at me for the first time. He observed me attentively, trying to assess who I really was and what I was doing at his house. I measured my words very carefully. I didn't want to cause more pain to a man from whom Africa had already stolen two sons.

'I'm not interested in the Sudan. I wanted to talk about the Congo.'

We store pain in boxes. It's surprising how a simple word can open them and release their contents. The two syllables of the word 'Congo' made the man who stood in front of me change into another man. Invisible fingers pulled the flesh of his cheeks downwards, as if the force of gravity had suddenly increased. His pupils grew larger. The Duke saw a horrible, private landscape. I didn't want to hurt him. But Craver was a career soldier and he reacted as such: taking the initiative when pain presents itself.

'What is your name?' he said with a suddenly energetic voice.

'Thomson, sir.'

'Your full name, please.'

'Thomas Thomson, General.'

'Were you a friend of my son William?'

'No.'

'Of Richard's?'

'No.'

Craver was beginning to lose his patience.

'Do I have to drag every word out of you one by one?'

After a few moments of hesitation, I decided to speak.

'I'm writing a book, a book on certain tragic events that happened in the Congo two years ago . . . But I can only reflect a very subjective perspective on the facts.'

Craver didn't quite understand what I was talking about. And since he didn't understand, he was getting more and more worked up. He was struggling to contain the fury that boiled within him. He took a step towards me. I had to resist the temptation to back away two.

'What book? What perspective are you talking about? Are you saying that . . .'

He understood.

I said, 'You did not invite me, I'm not your guest. There is nothing forcing you to listen to me. One word and I'll leave this house.'

'How dare you show up here and . . .'

He could have attacked me, but something restrained him. He looked at the floor for a little while. He rubbed his chin. Finally he raised his eyes.

'You don't mean to say you are writing a book for my son's murderer?'

'I think it's the last thing he will do in this life. And even a condemned prisoner has the right to some last words.'

It seemed he was hesitating between kicking me out or assaulting me and then kicking me out. Finally he raised a peaceful hand.

'I've always valued audacity. Even from an enemy.'

He turned and walked away so quickly that I had to struggle to keep up with him. I continued to talk to his back.

'I wouldn't want you to misinterpret me. What might seem like an intrusion is only an attempt at impartiality.'

'Do you have children?' shouted Craver, without stopping to look at me.

'No, sir.'

'Well done! Don't do it. They could die before you do. And of all the unnatural acts, the most aberrant of all is a father burying a son . . . two sons.'

We arrived at a large office, in shade, although it was midday. The large picture windows were covered with curtains made of heavy velvet. He pointed to a wall on which hung two framed photographs the size and shape of a flattened rugby ball. The first photograph bore an inscription: 'Richard Craver. Leicester Barracks, November, 1907.' In the dim light I had trouble making out all the detail of the images.

'Shall I draw the curtains?' I asked.

'No.'

Outside a magnificent sun blazed. I didn't understand why we had to suffer this gloom. But you don't question the Duke of Craver.

The photograph of Richard Craver was a close-up of his head and shoulders. In the vast majority of men's faces you can make out the traces of the child they once were. Not in Richard Craver's. The picture made you think more of a barracks sergeant than an aristocrat. Coarse features, of poorly sculpted stone, and a flaccid fringe of greasy black hair. There was no doubt that the Duke of Craver was someone used to giving orders from the day he was born. His son had also devoted himself to giving orders, but with a truncheon in his hand.

And his eyes. Richard Craver's right eye was noticeably larger, rounder, more open. His left eye indicated a more feminine side. The lid was lower, the gaze more sensitive, melancholy, almost defenceless. He had a slight squint, perhaps more obvious in the photograph than in person. A thick droopy moustache tried to reassert the masculine aspect of his personality. The attempt at camouflage was too obvious, and the moustache had the opposite effect of its intended mark of honour.

William was a very different sort of boy. The image showed a body and a character very different to those of his older brother. Craver guessed my thoughts and said, 'William took after his mother, may she rest in peace.'

This photograph showed the young man's entire body in a relaxed pose. Handwritten around the oval, you could read, 'Happy William Craver at his twenty-fifth birthday party.' William was dressed in white from head to toe. Even his shoes were white. The image had little contrast, but I would have wagered that his hair was as pale as his shoes.

All of William's facial features were projected outward, like a fox's head. He sat on an Empire-style armchair with one knee over the other. He was looking at something beyond the frame, at a vanishing point only he had discovered. Unlike Richard, the two halves of his face were as symmetrical as a spider's body. He held a cigarette and he appeared to be, more than just a smoker, a tobacco tamer, as if everything that came into contact with him became his natural accomplice. William was smiling, and I sensed that cunning was the first aspect of his being that had conquered adulthood.

'If men understood the risks of fatherhood, they would give it up. But that would be the end of the world. And we don't want the world to end. Isn't that right, Mr Thomson?'

'Yes, sir.'

The Duke jerked open the curtains.

'I don't like to see it.'

The curtain hid a large balcony. We went onto it. Craver took in a deep breath. From up there all the Duke's land could be seen. The Craver mansion was shaped like a croissant. The croissant's horns became walls that embraced a large garden. One entered the garden through a gate that united the two tips of the croissant.

Craver threw a question into the air. 'What is the point of happiness?'

'I don't know, sir,' I hesitated. 'I always thought that happiness was an end unto itself.'

'You're wrong. We want to be happy so we can bequeath our happiness.'

In the foreground a man was leading a horse to the stables slowly. We could hear the noise of the four hooves on the stone;

it was a very pleasant noise that blended with a stream of water from a fountain. In the background, very close to the tip of the right horn, there was some sort of cabin made of unfinished trunks of wood. Craver told me that, as a child, Richard played there for hours on end. At the tip of the left horn, there was a white summerhouse. A favourite spot for William's seductions, according to Craver. (What a sad smile he had when he mentioned these two buildings.) Between the cabin and the summerhouse, right in front of the entrance, was an oak. It was so broad they had been able to carve a great passageway through the trunk. I myself had passed through that opening on my way to the mansion.

'Murderers are the worst thieves. They steal the most valuable thing men have: their past and their future.'

Craver was no longer hostile. He rested his arms on the railing. The voice that spoke was desolate. Can one imagine how the stump of a tree cut down by a murderous hatchet would speak? I can, since that day, when the Duke of Craver said, 'Take a good look, Mr Thomson, take a long hard look. All of that will die along with me.'

FOUR

MARCUS'S CHILDHOOD AND HIS happiness elapsed at the same time. The day came when men were no longer moved by his performances. The women stopped crying. No one clapped. The audience were no longer watching a boy interpret Shakespeare. Marcus was now seventeen or eighteen years old. He had no idea how quickly his world was breaking apart.

Profits decreased. Arguments increased. Martha got sick. The fever prevented them from moving the wagon. When she coughed she left black and red sputum on her handkerchiefs.

Marcus was a witness to his father's flight. One night he was sleeping beneath the wagon, with Pepe as a mattress, when he was awoken by a noise. It was Mirno. He had a bag on his back and he was running. He fled like a thief that had just looted a house. Father and son have never seen each other since.

However, this isn't the place to judge Mirno Sevic. The fact is that Marcus was left alone. Not even six days separated Mirno's flight and Martha's death. Marcus's entire world collapsed in less than a week. The authorities in the nearby town took care of Martha's body, which they buried, and Pepe the bear was put down. Marcus related this succession of catastrophes to me without any emotion.

Everything indicated that the local authorities had been reasonably humane with the unknown orphan boy. Martha had a poor but dignified funeral. Marcus was accommodated in the parish and employed in the mines. He didn't last long. That claustrophobic underground world didn't agree with his outdoor spirit. Two months after Martha's burial he opted for adventure. The town was filled with young men with silicosis in their lungs; wire thin, hollow cheeks and huge purple bags under their eyes. All in all, that brief period seems to have left more of a mark on my notes than on Marcus's memory. By the time they asked him to register in the town hall, he did so as Marcus Garvey instead of Marcus Sevic.

He followed an erratic route, from west to east, with London as a vague idea of a final destination. On the way he worked as a labourer on several different farms, never staying more than two or three weeks. And that was how Marcus Garvey ended up at the Duke of Craver's mansion.

He was offered a decent salary, a bed, a roof over his head and board. But Marcus had London in his sights. One more step and he would be in the largest metropolis on planet Earth. He was young, the perfect time to open himself to the world. Why did he stay with the Cravers? He said it was to make his fortune. I think that there were other factors.

There, life was the exact opposite of his nomadic past. At the Cravers' mansion existence was perfectly regulated and compartmentalised. The masters were the masters and the servants were the servants. And, yet, Marcus discovered that he could find pleasure in human inequality, at least when it was accepted by both sides.

There was something else that justified Marcus's love for the Cravers' house, an attraction of which he was probably not fully conscious. I would surmise that Marcus stayed there because of the oak tree, that grand oak that rose between William's summerhouse and Richard's log cabin.

As a child I had always been drawn to the parable of the prodigal son. I admired the father's saintly attitude, his joy at the return of a son who had squandered half of his fortune. But I remember often thinking: what if instead of one prodigal son there had been two? Would he have received them with such joy?

Marcus's work was divided between the stables and the kitchen. But anytime he got the chance, he clambered up the oak tree. He was happy up there, halfway between the sky and the land.

Marcus knew the house's coachmen very well. They were honourable men, like all of the servants. But that day in late October, when they brought William Craver home, they had smugglers' faces. The car passed below the oak. William raised his cold pale eyes and saw Marcus up there, stretched out on a thick branch. Their eyes met. There are things that can be pretty and at the same time scary, like the mineral coldness of those light eyes. Marcus felt like a squirrel under the gaze of a poacher.

In the days that followed, contact between Marcus and William was minimal. William left his room rarely, and when he did, he treated the servants like ghosts. He looked at them as if they were transparent or as if they were furniture, and that was probably for the best: his other gaze was the one Marcus had encountered in the oak tree.

The servants spoke of William's past in hushed tones. He had devoted himself to some highly questionable financial enterprises. Someone without William's influence, someone without the Craver name behind him, someone like Marcus, for example, would have spent twenty years in prison. (It's also true that someone like Marcus Garvey would never have had access to a bank's board of directors.) The scandal hadn't yet cooled down and while William hid himself in voluntary ostracism, his father's contacts tried to fix everything.

Light shines differently if seen from above or below. The same thing happens with physical force. The force that moves some beings comes from up high, and the force that moves others, from below. Two bodies can have exactly the same amount of energy but they'll move differently depending on where that force comes from. It wasn't hard at all to guess where the forces that propelled William Craver came from.

One day Marcus and William met up at the summerhouse. Marcus was passing by and hadn't realised that William was inside, having a look around.

'You! Come here!' William shouted.

Marcus had once heard it said that only one out of one hundred thousand humans has grey pupils. Now he had one of them in front of him, almost close enough to touch, and it was as if he was looking at a crocodile: impossible to know what it was thinking, but knowing it couldn't be good.

'You're new?' said William.

'Yes, sir.'

'That's the only explanation. No one's yet told you that you have to take off your hat when speaking with a Craver?'

Marcus removed his hat.

'Are you the gardener?' asked William.

'No, sir. I work in the kitchen and in the stables.'

'Well, when you see the gardener tell him to fix all that.' With a vigorous finger William pointed at the summerhouse and its surroundings. 'It's filled with weeds. Tell him to fumigate them.'

'Yes, sir.'

William searched through the inside of his white jacket for his tobacco. He asked, distractedly, 'So, you are a stableboy?'

'Yes, sir.'

'And you also work in the kitchen?'

'Yes, sir.'

'Lately I've begun to understand labourers. I mean your economic position, at the base of the pyramid. Believe me, there's a good side to everything. It's very calming not to have anything, because that way you have nothing to lose.'

'That is true, sir.'

William pulled a silver cigarette case out of a pocket.

'What's your name?' he asked, placing a cigarette in his mouth.

'Garvey, sir. Marcus Garvey.'

William tried to light a match. As he struck it, it fell from his hands. William opened his eyes. He opened them wider, and wider, and wider, and he said with the cigarette still between his lips, 'Would you mind telling me what exactly you are waiting for, Marcus?'

Marcus bent down and handed him the match.

* * *

Richard Craver arrived at the house after his brother had been there, bored, for over a month, his angular face the colour of a peach, and with those enormous hands. Marcus was a witness to Richard's first act at the mansion. That large, robust body went into the Duke of Craver's office. He went in determined, but it was the decisiveness of someone facing the gallows with dignity. The doors closed behind him. Marcus, who coincidentally was below the window, was able to hear fragments of the conversation. And particularly the Duke's screaming and Richard's weeping. Marcus remembered it very well, because it was hard for him to imagine such a big bulky man crying. And what sobs!

Just like William, at first Richard had a reclusive period, as if he was embarrassed to expose himself to the world. The servants only saw him at mealtimes. When he looked, he was distrustful. When he wasn't looking, he was disdainful. Serious contradictions fought within him. Those who spoke to him were never sure if they were dealing with a buffalo or a batrachian. He spent whole weeks overcome by aboulia. Then all of a sudden he'd come out of that lethargy with virulent attacks against everyone and no one.

Richard Craver had been kicked out of the army. The only elements of the crime were Richard Craver himself, an empty stable and a six-year-old girl. Marcus couldn't comprehend how they had been able to accuse him of any crime. He talked about it with some of the other servants.

'If the stable was empty, how could he have stolen any horses? And if the girl was only six years old, what judge would admit her testimony against an officer of the military?'

Marcus didn't understand why all the servants shrank from the topic. And he soon stopped talking about it. What was discussed was the man's slovenliness and lack of willpower. Removed from military life, his body quickly grew fatter. He puffed up a bit more each day, and this change did not escape William's sarcasm.

'Soon they'll have to butter the doorways so you can get through,' he said.

Richard submitted, never challenging William's dominant role in their alliance. And yet, the interactions between the brothers weren't limited to a single pattern. There wasn't a vertical hierarchy between them in the strict sense. Richard was too brutal to allow that. When William crossed the line, Richard rebelled like an irate bull.

'If only your pockets were as big as your mouth!' Richard let loose, fed up with his insults.

But the same slight always repeated itself. Richard's subordination was not so much due to an inferiority complex as to an extraordinary lack of instinct. According to Richard: in case of danger, move quickly and don't think. According to William: in case of danger, don't move and think. Richard was incapable of coming up with any idea or initiative. His brother's might be absurd or crazy, but at least he had them. And one of Richard's few merits was being able to recognise his limitations, and so he enlisted under any flag that William was able to wave. That is a universal law: the clueless obey the insane.

William and Richard faced their ostracism with very different attitudes. Richard was a runaway train. William was a fox that hides, waiting for the dogs to get tired of looking for him. But neither one intended to stay there. They were just waiting for the occasion and the means to return to the world. For Marcus, that was incomprehensible: if someone could live in a mansion worthy of a king, why on earth would they want to leave?

One day Marcus heard the tail end of a conversation between the two brothers. Everything pointed towards it being the most vicious conversation that two brothers could have.

'From illness?' said Richard. 'You should know him better. That man only has attacks of good health.'

Marcus didn't hear anything more. But from that day on it was clear to him that the two brothers weren't chatting, they were conspiring. They started to show changes. Richard slimmed down. He did exercises and lifted weights like a strongman in the circus. William seemed more optimistic and incredibly friendly. Now his voice tickled you when he spoke. And when he smiled, all his teeth showed. Of course they were white.

I should also mention a simple but crucial anecdote, from around that same time. Marcus couldn't have known that it would change his life forever.

William received a French friend who had come to visit him. They strolled through the expansive grounds and, when they were in front of the large oak, William had trouble translating a word. Marcus was very close by and he said, spontaneously, in French, '*L'arbre.*'

'Well!' William was surprised. 'Do you really know French, Marcus?'

'A bit, Mr Craver.'

'And why is that?'

'My mother taught me.'

William gave him a probing look.

'From now on call me William, Marcus. William.' And he went off with his guest.

Two days later William and Richard called him into one of the house's large rooms. Marcus came in with his hat in his hands. William was playing the piano. Richard was playing billiards. They laughed when they saw him. They were in a good mood, and at the same time that laughter was setting the stage for a strange complicity.

'Hello, Marcus,' said William, still playing the piano. 'Do you like piano music? And billiards?'

'I don't want to take part in any crime,' was Marcus's terse response.

Marcus hadn't been able to sleep all night. Since he had heard that strange conversation between the two brothers he had become convinced that they were planning parricide. And that they wanted his help.

William stopped playing the piano. Richard put off the next cannon. They looked at him.

'Crime? What crime?' said William. 'What are you talking about?'

And the two brothers laughed. William got up from the piano bench and approached Marcus. He walked him around the room with a kindly hand on his back.

'Come, Marcus, come look at this,' he ordered, pointing to the piano. 'Have you ever stopped to think what piano keys are made of? Or billiard balls?'

'Well, no,' admitted Marcus.

'Ivory,' said William. 'Ivory is elephant tusk, and elephants are in Africa.'

Richard tried to do a cannon. He failed. He took a slug of brandy. 'You're right. I had never stopped to think about it, but the world is full of pianos and billiard balls,' he observed, resting the cue on the ground like a spear with a contemplative air. 'How many billiard balls must there be in the world? And piano keys? I'm sure if we lined them up they could reach the moon.'

'Would you like to come with us to the Congo, Marcus?' asked William. 'You know how to cook and you speak French. And we need an assistant.'

The Duke of Craver couldn't oppose his sons' trip, or he didn't know how to. The most pathetic thing of all was that that trip to their deaths wasn't a preconceived venture. The idea of Africa was shaped as the *tour de force* between the two brothers and their father progressed.

Sick of living at the Craver mansion, William and Richard asked him for a loan. That way they could start a new life, they assured him. The Duke refused. They had ruined their careers and they still had the cheek to ask him for a small fortune! A new life? The Duke knew full well that for his sons 'life' and 'vice' were synonyms.

The two brothers changed their tactics. The new argument was that they wanted to run a business together. But the reply was once again no, a curt no. William insisted. He explained to his father that they were thinking of going to Africa, specifically to the Congo. They thought that it would be the last place where they could still make some easy money, either in ivory, rubber or diamonds. 'Shut up, you lunatic,' was the reply. 'What do you know about Africa?' The Congo was the only place where there were still virgin territories, right in the middle of the African continent, replied William, and where there were no men there would be a lot of opportunities for the first ones that arrived. 'It's not even a British colony,' roared the Duke. 'Even better,' pronounced William, 'we aren't on the best terms with the English legal system.'

When they all sat down at the table, William and Richard talked about the Congo as if they were already there, ignoring their father. It was the familiar childish strategy of children who shout: 'You don't want to buy us some gloves? Well then, we'll freeze our fingers off!' They were going to go there, with his help or without it. What could the Duke of Craver do? When he understood that their decision was firm, he relented. As their father, and in order to guarantee his sons' safety in such an exotic land, he could only do one thing: pay for them to travel in the best possible conditions.

Looking at it with some perspective, everything about it makes one think that, actually, neither William nor Richard really intended to go to Africa. At least at first, the idea of the trip was just a charade to squeeze their father's wallet and get away from the family mansion. But at some point, inside William Craver's head, the farce must have become a real possibility. Swindlers and card players have a lot in common. William's bank scams prove it. His instinct led him to bet it all on one card. And that African expedition had all the makings of a huge gamble. The Congo was an open door for the bold. Why couldn't they find a gold mine, or a herd of ten million elephants, or appropriate a forest of rubber larger than Essex? What did they have to lose? William Craver had worked so hard to convince his father that in the end he had convinced himself that it was worth a shot going there.

Their luggage comprised over one hundred trunks. William remained faithful to his monotone wardrobe: several trunks contained dozens of shirts, made of cotton, wool, linen and silk, all of them white. This purely anecdotal fact upset Marcus Garvey slightly. All his belongings fitted into one small bag, and the Craver brothers needed more than a hundred trunks. But there was something good about the situation, too. Marcus felt like he was part of a great endeavour. At one level, of course: William and Richard travelled to the Congo in first-class berths on the steamship; Marcus, in third.

The only novelty of the passage was the entrance into the port of Leopoldville. For days Marcus had been impatient to disembark and he would spend hours at the prow, as if he were waiting in a box seat for a première to start.

And one evening, finally, the African coast appeared. At first Marcus thought that he was experiencing a mirage at sea. In the light of dusk the port of Leopoldville looked like an anthill. Hundreds of black figures moved rapidly in rows through the wharfs, carrying white loads on top of their heads like little ants transporting breadcrumbs. As they approached the port, Marcus could see that they were indeed men. Black men. And the white bundles that they carried on their heads, ivory tusks, which disappeared into the holds of the anchored ships.

They were welcomed in Leopoldville by an old friend of the Duke's. Marcus had forgotten his name, but he had a clear memory of the evening they spent together. The man was a high official of an import–export company who lived in a house of green wood, with mosquito nets on the doors, windows and beds. After dinner all four of them sat in wicker armchairs. The host gave them cigars and French cognac. He didn't make any class distinctions and Marcus was able to enjoy the same pleasures as the other men.

Their host expressed his doubts about William and Richard's venture. He said that the ivory was becoming scarce, that the rubber was a government monopoly, and that finding a mine deep in the Congo would be a stroke of luck as improbable as a lost ant finding an oasis in the Sahara. He added that William and Richard were nothing more than a couple of amateurs, and that the Congo was the most savage place in the world. But he said it all in such a cordial and funny way, that even the Craver brothers, as insulted as they may have felt, laughed heartily. He also said that the 'niggers' were the worst workers in existence, lazier than the Latins, more shifty than the Arabs, and stupider than the Chinese.

'Treat them without ceremony and with forceful methods,' he recommended between the smoke rings that came out of his mouth. 'It's the only language they understand.'

The house wasn't very big, with no extra bedrooms, and Marcus anticipated spending the night with the servants. The man dismissed the idea with a guffaw.

'No. That's unthinkable. White people don't sleep with Negroes.'

'I don't mind,' murmured Marcus, who didn't want to cause any problems. But that was what made the man raise his voice in a very unpleasant tone.

'Well, I do, my friend, I definitely do mind! If I allowed that, the entire European community in Leopoldville would incriminate me, and rightly so. A European can't mix with Africans. In this life, everyone has their place, and they have to stay there.'

That created a problem. Today it's hard to believe that our formalities were so strict, but in 1912 it was unthinkable that the Craver brothers spend the night with someone like Marcus. It was one thing to share tobacco and a cognac with a servant, and quite another to share a room. But Marcus couldn't sleep with the Negro servants of the house either. There was a moment of hesitation.

Finally, three of the servants accompanied him to a guesthouse at the port, poor but respectable and very clean, which was frequented by sailors and European staff of inferior rank.

First thing the following day, Marcus had to return to the house to meet with the Craver brothers. We'll have to forgive him the bewilderment he suffered. Marcus was unfamiliar with that phenomenon so often spoken of by travellers. They say that Africa shows us that in England everything is more tenuous, more trivial, as if we Northerners lived with ghost feelings, apathetic and mollified, uncultivated. On the other hand, the Congo amplified the world's power. The light didn't fall from the sky, it came from every side. The smells were fetid or splendid, nothing in between. The mouths spoke a language of bubbles.

The streets were filled with Negro men, women and children. He never would have thought there could be so many Negroes in the world. And he realised that a lot of them were looking at him as if he were the oddity. Suddenly he noticed that, as crowded as those red dirt streets were, no one ever bumped into him. They kept their distance, as if he were a leper. Why? He collided with a woman.

I remember that Marcus sat in front of me, at our rectangular table. He raised his handcuffed hands above his head.

'You could never imagine, Mr Thomson, the amount of things that Negro women can carry on their heads!'

The woman hadn't seen Marcus. Her bundle of firewood lay scattered on the ground. Marcus acted as any civilised person would: he bent down to pick up the firewood, feeling ashamed at having caused the incident.

'Excuse me a thousand times over, madam!' he proclaimed. 'I'll carry the wood to wherever you say. Forgive me, forgive me . . .'

But the silence made him forget about the firewood. He was surrounded by perhaps more than a hundred people, all silent. They couldn't understand what he was doing there, in the middle of the street. But above all they couldn't understand what a white man was doing stooped down and gathering a Negro woman's firewood. He looked at the woman. What he saw in her face wasn't indignation. It was terror.

The stay at Leopoldville extended longer than had been anticipated. Even to Marcus it was obvious that William and Richard were doing something more than enjoying the hospitality of their father's friend. The three men met frequently so that the new arrivals could learn the rudiments of life in the Congo. Since Marcus was excluded, the days dragged for him. So he was very happy when the expedition prepared to set off, fifteen days later.

That same day they introduced him to Godefroide, a thickset Negro man, as tough as a crab. His bones seemed twice as thick as normal. He wore short trousers and you could see that he had the brawny thighs of a wild boar. He wore a cylindrical, Turkish-style hat. His face was lined with fissures, very similar to the ones seen on soil that has endured a long drought. But the cracks followed an intelligent geometry, as if an iron spider's web had become encrusted on his face. He came recommended by a friend of the Duke. He didn't talk much.

'And the mules?' asked Marcus.

William made a vague gesture with his hand. Marcus saw a hundred Negro men beside the bundles. They only wore long underpants. They sat apathetically, squatting like frogs with their elbows over their knees, waiting for someone to give them marching orders.

'Bearers are in short supply,' said William. 'It took all of my father's friend's influence to be able to recruit them.'

I would never have thought that the jungle would be so close to the city. Two hours after they set off, there was no visible sign of human life. Leopoldville could have been right behind them, or very, very far away. The jungle had swallowed them up.

I'll skip the detailed account of their march through the jungle. Stanley has already described it quite well when he baptised it the 'green hell.' However, I will note, that exoticism and monotony can co-exist very well. The first twenty days they didn't report anything new. They advanced all day long in an extended row of humans. Since the path was so narrow and there was a very dense ceiling of vegetation above their heads, it was as if they were travelling through a tunnel. In certain spots the verdure was an impenetrable shield, and in others it became a sword that wounded everything it touched. The plants prevented any natural light from reaching the ground, so there was little difference between the days and the nights. At the end of each day, the expedition camped in any clearing, and first thing in the morning they set off again. Every day was the same.

William wore white, as always. White pith helmet, white shirt, white trousers. The only exception was the high black boots that made his figure even more svelte. Richard wore a khaki uniform and a wide-brimmed Australian hat. A thin ribbon of white fabric hung from the hat down his entire back, a precaution against the strong sun. At that time it was believed that the tropical sun ate away at the European spine. Each man's weapon matched its owner's body. William carried a light Winchester repeating rifle, Richard an enormous shotgun that according to the manufacturer's advertising could fell an adult elephant with one shot. When the ceiling of the vegetation allowed it, William and Richard travelled in portable chairs, borne by four bearers, similar to the ancient Romans' sedan chairs. And Marcus? Were his little legs built to withstand exhausting marches in such a hostile environment? Against all expectations, yes. Ducks have short legs too and they are great swimmers. With Marcus it was something similar. His workman's cap was enough to protect him from the heat. He rolled up the sleeves of a light linen shirt, on top of which were only the leather braces attached to his trousers. His worker's boots seemed to have been made to walk through the jungle. Moving among trees filled him with a new vigour, as if the jungle was his natural environment.

The trees. Godefroide taught him many things. It was him who explained to Marcus that the thunder they heard on their march wasn't actually thunder. Every once in a while a long boom would erupt, a cannon shot that ripped through the earth. But it wasn't the prelude to any flood.

'That's not thunder,' explained Godefroide impassively. 'Those are large trees dying. They fall and the sound spreads throughout the entire jungle, far, far away.'

There were trees whose trunks had thorns larger than bayonets and wider than axes. There were trees with iron bark and trees with velvet creases. Some projected their roots along the path, and blocked their way with a wooden barricade they either had to jump or climb over. And there were also killer trees, that grew up around other ones, coiling around them just like a snake. On many stretches of that tunnel of vegetation the atmosphere was so dense, the air so short of oxygen, that men suffocated. It was like breathing hot gas. The column had no choice but to speed up and hold their breath, as if they were underwater and trying to make it to the surface before drowning.

And the noise. A sort of uninterrupted whirling buzz with deep tones superimposed. The jungle might raise the volume at any moment, slowly, imperceptibly, constantly. Sometimes the sound's insistence made men drunk with fake energy and, as if they were spurred on by the drum that marked galley slaves' pace, they covered ten miles with the effort of only one. Other times, the sound passed through their clothes and their flesh and turned their bones into steam.

William's fair eyes made him suffer. In the Congo, the light has no gradation. Within the jungle, days were green darkness: the leafy ceilings sealed off the sun. Then, suddenly, the caravan would enter a clearing. There the sun would burst through in full force. Opaque darkness and then blinding light. The contrast hurt those delicate grey pupils.

William had always been an artist of cold violence. Now the excess of light provoked in him attacks of hot-bloodedness. On one occasion he directed his discomfort at Marcus. This was how it went.

One day, during the break for lunch, the bearers were ordered to open some boxes. They pulled chains and stocks from them. If they wanted to eat, they had to put the stocks on their necks. Godefroide translated William's words.

'Every day there are more disturbances around the pot. From now on you'll queue up like this. No more pushing.'

The men were hungry and they obeyed. A few moments later Godefroide and Marcus distributed the food to a row of one hundred shackled men. Each neck was attached to the next one and the previous one, no one escaped the irons. William approached the large pot where Godefroide filled the wooden bowls. William blinked, his eyes smarting in the intense light of the Congo. He scolded him, yelling, 'What are you, Marcus? A kitchen hand or a French chef?'

It was easy to imagine Marcus, moving his head from right to left, looking at the pot and the wooden bowls, not understanding what William was talking about.

'Save food!' he clarified.

Marcus looked at the row of men, each one similar to the next like one hundred sardines.

'But they're very weak,' said Marcus. 'They carry forty pounds all day long.'

'Do what you're told, halfwit!' shouted William. And before turning to leave he spat out, 'This isn't a picnic!'

They spent the rest of the day in the clearing. But after the meal no one took the stocks off of their necks. Drenched in sweat, William and Richard smoked, seated in folding chairs some distance away. They didn't say anything, they didn't do anything. They acted as if the Negro men had been chained up since day one. The strangest thing of all was that the bearers didn't complain. One, only one, made a gesture, picking up the chain with one hand and showing it timidly to the white men. But William and Richard just kept smoking. The one who held the chain up looked around him. No one seconded him and he let it go.

Marcus didn't understand it. The men had let themselves be chained up without offering any resistance. Why? For a bit of millet soup. They didn't protest, they didn't demand that the chains be taken off. They lay there apathetically like a flock of sheep. Nothing more.

What ideas went through Marcus's mind? We don't know what he thought, only what he did. In the middle of that small clearing there was a tree, only one. It reigned like a sole emperor that keeps the plebeians at a distance. Marcus had never seen anything like it. Compared to that tree, the oak at the Craver mansion was like a blind man's cane. The base was shaped like a monstrous, open frog's hand. Lateral planks of wood projected from the trunk, like shark fins, and plunged into the earth. Just one of those planks was larger than a child's toboggan. Marcus looked up, but the density of the branches kept him from seeing the tree's peak.

He climbed into the tree. He got up the first few feet thanks to some lianas that fell parallel to the trunk, which were stronger and more secure than iron cords. William and Richard laughed, 'What are you doing, Marcus? There's already enough monkeys in the Congo!'

Marcus didn't answer. He continued going further and further up. Instinctively, he used a technique sailors use when working on the ship's mast: of his four limbs, hands and feet, he steadied three before moving one. When he had climbed about fifty feet he could no longer see the ground. Further up. He heard William and Richard's sarcastic voices grow weaker as he climbed. Before he realised it he could no longer hear them, nor any other human sound.

Up there life was nothing like down below. He encountered birds, which were astonished by his presence. He wasn't afraid of falling. The branches made a wider, safer structure than any scaffolding, no one would have believed he was over one hundred and fifty feet high.

He continued. The trunks were now slimmer. The leaves whipped his face and scratched his hands. Marcus wanted to go a little bit higher, just a bit more.

Finally he stretched out his arm and a small branch broke in his fingers. It was if a skylight opened up: the greenest eyes in Africa met with the bluest sky in the world.

From that natural watchtower he could see a green carpet that extended into infinity. He was so high up that the jungle looked like a layer of moss. But it wasn't grass, it was trees, trees, trees. Here they rippled, further on they waved and above floated the jungle's vapour, rising with the density of a cotton fog.

The trees dominated everything. There was no desert, no ocean, no tundra that could compare. And in that moment, at the top of that tree, Marcus knew the world could be a very large place, but that the Congo would always be larger than the world.

Out loud he said, 'My God, where are we going?'

I think that Marcus sensed the answer: on beyond the grace of God.

FIVE

FIVE DAYS LATER THE bearers started dying off. The process was very simple. When a man fell weak, they tried to revive him by beating him with the butt of a gun. If he didn't respond, they opened the shackles, left him right there and the caravan continued forward.

Death begat death: the more bearers that died, the more weight the remaining ones had to carry, and so, even more bearers died. But the losses only revealed the Craver brothers' most inflexible side. During a break Richard surprised a man holding a jar filled with formol. He was looking at the liquid and the beetles that floated in it against the light. He was so fascinated he didn't realise that Richard was watching him.

'You opened the luggage!' shouted Richard angrily. 'How dare you?'

William came over. After briefly reflecting he gave his judgement. 'Tomorrow, this man will haul the champagne.'

That night Marcus spoke with Godefroide.

'Why are they so stupid? They are all tied up, and even so they steal.'

'He wasn't trying to steal,' said Godefroide.

'No? Then why did he open the trunk?'

'Out of curiosity.'

'There were only beetles in the jar.'

'He didn't understand what interest the white men could have in some dead beetles. And for that, now he is the one who'll die.'

Godefroide spoke little and always expressed himself with artistic ambiguity. Either due to his Bantu syntax or some unique inclination of his personality, it was impossible to know if he was just stating a fact, if he was condemning it or if, just the opposite, that he fully supported the authority that ordained it.

Carrying the champagne was the equivalent of a death sentence. There were sixty pounds of French bottles with thick glass. They couldn't distribute the load into other boxes, because that one had special cushioning to protect the bottles.

The champagne was like a mark of death. They all knew that the man who carried the champagne would die before the day ended, from total exhaustion. So, at the start of each day the Negro men would try to grab any bundle before that one. There were fights. The result, as logical as it was inevitable, was that the weakest ended up bearing the heaviest load. But William and Richard were pleased with the situation, because it ensured that the bearers made sure to wake up nice and early to avoid that crate.

Here, I'll interject: I had promised myself that I wouldn't open my mouth during our sessions unless it was vital. But when I heard about the first deaths I began to suffer a dreadful nervous excitement. Listening to Marcus was like drinking a thousand cups of coffee. My heart beat faster, my veins got wider and torrents of blood ran up and down inside me. Even still, I kept quiet. And I assure you that the effort of maintaining that silence was not healthy at all.

Marcus referred to the victims without any feeling. As if all that carnage was a minor incident. The bearers were human beings. They treated them like dogs, and when they died they left them like dead dogs. But Marcus showed no emotion. I was saying all that to myself, and the word 'Pepe' made me open my eyes.

At some point on the journey Marcus changed Godefroide's name to Pepe; it was shorter and easier to pronounce. William and Richard laughed at the joke. And Pepe stuck. That familiarity wasn't as strange as it might seem. Because of their daily tasks, Marcus and Godefroide had a very intense relationship. Godefroide (we'll call him Pepe from now on), was the Negro man who held the highest rank in the expedition's hierarchy. And Marcus was the white man with the lowest. They were very close to each other. There was always some sort of invisible dividing line between them. Like two men separated by bars, each on one side. But that didn't keep them from being the two closest men, each on their own side of the bars.

William and Richard slept in the same tent. Pepe, at first, slept out under the stars, like the bearers. One day he had a bad toothache. Even though he had a very stoic nature, William decided that Pepe should share Marcus's tent. He didn't want the bearers to see any weakness in the man, who was both guide and guardian. Marcus slept in a more humble tent, along with some piled-up trunks that had to be protected from the weather. He made a spot for Pepe and when the toothache subsided, no one thought of kicking him out.

In some corner of Marcus's mind, solid parallels with his childhood were established. He slept with Godefroide as he had slept with Pepe the bear from his youth. In a world where men were treated like animals, it could at least be said of Marcus Garvey that he shared his life with one of those animals.

It became necessary to replace the dead bearers. But that was easier said than done. All the towns were identical: a handful of round cabins with adobe walls and thatched roofs. And all the towns were deserted by the time the expedition reached them. There were plenty of signs that indicated the inhabitants had fled as fast as their legs could carry them. They must have had enough experience with what happened on the caravans. Later, an unforeseen crisis hovered over the Craver brothers' expedition: the bearers had no value compared to the load they were transporting; but until they found a mine, the load was of no use to them.

Their boldness was their main asset. At that point they had gone so far, so deep in, that their feet were treading on regions where the white man was only a rumour. People didn't flee in fear, they approached curiously, like penguins, without suspecting the threat those white men represented. The only ones that panicked were the children. They had never seen beings so ghostly pale and they cried from fright. The cruellest thing of all was that the inhabitants of those towns laughed at the poor devils on the caravan. They tortured them in a thousand ways: dancing around the captives, rubbing their penises on their buttocks to humiliate them and piercing their cheeks and the palms of their hands with burins. It didn't occur to them that they could be the next victims.

William and Richard always used the same tactic. They arrived in a village and assembled everyone. Before speaking they demanded a respectable distance between them and the indigenous mass, who laughed, jumped and danced, awaiting some gift or other. Finally they would manage to get all those black bodies and all those white smiles to gather before them, neatly collected. That was when they would throw a stick of dynamite into the crowd.

Red dirt erupted. Arms and legs flew. Shouts and moans. Pepe and Marcus would fall upon the wounded throng. Jumping with rapid movements, they chose the most stunned men, who had a hard time understanding what was going on. They shackled their necks while William and Richard beat them with the butts of their guns. In this fashion the caravan became restocked with bearers.

I remember Marcus explaining all that to me on a day of heavy rain. The noise of the water chiming against the walls of the prison could be heard in our inner cell. Marcus raised his arms as he reproduced the dynamite's explosion, 'Boom!' I involuntarily made a fist, a small nervous spasm, and my wooden pencil made a dry cracking noise. While I looked at the two pieces I said, with an iron voice, 'And what did you do to prevent it?'

The words were still crossing the border of my mouth when I regretted having spoken. Too late. Marcus was very surprised. I had never interrupted him when he was speaking. His magnificent green eyes blinked, like the wings of a butterfly, and he very politely asked, 'Could you repeat the question?'

I snorted. 'What did you do to stop William Craver and Richard Craver from blowing up a handful of helpless men, women, old people and children with sticks of dynamite?'

Marcus looked from one side to the other, for some assistance that wasn't there.

'Stop them?' he said finally. 'I don't think you understand. I was the one who threw the dynamite.'

I had been listening with an electrical tension in my spine. But when I heard that I felt a shot of sulphur enter my bloodstream.

'After the explosion Pepe and I were very busy chaining up survivors. William and Richard shot off their guns,' explained Marcus. 'The shots made them more confused and upset, and kept them from resisting at all. William and Richard enjoyed it. For them, recruiting bearers was the closest thing to a sport that one could practise in the Congo. While Pepe and I rushed about tying up the captured men, the Craver brothers examined them. The explosion had torn off those tattered straw rags they wore, and Richard often laughed as he pointed between their legs with the tip of his rifle, saying, 'Oh, oh, oh, look at that! That is something! What big cocks on these fellows!'

Marcus Garvey stood accused of killing two men. For that he was awaiting trial. But dozens had been killed by his hand, maybe hundreds of men, women and children. And no one accused him of those crimes.

Marcus raised his eyebrows high.

'And what exactly would you have done, Mr Thomson?'

My body recoiled, searching for the back of the chair. It had been a mistake to ask him anything. Now Marcus had every right to ask me questions. Once the question was posed, I couldn't avoid it. My hostility towards Marcus dissipated as quickly as it had risen, replaced by immense doubt. I wasn't at all sure where his guilt began. William and Richard had ordered him to throw the sticks of dynamite. And if he had refused? William and Richard were the heads of the expedition, and he was just a stableboy.

When the book finally came out it was described by some as a magnificent portrait of human degradation. They were wrong. The most incomprehensible aspect of horror is that there is nothing to understand. Horror is incredibly shallow and common. One only needs two things in order to kill: the ability and the desire. William and Richard could kill and they wanted to kill. From that point on I didn't count the number of dead. I would have loved to write the story of three healthy English youths that progressively degenerate, three youths that become more and more morally dissolute the further into the jungle they get. And yet, Marcus never mentioned any of that, not actively or passively. There was no process of conversion to barbarism. William and Richard were the same men in England as they were in the Congo. But the Congo was not England.

Marcus was convinced, and with reason, that recruiting bearers with explosives was a regular practice in the Congo. Neither William nor Richard was breaking any law; the question was if such an disgraceful act could be morally accepted? In this case, where does the decency of a reasonably honest man begin? Would Garvey have had to refuse the food restrictions that William had demanded a few days earlier? Or perhaps, at the house in Leopoldville, he should have insisted on sharing a room with the Negro servants? We must also keep in mind that Marcus Garvey couldn't oppose the Craver brothers' authority lightly. For a stableboy to rebel against two aristocrats, alone and in the middle of the jungle, would have required Marcus to be endowed with some inconceivable type of heroism.

But the core of the problem was something else. We have a tendency to think that the magnitude of pain inflicted is directly proportional to the effort required to cause it. No. The Congo had placed Marcus in an unusual position: active collaboration in evil was a matter of a concession as simple as holding out your hand. Now, a lifetime later, I have no doubt: that hand was the essence of the twentieth century.

Marcus's question awaited reply. I rubbed my eyes with my closed fists, and I could only say, 'I never would have gone to the Congo.'

SIX

LIKE COLUMBUS, WILLIAM LIED to the others about how far they had gone. And like Hannibal, he always promised them that their goal was around the next hill. Who was he trying to fool? The bearers' opinions meant nothing to him. Marcus and Pepe were subordinate voices. And, in fact, the one who decided when and where they would stop was Richard. In the army he had served in a logistics unit; he had also studied a bit of mineralogy, and it was he who carried out the prospecting. But the diamonds never showed up.

Richard was desperate; William, furious. Sometimes they were both desperate and furious. William screamed; Richard cried and screamed. Worst of all, they had gone so far looking for their imaginary treasures, so deep into a virgin jungle, they no longer found any towns, there were no more human beings to replace the losses. There were only trees, thorns and animal noises. But whether led by the constancy of the bold or of the demented, they continued.

Those who create a problem are the first ones to look for the guilty party. And the loudest. William and Richard accused each other. The jungle had never heard such horrid abominations.

Marcus realised that Pepe tended to keep his distance from the two brothers, at the tail end of the expedition. One day he too placed himself at the back.

'Why do you always stay at the end, Pepe?'

'William and Richard are like two elephants. One is fatter, the other has longer tusks,' replied the Negro man. 'And I know who loses when two elephants fight.'

'Really? Who?'

'The ants.'

Marcus couldn't recall the exact day when the expedition arrived at that clearing. He had lost count of the days and nights. And everyone had changed somewhat. Especially the Craver brothers. They were no longer half-penny explorers. The jungle had put them through some sort of aesthetic erosion. Their clothes, bought in London's finest tailors, had become frayed and faded. Large rings of sweat had overtaken their armpits, chest and back. With the exception of the bottles of champagne, no other glassware had survived. And that was how the caravan arrived at the clearing – that clearing.

Someone gave the order to halt. The bearers let themselves drop, exhausted. Marcus sat on a rock. Further on, William and Richard argued fiercely. One chased the other, who would withdraw and refuse to listen, until an insult too crude would make him attack and the other withdraw. Who would have imagined it? Two English noblemen arguing with the gestures of Italian greengrocers. Any moment they might unsheathe their revolvers and shoot each other.

The clearing was unusually large. More or less like a rugby field. The ground was welcoming, half covered by patches of green grass and in stretches by that red African sand, finer than any tropical beach. Marcus lay flat, absorbed in looking at the sky, that sky so blue which they could only see in the few moments when they went through a clearing. He lowered his eyes. His gaze fixed, by chance, on a random blade of grass. It looked like an asparagus. Marcus wondered, 'Is there asparagus in the Congo?' He brought his hand closer, and below the asparagus appeared a glow, a yellow light that hurt his eyes.

Marcus interrupted the Craver brothers' fratricidal war. With one hand raised, he said, 'There's something shiny here.'

It was like two people arguing over a stolen wallet when a third person shows up saying he found it on the ground. Marcus offered the golden grain to Richard.

'Where did you find this?' said Richard after a quick look.

Marcus gestured vaguely and said with a certain indifference, 'Here, in the clearing.'

If the bearers hadn't been half-dead with exhaustion they would have laughed. They had gone to the ends of the earth, and even further, and the white bosses spent their time pacing through the clearing like hens, their backs hunched as if they were looking for little worms to peck at.

'Here!' shouted William.

'Here!' shouted Richard.

'And more here!' said Marcus.

And even Pepe found a golden chickpea, and he held it up with two fingers very close to his eyes, looking at it as if he were an expert watchmaker. He raised it above his head, and said, 'A little yellow stone. They're everywhere.'

A few days later they had set up a permanent camp in the clearing. Since a large part of Garvey's story took place in that extraordinary clearing, I should devote some lines to describing it.

The clearing was shaped like an egg. In its exact centre they made a hole that grew deeper by the day: the mine itself. The Negroes got orders to dig and dig, and not to worry about anything else. And when the hole was deep enough and wide enough William freed them from their chains. The shackles were no longer needed: from that moment on they would sleep inside the mine. During the day the Negroes worked overseen by rifles, during the night the ladder – a trunk with sticks going through it like a fish bone – was taken away. The mine's exit, way up high, was just a hole in the ceiling. No one could get out through there. It was a mine and a perfect prison.

William and Richard, Marcus and Pepe soon began to refer to the hole that was the mine's entrance as the 'anthill'. Many feet stamped each day on the sides of the hole, so that the mouth of the mine took on a conical shape, like a dwarf volcano. Or a giant anthill.

The inside was shaped like a pumpkin. The Negroes pounded at the walls and expanded the hole. As the space got wider, they placed vertical beams to prop up the ceiling. From some of the beams they hung oil lamps. They gave off a cold light that amplified the wall's scarlet colour. Inside it was unpleasantly hot. And it smelled dirty, like burnt cheese.

The workers were distributed into three rotating shifts. Most scraped at the walls with short sticks. There were no picks: the Negroes' capacity for submission seemed infinite, but William and Richard didn't trust them. The earth was porous and came away easily. Some others, not many, filled wicker baskets and had permission to carry them up to the outside, taking turns going up the ladder. And a third group, much smaller and even luckier (because they could leave the mine), removed the gold from the dirt.

Richard had built a rudimentary bathtub at the foot of the mine with caulked wood. There they washed and separated the dirt from the gold. Not far into the surrounding jungle, there was a small stream. With trunks hollowed out by machete strikes and connected to each other, like tiles, Richard made some pipes that brought water. He had them lead to the bathtub and then return to the stream so that the clearing wouldn't flood.

In any case, as far as the Negroes were concerned, one would have to say that the establishment of the mine had brought them more benefits than adversity. The Cravers had gone far, incredibly far. They had gone further than the natives, to a latitude empty of men. If the Negroes died, who would replace them? So, in general terms, and even though it was only from self-interest, the treatment became more benign. The work in the mine was less punishing than hauling. And their food increased thanks to what the forest provided. Now the two brothers had much more free time, and they spent it hunting. Marcus cooked meats that were strange, yes, but nutritious.

Fifteen days later, William drew up some careful calculations in order to establish the mine's output. Each day of work yielded ten and twenty ounces of pure gold. That meant daily profits of around two hundred pounds sterling. Tax free, of course.

Up until then the Cravers had exploited the Negroes' feet as bearers. Now they exploited their hands as miners. No one bothered to count the deaths that it had cost to get there.

There are days when, before getting out of bed, we sense, we know, that everything is going to go wrong. That was how that Sunday began. I was running late. I had to be at the barrister's office with a copy of my progress and I was still getting dressed. I rushed to the bathroom as fast as I could and in the hallway I met up with Marie Antoinette, the turtle. I hadn't seen her, and I almost twisted my ankle for the umpteenth time.

Enraged, I kicked her, making her fly like a rugby ball. It might seem like excessive treatment for a turtle without a shell. It wasn't. In Mrs Pinkerton's boarding house, there were only two certainties: that the landlady was already old when Tutankhamen was born and that her turtle hated me with an unfathomable passion. And that Marie Antoinette had powers, yes, that too. For example, my kick had sent her flying through the air from one end of the hallway to the other. Any other turtle would have shrunk into its shell. Not her. Since she didn't have one she had acquired a cat's instinct and landed on her feet.

Marie Antoinette turned around, very worked up. She was looking for the perpetrator of that attack. She saw me, and when she had me in her line of vision she attacked me with rage. All turtles have ugly mouths but Marie Antoinette's was particularly ugly, a real crow's beak. She came towards me like a Roman battering ram.

Some might think that turtles don't do cavalry charges but if we were to look at the world from a turtle's perspective, we would surely find that some were quick and some were slow. Well, from a turtle's point of view, Marie Antoinette was charging.

The hallway was narrow. If I wanted to leave the house I had to get past her. Naturally, I wasn't going to give up an appointment with Norton just because an hysterical turtle was attacking me. I couldn't believe it: there I was, Tommy Thomson, going face to face with a turtle as if we were two knights in a medieval joust.

She charged towards me, and I went towards her. She had some horrific white foam coming from her mouth. We approached each other. I was above her. I thought: now I'll step on one of her feet, and she'll cry out, and Pinkerton will have to spend my rent money on vet's bills. But at the last second, in an agile manoeuvre, Marie Antoinette turned and wrapped herself around my ankle. I abhor any reptilian contact and I jumped. She fled. I stumbled. I staggered. I fell!

The direction of my fall coincided with the hallway window. Even still, I didn't have to fall. But I made two mistakes. Underneath my arm I carried the portfolio of written pages. I refused to let go of it, thinking I could easily keep myself from falling with one hand. My first mistake. The second, forgetting the lesson all children are taught, that the upper part of the body weighs more than the lower. I didn't realise the danger until I had my head and chest suspended outside the open window. I let all the pages drop, like a shower of confetti. And before I could do anything to prevent it, I was hanging over the void. I held on to the window frame, sustained only by my ten fingers.

This was definitely one of those occasions for which expressions such as 'Help!' were invented. But the truth is I have never known anyone who shouted 'Help!' in a dramatic situation. Nobody. The only thing I could utter was, 'Eeeh! Eeeh! Eeeh!'

I don't know how long I was there, hanging over the abyss and shouting. Finally a huge, solid figure appeared, framed by the window. It was Mr MacMahon. Thank God! He had a towel over his shoulders, he had just woken up and had that bovine face that people have when they're half asleep. He looked to my left and to my right, absurdly, then rubbed the sleep from his eyes and said, incredibly calmly, 'Tommy, old boy, what are you doing out here?'

I could only answer, 'Eeeeeeeh!' then, in a whiny tone, 'MacMahon!'

He got me out of there, eventually. I sat down, trying to pull myself together after the scare. Marie Antoinette had taken the precaution of hiding after her victory. I was running late and I didn't have time for retaliation. I had enough work to do recovering the scattered pages before the wind carried them off.

Norton was impatient. Because I was late and because he had been wanting to read the first few chapters of the book for days. He received me with very few words. It was his way of showing his displeasure. We sat down.

He didn't like it. He read my typescript and I read his face. He got more and more nervous. He turned the pages faster and faster. He started to talk to himself. He pointed to the most troublesome parts with his finger and said, 'But this . . . What is this? . . . And that? . . . And that?'

And after reading a few more pages he concluded, 'This is Zola in the Congo! Bakunin in the Congo! Catiline in the Congo!' He waited for my reply but seeing that it didn't come, he continued, all fired up. 'Don't you see what image we're reflecting of the English aristocracy? What do you want me to do with all this hatred for socicty? I'll never find any way to exonerate Garvey with this. There's enough to hang him ten times in here!'

'I don't want to start any revolution, I only want to write a book,' I said in my defence. 'And that is an exact account of the facts according to Marcus Garvey.'

'Do you want me to attack the most powerful people in Great Britain? Who do you think presides over the British courts? Robespierre?'

I could easily have kept my mouth shut. But I didn't.

'I also wanted to tell you that I went to visit the Duke of Craver.'

Norton put his hands on his head. Very slowly. He raised them little by little, until they were hugging that spherical capsule that was his bald skull. I continued, 'You haven't heard the worst of it yet.'

Norton held his breath. He didn't take his hands off of his head. And, after a brief pause that I used to gather my strength, I said, 'We came to a gentlemen's agreement. He'll help me with the facts and dates of the case in exchange for my sending him copies of the work as it progresses. I've been sending him certified envelopes for two weeks now.'

'What kind of irresponsible oaf have I hired?' shouted Norton. 'Don't you understand, for God's sake? Craver is the enemy! The only interest he could have is in seeing Marcus hanged.' And, even more furious, he yelled, 'You are insane! No! Pardon! I'm the one who's insane! I assigned this job, and I assigned it to you! A mercenary who, first chance he gets, gives away all the secrets of war to the enemy!'

He stood up, paced incessantly from one end of the office to the other, with one arm behind his back and gesticulating with the other like a dictator in an operetta. His accusations became a monologue: 'You are an untamed anarchist! Most writers are professional sycophants. And I have the bad luck of hiring a terrorist of the written word!'

I had never seen him fly off the handle before. I had a different man in front of me, an Edward Norton I had never known. He was overflowing with rage. I realised that he must have learned to hide this more passionate side to his personality. In his daily life he must have made a huge effort to channel that primal fury towards legal empiricism. I got up from my chair too.

'I won't oppose the cancellation of our contract.' I headed towards the door.

'Thomson!'

I turned. Norton was at the back of the room, still, firm, legs firmly together. Not even his violent rage had managed to add a single wrinkle to his clothes. He said, 'Sit down.'

He sat too. He had recovered his authority. His gaze softened a bit. He became that man I had met at the cemetery again, disinterestedly friendly.

'You want to know something, Thomson? I've always hated team sports. You could be the best cricket player in the world, but if your teammates are a bunch of losers you'll never win anything. That is why I devote myself to the art of law. I thought that as a barrister I wouldn't have to depend on anyone, only on my own abilities. Now I see that I was wrong. Life is full of imponderables.'

'I'm sorry I disappointed you.'

'From now on, just write. That's what I pay you for.'

'I can't,' I said immediately, with a decisiveness that surprised both Norton and me. 'I gave my word to the Duke of Craver. While I'm the one writing Marcus Garvey's story in the Congo, the Duke of Craver is going to receive copies.'

Norton was intelligent enough to realise that he was up against a wall. He made that pyramid with his fingers. He was coldly analysing how to get the situation back on track. Before me was more a rational machine than a man. He ignored my presence to such an extent that I felt like an object. Finally, I got tired of it.

'If you prefer to indulge in solitary reflection, I won't disturb you.'

'Sit!' he ordered for the second time. 'How do you expect me to find another writer? I can't start from zero at this point.'

'There are thousands of better writers than me. Everyone would want the chance to write a story as incredible as this one.' And I stressed my point by saying, 'And they are all sycophants. They won't argue with you about your strategy.'

But Norton preferred to ignore my sarcasm. He wasn't listening to me anymore.

'So the Duke of Craver wants to read the adventures of his pups in the Congo, eh? Well, it looks to me like he's going to get a lot of surprises.'

'Even more? I haven't been at all indulgent with the Craver brothers' exploits in the jungle. You just read it.'

Norton punctured me with his eyes.

'Yes, even more. He has many more surprises awaiting him.'

And then he addressed me informally. I remember it very well, because it was the first and only time that he did so in all the years of our relationship.

'You don't know it, Tommy,' he murmured, 'but the real story of Marcus Garvey in the Congo hasn't even begun.'

And, in essence, that was that. He didn't like me or the book, but I was still his writer. As I returned home lost in thought, I could sense the weight of his displeasure on my back as if I carried a child on my shoulders. I was thinking about the book, about Garvey, about Norton, about the Congo. I was incredibly mixed up. From nowhere my life had taken a turn, and I didn't know where that turn would lead me. This wasn't a book, it was a war. And I was one of the forces involved, not exactly the most powerful one. On the other hand, it's also true that there are things that we don't like but which attract us all the same. When I arrived at the boarding house I was still swimming in that sea of thoughts. As I went through the hallway I discovered her, lying in wait behind the leg of a wardrobe.

It was her, Marie Antoinette, scrutinising me, satanically silent. Some would say that Marie Antoinette could only express her hate in silence because she was a turtle. To these naïve souls I would reply that hate, like laughter, makes less noise the deeper it is.

This turtle had gone too far. It was one thing that we hated each other and quite another that she had gone to the extreme of trying to murder me. I picked her up with one hand and launched her off the balcony in the style of a javelin thrower.

Three seconds later that simulacrum of a human being named Mrs Pinkerton appeared in the hallway.

'Did you say something, Mr Thomson?'

'Who me?' I remarked in the most evasive tone. 'Nothing at all, Mrs Pinkerton.'

'I'm looking for Marie Antoinette. You wouldn't happen to

have seen her, would you? Lately she's had me worried. She's a little sad . . .'

Pinkerton began to look for Marie Antoinette in all the corners, waving a lettuce leaf as a lure. I did too. I shook a rotten leaf of lettuce and with my back hunched I called out her name; it was glorious hypocrisy. The door opened. It was Mr MacMahon, appalled.

'Mrs Pinkerton! Look what fell on top of me!'

'Marie Antoinette!' exclaimed Pinkerton when she saw the turtle in MacMahon's hands. 'What have you done?'

MacMahon's shouts ratified Mrs Pinkerton's suspicions.

'She tried to commit suicide! I saw her as she fell from the window! I was coming back from mass, I was right below and I opened my arms. We're so lucky!'

At this point I'll omit the jumping for joy and fussing those two did. Especially Mrs Pinkerton. Her eyes even grew damp! I had never seen her like that. She congratulated MacMahon as if he were Noah in the flesh. She wrapped Marie Antoinette in a tiny scarf and brought her a plate of warm anise so she could inhale the vapours. While Pinkerton wiped dry two little tears with a handkerchief, MacMahon asked us to wait a moment and he disappeared. A few seconds later he came back with a curious artefact in his hands.

'Look what I brought for her!'

MacMahon placed some sort of clog on the table, or that's what it looked like. It was like a child's wooden shoe, but wider and with some holes distributed along the structure.

Pinkerton, or me, I don't remember, asked what it was.

'But can't you see?' MacMahon was surprised. 'It's a new shell for Marie Antoinette.'

'You don't mean to put poor Marie Antoinette in a wooden device!' grumbled Pinkerton, who had only taken five seconds to recover her usual mood.

'You offend me, Mrs Pinkerton,' said MacMahon with his little eyes horribly sad. 'When my hands make something, whether it's a metal piece that weighs a ton or a wooden shell, the only thing that matters is the opinion of those affected: if Marie Antoinette doesn't want the shell, I won't insist. Let her be the one to decide.'

And MacMahon himself picked up the turtle and put her down beside the wooden shell. All three of us leaned forward over the table as if we were bowing, very, very interested in Marie Antoinette's reaction.

MacMahon had designed the shell very skilfully. The back part was open like the neck of a pullover, so that the turtle could go in and out as she pleased. At the front, it had a hole for her head and two for her front legs. The upper part was painted with very simple geometric shapes in red, blue and yellow. While Marie Antoinette hesitated, I asked MacMahon, 'So why did you paint the shell in bright colours?'

MacMahon scratched the back of his neck. 'Because it's pretty. Don't you think?' He wavered and then added, 'Wouldn't you paint the roof of your house with bright colours if you could?'

Marie Antoinette sniffed out the shell. She approached it with a grin that was uglier than usual. After much vacillation she stuck her head into the back entrance. MacMahon had measured very well. We saw that the turtle's head and feet came through the pertinent holes, that they fitted perfectly.

'It looks like she's dancing,' I said a few seconds later.

It was true. It looked like Marie Antoinette was dancing the foxtrot, twenty years before it was invented. Which is to say, she liked it.

MacMahon clapped. I didn't say anything. Neither did Pinkerton. I was surprised that she wasn't pleased. After all, it was her beloved turtle. But I was forgetting that Pinkerton was Pinkerton. And that woman, an artist of contemptible turns of phrase, managed to outdo herself.

'Not bad,' she said, stuck-up as usual. 'If Marie Antoinette likes her new shell so much, Mr MacMahon, I'm willing to negotiate a fair rent.'

'Mrs Pinkerton, I don't charge rent to little turtles without shells,' said MacMahon. And he added, in a raspy little voice, 'It's a gift. I wanted to give it to you on your birthday, but when I saw you so sad and weepy I couldn't wait.'

Astonishment turned Pinkerton's face into a bank note, flat and green.

So, if all that hid some moral lesson, that evening I didn't have the energy to discover what it was. I remember that I went to bed, I turned out the light, I fell asleep and I had a particularly agonising dream. In the dream I was Doctor Flag's ghost writer again. I had a question about an outline. And as much repulsion as Flag's tyrannical figure caused me, I had no choice but to ask him, 'In the Congo are there turtles like Marie Antoinette?' And Flag, threatening me with his ivory-handled cane, answered, 'Obviously not! Even a ghost writer as incompetent as you should know that in the Congo's jungle there are only animals!'

SEVEN

THAT DAY I ONLY half listened to Marcus. That happened to me sometimes. His narrative thread was labyrinthine, he had a strong tendency to abuse details to the detriment of the core of the story. He would make me fill entire notebooks with futile notes that didn't contribute anything to the story. And since I avoided interrupting him except in cases of *force majeure*, my mind tended to wander.

I was jotting down some vacuous, foolish thing, when Marcus said, ' . . . and the next morning, in front of the mine, there was a stranger.'

I looked up from my notes.

'Pardon?'

'A man, planted right in front of the anthill.' And Marcus imitated him standing up, very rigidly, with his hands glued to his sides, looking out into the distance.

From the other side of the bars Sergeant Long Back watched

us, more suspicious than curious, unblinking. A peculiar duel between static forces began, Marcus looking like a general in formation in front of the Queen and Long Back, as always, looking like a wax statue.

'At the mine? A stranger? I don't understand,' I said.

'We didn't understand either,' said Marcus, sitting down again.

'Was he stealing the gold?'

'No. He was outside the mine, I already told you that. Outside, standing, still.'

'Was he spying on the mine?'

'No. His back was to the anthill. He was facing the camp.'

'A Negro man?'

'No. He was white.'

'A white man?'

'Yes, white. But not like us.'

'But didn't you say it was a white man?'

'I mean that his skin was whiter than milk fresh from the cow.'

The first ones to notice the unusual presence were the miners. It was very early, the work day had not yet started. Marcus was reviving the previous night's fire. William and Richard had risen even earlier, bent on scouring the entire forest in search of some memorable specimen, maybe a gorilla, and had set out a while ago.

The Negroes' shouting made Marcus forget about the fire. The tents obscured his view of the mine, so he couldn't see what the disturbance was about. Right away he sensed that it was something serious. Those screams reminded him of the ones heard in the villages when the dynamite exploded. He left everything and ran towards the anthill.

Terrified, the Negroes shouted, moaned and gestured. Somehow they had managed to get out of the mine. The only thing that kept them from going even further was Pepe's rifle. He was also half paralysed with fear. All the arms pointed to a human figure, thin and long like a celery stick, who observed them indolently from the mouth of the mine.

The white man was, in general terms, a man. His entire body was covered with some sort of chestnut-coloured clothing, which ended in long tails that reached his ankles. Geometric motifs went around the clothing at belly-button height. He had a skull a bit more oval and pointy than ours, like the mummies in Peru. Bald, very bald. 'And his ears were turned around. Write it down, write it down!' Marcus insisted childishly, pointing at my notebook with his finger. 'Our ears end in a hanging lobe; theirs were like bats', with a fleshy point on the top!' His face was full of angles and corners, bringing to mind a chiselled diamond.

Marcus focused on the length of his fingers. And he saw that this creature had an extra one. A total of six on each hand. But the most enigmatic of all were his eyes. They scrutinised our world from caves of flesh, sunken into his face. That creature didn't look, he focused in on things. His eyes collected information, they were as uncritical as two telescopes or, even worse, like two microscopes. Marcus understood perfectly why the men fled. Seeing a creature like that only brought one single idea to his head: to take off in the opposite direction.

'Who on earth is it?' Marcus asked Pepe.

Pepe's voice trembled, 'I don't know.'

The stranger turned his attention to the trees that enclosed the clearing. His mouth opened in a look of surprise. Then he raised his gaze to the sun. His mouth opened even wider. He kept his eyes fixed on it without blinking, and Marcus thought he would go blind.

But he didn't go blind. The man's body shook, as if he hadn't quite digested that natural spectacle, and he headed from the anthill towards where the Negroes were. The men moved away shrieking, even with all Pepe's threats to keep them still. And, in that moment, the intruder spoke.

Such a strange language had never before been heard in the Congo. It sounded as if he spoke with his mouth filled with stones. He expressed himself with a dry, and not at all friendly, passion. It was obvious that the intruder was struggling to communicate some message. He did so with both arms held high and all twelve fingers spread open, ranting with the full force of his lungs. At one particular moment he pulled out an object that he carried hidden amongst his clothes: a metal pole almost two feet long, whose upper part was crowned with two smaller sticks in the shape of a cross. The white man stuck the pole into the ground and, with great solemnity, started shouting out a speech. Naturally, no one understood a word. But the image itself was extraordinary: an individual of the most unknown origin making an appeal with his arms open wide and stretched out parallel to the ground. Slowly their fear became mixed with curiosity.

'Mr Garvey, what should we do?'

Pepe's question was not poorly timed. The work at the mine had stopped and the miners, now free, could get into all sorts of trouble. He wondered what William would do. Shoot him in the liver, of course. But William wasn't there, and Marcus had never shot anyone. At least not without a direct order.

Pepe insisted, and he was right, because they were running a much more serious risk than it seemed. There were more than a hundred Negroes. For the first time since they had arrived at the clearing, they were free. The only defence that Marcus and Pepe had was the shotgun. The shotgun and the fact that the miners were still stunned by the newcomer's presence. Anything could happen. For the moment the Negroes looked at the man with their mouths agape. (Garvey didn't understand that the Negroes could be attracted to the two diagonally crossed sticks. I could. I wasn't surprised at all that they were willing to take an interest in any novelty that allowed them to avoid, even for only a little while, the life imposed on them by the Craver brothers.)

Marcus walked across the circle formed by the miners. Not even he knew what he wanted to do. But he was bold enough to grab the pole and gauge the weight of it with his hands. He brought the object close to his eyes and observed it carefully. He didn't find anything. It was only what it appeared to be: a pole with two little sticks on the upper part.

He began with timid laughter, which soon became riotous. At first the miners didn't understand. Pepe did and he soon joined in. They looked at each other and then at the white man, and they both started laughing at once. After all, if you took away the newcomer's noisy speech, and the exoticism of his skin and clothes, he was just an old man. A loud-mouthed, stubborn old man that worshipped a cross. Nothing more.

Some of the Negroes also began to laugh. They pointed to the white man and the pole and they laughed. Little by little, more voices joined the laughter. It was as if they were waking up slowly from a ridiculous dream. The white man became annoyed and his tone became more aggressive. Too late. The entire clearing had already become clamorous laughter. In fact, his irate efforts to stop the howls became the main reason for it.

The wild laughter of the miners, Pepe and Marcus all blended together, and no one could stop it. Some of them lay on the ground splitting their sides, others smacked their thighs with their palms or grabbed their stomach with both arms. Marcus collided with Pepe. They hugged and fell on their knees without letting go of each other.

Garvey remembered that group laughter very well. I could understand him. But, from my perspective, the reason the laughter spread that way wasn't because of the intruder. It had been months since those men, Marcus included, had laughed. Not once, not even a sad smile. They had no reason to, slaves to a jungle mine. And now, for a few brief moments, all the hierarchies, suffering and punishments vanished behind a veil of laughter.

They could have continued laughing for hours and hours. But the sound of a shot into the air above the clearing stopped them. It was the Craver brothers. William had shot his rifle into the air and came towards them, followed closely by Richard. It was so unimaginably chaotic that even William Craver was surprised. He asked, more into the void than to Marcus, 'Do you mind telling me what's going on?'

William still hadn't noticed the intruder's presence and he started screaming at Marcus.

'Have you gone mad? The Negroes are out of the mine. And unchained! Are you drunk or are you . . .'

He didn't finish his sentence. The Craver brothers had just seen the white man.

'My God . . .' said Richard.

William didn't allow himself to be impressed. He went up to the intruder with the authority that his long stride gave him. He only stopped when his nose was less than a palm's length away from the man. He looked at him with aggressive curiosity. William was a master of insolence, he knew how to offend without even speaking. But he didn't manage to make the man bat an eyelid. When the Cravers saw the newcomer their vehemence turned to silence. The two brothers' entrance into the clearing was a clear demonstration of their power. He had understood his inferiority and maintained a passive attitude. William touched him with four fingers. He jabbed his chest a little and said, 'You! Who are you? What do you want?'

He got no response. The man moved his head looking alternately at William and at the hand that touched him. Richard approached them and took over for his brother, shouting right into the newcomer's ear, 'Do you mind telling us who the hell you are? You! Yes! You! Answer!'

Suddenly, with an unexpected gesture, Richard raised the butt of his enormous shotgun threateningly. Anyone would have ducked their head, even just as a reflex. Not the intruder. No one could be totally sure if his attitude was arrogance or idiocy.

'We'll start again. Who are you?'

He thought about it for a long time, but this time he answered.

'Teeec Tôn,' he said. 'Teeec Tôn.'

'And now what's he saying?' asked Richard, scratching the nape of his neck.

'How do you expect me to know?' roared William. 'It's the first white monkey I've ever seen.' And turning towards Pepe, 'Pepe! Do you understand him?'

'No, Mr William.'

'Well then, at least make the monkeys shut up!'

The Negroes started making a ruckus again. The Cravers' arrival had made the humorous aspect of the situation fade. That's the problem with general boisterous laughter. It can be very democratic and very amusing, but it doesn't solve anything. On the other hand, in front of the Cravers the man had a different tone. Less passionate, much more dangerous. He no longer wanted to convince anyone. He was just introducing himself. And that word, 'Tecton', became the detonator for a new outbreak of panic.

Pepe had to distribute many blows with the rifle butt to re-establish silence. Meanwhile, William forced the man to take off his cassock, which ended up in Marcus's hands. It wasn't made of cloth. It was a mosaic of tiny pieces, like a reptile's scales. He admired it. Thousands of little sewn stones, smaller than a baby's fingernails. The result was an incredibly flexible suit of armour, light and compact. It didn't seem to be designed to resist the impact of any weapon, but rather to surpass natural obstacles. Marcus saw dirt stuck to the little stones. He smelled it. A warmth and smell entered his nostrils that he would have recognised anywhere: the stones came from the mine.

Beneath the tunic there was some sort of pyjama. A red hide, extraordinarily thin and very tight against his skin. William ordered him to take it off. The skin that appeared under the red pyjama was unusually white. Marcus thought of a white mouse. His pectorals were somewhat fallen, his musculature aged but still firm, the mass of his thighs shrunken. It all spoke of a body that had entered the autumn of life. No one mentioned his pubic hair, but all eyes went to those hairs, as white as his skin.

William ran out of ideas. By stripping him he had wanted to diminish the man's dignity, but it was as intact as before. After a second's hesitation, William pulled Richard away. It was a very unique moment. William and Richard spoke in private, a few paces beyond the newcomer, who was left alone. He continued looking at everything with those absorbent eyes, without moving or reacting. Pepe held his rifle very tightly and kept it trained on him. Marcus, without getting even an inch closer, asked him, 'Tecton? Is that what you're called, sir? Is that your name? You are Mr Tecton?'

The man moved his neck slowly, like a periscope turning on a poorly greased axis, and he placed his eyes on the mouth that questioned him. His eyes were more feline than human. Marcus would never forget that gaze. He had the sensation that this man saw things in him that even he hadn't known existed.

'Teec Tôn,' repeated the man.

And he didn't bother to add anything else. William and Richard aborted the halting dialogue then. Richard grabbed the man by the arm, William ordered, 'Pepe, Marcus. Set up the little tent.'

They obeyed. It was a very small tent, unused. Once it was erected, they nailed a stake into the ground in the centre of the tent. There they made the man sit, tied to the stake by the wrists and waist.

For William and Richard all this was an unforeseen and annoying occurrence. For the moment they preferred to concentrate on getting the mine up and running again. They sensed that the visit would create problems for them. And they were right. Even though the intruder was tied up, and very securely tied up at that, far out of the Negroes' sight, he brought about an incident that was the closest thing to a mutiny that the expedition had seen. The men refused to go back to the mine. One hundred voices shouted in unison the only white word they knew: 'Champagne! Champagne! Champagne!'

Pepe didn't know how to contain the uproar. William did. He approached the loudest one and emptied six bullets from a revolver into his head. All six. Marcus was reminded of a watermelon that his mother had thrown to the ground with all her strength during an argument with his father.

'You don't want to go back down into the mine?' said William. 'Fine, we'll give you a day off. Pepe, Marcus, tie them to the trees that surround the clearing. By the wrists and ankles. I'll check the knots.'

Marcus couldn't sleep at night. He knew that Pepe wasn't sleeping either, even though they had blown out the oil lamp a while ago. He turned to him and said, 'What about you, Pepe? What are you thinking about?'

'I'm doing everything I can to not think about it,' he responded from the darkness.

'We thought that this region was uninhabited,' Marcus sighed, 'but maybe a bit further on, beyond the next hill, there's a tribe of white men.'

And he turned over. But Pepe had something else to say, 'He didn't come from beyond, he came from below.'

'What? I don't understand you.'

'I saw it,' said Pepe's voice. 'I was standing guard and the men started shouting. When I stuck my head out, when I looked inside the anthill, he was already in there. There below, among the men, who shrank from him, deathly afraid. He was dusting off the dirt that was stuck to his clothes.'

'If that's the case,' asked Marcus, 'where did he come from?'

'I felt sorry for the men. I let them out of the hole myself, I lowered the ladder. Then no one thought of taking it away, of course. They just wanted to flee the mine. I had to keep them from going too far. And meanwhile up he climbed.' Pepe lowered his voice, as if afraid that Mr Tecton might hear him, 'No, I don't know where he came from.'

There was a very long silence. Marcus broke it by saying, 'And don't you feel sorry for him?

'Sorry? For who?'

'Mr Tecton,' stated Marcus. 'If you really look at it, he hasn't done anything. He was just there. And for that they made him a prisoner, because he crossed William and Richard's path, nothing more. I'm sure they're going to kill him. Sooner or later.'

Pepe lifted his head from the pillow. Marcus couldn't see him but he guessed his movements, the breath from that black mouth only inches from his face.

'Can you see me, Marcus?'

'No, Pepe, of course not,' said Marcus, a little offended by the simple question. 'It's pitch black, Pepe. And you're black.'

'That's the problem with white people,' said Pepe, lying back down. 'You can't see darkness.'

A little while later Marcus left the tent. The most significant thing about the episode that followed is that as he told it, he made excuses for each and every one of his actions. First, he insisted that he was only going to urinate at the edge of the clearing. Impossible. Each one of the trees that marked the limits of the camp had a black man tied to its trunk. The entire perimeter was filled with prisoners that moaned softly. With mute gestures and without much hope, they begged him to loosen the cords that William had forced them to tighten sadistically. But Marcus couldn't help them. If he took pity on one man the others would demand the same treatment, getting louder and louder until William eventually woke up.

He headed towards the prisoner's tent. He swore he only wanted to give him water. No one had taken care of him all day, and Marcus knew that the tropical heat could be very cruel beneath a closed tent. Once he was inside he lit an oil lamp. It was a big mistake, because the light showed him a naked, bound man. Nothing more. Mr Tecton focused his eyes on the oil lamp. His eyes were round like coins. Before the flame his pupils narrowed until they were thinner than a hair. He didn't speak. Defenceless, captive, lacking the rhetorical grandiloquence he had had that morning, he seemed like a different man. Before Marcus could ask himself what he was doing, he had already set him free. Why? Out of pity?

The man didn't thank him. He didn't say a word. Marcus took him by the arm and escorted him out of there. Once they were at the door to his tent, he gestured to him to wait while he looked for the red pyjama and the clothing made of little stones. He felt his way along in the dark so he wouldn't wake up Pepe, which was ridiculous. He could see Pepe's eyes blinking in the darkness. Even though the Negro man was the soul of discretion, Marcus whispered, 'Don't say anything.'

He left with what he had come to find and he took Mr Tecton to the mine. He asked him for help setting up the ladder, but the man continued to be completely apathetic.

Marcus carried an oil lamp, which he used to illuminate the mine, and as he brought it close to the walls he realised that he was inside an enormous Gruyere cheese. The excavation had uncovered a curious geological landscape: some kind of round-mouthed tunnels opened up everywhere, of all different sizes. Some were as small as apples, others larger than the diameter of a large tree. It was such a curious sight that he almost forgot about Mr Tecton.

'This is yours,' said Marcus.

He kindly handed over his clothing and went back to investigating the holes that spotted the walls. Perhaps he shouldn't have turned his back on him. In that case he would have seen someone who, once dressed, had recovered his earlier personality. The clothes did more than just cover his nudity. He left his captivity behind and once again became that arrogant creature.

Right before the attack Marcus heard something. A rough voice that whispered sweet things into his left ear. He didn't have time to say or do anything. An arm went around his neck with extraordinary force.

That aggression was the last thing Marcus was expecting. He had freed him, he had dressed him, he had helped him get home. And Mr Tecton had repaid him by attacking him from behind. Why? Why? The sleeve that constricted his throat, wrapped in that cloth made of flexible stone, felt like an iron snake. A burning rattle came from his lungs. He felt the arm lift him off the ground like a hangman's noose. He realised that they were both entering one of the wider tunnels. Mr Tecton wanted to take him with him!

Marcus's sight became obscured. Because the arm was depriving him of oxygen and because he already had his whole thorax inside a dark lair. Behind him, all that was left of the Congo was a point of weak light. Ahead, pure blackness. And beyond that? Where was Mr Tecton taking him?

'No!'

Mr Tecton was on top of him. He pressed him into the ground and dragged him with his free arm, further and further into the tunnel. Marcus struggled with his fists and feet. With his heels he tried to hit his rival's ankles. He used his hands, his head, neck, shoulders, anything he could to get free. But in such a narrow space, and in that captive position, it was very difficult to do any damage to anyone. What's more, he was an incredibly strong man for his age. Marcus only managed to irritate him. He grunted something and squeezed his neck a little tighter.

They had already travelled three feet, six feet, nine feet. But when air no longer entered his throat, a second before losing consciousness, he felt his hand grasp Mr Tecton's ear. One of those bat ears, with long lobes rising from both sides of his face. Marcus pulled with all his might. He must have hurt him, because he shrieked. He pulled harder, and with the energy he had left he jammed his nails into his flesh as much as he could.

Mr Tecton cursed sharply and loosened his grip. Slightly, only slightly. Marcus took the opportunity to slip beneath his body and he felt the stone tunic tear the back of his shirt. He fell to the mine floor, the sand grazing his bare back.

He looked up, flat on the ground and breathless, ready to fight like a cat on its back. During an indefinite interval Mr Tecton scrutinised him, wondering if he would attack again or not. He was only four feet or so above Marcus. He looked like a spider, with half of his body outside the tunnel and his hands free. The light from the oil lamp bathed the dark garnet walls. Marcus grunted with his fists clenched in front of him, terrified. The struggle and the mine had covered him in a layer of unnatural warmth.

Mr Tecton clicked his tongue in displeasure. He turned around, twisting his waist with leathery flexibility, and disappeared into the hole.

I remember it as if it were yesterday. After Marcus explained all that to me he covered his face with both hands, one palm over each eye. I wasn't at all sure if that gesture meant he wanted to forget everything he had just told me, or the opposite, that he wanted to keep the memories from fleeing. The chains he wore on his wrists squeaked like a child's swing. Later I would feel ashamed of having jumped up, of crossing the entire length of the long table that separated us, and of the lack of restraint with which I demanded of him, 'But who was the man? Who was Mr Tecton?'

Marcus slowly moved his hands from his face. He softly said, with the voice of someone who had just been crying, 'A Tecton.'

I wanted, demanded more information. Marcus only added, 'The first Tecton that saw sunlight. And the least dangerous of all those who set foot in the Congo.'

EIGHT

THE NEXT MORNING WILLIAM went mad with rage. He was unhinged: instinctively, irrationally, he accused the Negroes of Mr Tecton's disappearance. It didn't even occur to him that, if they could, they would have been the first to run away. When William threatened them with the revolver, Marcus admitted his guilt. He knew very well what that revolver was capable of.

'It was me. Last night he got away from me.'

'You?' barked William. 'Why did you let him go?'

'It was very hot under the canvas. I offered him water and he took advantage and hit me.'

'Idiot!' William slapped Marcus. 'Where did he run off to?'

'Into the forest,' lied Marcus, pointing in some direction.

'Why didn't you wake us up?' asked Richard.

'Because I was afraid that William would smack me,' said Marcus ironically.

William smacked him again. 'Well, now you've got it on both cheeks.'

After a little while they returned to their daily tasks.

'One minute,' I said, interrupting Marcus's story. 'They didn't investigate the escape? Not even to go into the forest where you had pointed?'

'Well, no.'

'Let me see if I understand. One fine day a man appears in front of the mine, someone that could have fallen from the moon. William and Richard tie him up inside a tent. At night you help him escape. William and Richard realise and all they do is give you a couple of smacks. They go back to work and forget about the whole episode.'

'Well, yes,' allowed Marcus, frightened by my interrogation.

What I had to remember was the Craver brothers' nature. If I didn't keep in mind the gold, or the gold fever, their actions in the Congo made no sense. Marcus himself was subject to the pace and logic of the two brothers. I have already mentioned that Marcus was very surprised when I questioned him about the morality of his behaviour and when I pointed out to him the absurdity of some of the Craver brothers' decisions. His small acts of rebellion – climbing a tree when he shouldn't, setting free an undervalued prisoner – were as unconscious as they were sporadic. Even still, why didn't they punish him more harshly? Once again we have to judge the facts from the perverse and narrow mentality of the Cravers. We can assume that they didn't give any more importance to the escape because it saved them a problem. They were in the deepest depths of the Congo, they concluded that Mr

Tecton must be a member of some strange tribe and they went back to their business. Neither William nor Richard wanted to know anything about the intruder. They didn't want to think about him, because thinking about him seriously implied having to face an unsolvable problem. But ignoring reality, on the other hand, isn't usually a solution at all.

Three days after Mr Tecton's visit, the Negroes again came hurrying out of the mine as if shot from a gun. It was midmorning and Pepe hadn't been able to keep them from rushing up the ladder. The Craver brothers feared a mass, premeditated breakout. Richard shot into the air and the fugitives hit the ground like a human rug. They shouted, 'Champagne! Champagne! Champagne!'

William demanded an explanation from Pepe.

'I couldn't hold them in,' was Pepe's excuse. 'They all threw themselves at the ladder at once. I would have had to shoot to kill.'

'Don't they realise they can't go anywhere? We're a thousand miles from any civilised place. Without provisions they won't get anywhere, they'll be swallowed up by the jungle. Tell them that!'

'They don't want to go anywhere. They only want to get out of the mine. They say that they hear noises in there.'

'Pepe!' William reproached him. 'What do they say they hear?'

'Noises.'

William was so furious that the insults didn't make it out of his mouth.

'I've heard them too,' Pepe said in his defence.

'Damn you!' shouted William. 'What kind of noises?'

'Noises.'

'Stay here!' ordered William. 'Since you couldn't keep them from abandoning their work, at least make sure they don't go any further.'

William and Richard entered the anthill armed with rifles and revolvers. Marcus went with them. They didn't notice anything out of the ordinary. Just the same old cave, with scraped walls. Marcus hadn't been in there since the night with Mr Tecton, and in that time the underground bubble had expanded considerably. There were also more tunnels.

'I don't see anything here,' said Richard.

'Of course not!' cried out William. 'What were you expecting?'

'Pepe said something about noises,' added Marcus.

'Well, I don't hear anything either,' said Richard.

'Shut up!' said William. 'Both of you shut up!'

And they all three listened very carefully. Marcus was the first to break the silence. 'I hear noises.'

'Well, I don't hear anything,' insisted Richard.

'Would you mind shutting your bloody traps?' said William.

Yes, you could hear something. A whispering. It stopped. And then they heard it again. It was a fragile voice that could only make sad vowel sounds. It seemed like it came from very far away, or maybe very close by; they weren't at all sure. Within that enclosed atmosphere the sound bounced and was absorbed. It was like hearing a radio hidden under a mattress.

'It must be the Negroes outside, singing,' said Richard.

But Marcus knew very well that the voice wasn't coming from outside the mine. The idea of lighting a match and bringing it close to the holes was his. He looked inside the tunnels, sheltering himself in the weak light. With each new match he leaned over another hole, then another, and another. But the only thing he saw was infinite darkness.

At the height of his knees there was a perfectly round hole. It couldn't have been larger than the mouth of a cannon. He knelt down.

'What are you looking for in such a small hole, Marcus?' Richard laughed. 'Mice?'

'Now I understand!' said William. 'It must be field mice. When they fight they can make more noise than a herd of pigs. We'll put some mousetraps down there so the monkeys don't get scared.'

The Craver brothers laughed. Mice fighting. That's all. Marcus's match went out. He lit another without moving from that tunnel, so low that he had to get on his knees. He stuck the arm that held the match and his head through the hole. Half his body was inside the tunnel. He lit another match. The sudden flare of its combustion blinded him for a second. He blinked.

'Oh my God!' shouted Marcus, jumping back. 'My God! My God! My God!'

NINE

THERE IS AN EPISODE in classical history in which Marc Antony offers Caesar a royal crown. But he refuses it and the people applaud his gesture. Actually, Caesar was dying to get that crown. It was all a strategy to learn the plebeian opinion without risking anything. That day, at Norton's office, I saw a similar scene. Because Norton was one of those men that, either out of prudence or strategy, only spoke about his convictions when he knew what the convictions of the people he was dealing with were.

He liked the next few chapters much better. This time he turned the pages and nodded his head. I could even hear him accompany his reading with some good, good, yes, yes, good, good. He stopped. He had reached the paragraph where the Tecton appeared. He inhaled. He read a bit more and he said, 'Hopelessly insane, isn't he? One of those lunatics that need a whole asylum just for them.'

'Crazy?' I said. And after a long hesitation, 'No, I wouldn't say that. Not at all. Marcus is not a lunatic. I hate to admit it, but I have to say I believe in him. And even though it seems like a lie,' I confessed, 'I also believe his story.'

'Bravo!' said Norton all of a sudden. He banged his fist on the table, spilling water from a glass. 'I knew it! I knew you'd agree with me!'

'Marcus isn't lying. I'm not an expert interrogator, but I judge his story from another point of view.' I shook my head. 'I'm a professional in stories. And this story's sutures are perfect. There are many angles, and each one confirms the others. Marcus is too inept to make up such a sophisticated story. Actually, I don't think there is anyone sick enough to make up such a twisted plot. Don't you agree?'

I paused and warned Norton, 'On the other hand, the Craver brothers are still the same characters. I don't plan on watering that aspect down.'

'And I'm not asking you to compromise,' said Norton. 'I'm just glad that the Cravers' evil has faded into the background a little. That makes Marcus's stance more elegant and, as a result, easier to defend.'

There was something that Norton hadn't quite understood. He no longer referred to the writing as a sworn declaration *in extenso*. He was talking as if the work had a life beyond the legal realm. I asked him, 'Do you think that my work contributes to Marcus's legal defence? Do you see any hopeful signs in it?'

'It is an extraordinary story, as I told you. Only a pedigreed writer could raise it to the level it deserves.' He smiled. 'Let's hope, then, that you are worthy of it. You do your job and write, Mr

Thomson, write. A good book needs to come out of this. But I'll decide on the legal strategy.'

I didn't quite understand, but that wasn't my problem. I stuck to what was.

'I want you to know that this book is going to take time. The story is getting more and more dense. And since I only have an hour every fifteen days to interview Garvey, the writing could take forever. Before, I had more time with Marcus,' I explained, 'but for a while now he's been getting visits from someone else. He says that it is the only friend he has left in the world. Do you know anything about that?'

Norton made a noncommittal gesture. That didn't interest him. He pulled himself back, his hands at the back of his neck. Then he moved five fingers in the air as if he were unscrewing a bulb.

'Can we deny him some friendly company? It wouldn't be humane. A prisoner's diet is made up of potatoes and chickpeas, meat once every three weeks. If these visits give him some spiritual nourishment, the book will benefit.' And then he immediately returned to my reply. 'Yes, I know, we don't have time, but legal proceedings are subject to a thousand imponderables. I trust some procedural triviality will give us the time we need so badly.'

He had said all that while continuing to read the last few pages I had written. He looked at the ceiling.

'I don't understand,' he thought aloud. 'At this point in the story she should have already appeared.'

'She? Who are you talking about?' I asked.

Norton was about to answer me, but just then we heard a distant noise. It was the hoarse shouting of a crowd, reminiscent of the tumult of a big shipwreck. The noise grew and grew. When we opened the window the noise entered the office like a living creature.

A human flood filled the entire avenue. People were singing patriotic songs and marching towards Trafalgar Square. Next to us, on the façade, the window of an office adjacent to Norton's flat opened. An office worker was observing the human mass as we were, leaning on the windowsill. Norton asked him what was going on.

'You really don't know?' The man was very close, but he had to shout to make himself heard. 'The war's broken out!'

'What war?' I asked.

A million lungs lifted in patriotic song. They resonated so loudly that Norton's neighbour brought a hand to his ear. 'What's that you say?'

'I asked,' I said, also shouting and making a trumpet with my hands, 'who are we at war with?'

The man opened his arms. 'Everybody's at war with everybody else! Right now all of Europe is at war!'

Norton went into his office. He made a few solitary dance steps; he was euphoric. I closed the window to keep out the shouting and said, 'I didn't know you were so patriotic.'

'You should be happy too.'

I didn't agree at all. 'In my opinion wars aren't led by patriotism, but rather by the desire for lucre and the rapacious instinct.'

'You are and always will be an antisocial type,' commiserated Norton, smiling. 'But I wasn't talking about high politics, I was thinking of the Garvey case.'

'Now I'm definitely not following you,' I said with resignation.

'Didn't you say you didn't have enough time to write the book?

Starting now you'll have all the time in the world. This war is the procedural triviality that we needed.'

Norton was right, as always. The Ministry of Defence swelled out of proportion. As a result, the other ministries saw their staff and budget reduced. The fact that the Ministry of Justice was the most affected is a perfect symbol of what a war means. Norton, who was a genius at creating legal obstacles, wrote dozens, hundreds of instances on Marcus's behalf. I think that in the first year of the war more resources fell on the judge in charge of the Garvey case than bombs on Belgium. The majority were technical objections. Norton didn't have even the slightest hope of winning any of them, but he knew perfectly well that the lack of staff would slow things down and that the trial date would get pushed back. I said it already: Norton was a genius. Most geniuses are geniuses because of the way they manage their natural talents. He was one because of the way he took advantage of the world's defects.

Marcus had fallen flat on his back in surprise. The voice could no longer be heard. Now they only heard the noise of a body being dragged. Then another silence. And later they could hear breathing mixed with groans. William and Richard aimed at the hole with their guns. Marcus, panic-stricken, ran to hide behind Richard's legs.

Something white emerged. The first thing they saw was the crown of a skull. William and Richard took aim. Probably the only reason they didn't shoot was curiosity. Could a body fit in there, through such a narrow opening? It was like seeing a snake come out of an egg. The arms and legs slithered through the hole as if they were made of rubber. And finally the body fell to the ground with a sound like mashed potatoes being dumped on a plate.

It was a woman. She wore a tunic similar to Mr Tecton's, but her features were much younger, much softer. She lay on the ground and was as surprised as the three men. Her hair was in woolly plaits and fell from the nape of her neck. 'What big round eyes,' thought Marcus. Because they were literally round and, unlike Mr Tecton's, weren't sunk into the surrounding flesh. Richard brought an oil lamp close to her and the artificial light made her pupils narrow. The rest of the ocular sphere was a honey-coloured sea, like liquid amber. But the most peculiar thing about her eyes was not their feline shape. The most peculiar thing was that they showed no fear of the rifles.

Marcus watched as the woman moved her shoulders. Richard asked, 'What's she doing?'

'She put her bones out of joint to get through the hole,' said William. 'Now she's putting them back in place.'

'I don't understand.'

'And you call yourself a soldier? In the Boy Scouts they taught us that if you can squeeze your head through a hole, you can squeeze your whole body.'

'Oh, shut up!' spat out Richard. 'You want to give me lessons on human anatomy?'

'Human?' questioned William, making a slight movement with the tip of the rifle. 'Take her clothes off, Marcus.'

'Who, me?' said Marcus.

'Yes, you. The old man didn't have any hidden weapons. But you never know.'

'I'm unarmed!' protested Marcus.

'Exactly,' said William cynically. 'We'll cover you.'

Marcus had a lot of reservations. But it was a direct order from

William. And it was just a woman. Why should he be afraid? He asked himself that question and he realised that he wasn't afraid, he was just ashamed. Finally he decided to go ahead. He did it half stooped and with one hand open in front of him as a sign of peace, as if to say: I don't want to hurt you. She was seated, and kept her back against the wall and her knees against her chest. Yet she seemed more inquisitive than frightened. It was hard to understand; she was surrounded by such different beings, who were armed, and she wasn't afraid.

When Marcus got a little bit closer, always leading with his conciliatory hand, she intercepted it with her own. She wasn't trying to stop him. She was just greeting him. Their fingers intertwined like two hands praying. It would have been a union of two perfect pieces if not for the fact she had six fingers. But there was more, much more: the woman's hand was incredibly warm. Fever? No. Marcus knew that the woman wasn't sick, that was just how she was. Marcus received that warm charge and he understood that she belonged to another world.

Richard needed Marcus's attention. He didn't hear him. He was too wrapped up in her, in that unexpected warmth. William had to shout his name. For Marcus it was as if someone had broken the glass of a shop window with a hammer blow and, finally, he turned his head. William again insisted, 'Take her clothes off.'

Marcus didn't know how to do it. Her armour was even more delicate than Mr Tecton's. It fitted round her neck and wrists perfectly. Marcus ran a hand along her shoulders, breasts and belly, searching her, looking for some hidden button. The armour was incredibly compact, of one single piece, rough to the touch. No button appeared. She understood Marcus's intentions. She turned to show him her back. At first Marcus thought that that was her way of refusing to be stripped naked. He panicked. William and Richard's rifle barrels were still there, just feet away. Fortunately she wasn't refusing, she was showing him how to take off her armour. Marcus looked more carefully, and on the woman's back he could see some tiny clasps. He tried to undo one, but all ten of his fingers trembled.

'Don't be afraid,' said Richard, mistaking Marcus's feelings. 'We've got a close eye on her.'

She had to help him. Her arms were very long. They moved back in a contortionist's pose and undid the ten clasps in five seconds. The only thing Marcus did was finish taking off the tunic. She had extended her arms so it would be easier for him, and the whole armour came off like a banana peel.

'All of it!' shouted William. 'Take it all off!'

Below the tunic the young woman wore a vest and some skin-tight red trousers. Marcus moved a hand towards the shirtsleeves, but he stopped halfway. Instead of touching her he brought his hand to his cheeks. They were very warm. Especially his ears, which burned as if he had stuck his head in an oven. Had the touch of her hand made his whole body warm? No, that warmth had a different source: the embarrassment of taking a woman's clothes off.

'Marcus!' shouted William.

And with the tip of his rifle he poked him twice in the back. Luckily the young woman understood what the Craver brothers were demanding and she helped him. Her shirt came off over her head pulled by four hands at once. Then she stood up. Until that moment they had only seen her lying down. She was very tall, almost six feet. Marcus bent down and lowered her trousers, grabbing them where the pockets would have been. Her white thighs went on forever. She stood and looked at him as if she didn't quite understand why he was doing that.

From the beams hung nine oil lamps. But the woman's body would have been completely visible anyway: it was so white that just a speck of light would have been enough to see her. She was even whiter than Mr Tecton. Her nipples, for example, were also white. And in her pubic area there was a small rug spread, like while velvet. Only some crusty traces of ochre mud, on her hands and in her hair, attenuated that whiteness.

'That's what the monkeys were squawking so much about?' said William. 'A little white albino, dirty and lost.'

'Albino?' asked Richard.

'Didn't you see any in Leopoldville? Black albinos are very strange. Like white Negroes, or black whites. There must be a fair lot of albinos around here. That must be it.'

'And they live underground, these black albinos?'

'Of course not.'

'But we saw her come out of the hole,' insisted Richard with his ox-like stubbornness. 'Marcus saw it too. Didn't you, Marcus?'

'So?' William was losing his patience.

'So she must have come from underground.'

'No, Richard, that can't be,' said William with a sarcastic ring to his voice.

'And why not?'

William answered with deliberate intonation, dogmatic and violent, dragging each syllable. 'Because underground there are no people, Richard. People don't live underground. Underground there are only dead people buried in cemeteries.'

Richard still dared one last dissension. 'Perhaps not. But in that case, what was she doing underground?'

'Think about it for a second! The most likely scenario is that she came with the old man. For some reason she must have stayed back. When she saw that we tied up the old man, she hid in the mine. Then the Negroes went into the mine, and she must have gone into the hole where we found her. Three days ago. What she wasn't expecting was that the Negroes never left the mine. She was exhausted and in the end she had to come out.' He picked up the young woman's armour with the tip of his rifle. 'Look at these clothes! Why are they so dirty and wrinkled? Because she's been stuck in these catacombs for three days.'

'Or because she comes from far away,' murmured Marcus.

'Did you say something?' demanded William.

Marcus, naturally, didn't repeat himself.

'Have her put the red pyjamas back on,' William ordered. 'I don't want the monkeys to see her naked. They're capable of anything.'

And he took her. Richard and Marcus followed him. Once they were out of the mine, William had the Negroes surround her. He stood firmly with his legs apart and his hands on his hips. Pepe translated what he said.

'This is what you were so afraid of! A little girl. Look at her! And you, one hundred men, whining with fear because you heard a creature moaning. Aren't you ashamed of yourselves?'

In the light of the Congo the woman's whiteness hurt their eyes. William's speech managed to have a certain effect on the miners. William was a master when it came to taming logic. He knew how to choose his arguments in such a way that reality always worked in his favour. William never tried to convince his opponent, just crush him. And so listening to him was obeying him. He even went much further, perversely far.

'You worked very hard,' he said to the Negroes. 'Perhaps we haven't been considerate enough to you. If you've made it this far you also deserve to take part in the success. We have decided that if the gold mining goes satisfactorily, you'll get fair and generous compensation. And now let's celebrate that our fears have vanished.' William moved a hand, 'Pepe, Marcus, bring a little table and some bottles of champagne. And be quick about it.'

So they did. William himself served the first swigs of champagne. Each man held out the wooden bowl for food and got a small stream of champagne. Happiness.

'Champagne for the monkeys?' asked Richard, surprised, while the Negroes drank and laughed.

'That will motivate them. But don't untie them.'

'And the white girl?' asked Richard.

William thought it over for a while. The woman hadn't moved. Finally he said, 'Me first,' handing over the bottle so he could continue serving champagne. 'Meanwhile, you keep watch.'

And William went into his tent with the woman. Richard left Marcus as the waiter and he kept watch to make sure the Negroes didn't do anything crazy. He paced slowly up and down, smoking, with his rifle at his back. When Marcus had filled all the bowls, Pepe whispered to him, 'Mr Marcus, there's a man here who wants to speak with you.'

'With me?'

'Yes,' and Pepe pointed with his finger to a very old man, perhaps the oldest of all the Negroes.

The champagne didn't interest him and he stayed at the margins of the celebration. The other Negroes drank and danced as much as their ankle shackles allowed. Marcus and Pepe approached the old man. William was inside the tent, but Richard could see them, so Marcus took the old man behind a tree. While they were there, Marcus asked Pepe, 'He's a poor devil just like the rest. Why are you making me talk to him?'

'One always has to listen to the elderly.'

Marcus looked behind him. Richard had one eye on the Negroes elated by the champagne and the other on the tent, waiting for his turn. The old man spoke with a profusion of gestures and curtsies. He had been going on for a minute and Pepe hadn't batted an eyelash.

'Why don't you translate for him?' demanded Marcus.

'Because he hasn't said anything yet. He's introducing himself.'

The old man changed his tone. And Pepe said, 'He says that he has nothing to lose, that he is an old man fed up with life. He says that he has seen six children and nineteen grandchildren die at the hands of white men. Some died on the caravans, others collecting rubber, others as punishment. He wanted to die, once and for all. That's why, when the people in the village fled, he didn't move from the door of his hut.'

Marcus remembered that. In one of those empty villages they only found an old man with a cane that sat, indifferent to everything. They were very short on bearers and all arms were welcome. Pepe had handcuffed him.

'He says that he doesn't understand why he has lived so long. Dying, when you really look at it, isn't so bad. People live until they die, and when they die they turn into ancestors.'

'The abridged version, Pepe!'

'He says that he doesn't mind dying. But now, here, he can't understand what he has done to deserve such a horrific death.'

'Pepe! What does he want from me?'

'He says that he wants to choose his death,' translated Pepe without any sign of emotion. 'He says that he wants you, the least white of the White men, to kill him.'

Here, in my role as the story's transcriber, it would have been very easy to do Marcus a favour. This small episode had no bearing on the general course of events. Therefore, I could have said that Marcus Garvey took pity on the old man and set him free. But that's not what he did.

'Make him shut up!' shouted Marcus. 'Kill him yourself, if that's what he wants. You're even less white than me!'

'He says that white men are more dangerous than danger. He says that they kill when we don't ask them to and never when we do.'

'Don't translate any more for me!' yelled Marcus with his hands over his ears. 'Why are you doing this to me, Pepe? Why? I thought we were friends!'

They heard Richard ordering the men back to the mine. Soon he would notice their absence.

'You heard Mr Richard, Pepe,' said Marcus exasperated. 'Everyone back to work!'

William took a long time to come out of the tent. When he did he looked like a different man. His eyes were even more piercing than before. Also sadder. Marcus was very surprised to see him with that expression, because William was a man who was unfamiliar with sadness, he only knew disappointment. But he took a good look at him, and the longer he watched William the more incredible he seemed to see him.

He had the feeling that William had come out of the tent twenty years younger. He was a child, a mischievous child. An enraged and at the same time frightened child. He took a few, strangely staggering, steps. He looked vaguely into the distance. He took a revolver and aimed randomly, as if he was trying to remember some forgotten notions of target shooting. He looked like an actor rehearsing a role that he had played years earlier. He lowered the gun. He opened and closed the fingers of both hands to awaken sleeping limbs. Richard didn't see any of that. He only wanted to go in the tent. He trotted with those elephantine steps so particular to him, stomping on the world, anxious and lighter than one would think seeing his robust body. But William blocked his path.

'No.'

'No, what?'

'I'm keeping her.'

'Why?' asked Richard, indignant.

'I've changed my mind,' was all William said.

'It's been too long since I was with a woman!'

'You've never been with a woman, just with girls,' said William. 'And what's in that tent isn't good for you.'

The entire clearing was witness to a very bitter argument. Finally, of course, Richard relinquished the white woman. His strategy changed, now he scorned his brother's conquest. His demands became sarcastic remarks. It was like that fox in the fable that decided the grapes too high to reach were too green. But that wasn't the end of it: William kicked him out of the tent! More arguments. As was to be expected, Richard gave in. And there was a movement in the camp like dominoes. William took the tent that had been both of theirs, to share it with the white woman. Richard moved his luggage to Marcus and Pepe's tent, where he would sleep from that night on. And Marcus and Pepe, evicted, were ordered to set up in the smaller tent, which up until then had only been used to store packages and to tie up Mr Tecton. The rest of the day was, apparently, normal. They worked on their usual jobs, but everyone could feel William's anxiousness for the night to arrive.

He was the absolute king of the clearing, of that miniature world. He didn't need anyone's permission to go to his tent when he wanted to. Even still, he held himself back. Probably he was measuring the limits of his own desire, of a new and unknown sensation. All day long no one dared speak a word to him. Everyone chose to avoid him. He was like a lightning conductor after an electric storm. They could almost see sparks at the tips of his fingers.

At dinnertime William couldn't contain himself any longer. He drank a few sips of coffee that was still boiling. Streams of black liquid flowed from the corners of his mouth down his neck. He stuffed a few pieces of half-raw meat into his mouth, like a cannibal, and he went to his tent, with her.

The others didn't wait long before heading to bed themselves. Inside their new tent, Pepe and Marcus didn't say anything to each other. The oil lamp was out, but they didn't sleep. Marcus was listening intently. He wanted to know what was going on in William's tent. He couldn't help that childish, malicious snooping. But he didn't hear anything. Nothing. No yelling or moaning, not from her or from him. Just the sounds of the African night.

TEN

POSSESSED BY A CALVINIST mentality that they had discovered in the tropics, the Cravers started work first thing in the morning. Marcus was ordered to bring breakfast to the captive as soon as William had left the tent. He always found her barefoot, dressed in some trousers and one of William's white shirts. And with a hand cuffed to one of the poles that held up the tent's canvas. So much whiteness hurt his eyes.

One day he took pity on her and freed her wrist. It wasn't, in fact, as risky as it might seem. William worked all day long. If he left the mine it was only to go hunting, so he didn't return to the tent until the evening. As for the woman, Marcus knew perfectly well that she wouldn't go anywhere. He was convinced that she came from the depths, and so the only place she could flee to was the mine, watched over by a hundred men.

'The jungle is enormous, enormous!' Marcus explained to her, stretching out his arms. 'Go round wherever you like, but come back here before it gets dark. Do you understand?'

It seemed to him that she agreed. That first day of limited freedom, though, he kept one eye on her while he cooked. The woman didn't go very far anyway. For her it was a new world, and she walked through it with the cautiousness of someone afraid that they'll break something with each step. She admired a blade of grass as if it was something fantastic and new. She lay down anywhere and passed her hand along the ground, astonished by the carpet of grass. Marcus thought: 'If the grass goes to your head, dear, wait till you see the jungle. You'll be drunk on trees.' And indeed, a little while later the woman disappeared from his sight, into the jungle. Marcus followed her, just in case, and he found her hugging a tree. She had her ear to the trunk, as if she was listening for a heartbeat. He noticed the woman's feet, which gave him a start.

'Get out of here!' he shouted, pulling her away.

After he had gotten her a few feet away he showed her the thick boots he wore on his feet. She didn't understand. Marcus took off his boot and placed it in front of her eyes.

'Do you see it?'

But the woman looked at the boot without understanding.

'Ant,' said Marcus, pointing to a small black body stuck to the leather, which moved its legs frantically. 'That place was full of ants. They are very small but they can devour a live goat.' He pointed to the insect. 'This one has been chewing on my boot for two days. If you go near them, they attack you. Watch this.'

Marcus grabbed the ant's body with two fingers. Only the body. The head remained there, chewing on the boot with its jaws.

'Do you understand now? They are bad.'

She made a disgusted '*ach*' sound. It was the first time she had opened her mouth. Marcus hadn't ever heard her before. The young woman turned her neck and then her whole body. She sat, crossing her legs. She usually sat like that, with her heels touching the inside of her thighs. Now she did it with her back to Marcus. She was displeased, strongly displeased. Marcus felt perfectly stupid, with a dead ant on the tips of his fingers and asking for forgiveness.

'It was just an ant . . .' Marcus stammered. 'And it could have hurt you . . .'

He didn't know what else to say and he returned to his work.

For Marcus, work was a way to avoid the mine, the Congo, everything. When he was working the world faded away. They had a huge mud pot shaped like an upside-down spinning top. It was so big that half a buffalo could have fitted inside. Marcus wasn't too refined with their diet, but he didn't torture the Negroes either. He filled the pot with chunks of different meats and with vegetables, a handful of salt and pepper, and he let it boil, stirring it every once in a while with a cane shaped like an oar. The Craver brothers' menu, obviously, was very different, and Marcus prepared it in more delicate vessels. The European ingredients had run out almost completely a while ago, and Marcus had had to adapt the Cravers' palate to the jungle produce. Both brothers liked ladies' fingers, dwarf bananas served fried, and children's ears, very wrinkled peanuts shaped like fava beans, which he boiled. The meat was usually Scottish liver, which was what they called the liver of a bird very similar to a pheasant that Richard hunted whenever he could. (They called it Scottish liver because according to William those large birds had livers more swollen than a Scottish drinker.) But an hour after his run-in with the woman, he heard her again, '*Ach, ach, ach*!' The voice came from the jungle. Marcus ran there as fast as he could.

It was her, of course, in the middle of four trees laid out in a perfect rectangle. She had sat on another anthill and she struggled frantically against a handful of ants that were climbing up her trousers. On such a white body the ants stood out. He helped her.

'Why didn't you listen to me? I told you! No, it's not enough to shake them off. You have to take them off one by one, or they'll never leave. And if you get a lot of bites, you'll have spasms.'

Marcus began to curse himself. He should have guessed that freeing her would only bring problems. He couldn't watch her and the pots at the same time. He didn't want to tie her up again either.

'Wait here, please,' Marcus said to her. He came right back.

'Look!' he said, sitting down by her side, among the trees, and putting a photograph into her hands.

She drew the photograph to her, passing her eyes over the image, very close to the paper.

'That animal is the best friend I've ever had. His name was Pepe, he was a bear and this is the only picture of him that I have,' explained Marcus. 'Well, actually it's the only picture I have of Pepe or of anyone. I'd like to have one of my mother, but I don't. Do you have any pictures of your mother? No, of course not, what a stupid question.' He pointed to the animal's head with his finger. 'Look at that hat! Whenever Pepe danced he wore a hat. He liked hats a lot. You can't tell from the picture, but it was a red hat. Like Pepe's. I mean the Negro Pepe, the Negro man that you know, the one who sleeps with me. I used to sleep with Pepe too, the bear Pepe, I mean. Negro man Pepe is a good man, even though he's not as good a friend as Pepe, I mean not as good a friend of mine as the bear Pepe. Do you like my picture?'

He realised what a jumble of information he had just spouted, and in a language that the woman didn't know a word of.

'You understand, don't you?' he asked her.

I remember that after he explained that scene to me, Marcus made a sceptical face, as if he still wasn't sure if she had understood him.

I'd bet anything she did understand him.

The next session didn't continue in chronological order. I preferred instead that we focus on the character.

'Tell me about her.'

'About who? The white woman?'

'Yes. The white woman.'

Marcus looked from one side of the table to the other, his indecisive act.

'Do we have to talk about her?' he asked me with some regret.

He didn't want to. But my job granted me some prerogatives.

'Yes, Marcus,' I replied, implacable. 'I think so. I want to talk about her.'

According to Marcus she was called Amgam. But I forced him to reconstruct the scene in which she introduced herself and I came to the conclusion that surely Amgam wasn't her real name. Marcus must have christened her that way based on a linguistic mistake. Marcus told me that, late one evening, she extended a hand towards him, pointing to him, and said, 'Amgam.'

'Amgam? I am Marcus,' he said.

But when I demanded more details of the scene, Marcus said that that evening he had lit a gas lamp. The white woman reacted as if the match had created a miracle. The flame danced behind the glass walls. She laughed. She brought her large palm, with those six long fingers, to the upper opening of the lamp and said, 'Amgam.'

Marcus thought that those six fingers were pointing to him, addressing him. But when faced with my scepticism, Marcus hesitated. Finally we concluded that she was only exploring the warmth of the lamp. Which is to say, she wasn't actually introducing herself, she was only referring to the lamp with a Tecton name. But Marcus thought it was an official introduction.

'Marcus,' he said.

'Amgam,' she repeated.

'Amgam?' said Marcus. 'Amgam.'

So, the most likely conclusion is that Amgam was nothing more than a Tecton word for 'light' or 'fire' or both things at once. But Marcus began to call her Amgam. And the name stuck.

In that period the heroines in novels were usually angelic beauties, and one of the most surprising aspects of the tale was that Amgam wasn't.

Did Amgam follow our ideals of beauty? A vague portrait emerged from Marcus's description. Some parts of her body surpassed our highest feminine ideals. When Marcus remembered the svelteness of her body and her hips, for example, he blushed. Always. Or when he talked of those Egyptian eyes, terrifyingly large and round, with gigantic black pupils at night that became as thin as a hair when bathed in the light of day. One imagines, then, that in the evenings, and in such a white body, her eyes must have stood out like two lighthouses that beamed black light. Marcus described them in a very curious way, he could only say what they weren't. He said that her eyes were the exact opposite of William's.

But, as for her general figure, and if we limit ourselves to purely aesthetic criteria, we would have to conclude that some parts of Amgam bordered on the disastrous. Her legs and arms, for example. Her long legs affirmed a gazelle's silhouette. Unfortunately, excessively long arms ruined the overall impression. When she held them against her body she could touch her kneecaps with the tips of her fingers. Her hands and feet were also very large. If Marcus put his palm on top of hers, every one of Amgam's fingers went beyond his. William's trousers and shirts were too short for her: she was a tall woman, very tall. She was a head and a half, maybe two, taller than Marcus. Men are used to looking at women from above, and the perspective that Amgam gave, the opposite of the usual one between men and women, made Marcus extra timid. Small breasts, almost non-existent, nipples like buttons. Nose thin and long, with the skin tight to the bone. And since her lips were also very long, her face was designed around a sort of upside-down capital T.

And, yet, any aesthetic judgement of Amgam would have to take into account the magnetism that that creature of lime radiated.

She was a complete foreigner, and as such the most impartial witness to life above ground. If Amgam formed an opinion about our world, it would be an entirely disinterested judgement, without prejudice or prior sympathy. During our sessions, Garvey never used that reasoning. I arrived at it on my own. (It was an inevitable conclusion.) The Craver brothers didn't think of it because they were blinded by the pirate's gaze: they couldn't see the treasure, only the booty. Garvey, who was much more humble, at least saw her as a woman.

One morning Marcus realised that Amgam wasn't in the clearing. That wasn't exceptional. She often disappeared from his sight, into the jungle, and came back after a short walk. That day it started to rain. The way it does in the Congo, in a torrent that threatened to flood the world. The drops made the jars and cans ring as if they were being shot at, and the clearing became an immense pool of mud. But Marcus had already learned that the storms in the Congo were as brief as they were apocalyptic. Normally the Cravers took refuge under a large piece of fabric suspended between four poles near the mine. But if the rain didn't stop it was also highly likely that they would decide to take shelter in their tents. And in that case William would discover the absence of his prized white woman.

The sun came out, thank God. After a storm William and Richard were more irritable. Before starting the digging again they had to evacuate the water from the mine. Which, naturally, meant wasted time, and if they wasted time they wasted money. From where he was, Marcus could hear the Cravers' howling and the lash of their whips.

But Amgam didn't return. The mud had already solidified. The jars flooded with rain were already filled with stupidly drowned insects. After a while he started to really worry. He left the pot and he went into the jungle.

'Amgam? Amgam?' he shouted.

There was no reply. All he could hear were the sounds of the jungle and the cracks of the branches he broke with his steps. Damn! Why had he taken for granted that Amgam wouldn't run away? The jungle was filled with dangers, she would never manage to get anywhere. For some reason it had seemed absurd to him, he had considered her intelligent enough to reject the idea of running away. But maybe Amgam had a different perspective. As bad as the jungle was, nothing could be worse than William's tent. Yes, William Craver. He would kill him. It was one thing to set free Mr Tecton, and quite another to lose his night-time plaything.

'Amgam!'

She could be anywhere. And it was useless to follow a woman with such long legs. He threw his hat down and stamped on it, furious. Luckily, in that part of the jungle the vegetation was thin enough to allow him about ninety feet of vision. And there, on a rock, he saw a white figure.

Amgam sat on a rock high enough that the grasses hadn't completely triumphed over it. In that corner, just above the rock, the jungle's ceiling was thicker. That was why the weeds hadn't devoured it, because of the excess humidity: the upper strata accumulated so much water that it filtered down all day long. So it was no longer raining in the clearing, but on Amgam a fine, regular shower fell. The vault of vegetation had converted the spot into a shady place. All the light was reduced into thin, compact rays that fell erratically onto the rock.

She was naked. She sat on the moss that covered the rock with her legs crossed and her eyes closed, turning her neck so that the water was distributed all over her body. Her hair, now clean, shone as white as the rest of her body. Marcus approached her. Now that he had found her he was embarrassed to disturb her while she was bathing. No, it was something more than just bathing. She seemed like a different woman.

When he was close to the rock he cleared his throat to announce his presence. She ignored him. Marcus saw a fine film of white smoke surrounding Amgam. It was the water itself, evaporating from the contact with such hot skin.

Marcus was getting wet. He stretched out an arm to touch her knee.

'Hello.' And pointing to the clearing. 'We have to go back.'

Amgam opened her eyes. Her eyelids had an enormous span, compared to ours. When she raised them it was with a mechanical slowness, like an opera curtain.

She looked at him from the height of that tropical moss-covered rock, and what Marcus saw in those eyes was pure intelligence, pure in the same way that gold could be pure. She didn't obey him. Instead of coming down from the rock, she spoke.

Of course, Marcus couldn't understand a word. But he did understand the tone. She wasn't a resentful woman, just severe. It was a recriminating, accusatory voice. Amgam had lived in the clearing long enough to understand the essence of the power that ruled it. And when she spoke that way, when she looked at him that way, what she was saying was: you also form part of the established order, Marcus Garvey, you cook for the murderers.

Marcus denied it vigorously with his head. 'I can't do anything about it. I can't.'

Amgam didn't say anything more. The water slid down her forehead, went into her eyes, and even still she didn't blink. Marcus took a step forward, intimidated and ashamed.

'I can't do anything to the Cravers. No one could.'

He had gone into the jungle after her, and now he was the one who was fleeing. Back to camp.

One day I typed until well into the night, and at half past one strange things started happening. I couldn't get Amgam out of my head. I was thinking that the judge's clerks had written thousands and thousands of procedural pages, but the most determining person in the Garvey case didn't appear in them. Amgam, yes, a critical eye that had a disruptive effect on those she cast it on. Marcus Garvey had come up against her, and once he had been interrogated by Amgam he couldn't go back to being the way he was before. I remember that I lifted my hands off the keys and covered my mouth.

Even though it was very late, I went into Mr MacMahon's room.

'Mr MacMahon . . . Wake up, Mr MacMahon . . .' I whispered, shaking his shoulder.

'Tommy? What's going on, son?' MacMahon was frightened. 'Is the building on fire?'

I sat on one side of the bed. MacMahon had only had time to sit up.

'Mr MacMahon,' I said, 'how do you know when you are in love with a woman?'

'What did you say?' he asked, wiping the sleep from his eyes. 'For the love of Saint Patrick, Tommy! Do you know what time it is?'

'Please, tell me.'

'I'm tired, Tommy. Can't it wait until the morning? Tomorrow I'll tell you about Mary.'

'No, please, now.'

MacMahon wiped his eyes. For a second I was afraid he was going to let out some resounding wind. He scratched under his armpits and the nape of his neck.

'Well, look,' he said as he organised his thoughts, 'I wanted a woman that was young, clean, gentle and happy. And one that could give me many children, obviously. So I started to look for her. First in my village and then in all the villages of the county.'

'But what were you looking for, for God's sake? To get married or to buy a cow?' I protested.

MacMahon replied with a suddenly firm voice. 'Mary is the best woman ever. I would have travelled the world over ten times to find her.'

'Do you mean that?'

'Yes, son, yes. It's true.'

'Was it love at first sight?'

'No. It was more than that, much more. I loved her before I saw her.'

'Before? How's that possible?'

'Because I had spoken with her. That's how villages are. Everybody knows each other. And voices are very important. They had told me a lot about Mary, and all good things. Before I saw her I was already walking like a dog, with my head bent and my mouth half open. And one day, while I was getting spruced up to go to the festival in her village, where some mutual friends had arranged for us to have a date, I knew that Mary would be the love of my life.'

'How could you be so sure of that?'

'I was.'

'Yes, I can understand that,' I acquiesced.

'No, you don't understand it,' said MacMahon, contradicting me. He looked directly into my eyes, he pointed to my nose with his finger and said, 'Love is very difficult to understand. And do you know why? Because love is the most idiotic thing in the universe, Tommy, but also the most important. That's why it's so hard to understand.'

ELEVEN

I'VE ALREADY MENTIONED THAT William and Richard were very fond of hunting. And since the work at the mine had become more routine, they had more free time. Pepe could handle controlling the workers inside the mine, and the few that worked outside, on the rotating system, washing the gold in the tub, showed an infinite capacity for obedience. In addition, if he needed to, Pepe could always ask for help from Marcus, who was boiling the pot very close by. But Pepe never needed to. A less distrustful and more realistic look at the situation would have made the Craver brothers see that the Negroes didn't show even the slightest hint of revolting, that they didn't even attempt to take an ounce of gold.

One morning Marcus went hunting with Richard. They were looking for something large, some buffalo or deer that they could use to feed the troop of miners. Richard knelt down to examine some footprints in the mud. He turned towards Marcus, very excited, and said, 'Tell William! There's a lion close by.' And getting himself excited, 'Damn it, we're going lion hunting!'

'And what if William's in his tent, very busy?' said Marcus. 'I'm sure he doesn't want us to interrupt him.'

'Do what I tell you,' ordered Richard. 'What do you think would interest William more? Hunting a lion or screwing the white girl?'

Marcus obeyed, but he was positive that his prophecy would be fulfilled. And William did curse his name when Marcus interrupted him from the other side of the canvas. But Richard's assumption was also correct, he was thrilled at the idea of shooting a lion. William came out of the tent completely naked. And while he got dressed as fast as he could, he ordered, 'Ah, Marcus. The tent is dirty. Sweep it out.'

William disappeared into the jungle. Marcus went into the tent. The ceiling was very low and he had to get down on his knees. He used a brush of black hairs to sweep. It was made from the eyelashes of an elephant the Craver brothers had shot. He had put together the eyelashes from both eyes and had made a very handy little broom for cleaning corners.

He swept and, out of the corner of his eye, looked at Amgam at the back of the tent. He was embarrassed to look at her. William could have been raping her just a few seconds earlier. He was getting further and further inside the tent, and sooner or later he would reach where she was.

She didn't seem especially hurt. Naked, with her eyes open and looking up at the ceiling, Amgam ran a hand over her chest and belly, very slowly. Her fingers reached her white pubic hairs and went back up. It was as if Amgam had ordered her senses to hibernate. She wasn't in that tent, only her body was.

Amgam didn't fight against the pain. Instead she extracted it from inside her and watched it as if it were something foreign and alive. A large part of her secret, thought Marcus, was that she understood pain differently. And in that same moment he knew that Amgam was an infinitely superior being to all the others gathered there in the clearing. And he knew it with a clear, pure logic, just as he knew that England was very far away or that there were trees in the forest.

Marcus was still sweeping the tent. He was a slave to the automatism that months in the service of the Cravers had instilled in him. The brush dragged a strange object. He couldn't tell what it was and he held it up in the air with two fingers. It was a small bag of flexible rubber, filled with liquid. Marcus dropped the condom with a shiver of disgust.

He was getting dizzy. In that clearing in the Congo reality and fantasy were two nations at war, invading each other. William raped Amgam, and the one who was afraid of catching something was William. And meanwhile, while all that was going on, he, Marcus Garvey, swept the ground with elephant eyelashes. He felt strangely drunk, as if the air in that tent was alcoholic. He felt like laughing, but he held it in. He sensed that if he let that laughter loose, he would go mad. He grabbed his skull with both hands: if he didn't, his ears would grow wings, he was sure, and his head would go flying. Near him he saw a flask of whisky. He took a very long sip. Then he tossed a shirt and some trousers toward Amgam's naked body.

'Get dressed,' he said, still drinking whisky. 'You're going home.'

At first she didn't understand. But Marcus was resolute. He even helped her with the buttons on the shirt to hurry things up. They left the tent together. Marcus moved with firm steps toward the mine. He brought her with him, holding her by the elbow. He was moving with such momentum that he was almost dragging her behind him.

Pepe saw the startling pair. She was at least a head taller than him, and so white next to his olive-coloured skin, while he set the pace with his short legs.

'Mr Marcus? Where are you going?'

Pepe was speaking to him formally. That sign of respect could not be good. Marcus didn't answer. Pepe insisted.

'Please, Mr Marcus, don't do it.'

'Why not?' said Marcus without turning around, almost at the anthill.

'Mr Marcus! She is different. She belongs to Mr William. We'll have problems, many problems. Don't do it!'

Marcus went down the ladder to the mine behind her. The men had stopped working and were watching them, dumbfounded. When they stepped into the mine all the Negroes moved away.

'Will you shoot me, Pepe?' challenged Marcus.

He took Amgam to the hole through which she had come into their world.

'Mr Marcus!' shouted Pepe. 'Leave it alone! I won't warn you again!'

Marcus raised his head. Up there, at the mouth of the anthill and silhouetted against the clouds, was the brawny figure of Pepe, aiming at him with his old rifle. Marcus stopped. But in the end he decided, 'You won't shoot. I'm sure of it.'

Pepe hesitated for a few incredibly long seconds. Then he lowered his gun and said resignedly, 'No, I won't do it. Obviously I won't do it.'

But Pepe's resignation was not Marcus's victory, far from it.

When Pepe talked to the Negroes it was as if he did it from underwater. And now he spoke to them in that language filled with bubbles. It didn't take much for him to convince the Negroes to hold down Marcus and the fugitive.

'Are you happy, Pepe?' bellowed Marcus, flailing uselessly among twenty arms. 'What did you promise them? A plate of lentils?'

'No,' said Pepe. 'Sardines.'

There was nothing he could do. Those men hadn't fought for their freedom, but they were willing to keep Amgam from having hers. And why. For half a tin of sardines. The saddest part of all was that day they were having sardines anyway. Marcus had found fifty tins recently in a trunk that he had thought was empty. With the treachery or without, they would have eaten sardines.

Amgam and Marcus emerged from the mine. When he had climbed the last step of the ladder and was passing Pepe, Marcus leaned close to his ear and said, 'I'll never forgive you.'

Once he was out of the mine, Marcus didn't dare look her in the eyes. He continued his route as if she didn't exist, heading into the jungle. When he was far enough away from the camp, he let himself fall. He curled up like a praying Muslim and he started to cry.

A man's collapse should be as private an act as his death. When a man falls, when he fails, he has to be protected from public inclemency. But sometimes an apparent failure is a success, when men save their dignity simply by having tried to save it.

Unexpectedly Marcus felt six fingers caressing the nape of his neck. Before they realised it, they were already embracing.

* * *

I remember interrupting Marcus.

'It's not possible!'

'What's not possible?' asked Marcus with interest, looking from one side of the table to the other. 'Did I say something wrong?'

'Are you saying that you made love to her? That she became your lover?'

Marcus's face turned the colour of a ripe tomato.

'I should have kept it to myself, you mean?'

The upper part of my body very tense. I relaxed a bit, resting on the back of the chair.

'No, it's not that,' I said, regretting my outburst. 'It's good that you explain everything to me. It's very good.'

'So? If it's not that, what mistake have I made?'

Marcus couldn't understand that he hadn't made any mistake, that he had only hurt my feelings. At first the image of Amgam's fingers on his neck had seemed unbelievable to me, then unbearable. Those six fingers, so white, so thin, so long. I didn't ask him any more. I didn't want to hear it. But, inevitably, I imagined Marcus and Amgam holding each other in the middle of the jungle. I felt a cold fire in my heart, a thin, compact blowtorch flame that scorched my chest.

Why did it upset me so much? I didn't consent to my feelings for Amgam. Actually, I hated them. They had cropped up recently, a few nights earlier, in Mr MacMahon's room, and in that very moment I sensed the problems they would bring. More ridiculous feelings couldn't possibly exist in the entire universe. And at the end of that session, sitting in front of Marcus Garvey, I said to myself, 'Tommy, boy, how can you be jealous of a prisoner, and over a woman that you have never seen and you never will see?'

But I was also clever enough to realise that the question could have been another one: where did Garvey's ability to hurt me with words come from?

Marcus Garvey's story exposed my defects and limitations. Until he had explained that he had been with her, I hadn't understood to what extent I despised him and felt superior to him. It's very easy for us to be compassionate with someone who is no competition. I had allowed myself the luxury of being so indulgent and generous with him, a poor gypsy awaiting the gallows. But now my feelings conflicted with his biography. That someone like him could gain access to Amgam's love upset me. He had had something that I could never have. Never. And never is a very long word. But, in fact, there was nothing extraordinary in that episode. Amgam moved with magical clarity, that at the same time was perfectly logical. What would have been strange was if Amgam had acted any differently. That Marcus was a subordinate, a short-legged gypsy creature, was unimportant. At least for her. Amgam came from another world, she was free of our prejudices. And Marcus was the best man in the clearing. That's why Amgam loved Marcus. And seeing that Amgam was capable of loving someone like Marcus made me love her even more. And him, a condemned man, I envied.

While I was reflecting on these things, Marcus was still waiting for me, without having the remotest idea of the course my thoughts had taken. He insisted once more, 'What was my mistake, Mr Thomson?'

I cleared my throat sonorously, trying to cover up my discomfort, and I said, 'You said earlier that William and Richard had gone out to hunt a lion.'

'Yes, indeed. Richard had seen lion tracks in the mud. They went out together to look for it. But they didn't find it.'

'There are no lions in the jungle,' I said. 'It must have been a leopard.'

'A leopard?' pondered Marcus. 'Could be, maybe Richard was talking about a leopard. I don't remember that well.'

The Craver brothers' fervour for the mine grew day by day. On the other hand, Richard's interest in hunting buffalo diminished like a child's fever: suddenly. William's sexual passion also slackened. The only reason he didn't turn her over to his brother was out of a sense of ownership. William was clever, and he knew that the Negroes' hierarchical instinct was reinforced by that image: the whitest man in the world controlling the whitest woman in the world. Or the underworld. But there was something hard to define in William's attitude.

Sometimes, only sometimes, it seemed to Marcus that William didn't use his power over Amgam to control her, but just to keep anyone else from getting close to her. But such ideas were too subtle for Marcus Garvey, they passed through his mind like shooting stars on a clear night, sporadically and without stopping.

Often, injustice is revealed when the just suffer an unforeseen misfortune. It can also be exposed by the opposite: when fate bestows unexpected good fortune to the corrupt. Because that seam was bountiful. Every day the bathtub washed clean more gold. From an average of fifteen ounces a day it had become eighteen, then twenty, and then twenty-five. And the more gold they extracted, the more earth the Cravers demanded the miners remove.

Sometimes they would yell at Marcus to come and help inside

the mine. Every day the space widened and someone was needed to help direct the work of installing wooden beams.

He realised that the inner landscape had gone through great changes since his last visit. The bubble was now wider. More, larger holes appeared on the walls. Marcus stopped in front of the tunnel through which Amgam had come into the world. Its mouth was wider. Due to the miners' work? No. They picked uniformly in every direction. When they loosened earth the only thing they did was leave uncovered the pre-existing tunnels, which widened as they went further into the earth.

The miners didn't need much instruction to position the beams. Since no one was paying much attention to him, Marcus took the opportunity to approach the largest of all the holes. He lit a match. That little weak light only illuminated a few feet of the tunnel. Enough to see some sort of tube that had the relief patterns of the roof of someone's mouth. Further on, the tunnel twisted like a worm heading into the earth. He suddenly felt air on his face. Just as he wondered if that wind was the product of his imagination, the match blew out. But if the tunnel went into the earth, how was it possible that a gust of wind could come out of there? Marcus didn't ask himself anything else. The memory of Mr Tecton was too distressing. When he got out of the mine he was happy.

In that period, the two brothers' normal mood was euphoria. The mine was bringing them closer to their own particular social revenge. William wanted to buy himself a bank. Richard, an army. And euphoria, often, expresses itself through volcanic resentment. At night they got drunk, shouted and shot their revolvers into the air. More than once Marcus feared that a bullet would come through the tent canvas and injure him or Pepe.

The Africans were turning into some sort of Negro Nibelungs. And I don't intend that as a metaphor. The Cravers had brought a gramophone close to the anthill to which they attached a speaker shaped like a giant carnation. Wagner was what was most listened to. The mosquitoes of the clearing wrestled with the music, excited into a state of insanity, and attacked the men like small flesh projectiles. But William was convinced that the music motivated the miners. It goes without saying that a few lashes of the whip also contributed, and not in small part, to the acceleration of the work pace.

Each day they worked harder, each day more gold was extracted and the mine grew larger. The following fortnight, a false, but tangible, peace reigned. It was as if the mine and the two brothers, encouraged by common interests, had decided to row in the same direction. And, as a result, it was no longer clear if the Craver brothers had found the mine or the mine had found the Craver brothers.

Meanwhile Marcus lived in another world. He had first tasted love there, in the jungle, with her, with Amgam. The Congo was a strange place. A place where pain and pleasure came together and became superimposed, just like the organic layers of humus.

The Cravers' obsession for gold created many rifts that made them avoid each other for long periods. The daily routine was unbelievably monotonous. William spurred on the miners as if they were oxen tied to a plough, driving them to extract more dirt, more gold, while Richard supervised the workers at the bathtub. Marcus's basic obligation was to cook the Craver brothers' meals and the miners' mess. Often, when he had already cooked William and Richard's delicacies, he left the large pot boiling and went into the jungle to a corner he and Amgam had agreed on earlier.

Marcus wouldn't have traded one of those times with Amgam for all the Craver brothers' gold. She made him touch her; she took Marcus's hands and placed them on her body. She also touched him, she knew no shame. The first few times she embraced him with that hot skin, Marcus had the feeling that he would burn like an apple in the oven. And at first he didn't find the way Amgam loved him pleasant at all. He felt like an animal manipulated by veterinarians. It was as if she was saying: do that, do it like this. And Marcus wondered: is that normal, is it always like this?

Very quickly though, that apparently crude contact revealed an erotic finesse. She stopped guiding him much sooner than he could have imagined. He investigated her body with as much insolence as she had examined his days earlier, perhaps even more. Each time they got together Marcus discovered a different layer of pleasure. And one day he said to himself, 'Great God Almighty, before this woman and I exhaust all the possible pleasures, a single woodworm could eat all the wood in the Congo.'

Understandably, Marcus's accounts caused me a double-edged discomfort. He never held back, his stories were filled with verbal abandon. We have to keep in mind that Victorian morality was still in effect. Now it might seem unbelievable, but in that period the social rules of the well off recommended that the words 'leg' or 'arm' only be used for a good reason, as they were immodest. I didn't know anything about life. And I had Marcus Garvey in front of me, loaded down with chains, but telling me of moans and shivers with an expansive freedom that I wouldn't have been able to find in the most pornographic fiction. It was as if that man, after the Congo, had forgotten that life and sex are separated by the walls of civilisation. And all I could do was take notes with a sporadic smile on my lips.

It didn't take much effort for me to imagine them. A little gypsy like Marcus Garvey in the heart of a tropical jungle, drenched in sweat, embracing a woman with skin like snow but of a temperature five or six degrees higher than ours. The second source of my discomfort, naturally, was that I was forced to listen to the details of that singular love, a love that I wanted to have lived but I was only allowed to transcribe. They were lovers, and I was just a typist who couldn't get over it.

In any case, furtive love has its inconveniences. Marcus worried that William and Richard might discover that the two absences were related. He didn't even want to imagine William's revenge. And he also worried about Amgam. Before or after making love she demanded that he pay her attention. Sometimes she even grabbed him by the wrist and made him sit up so that he would be more attentive. She wanted to explain something very important to him, yes, but what? He didn't understand her. Marcus felt like a dog that was trying to learn: the dog knows that he is faced with a superior intelligence, but he is incapable of understanding what is expected of him. Amgam always took the initiative: sit, listen to what I'm telling you, do you understand, do you understand? It's important that you understand it! Amgam spoke and gestured, she was as often vehement as she was slow and explicit, and Marcus didn't understand a thing. The Tecton language had extraordinarily rich phonetics. When she spoke with a thousand vowels it was impossible to retain a single word. Other times, though, Amgam's voice slid with the descending tone of an hourglass.

With great effort, and even more imagination, Marcus tried to decipher her gesticulation. But all his efforts never amounted to more than pure speculation. One day he thought he understood a completely different story: that Amgam had travelled there impelled by the desire to get to know other forms of life. Marcus laughed. No, not that. It was obvious that he would never admit that. What interest could the Cravers' life have, or the Negroes, or his? The routine in the clearing, the slavery in the mine? Anyway, the reasons that had brought her to our world were anecdotal. Amgam's real interest was in communicating some other idea to him, something much more urgent. She kept insisting on it. And Marcus, desperate, naked, could only grab his head with both hands and whine, 'What do you want, beloved? What do you want? What are you trying to tell me?'

A few days later the noises inside the mine returned. Everyone was sleeping and at midnight they were woken up by screams.

'Champagne, champagne, champagne!' was the outcry that spilled from the mine's hole.

William, Richard, Marcus and Pepe came out of their tents at almost exactly the same time.

'Now what's going on?' said Richard.

'It better be important or I'll cut off their tongues with the meat scissors,' said William.

When all four reached the anthill, Pepe quietened the miners with a dry shout. The Negroes' language could boom louder than a whip, recalled Marcus. Then he asked them why they were shouting.

'Noises,' translated Pepe. 'The noises again.'

'Banging.'

William was very sleepy and those damn Negroes had woken him up. He rubbed his eyes. Marcus thought he would pull out the revolver, that he would shoot it into the air, or even worse, at someone. But William was unpredictable. His response deserved a place in some anthology of mental aberrations.

'Tell them to fill their ears with damp dirt. It will make a plug and that way they won't hear anything.'

And he went back to his tent!

According to Marcus, as implausible as it may seem, the tactic worked. Prisoners and children have many things in common: the Negroes shouted because no one paid attention to them; they got no response and finally, like children that cry and aren't comforted, they grew tired. And, of course, no matter what they did they couldn't get out of the mine without the ladder.

The next day, though, all of their faces reflected that consumption that constant fear creates. William understood that the Negroes needed a few words of comfort.

'Listen to me, everyone!' he shouted at them. 'The jungle is filled with noises. The noises never hurt anyone. I don't want any more nights of screaming!'

A new workday was beginning. Richard took William to one side. Even still, Marcus could hear what they were saying.

'You're not fooling anybody, William,' said Richard in a soft voice. 'Every time they've heard noises something was going on. That's the truth.'

'An old man and a girl,' said William. 'That's the only thing that's happened.'

'I've never seen anything like those people. They're not normal. And you know it.'

'Don't be an idiot. They can't come from underground. There must be some explanation that's so simple we haven't even realised it.'

Richard shook his head sadly. 'For the love of God, William. You've seen it more than anyone, you've slept with her. You sleep with her! Maybe there is some simple explanation, as simple as this one: that in the Congo there are people who live under the ground. Who knows what else is hiding down there?'

'What do you want me to tell you?' yelled William with the beginnings of rage in his voice. 'Strange things are happening, that's true. But this is Africa, Richard, Africa! Strange things happen here. The Negroes are black. Have they kept us from getting to the gold? No. We've seen a white old man and a girl. You want us to give up because of that, Richard? Of course not!' William changed his tone. He placed an arm on his brother's shoulder. 'This is our opportunity. We are making a fortune! I don't plan on going back when I'm making so much money. And neither should you.'

Richard sat with the rifle between his knees. He hugged the butt of the weapon. Seconds later he admitted, 'Maybe you're right. What else could happen?'

'That's what I like to hear.'

And they joined in a very intense embrace. It was the only time that Marcus saw true brotherhood between the Craver brothers. Then William pinched Richard's cheeks lovingly. 'And now go and take care of the tub. Or maybe you want the monkeys to see us arguing?'

Marcus didn't wait long at all. The first chance he got he took Amgam to the jungle. He pulled her by the elbow and kept looking behind them. When he was sure they were alone, he spoke.

'That was it, what you wanted to tell me, wasn't it?'

She didn't understand.

'Amgam!' Marcus tried to draw the mine in the air. 'Who's down there? Who? Are they your friends? Do you know them? What you wanted to say was that your friends, sooner or later, would come up.'

But that time she was the one who didn't understand. Amgam's eyes moved as if they were trying to follow a fly in flight. They went from Marcus's hands to his lips, and back. Marcus motioned her to sit on the grass and joined her. He spoke very slowly. He pointed to the ground with his finger and said, 'Friends? Of yours? Your Pepes underground?'

'Pepe . . .' she understood finally.

Marcus smiled.

'Yes, of course, that's it. Pepe, Pepe, Pepe! Amgam's Pepes.'

But she was silent. She didn't share Marcus's joy. In fact, quite the opposite. Her face looked like a granite screen. She stood up with a jolt. She was so tall! Marcus was still at ground level and she stood before him, thin, infinitely tall, reaching up to the clouds like an ivory tower.

'Champagne!' shouted Amgam. She moved her arms up and down to emphasise her words. 'Champagne! Champagne! Champagne!'

Marcus leapt up. He was afraid that they would hear them from the camp and he covered her mouth with his hand.

That day Marcus couldn't explain any more to me. Our time was up and the guards ordered him to stand.

'People use the word "fear" too loosely,' he said while they searched him to make sure I hadn't given him anything. 'Children fear the dark; women fear mice; men fear their bosses. People are afraid that the price of bread will rise or that there'll be a war. But that's not fear. And in order to know what fear is, it's not enough to have heard it talked about.'

Marcus was already in the hallway. The two guards escorted him, one held him at each elbow. He continued talking. That day he talked until he disappeared from the hallway, calmly, like an orchestra playing on a sinking ship. With his neck turned, as he got further away, he was still telling me, 'Amgam shouted "Champagne, champagne, champagne!" and when I was covering her mouth I knew that for the first time in her life she was afraid. I mean, really afraid. Do you understand me, Mr Thomson? Do you understand what I mean?'

As I headed back to the boarding house I convinced myself that the book was beyond my abilities. I walked aimlessly, having a discussion with myself. How could anyone describe all of Marcus's horror and all of his love, there beside Amgam and awaiting the Tecton? It was impossible. That story couldn't be made into a book. At least not by me. On the other hand, the book was getting too big. It was bigger than me, than Norton, than Marcus himself. I had to finish it. It didn't even matter whether I was talented enough or not, just like no one asks a soldier if he's brave enough to complete a mission. I didn't get back to the boarding house until it was dark. There I bumped into Mr MacMahon. Unexpectedly, because it was late at night and MacMahon was very strict about his schedule. He was sitting in the dining room accompanied by a half-empty bottle of cheap whisky. He told me that his wife was sick. And he, so far away, could do nothing to help her. It wasn't so much the seriousness of the illness that worried him, but that the poor woman had to continue taking care of the children. I drank a whisky, in solidarity. I refilled his glass, and mine too. I drank too much. MacMahon couldn't help his wife and I couldn't help Marcus Garvey. Since I was a little tipsy I spoke with the voice of a little frog, 'Well, you don't know the worst of it.'

'Oh no?' answered MacMahon after a long pause. He too was staring absently at his glass.

'No, you don't know it. It's very likely that soon all humanity will be wiped out by a murderous race.'

'Is that so?' said MacMahon, indifferently. He jerked his head up and down as if he were digesting the news. He scratched the short thick hair, like a wild dog's, that covered the nape of his neck, and he asked dispassionately, 'And there's no way we can stop them?'

'I'm afraid not.' And after thinking it over a bit I stated, 'No, not a chance. We'll be pulverised, annihilated, snuffed out. The human race will become dust in the winds of time. Not even ruins will remain to show that we ever existed.'

We immersed ourselves in the contemplation of our glasses.

'Maybe we don't deserve any better . . .' I philosophised. 'It'll all be over.'

MacMahon nodded. I wasn't expecting a prudent proletariat like him to say, 'And to hell with it!'

He was right. One day we would be exterminated, by the Tecton or by time, sooner or later. We would all disappear. Us, those that depended on us, those who haven't yet been born and who one day would have to depend on those that now depend on us. Everybody.

'And to hell with it!' I said.

'And to hell with it!' said MacMahon.

Laughter came out of me like a hiccup. And it spread to MacMahon. Everything would go to hell any day now. And thinking about it, suddenly, was funny.

We laughed so hard that the other boarders shouted at us from their rooms to shut up. We couldn't stop. The boarders' doors became drums. They made me think of the tom-tom drums in the jungles of Doctor Flag. They announced the big news. To hell with it! We laughed till the whisky ran out. Then we went to bed. What could we do? The Tecton were about to invade the world. But our whisky was all gone. These things happen.

TWELVE

THE NEXT FEW DAYS set everyone's nerves on edge. The screams that came out of the mine at night were a thermometer of the noises within. Some nights the racket didn't stop until daybreak. William didn't want to deal with it at all. He ordered Marcus and Pepe to take care of the incidents at night. They were only to notify him in case of a real emergency.

Marcus couldn't stand waking up with nightmares. Now he found out there was something worse: waking up for other people's nightmares. He could only sleep for a little while, until the explosions of howls ravaged his mind. The sound travelled from the mine's opening and spread through the clearing. There were one hundred mouths shrieking desperately, like pigs that had a knife to the neck. Marcus opened his eyes, disconcerted, terrified, wet with a sickly sweat. His numb brain had trouble accepting what was going on. He learned to ask himself four questions before moving: 'Who am I? Where am I? Who's screaming? Why are they waking me up?' And he answered: 'I'm Marcus Garvey. I'm in the Congo. I'm an overseer of Negroes. The Negroes are screaming because they're afraid of a Tecton attack.' And when he had obtained those four answers he told himself: 'Calm down, everything's normal.'

Marcus and Pepe went to the anthill on many occasions. When the shouting exceeded the normal levels they would leave the tent, stick their heads into the mine opening with the rifle at hand and ask the men what was going on.

'Noises,' translated Pepe one day. 'As always.'

'And they are screaming so much because of that?' said Marcus.

'The sound of blows.'

'Blows, blows, blows . . .' cursed Marcus. 'And doesn't it seem like a big coincidence that they only hear them at night? They're just trying to kill us with exhaustion!'

'They hear them during the day,' explained Pepe. 'It's just that during the day the sound of their work covers them up.'

Marcus snorted. Annoyed, even though he wasn't sure with whom, he shouted, 'Push the ladder down! Lower it!'

'Are you sure?'

'Do what I tell you.'

The ladder fell and Marcus descended. Pepe stayed up above, with his rifle at the ready. Even though the moon was full, Marcus could only see eyes around him, white eyes everywhere. They trembled and moved away from him like a herd of eyes. The mine stunk.

'Where does this bloody noise come from?' asked Marcus.

'To your right, at the back,' translated Pepe from above. 'They say that the sound comes from one of the tunnels higher up. Above your head. Do you see it?'

Yes, he saw it. It couldn't have been long since the excavation of the wall had uncovered this hole. It was round and very high up for someone as short as Marcus. He hung his shotgun on his back and pulled himself up with the strength of his arms.

He felt as if he were sticking half of his body into a whale's windpipe. But he hated himself for having paid any attention to the Negroes, for not having paid himself any attention, and he shouted, 'I don't hear a thing here!'

He was lying. He still hadn't heard anything, but he was convinced that sooner or later he would hear something. Like when a stone is dropped into a well of unknown depth, the sound of the impact might come earlier or later, but it would always come.

And he heard it. Of course he heard it. The noises came from deep inside, from the depths of the earth. Marcus placed the palm of his hand inside the tunnel. It was vibrating.

At first he thought that all the sounds were one sound. But his ear could soon differentiate layers of sounds. The most grating one reminded him of paper being torn. Below that one he heard some sort of rhythmic echoing, like many horse's feet on hard sand. And there was even a third sound, harder to define, less precise.

Marcus let himself fall to the mine's floor and he climbed up the ladder. He moved quickly, that was what gave him away. The Negroes broke the expectant silence they had maintained while Marcus listened to the depths as if with a stethoscope. They started shouting again with fear, and some hands had the audacity to hold him by the shirt, more like shipwrecked men that beg to be let on board a boat than with real aggression. Marcus brushed them off without thinking or stopping. When he was above ground Pepe helped him pull up the ladder.

'We have to wake up William,' said Marcus.

He himself took care of it. He sat in front of William's tent and said, raising his voice a little more each time, 'William? William?'

The canvas door opened a crack. William was naked. He only wore a thin silver chain around his neck. His light eyes blended very well with the African moonlight. Even Marcus could appreciate the beauty of William's body, a beauty created to live by night. Marcus saw the silver-coloured pubic hair of the younger Craver brother. And behind him, Amgam, seated as always, with her legs crossed. She wasn't tied up. Inside him he felt a stab of love and hate in equal parts, the same way that blue and red can co-exist in the same flame. Marcus had thought that William always tied her to the pole so he could take her. Did it really matter if she were tied or untied? Not really. William could rape her when he wanted and how he wanted. What worried Marcus was that maybe, just maybe, he didn't need to rape her. When he really thought about it, he had no way of knowing what went on inside that tent. It occurred to him that he knew as little about the relationship between William and Amgam as William did about the relationship he had with her. He lowered his eyes, hoping not to betray his feelings.

'I come from the mine,' reported Marcus, speaking with his gaze lowered. 'And there really are noises.'

'Really?'

'Yes.'

'And what's new about that, Marcus?' said an irritable William.

'The noises are very loud.'

He was lying. What was really new was that Marcus had heard

them for the first time. But what he was trying to communicate was not a fact, but a fear.

'How loud?' replied William sarcastically. 'Loud as thunder? Loud as a shot from a cannon?'

'Not that loud,' said Marcus, a bit disoriented. 'But they're there.'

'So, what do you suggest I do?'

Marcus moved his head from side to side. 'You told us to let you know. It's not the sound of a flute. It's like the sound of a large factory. The Negroes are right.'

William interrupted him. 'Marcus, the Negroes are never right. Can you understand that?'

'I suppose so, William,' said Marcus. 'The Negroes are never right.'

'No. You don't understand. Let me explain something to you: if the Negroes were right they would rule Europe and we would be in the Welsh mines extracting coal for them. But it turns out it's the opposite; we rule Africa and they work in the gold mines in the Congo, under our orders. Do you understand now, Marcus?'

'Yes, of course.'

'Good night.'

And William closed the canvas with an abrupt gesture.

At that point anyone would have been able to see that a horrible threat was approaching. Or better put: rising. Anyone except William and Richard. Marcus felt as much a prisoner of the mine as the Negroes themselves. Or maybe more. They, at least, could complain. He didn't know what to do. The Craver brothers had created that peculiar atmosphere where the profit outweighed the risk, and they had never asked him if he agreed. Marcus was afraid. Of the mine and of the Cravers. The fear he felt about the mine was too vague to fight against. The fear he felt about the Cravers was worse: the type of fear that pushes the victim to join forces with those who terrorise him.

Then there was Amgam. Marcus was a slave to some sort of contradictory paralysis. Flee together? To where? To the jungle? Into that harsh green ocean? To the Tecton world, where she would be well received? Marcus couldn't know what lay below the mine and beyond. But whatever it was, it was the last place in the universe he would go of his own free will.

Some nights the Negroes shrieked with a horror that never tired, for hours and hours. Marcus never learned to tell their voices apart. For him they were an anonymous mass that only said: we're afraid, we want to get out. Or maybe: they're coming up, they're very close.

Sometimes he didn't hear them all night long, who knows why. That unpredictability didn't ease Marcus's soul. He was the one who kept watch, he was the one who had to go to the anthill. But nothing ever happened, just the shouts, and the repeated warnings made them lose their effect. Finally Marcus made that mistake, so human and at the same time so cruel, of accusing the victim of the crime. When the Negroes shrieked Marcus cursed them from his tent, jerked Pepe's elbow and ordered him to go and have a look.

One night the Negroes raised a unanimous and uniform cry. They started at dusk and they didn't shut up all night. Marcus could only half sleep. He remembered only vaguely the order of events. When the intensity of the moans became unbearable, he ordered Pepe to see what was going on. Pepe returned without news. The Negroes, though, were shouting again. Even still, precisely because the shouts were continuous, because they maintained a tone of monotonous horror, he was able to fall asleep. Like those who live by a waterfall who become so accustomed to the sound of the water crashing that they end up incorporating it into their dreams.

Very early in the morning he was awakened by the silence. An absolute silence, if there was such a thing as absolute silence in the Congo. No sound came from the mine. His mind had grown accustomed to those hundred throats coordinated by fear. He had grown so accustomed that the silence was novel.

He opened his eyes. Beside him, Pepe also had his eyes open. Pepe looked at the canvas that served as the door. But he looked with the eyes of a mummy, fixed on an eternity beyond his grasp.

'Pepe?'

Pepe didn't answer and Marcus followed the direction marked by his gaze, fixed on the canvas door.

There was a round, white, bald head there. The khaki canvas of the tent was opened halfway to show that head with puffy cheeks and eyes round as tennis balls. Just one head, which moved its pupils at full speed, as if it had very little time in which to see everything. The lips traced a letter V, but no one would have called it a smile. The head made a face. It stuck out a violet, triangular tongue. And suddenly it left, as if it had been sucked out.

It was such a fleeting vision that Marcus didn't even have time to be frightened. He shouted to Pepe, 'Did you see it? Did you see it?'

Pepe didn't answer, immobile on his cot. Marcus left the tent.

A plague of human locusts were looting the camp. There were Tectons everywhere. Five, six, ten, twenty, more, much more. He didn't know how to count them. There must have been more than twenty, but they moved so quickly that he might have counted them twice. Marcus had never seen such frenetic activity. They wore tunics covered with red earth and they searched through everything with very proficient monkey hands. They communicated their findings with incredibly hoarse voices, like cows speaking very quickly. It was hard to believe they were of the same race as Amgam.

Human life didn't exist for those Tectons. Like someone who's colour-blind and can't distinguish colours well, they suffered from some sort of visual deficiency that impeded their perception of human beings. They only saw objects. And all their activity was concentrated on separating the useful from the useless, that one yes, that one no, that one yes, that one no.

Richard had come out of his tent. He was as dumbfounded as Marcus. The Tectons were going through trunks, emptying out sacks, opening bags and suitcases. In just a few minutes they had turned over the entire camp. Soon the first incident would happen.

A Tecton approached Richard. Or more precisely, the wristwatch he wore. The Tecton leaned over his wrist. He really didn't use any direct violence; he only had eyes for the watch. But Richard, terrified, took a few steps back. The Tecton persevered, advancing as Richard moved back and all the while working on the watch's band. Finally Richard lost his balance and fell on his back. The Tectons stopped suddenly, like puppets moved by the same strings, and great peals of laughter came from their mouths. The watch thief even imitated Richard, his crude movements and his spectacular fall. More laughter. Richard, flat on the ground, but unhurt, was crying. Meanwhile another Tecton approached Marcus, attracted by a lighter wick that stuck out of his pocket, and he put his hand in there.

'No!' said Marcus, pushing him softly but firmly.

The Tecton looked at him with an annoyed grin. He offered him a stone cube the colour of ash. Inside Marcus's repulsion mixed with controlled fear. It seemed to him, at that time, that the best thing he could do was to take what he was being offered. It was just a rock, or maybe a piece of ceramic sculpted into a small cube. The Tecton confused Marcus's hesitation with a bargaining strategy and he doubled his offer. This time he offered him a long stone, similar to school chalk. What was he supposed to do with that? He didn't have much time to think it over. Amgam had appeared from somewhere and, with a smack to his wrists, had made the stones, or pieces of ceramic, or whatever they were, fall. Then she dragged him towards the edge of the clearing.

In one of the trees that marked the boundary of the clearing there was a Negro tied up. William had grown fond of that punitive method since the day he had tied up all the miners. The man was there for some minor infraction. With both hands Amgam turned Marcus's head so he had to look at the five Tectons that the African had on top of him.

The Tectons had found the poor devil tied up and had taken advantage of his helplessness. They didn't need to negotiate anything. Two Tectons were pulling out his fingers and toes with the help of some pliers. Another was boiling a small vessel shaped like a small pot where he diluted powdered chemicals and stirred the contents. The fourth emptied the fingers into the little pot, and with the help of some tweezers he extracted them once they were cleaned of skin and flesh. When the bones had cooled down, he gave them to the fifth Tecton, an individual seated on the grass that worked with jeweller's tools. The Tectons seemed deaf to the screams of the man they were mutilating. The pliers kept pulling off fingers, the streams of blood didn't seem to bother them.

Marcus lost control. His first impulse was to run from that scene in the opposite direction, which brought him back to the centre of the camp. He was approached by the same Tecton as before. He grabbed him firmly by the front of his shirt with one hand, and with the other he offered him three small stones, three. And, finally, Marcus understood what material the Tecton currency was made of.

'Let me go!' begged Marcus. 'Leave me be!'

But Marcus couldn't get the Tecton's breath from his ear. He didn't know how to get free of him. Until, without warning, the Tecton's head burst like a melon hitting a cement floor. Skull fragments flew like shrapnel. Marcus became frightened when he saw his shirt wet with Tecton blood.

William had been the last to wake up but the first to react. In his own style, naturally. He moved with a revolver in his hand and shot all the Tectons that made the mistake of coming too close to him. It was like walking through a shooting range. One step, two, bend the elbow and shoot. The Tectons took a long time to realise what was happening. It was as if they couldn't comprehend that someone had dared to attack them. There was one who even planted himself in front of William with his arms in the air and shrieking something very angrily. William stuck the barrel of the gun into his mouth, shot and continued advancing, his face spattered with blood, dauntless, choosing victims at random. Encouraged by William's example, Richard grabbed his shotgun. And soon more bullets than mosquitoes flew over the clearing's airspace.

There was a certain grandeur in the cold-bloodedness that

William Craver showed that day. Not a single muscle on his face moved. When he ran out of ammunition he opened the revolver's pan, ignoring the Tectons, the screaming and the chaos that surrounded him. He filled the chamber and continued his target practice. One step, two, stop. The arm extended, aimed, *bang!*, a dead Tecton. And another, and another. His shirt and trousers became stained with the blood of his victims. But William, impassive, didn't stop. He had in his favour the fact that the Tectons didn't defend themselves. Many didn't even realise they were dying; a bullet went through their chest and they fell right there, with their booty still in their arms. The last two were smarter and they fled.

The entire massacre lasted only a few minutes. The pair of Tectons fled towards the anthill. The lifted their skirts with both hands so they could run faster. To Marcus they looked farcical. Which made William's order to Richard sound so cruel.

'Kill them, Richard! Don't let them get away!'

William had run out of bullets. Richard aimed calmly with his elephant-killing shotgun. A spout of blood came from the side of one of the fugitive's heads and the Tecton collapsed. But his gun jammed and he couldn't repeat his success with the second fugitive.

'Marcus! Grab him!' said William while he turned his pockets inside out looking for bullets.

Marcus's short legs weren't made for chasing people. But the Tecton was let down by his skirts, so one could say it was a fair race.

Marcus was getting closer. When the fugitive went along the small mound made by the anthill, he only had four feet of advantage. He didn't really jump, it was more like the Tecton let himself fall into the void. Marcus stuck his head through the hole. 'Grab him before he slips away!' he shouted to the Negroes inside. 'Grab him!'

But none of them dared move. They all lay against the walls, trying to keep themselves as far as possible from the intruder. Marcus went down the ladder as if he were sliding down a firemen's pole.

The Tecton was already getting into one of the slits in the wall. Marcus jumped and with extreme force he managed to catch the Tecton by an ankle. The feet were the only part of the Tecton that still stuck out of the hole. The other one kept kicking, trying to strike Marcus's face.

'Help me!' shouted Marcus, who looked like a stuck chimney sweep.

Finally the Tecton's heel managed to hit his nose. It was a very painful blow. Marcus saw little yellow spots. He let go of the ankle for a few seconds, half blind, and the Tecton disappeared into the tunnel.

'Why didn't you stop him?' shouted Marcus, turning towards the Negroes as the blood began to gush from his nose. 'They'll be back!'

Seconds later William and Richard arrived at the mouth of the anthill. They came into the mine and shot into the hole the Tecton had fled through.

Too late.

THIRTEEN

On William's orders, the Negroes dug a large pit and dragged the bodies of the dead Tectons there. Everyone helped when it came time to dump the corpses and cover them with dirt. Burying them was a doubly painful operation, because the Tecton's eyes and skin made them appear to still be alive. According to Marcus, dead Negroes don't turn white, just grey. Something similar happened with the Tectons. Death made that white skin change very quickly into some sort of waxy white, and then to pearl grey. So, we can conclude that death is the great equaliser. But the Tecton bodies still had some peculiarity that was hard to pin down. Maybe it was their half-open mouths, like fish. Or their glassy eyes, the lids always raised, a damp cobweb on the retina. Hours earlier they were still looking at the Congo sky, so blue, without wanting to accept that they were already dead and had lost the right to look at the humans' sky. When he looked at those paralysed features he wasn't sure if they were really dead, or if they had ever been alive.

'From dust they came and to dust they return,' said William after the last shovelful.

No one could tell if it was a prayer, irony or a curse.

Pepe translated the Negroes' explanations of what happened in the mine. According to their statements, the Tectons had appeared from the noisy hole. They carried ropes and hooks that they used to climb up on the walls.

The rest of the day Pepe was even more silent than usual. In the evening, when Marcus met up with him at the tent, neither of them wanted to talk. Before closing his eyes, Marcus pulled a blanket over himself. Since they had been in the tropics it was the first time he had covered himself up to sleep.

'I didn't know it could be cold in the Congo,' reflected Marcus aloud.

'It's not cold,' said Pepe. 'It's fear.'

A little while later Pepe added, 'It's over.'

'What do you mean?' asked Marcus.

'I'm leaving,' was the reply. 'Tonight. I'll wait until William and Richard have fallen asleep. Then I'll get out of here, take the men from the mine and we'll run off.'

Marcus sat up. 'Have you gone mad? You can't do that.'

'Why not?'

Marcus didn't have an answer. He lay down again. He looked up at the tent ceiling and said, 'You knew it already, didn't you? You've always known. The Negroes know some legend about those people that live in hell.'

Pepe turned towards Marcus. He even seemed amused.

'Legend? What legend are you talking about? I don't know any legend.'

Pepe laughed so hard, and so much, that he had to contain himself for fear of waking up William and Richard, even with the distance that separated the two tents.

'No,' explained Pepe. 'Everything I know I learned from my grandfather. He talked about what he had seen. And he said that whites always behaved the same way, no matter where they came from.'

Marcus's curiosity was piqued. He turned his body towards Pepe, leaning his head on one hand.

'What do you mean?'

'My grandfather knew what he was talking about. The white men always do the same thing. First, the missionaries arrive and threaten hell. Then, the merchants come and steal everything. Then, the soldiers. They're all bad, but the new arrivals are always worse than the ones before them. First came Mr Tecton, who wanted us to believe in his God. Today the merchants appeared. And soon the soldiers will come up. I don't want to be here when they arrive.'

'What about her?'

Pepe hesitated. 'There are strange people everywhere.'

'Did you see what the Tecton did with that man's hands and feet?' said Marcus.

'White people are like that,' reflected Pepe. 'They make us work as bearers and miners. And they become rich that way.' He sighed. 'At least I'll have the pleasure of taking my brothers in the mine with me.'

'Now they're your brothers?' said Marcus sarcastically. 'I

remember when we chained them up you took part very happily. Oh, Pepe! We are more than five hundred miles from any civilised place, or even inhabited. If you find anywhere it will be one of the villages we attacked on the way here. You only have an old rifle and hardly any ammunition. You'll be alone. When they recognise you, they'll kill you. That's if the jungle doesn't kill you first.' Marcus sighed. 'Don't do it, Pepe. You say you want to free the boys in the mine and leave with them. How do you know they won't kill you the first chance they get? They've got good reason.'

'Maybe so,' said Pepe, 'but at least it will be them that kill me.'

From the jungle came some animal roars of an unknown, twisted beauty. The noises of the jungle, the lit oil lamp, the tent and each other's company combined to give them some pleasure. It wasn't until then that Marcus understood that it was all about to end, that Pepe was leaving.

'Come with me,' offered Pepe.

'No, I'm staying here,' said Marcus.

They put out the lamps. But they didn't sleep. Five minutes later, from the darkness, Pepe said, 'It's because of her, isn't it?'

After a little while Marcus answered, 'I'm tired, Pepe, very tired. Tonight I'm going to sleep soundly. So soundly I won't hear a thing.'

They didn't sleep. But they pretended to be sleeping. Three hours later Pepe got up, took his old rifle and his red hat, and before leaving the tent he put his lips close to Marcus's ear. He said, '*Du courage, mon petit, du courage.*'

And he left.

In the book I wrote another account of Pepe's farewell. What was it? It was the version that Marcus had recounted to me: that of a long-suffering Pepe, who stays with him even though Marcus begs him not to, fighting against the Tectons, protecting him with his life, until Marcus himself threatened him, pointing a revolver at him to get him to leave. I couldn't believe it. Pepe's attitude was so heroic that it was almost a caricature. So one day, when we revised that chapter, I took a stand at our table with my arms crossed and my elbows sticking out, and I surprised him by saying, 'Marcus, why are you lying to me?' He looked from one side to the other, hesitant, ashamed, and more unsure than ever.

I knew the answer. He was lying to protect Pepe's good name, the only friend that he had had in this world. Some will ask: if I knew he was lying why did I write the false version? The answer is: because I was fed up with Doctor Flag's Negro characters. For once, I said to myself, have a Negro that blows tons of white blokes to bits, the opposite of what rotten old Flag would have made you write. And since it didn't affect the narrative structure, I allowed myself that.

How could I be so simpleminded? It's the second version that describes the best of all possible Pepes. It shows us that Pepe was the only sensible creature in that camp.

Much has been said about the loneliness of those faced with the gallows. Less has been said about the loneliness of the executioners. Marcus would never forget William and Richard's expressions the next morning, when they discovered the mass flight. They had imagined all the possibilities – attempts at murder, revolts and thefts – except that one. Richard always slept with his long rifle lying by his side, like a lover, William with a revolver under his pillow. The little sacks of gold were buried under William's tent. But no one wanted to steal their gold or their lives. No one wanted to get rich. Or even to get revenge. They just wanted to escape, that was all. And the Craver brothers couldn't have anticipated that.

Marcus recalled the human desert the clearing had become that morning. The Negroes' bodies no longer filled the mine. Their voices weren't loud enough to disturb the noises of the jungle. Slaves without a master are free. Masters without slaves are nothing. They were alone.

The previous night's fire was still smoking, and that dying fire was a very good representation of the camp's spirits. Marcus and Richard sat in front of the dwindling smoke, looking at it apathetically. Further on, William found Pepe's canteen. He picked it up and weighed it in his hands and then he threw it to the ground with fury. Marcus and Richard didn't take their eyes off the embers.

'And now what?' said Richard.

'Now they'll kill us all,' answered Marcus spontaneously, as he smoked. Not even he had known that his voice could be so harsh.

'Kill us?' said Richard, startled. A sarcastic smile crossed his face. 'Who do you think will kill us, now that everyone's gone?'

Marcus raised his eyes from the ashes, he looked at Richard, he turned his neck and looked at the mine. Richard understood.

'Oh God, oh God!' whined Richard, covering his face with both hands.

'What's going on here?' demanded William, who had now forgotten about Pepe's canteen.

'Richard's crying,' was all Marcus said, with an uncharacteristically harsh voice. William realised that. And he looked at him as if to say: first Richard, then I'll take care of you.

'Come on, you're a soldier!' William said to encourage him, putting an arm around his shoulder. 'Where's your fighting spirit?'

But Richard wasn't a soldier, he was a wreck. William insisted.

'You are an officer of the British Empire!'

'This isn't part of the Empire,' said Richard finally. 'This is the Congo.'

William liked that. You can't talk to somebody who's not even listening. Richard had replied, and if someone replies that means they can be convinced.

'Richard! What did they teach you at the military academy? What should you do in a situation like this?'

'You don't want to understand,' said Richard, who in spite of all his limitations could be very lucid. 'No military instructor taught us what to do in case of a Tecton invasion.'

But William shouted. Marcus had a very vivid memory of that shout. He remembered it like he would have remembered an unexpected eclipse. It was a new, anomalous voice, halfway between ambition and brutality. It was a claim of ownership and it was a declaration of war. He was not leaving. He was not giving up the mine. Never, and to no one. Let them come for it. William yelled and it came as a nasty surprise to Richard.

'Richard!' he demanded. 'What should we do? You're an engineer. Tell me what we should do!'

Richard opened and closed his mouth a few times, but William was on top of him, not letting up on his demands.

'A fence,' said Richard finally, as if he were reading an instruction manual written on the air. 'We have to surround the anthill with a fence.'

'A fence?'

'Yes. We'll build a fort, but in reverse. It won't keep the Tectons from entering the mine, but it'll keep them from coming out of it.'

'You heard the man, Marcus,' said William, who approved the idea. 'Start chopping down trees. We'll need lots of trunks. Let's go.'

And he took Marcus to the forest while Richard stayed at the anthill taking measurements and reactivating his military engineer brain.

William and Marcus started cutting trees. They couldn't be too large or too small. They were looking for trunks between six and nine feet, tall enough that they couldn't be climbed once they were driven in vertically and formed the fence, but not so large that they couldn't be dragged to the anthill. They each had an axe and they worked very closely with each other. William said, 'You haven't been on our side for a while now. Don't bother denying it, I know. What I don't understand is why. Why, Marcus? Is it the money? You think you deserve more?'

Marcus didn't speak. William continued, 'Do you really believe we haven't been thinking of you? Don't be an idiot, you'll be compensated. You'll return richer than a tramp like you could ever dream of being. The Cravers never turn their backs on faithful servants.'

The trees fell. Once they were on the ground they chopped off the branches so that the fence would create a solid wall. Marcus maintained a stubborn silence.

'So it's not about the money,' concluded William.

They tied a few trunks together and then put the end of the rope on their shoulders so they could pull them like mules. But at the last minute William let Marcus drag the whole load by himself. He walked at his side, like a mule driver.

'Is it about the Negroes? Could it be that behind that gypsy skin lies a philanthropic soul? No, it's not that. There are no more Negroes now. And you're glummer than ever. So why then?'

Marcus collected the trunks in a pile near the anthill. Amgam sat in front of the tent with her legs crossed. William stopped. His grey pupils were two lead coins.

'It's about her,' he finally guessed. 'Her.'

William's head turned from Marcus to Amgam and from Amgam to Marcus. He was having trouble putting the two characters together. It wasn't often that someone like him found reasons for admiration.

'It's about her,' he repeated. 'It's about her.'

The three Englishmen spent five days and five nights building the little fort. But as hard as the work got William never forgot the feelings he had discovered in Marcus.

Richard began the work by driving in a stake right beside the anthill. Out of the stake came a cord twelve feet long, at the other end of the cord they had tied another stake. When the cord was taut he went around the anthill once striking the ground with the point of the second stake. The cord created the radius and Richard used the stake to mark the ground like a plough. That was how he drew a circle. William and Marcus dug the furrow marked by Richard until it became a small trench, and they put the trunks in there. They raised them vertically, they strengthened them and tied them together with cords; they built a solid wall. They used picks, shovels, axes and hammers. They were afraid and they had to work with their rifles on their backs. The butt constrained them; the rifles' bands, crossed on their chests, were an irritation; their mouths were filled with curses, their hands covered with cuts and blisters. No one would have ever thought that something so simple would require so much effort. They continued working at night lit by three oil lamps that multiplied the shadows by three. They appeared to be nine men.

William and Richard kept thinking about how to perfect the wall, how to make it higher, stronger, more impenetrable. And while they applied technical principles there was no room for spiritual arguments, which at the same time were obvious: that the fence was an aberration, and that anyone with a bit of sense would have fled.

There was a moment when Marcus was about to shout, to say that's enough. Didn't they see it? No fence would stop the Tectons. He dropped his tools and walked towards Richard with firm steps. He was the weakest of the two. Maybe if Marcus yelled at him he would see the light. Richard worked seated beside the fire. He was smoothing the trunks for the fence with a machete.

'Do you want something, Marcus?' said Richard as he saw him approach.

But before explaining his point of view about that ridiculous wall, Marcus couldn't help making a spontaneous observation.

'No, Richard, not like that,' he suggested. 'Don't cut off the branches that stick out of the upper part of the trunk. Trim them and sharpen them. That way if they try to climb up the trunks they'll cut their hands.'

'You're right!' acknowledged Richard. 'That's a very good idea. Good thinking, Marcus!'

From that instant on he didn't know how to oppose the project. Richard's praise, paradoxically, made Marcus feel more a part of it. His criticism of a small aspect of the fence implied a tacit acceptance of the whole thing. And Richard, who was so terrified that he would have accepted any help no matter where it came from, didn't hesitate from that moment on to consult with him on every detail with extreme affability. And so, without his really knowing how, it became impossible for Marcus to express his true feelings about the wall.

In all of those days he only had one chance to get close to Amgam. Taking advantage of an accident on the job, when the point of a stake he was handling opened up his whole forearm in a wound that was longer than it was deep, Marcus took a break to tend to his arm. Amgam, seeing his injury, went to help him.

They were standing next to a tent. Marcus emptied the water from a canteen over the wound. She brought him some bandages. That allowed their hands to touch. But Marcus knew that now William wouldn't take his eyes off them. She knew it too. All the love she could give him was a little pressure with her hand. She squeezed Marcus's hand with her six fingers a few seconds longer than necessary. It couldn't have been very intense contact. And, yet, it was.

He wasn't alone in the world. Those amber eyes thought of him. Squeezing his hand, conveying that supernatural warmth, let him know that Amgam's mind was only working on one thing: freeing him.

Besides that episode, though, they only lived for digging. They worked and worked, until a week later, one evening, when the wall finally stood, magnificent, with that undeniable beauty that constructed things raised in the middle of wildest nature have, Amgam approached it.

The night was particularly chilly and damp. Thousands of insects saturated the air with the clamour of shrill bursts. Around the anthill there was a wall of perfect trunks. It even had a little door that opened like a drawbridge. If the fence were a watch face, the entrance would have been at six o'clock. From one side to the other of the drawbridge, which is to say from five to seven, they had created some lookouts from which they could watch the anthill and loopholes to stick the rifles through. At twelve o'clock there was a third shooting point. Richard's idea was to create a system of crossfire, so that the invaders would be shot down as soon as they appeared through the anthill.

Amgam went into the space enclosed by the wall. For some reason, no one restricted Amgam's movements. Worn out by the long day of work, not thinking clearly, they let her do it. And they went in behind her. They watched as she observed the wall. Suddenly, without anyone really knowing why, Amgam's opinion had become important.

Three equidistant lamps hung from the inside of the fence, one above each loophole. Their cold light created weak, twisted shadows. The nine shadows, twelve if we count Amgam's, stopped. She had understood, finally, that the purpose of this construction was purely military. She approached the anthill. There she saw the work from the perspective of an attacker emerging from the depths of the earth. She sat, in her usual style, on her heels. Marcus, William and Richard couldn't take their eyes off her. Finally Amgam made a gesture.

Words were unnecessary; all three of them understood her. More than a gesture, it was a general prostration of her body, a spectator's sadness. They all comprehended that Amgam was feeling something unknown to the three men: she was feeling someone else's pain.

Richard was the most affected. 'Somebody get her out of here,' he whined in a defeated voice. 'Please, oh please, somebody take her.'

No one listened to him, and he was the one who ended up leaving. William and Marcus stayed by themselves inside the fence, each one on one side of the anthill. The three lamps made a slight sound of gas escaping that imposed itself on the jungle's nocturnal sounds. Now that William knew of his feelings for Amgam, Marcus feared that he would use them as another weapon. But that evening William seemed like a different person.

Marcus sat down, tired, his back against the fence. William's legs, sheathed in those white trousers, planted themselves before him.

'She came out from below ground . . . like a worm . . . and you love her . . . you love her . . .'

He didn't say it with disdain. He spoke more like someone trying to resolve the *Times* crossword out loud. William grabbed one of the lamps, which was surrounded by insects and moths. He put it on the ground between them and knelt down. With two fingers he captured one of the largest moths, one with white wings. He let it fall through the upper opening of the lamp. It lit up like a paper kite. He didn't take his eyes off the insect in flames.

'Tell me, Marcus Garvey, what is it that you like about her? I want to know.'

William had discovered the truth, it was useless trying to hide anything from him. And he didn't have the energy to start a dialectical duel with someone so superior to him, either. Above them, the Milky Way crossed over the sky of the clearing like a spinal column.

'I like touching her,' he said.

William's eyes had never looked so much like a shark's. Sharks' eyes show no love. But those eyes, that evening, were also conscious of their inability to be anything else. William left. He went to his tent, with her. He would surely force her with the coldness of a scientist experimenting with laboratory rats. That was the paradox that distanced William Craver from the human species: perhaps he wanted to reach love, but the only route he knew was rape.

A little while later Richard approached Marcus, who now lay on his back. Richard was the one who was most scared. Or, the one who was worst at hiding his fear. They smoked together. Marcus's thoughts were lost in that fantastically star-filled sky, and Richard said, 'I don't like to look at the stars. When I do, I have the feeling that the stars are closer to home than we are.'

Marcus sat up. But once he was upright he couldn't help looking at William's tent. What must be going on in there? He didn't want to know, he didn't want to hate William more than he had already learned to hate him. And while he observed the khaki canvas of the tent he had an idea: never before had someone so desirable and someone so undesirable been together. It was like sticking absolute good and absolute evil in the same bottle. Marcus closed his eyes. No, he definitely did not want to know what was going on inside there.

'Let me tell you an old family story,' said Richard. 'When I was small someone gave us a kitten. The only detail that differentiated it from the other cats was its white-tipped tail. William played with it a lot. My father did as well. That was very surprising to me, since I was used to having the very serious Duke of Craver for a father. My mother was already ill from the disease that would take her to her grave, and the pet thoroughly cheered her up. One day the kitten was found dead, in the garden. There was blood everywhere. If you looked carefully you could see that its body had been cut exactly into two equal halves. My father said that it had been crushed by the wheel of a cart, but it wasn't any cartwheel that split that kitten like a guillotine. It was an axe blow. Well, actually two blows. Even a child can use an axe.'

Richard sighed.

'I remember another time. The family was sitting at the table. William explained to us a discovery he had just made. He said that feelings weren't like opinions, because one could change an opinion when one wanted to, but that it was impossible to have a feeling if the feeling didn't want you to have it. That night I overheard my father talking to my mother about William. He said that William had a lot of talent. He said that William was like an extraordinary book. But that the good Lord had forgotten to write in the full stops, the commas and the accents in that extraordinary book. My mother asked him, "Do you mean to tell me that the boy has bad feelings?" And my father replied, "No, my dear, it's worse. What I'm saying is that he doesn't have them."'

We might think that the fact that Richard shared this with Marcus indicated a weak spirit, and that Marcus should have taken advantage of that to make him come back to his senses. No. Marcus didn't miss any opportunity, for the simple fact that the opportunity never presented itself. Richard was too dependent on his brother to stand up to him. Any independence of Richard's personality was mortgaged as soon as a crisis appeared. And who could imagine a bigger crisis?

The next day was the beginning of what was to be the last period of human life in that damn clearing. For William there was no contradiction between his objectives and his circumstances. Once the defences were established, according to his logic, there was no reason not to continue extracting gold. The day went like this: Marcus, inside, was in charge of picking at the walls of the mine and filling a large wicker basket with the earth he had extracted. From above, William pulled up the full basket with a rope. He went through the door of the fence with the basket in his arms and he headed towards the tub, where he emptied out the basket's contents. Richard was in charge of separating the dirt from the gold. William returned to the anthill. Meanwhile, Marcus had had time to fill up another basket. William lowered the empty basket and pulled up the full one.

The mine had become an enormous subterranean vault. At least for one man alone. Now the light of the lamps, spread out over the dozens of beams that held up the ceiling, struggled to illuminate the inner surface. Midday announced itself with a shaft of sunlight entering vertically through the anthill, falling like a theatre spotlight.

Before, one hundred Negro bodies had filled the mine. Now it was empty. Marcus's voice bounced against the spherical walls. Between baskets he opened a flask of whisky to have a sip, and the squeak of the cap unscrewing came back to him multiplied a thousand times. When that happened he couldn't help looking around him. It seemed like the tunnels were telescopes into another world. And that they were focused right on him.

But I have to say that what most impressed me about the story of that period, leaving to one side moral judgements, was the figure of William Craver. What extraordinary willpower, able to contradict and combat all the laws of the universe!

Why did he do it? Gold fever? He didn't even have any miners left. Richard might be a bundle of lethargy, but William was too smart a man. Why did he stay there, then?

I think that he was compelled by a hidden impulse, as powerful as it was invisible. I think that in William's recklessness there was a secret desire to die. He was a killer. And now, for the first time in his life, he was the victim.

Here's a story: a famished snake approaches a little bird, the bird sees the snake coming. Why doesn't the little bird fly away?

Because he wants to find out how the story ends.

FOURTEEN

WHAT MOST UPSET MARCUS about the recent events was that they kept him from Amgam. Without being able to camouflage himself among the Negroes, without being able to meet in secret in the jungle as they had before, Marcus was further from her than ever. He spent the day working in the mine, and at night she was shut up in William's tent. And William, ever since he had learned of Marcus's feelings, watched over her with a mix of hatred and distrust. No, that wasn't exactly it. No one could ever really fathom what William was thinking.

At night someone always had to watch over the anthill. The distribution of turns was a reflection of the established hierarchies. William was exempt from any obligation. Richard kept watch a third of the hours of darkness, while Marcus took care of the other two-thirds. In order to make up for his lack of sleep they let him have a nap after lunch. But he didn't get enough rest and every night his fatigue increased. Looking at it with that perspective, then, one could say that it was William who provoked it all. It was one of his favourite tactics, first he would create the conditions for someone to make a mistake, he would make it inevitable, and then he would punish the offender with utmost severity.

One night William surprised Marcus.

'You fell asleep, Marcus! What would have happened if the Tectons had appeared? It's incredible, they could come at any moment and you fall asleep . . .'

Marcus apologised. And apparently that was it. But in the evening, when they were about to end the workday, William took the ladder out of the mine.

'William! What are you doing?' shouted Marcus from the bottom.

'I'm sorry. It's the best thing for everyone.'

'You can't leave me here all night! Alone and unarmed!'

'Oh, no? Why not?'

'Because the Tectons could appear at any moment! You said it yourself!'

'Exactly,' said William's lanky figure. 'I want to make sure you won't fall asleep. If they come, let us know. But don't you dare cry wolf.'

'William! William! William!'

But William had already gone. Marcus couldn't believe it. William was probably with Amgam, and he was stuck at the bottom of the mine. He went towards the large hole from which the Tectons had appeared. Every day, while he worked extracting dirt from the walls, he looked at it out of the corner of his eye. Now he discovered that it was worse at night. Especially without the ladder nearby. When they returned everything would depend on whether or not

William and Richard could rescue him in time. But that wasn't worth thinking about: William had left him there because he had no intention of helping him. He put his head into the hole. Once again he felt that gust of cool air on his face. 'It's not air,' Marcus told himself, 'it's the devil's breath.'

He moved away from the hole. He leant on the wall opposite, whisky flask in his hands. He pulled his legs up and hugged his knees. He couldn't stop staring at the hole. He looked at it until his eyes hurt.

Would they come that night or would they wait a few days? The first Tecton wave had been preceded by strange noises. But Marcus doubted that they would be repeated. He suspected that the noises had been caused by tunnelling work. And now the tunnel that connected the lower world with the upper one had already been created, and widened. What's more, the Tecton knew how they would be received. One thing was sure: they would not be kind to the first human they came upon.

The Congo. Moisture that burns. And below ground, an oven. Marcus breathed in his own sweat. It slid down his forehead and nose to his lips, like a small stream that tried to re-enter the body it had come out of. He finished the whisky. Shortly after, the alcohol, fatigue and desperation made him close his eyes. He dreamt that he fell into a dark well, and he fell, and he fell, but the final impact never came. While he dreamt Marcus knew he was dreaming. He thought to himself that he hadn't had that dream since he was a child. But he also told himself: 'No, Marcus, no, the problem is that today you're not dreaming. This isn't a dream, it's reality.' He opened his eyes. And in front of him, coming closer to his face, was a six-fingered hand as white as snow.

Marcus went from horror to love in a split second: it was Amgam. They hugged each other. Marcus couldn't help wondering how she had managed to climb down there. He took her by the hand, the same hand that William, every night before going to sleep, tied to a pole in his tent with iron handcuffs. She understood, it was as if her smile said, 'My love, you have here before you a women capable of dislocating all the bones in her body to get to another world; and you doubt that that same woman could dislocate the bones of one hand to escape from some common handcuffs?'

Amgam had no time to lose. She examined the cave. She took charge of the problem, weighed all the options. Sophisticated machinery moved within her ample white forehead. Marcus could almost hear the squeaking of that Tecton brain.

Finally Amgam pulled Marcus's arms, tenderly but decisively. He understood what she was suggesting. She wanted them both to escape into the hole, to flee towards her world. The idea had a certain logic. When they met up with the Tectons, Amgam's intervention might save him. Of course, that meant going into the tunnel. Marcus loved Amgam as he had never loved anyone before, but since the night with Mr Tecton that hole had caused him insurmountable dread. He had to make up his mind. And so, there, deep in that abominable mine, absolute love arm-wrestled with absolute terror.

We shouldn't believe what romance novels tell us: fear won.

Marcus couldn't follow her. He would have gone with her to any place in the world. But not to her world. He would never go into that dark tunnel. Ever. Amgam sighed, disheartened.

They had to look for another solution. But what? She was more intelligent than him, she had already thought of everything. And the only alternative was to flee into the jungle. She pulled him by the hands. He objected to the idea, gesturing like an insane monkey. Amgam didn't know anything about the Congo, she couldn't know anything about it.

On the expedition to the mine William and Richard had left a trail of blood. The reverse journey, surely, would be as painful as the trip there: a million anonymous Africans must want him dead. Sooner or later they would meet with a revenge as just as it was misdirected. They would never get to Leopoldville alive. Perhaps if the entire expedition managed to clear the way with gunfire. But separately, unarmed and without provisions, never. It was possible that not even Pepe himself, who knew the country and had a rifle, had survived. How could those two, a little gypsy and a Tecton, the oddest couple in Africa, in the world, hope to make it? Wandering through the jungle Marcus and Amgam would be like two beetles on snow.

In her world they would kill him. In his world they would kill them both. And from Marcus's point of view that was all that needed to be said. They sat very close to each other. Amgam looked at the ugly floor of the mine, with her head bowed. Marcus had never seen anyone so sad. He felt responsible for it: he was the reason behind such a kind-hearted sentiment, and it filled him with a strange satisfaction.

'My beloved, I'm not dead yet,' said Marcus, caressing her cheek. 'Many things could happen.'

They embraced. Dead tired, Marcus fell asleep with her chest as a pillow. He didn't sleep long. Before the sun came up he opened his eyes. She was no longer there. At some point in the night Amgam must have gone back to the tent.

There was still an hour before the sun came up. How did Marcus Garvey spend it? Reviewing his brief existence on earth? Putting his soul in order? No. Marcus spent that hour suffering from horrid jealousy. Amgam's visit had made him think of many things, all of them bad. The binds with which William constrained her meant nothing to her. That had been very clearly demonstrated. Why then did she tolerate William raping her every night? What did William feel for her? And Amgam for him?

The Tectons were about to arrive. And he was jealous. I remember that as I took notes of that scene I thought, 'People can be incredibly absurd.'

The sun came out. A basket suspended by a rope was lowered into the mine. Above they had installed a pulley. It was too far from the mouth of the anthill to see who was handling it. The basket shook for a few seconds at the end of the rope. Then it stopped, as if to say: what are you waiting for? Fill me up. Marcus obeyed. The basket took off and shortly after came back, falling in the same spot, empty.

'William!' shouted Marcus. 'You can't leave me here. The Tectons could come at any moment. They won't be long now!'

The only response was a jerk on the rope. The basket jiggled like an impatient puppet. But this time Marcus ignored it.

The tunnel. Marcus started to fill it with rocks. Rocks and more rocks. But he only managed to create a ridiculous screen of stones. It was as if a man condemned to die were trying to delay the morning of his execution by covering the window of his cell with towels. Marcus raised his eyes.

'William! Will you let them kill me while I work as the devil's chimney sweep? Why, William? Why? What have I done?'

'No one wants to harm you, Marcus.'

It wasn't William's voice, it was Richard.

'Richard! Where is William?'

'Fill the basket.'

With Amgam, obviously. The whole thing was a deliberate, cruel revenge: the Tectons would come and they'd kill Marcus, and meanwhile William would have Amgam for himself. What a dark soul, William Craver's. Unlike other spiteful lovers, he wasn't jealous of the feelings she didn't have for him, but rather of the feelings he couldn't have for her.

'You're not like William,' Marcus flattered him. 'Lower the ladder, Richard!'

'Only if there is a problem. That's what William told me to do. Until then, work,' said Richard, still keeping himself invisible.

'A problem?' said Marcus with a desperate voice. 'An underground race is about to invade the Congo, the world! And you won't lower the ladder until there's a problem? You're as mad as a hatter, Richard Craver!'

Marcus didn't know how to interpret Richard's silence. Maybe it was merely the passivity of a morbid spectator. But what if behind that silence lurked feelings of guilt? Marcus was thinking very quickly. He guessed that William had never explicitly ordered Richard to kill Marcus. That wasn't the nature of their relationship. Surely William had only given him some neutral instructions that would eventually lead to Marcus's death. What other reason could there be, otherwise, for an order that prohibited helping a shipwrecked man until his head no longer sunk below the water? Because, obviously, the only possible 'problem' was the Tectons. And once they appeared, when they were already in the mine, the last thing that Richard would even consider doing would be to lower the ladder.

'Think, think,' said Marcus to himself, 'there are no desperate situations, only desperate men.' He had to take advantage of the fact that William wasn't there, and that Richard was free of his influence. He had to give him reasons that would justify disobedience.

'I'll remind you that three minus one makes two,' stated Marcus. 'If they kill me you'll only be two men defending yourself against the Tectons. Lower the ladder!'

Nothing.

'At least stick out your head. They told you to lower the ladder if something strange happened. Fine. But how are you going to know what's happening if you can't see it? Richard? Richard? Richard!'

It was useless, even though Richard had his doubts. If he was sure of his role he would have shouted at Marcus to fill up the basket. He didn't.

As foolish as it was, he piled up a few more rocks at the hole. After a while the first few feet of the tunnel were more stuffed than a Christmas stocking. He put a last little stone there, like a finishing touch. He sat down again. Right there, below the hole, with his back leaning against the wall.

Marcus thought about Amgam, about the things that William must be doing to her. He knew that William wouldn't be satisfied with raping her. His imagination offered him demonic scenes. All the Congo's perversion fitted inside there, inside a simple canvas tent. A cold melancholy nested in Marcus's chest. He hadn't died yet and he already missed life.

He felt something hit his head lightly. He saw something bounce off his head and fall to the ground. He took a good look at it: it was the last stone he had placed in the tunnel.

He got up.

'They're coming, Richard!' shouted Marcus. 'Stick your head in and you'll see it for yourself. Damn you, Richard Craver! Look!' he insisted when he got no response. 'That's all I'm asking of you. Look!'

The hole trembled. The wall of stones shook. Something pushed harder and harder.

'Richard, look! Just look!'

Now the stones fell like a cascade. Marcus had the impression that the wall would burst at any second.

'Richard!'

The bulky torso of Richard Craver appeared up above. Just in time to see the tip of some sort of black spear come through the stones. No, it wasn't a spear; it was a gigantic drill bit. Richard suffered some sort of hypnotic crisis. He couldn't take his eyes off the instrument that was destroying the fragile wall of stones.

'What are you waiting for? Lower the ladder now! Bloody hell! Richard!'

The last shriek woke Richard up. He looked at Marcus as if it was the first time he had ever seen him.

We mustn't confuse desperate acts with useless ones: that wall of rocks saved Marcus Garvey's life, because while the Tectons were breaking through it Richard had one critical moment to make up his mind. William hadn't counted on that extra minute. Richard saw Marcus begging for help and the black-tipped drill, and he remembered William's instructions: there was no reason not to lower the ladder. And he lowered it.

Marcus rushed to the ladder. At that moment the first Tecton's head emerged. It was completely covered by a helmet that had three small round openings, two for the eyes and one for the mouth. He used his head like a battering ram, pushing away the last stones that blocked his path. Behind the head appeared a furious torso, white armour, dusted with red earth. And two arms that held the drill. It was a perforating instrument, more than a weapon, but Marcus was sure that the Tecton would try to kill him, that he would grab him from behind as he was climbing up the ladder. He knelt down, then he threw a handful of red earth at the holes in that helmet and climbed like a lizard without a tail.

'The ladder!'

Richard and Marcus pulled up the ladder before the Tectons had a chance to climb up it. As they raised it they could see the inside of the pumpkin-shaped mine filling up with white bodies at an alarming rate. In less than a minute close to a hundred Tectons must have emerged.

'To the fence!' shouted Richard.

They took the ladder, then they went through the drawbridge door and closed it behind them. William had just come out of his tent.

He hadn't had time to get dressed. He wore only black boots and white trousers. We have to imagine that he must have been surprised to see Marcus alive. 'Richard, go to the twelve o'clock loophole,' ordered William. 'And don't shoot until I do.'

Richard obeyed and went round the fence to the northern loophole. When they were alone William had the audacity to give Marcus a rifle. He tossed it to him with one hand. The weapon crossed the space that separated them making a parabola. Marcus caught it so awkwardly that he almost tripped. William said, 'Do you know how to work it?'

'No.'

'You're a clever boy, you'll learn quickly.'

William and Marcus took up their positions. Marcus at seven o'clock and William at five, separated by the door. The guns went in through some slots in the shape of horizontal rectangles. That allowed each barrel to cover the entire space inside. On the other side of the fence, at the twelve o'clock position, emerged the tip of Richard's gun, which kept shifting from the right to the left within its slit, searching for a non-existent target. Because the anthill remained incomprehensibly calm.

'What are they waiting for?' wondered William. 'Why don't they come up?'

Time dragged. And it was unbearably hot. Marcus dropped his rifle to one side. The mugginess made him so dizzy he had to rest his forehead against the wood of the palisade. At the edges of his visual field he saw yellow lights. Rivers of sweat fell from his cheeks, they congregated on his chin and trickled to the ground in a small vertical stream. He felt the mosquitoes slide off his skin, trapped in sweat too dense for their tiny legs. The wall of tree trunks surrounded the anthill, the forest surrounded the clearing. Thousands of animal sounds went up to the sky like the smoke from a pot. There were also the squeaks of a train braking. And the creaking of an overloaded rocking chair. But that constant roar came from the insects, like grinding teeth, thousands and thousands of tiny teeth gnashing against each other.

Something caught Marcus's attention. He looked at the sky, as if checking the weather, and spoke.

'They're coming,' he said to William. 'Listen.'

Silence had fallen over the clearing like a meteorite. Since that day, so long ago, when they had left Leopoldville, they had always been accompanied by noises, night and day, day and night. Sounds shrill and harsh, wild and friendly. Irritating like a drill or sedating like flowing water. Noises of birds, of monkeys, of unidentified beasts. The sound was so constant that they had stopped hearing it. And now, all of a sudden, silence.

'Do you see?' shrieked Richard from his position. 'Do you see what I'm seeing? Oh, God!'

Three hooks now clung to the mouth of the anthill.

'Shut up!' said William. 'And don't shoot!'

They could see that from the hooks hung some hairy ropes. The ropes were taut. They held heavy weights: Tectons ascending. There was no doubt about it. Now they could also hear some military voices, very similar to the shouts that mark the rhythm on galley ships. On top of each hook appeared a helmet. One of those stone helmets that covered the entire face except for three round holes, two for the eyes and one for the mouth. The heads didn't move from the anthill. They hadn't expected the primitive fort that contained them. After a few very long minutes they decided to show themselves, standing up, still. Behind them appeared more Tectons. They all wore the same stone helmets and the same armour, with long skirts that went down to their ankles. The Tectons made a circle around the mouth of the mine. Disciplined and still, back against back, as if each one had to keep up individual combat with the tree trunks in front of it. More Tectons came out. The formation created the effect of a living sculpture. Suddenly, though, a guttural voice was heard, and all the Tectons took a step forward, expanding the circle. That was what William was waiting for. Before they could get to the trunks he shouted, 'Now!'

It was impossible to miss. Richard's enormous shotgun made some horrific holes in the stone armour; William's rifle shot with the cadence of a machine-gun. In such a small space and in the midst of that crossfire the Tectons had only one strategic option: to climb up the wall of trunks before they were killed. Impossible. They were shot down before they could even start climbing. Tectons didn't stop coming out of the anthill. It was as if the mine spat them out. They showed admirable discipline, complete indifference to the rain of bullets that killed them. The dead bodies piled up inside the enclosure. Then some sort of howl was heard, very similar to what would come out of a horn. It was a retreat order. When they heard it, the surviving Tectons returned to the mine. They had called off the attack. At least for the moment.

'They're leaving!' announced William. 'Cease fire!'

But Richard must not have heard him. Around the anthill there was a heap of dead. Richard shot and shot into those dead bodies.

'Richard! That's enough!' shouted William. 'Stop shooting, save your ammunition!'

Fear kept him from hearing anything. He continued shooting. Through the lookout, Marcus focused his attention on the pile of dead. And he was surprised to see that, indeed, he could still make out movements. What Richard didn't understand was that all that agitation was caused by his own bullets, which were designed to kill elephants. Each time a corpse received an impact the entire pile shook. The heads and appendages moved as if they were still alive and sprayed the inside of the fence with blood.

William and Marcus went around the fence to Richard's

position. There William shook his brother by the shoulders. Richard jumped. He thought he was being attacked from behind. With a horrific scream he moved his rifle like a sabre, attacking us dementedly.

'Richard!' shouted William, backing up. 'What are you doing?'

Even after hearing his own name it took him a second to recognise them. Then he collapsed. He sat leaning on the fence, his mouth open. Marcus had never seen a man sweat so much. His face shone as if it had been dipped in oil, his fringe wet, his khaki shirt absolutely soaked.

William and Marcus also sat down.

'Killing Tectons is tiring,' said William.

And the first giggles appeared. They had fought off the Tectons. But Marcus, without meaning to, rained on their parade. He asked, 'And what now?'

At this point in the story I had a little incident with Marcus. I want to mention it. He didn't follow the narrative thread. I insisted that he tell me the events, calmly and in order, and he just complained. I can't say he planned to defy me. It was some sort of passionate and spontaneous response. I kept asking him to stick to the story, and give details. Otherwise, we couldn't move forward. He didn't listen to me. His emotions overcame him, he was unable to do what I asked of him. He loathed William and Richard, especially William. He shook his chains, he was about to scream. But all that verbal incontinence was suddenly silenced.

Sergeant Long Back was standing behind Marcus. He had placed his cold truncheon on one shoulder, brushing his neck. Just that. But Marcus shut up, trembling. All the fussing had dissipated.

'Garvey,' ordered Long Back, 'answer what you're asked.'

I hadn't wanted that intervention. Long Back made me an accomplice to his truncheon. But I needed Marcus to clarify some things for me, and I had no authority over Long Back. I said, 'Marcus, you still haven't told me about the Tecton weapons.'

'What weapons?' said Marcus swallowing saliva, glancing sidelong at Long Back.

'You haven't mentioned what type of weapons the Tectons carried,' I said, examining my notes. 'You've told me about the stone helmets and the armour that protected their entire bodies. But I can't describe the attack against the fence without mentioning the Tectons' weapons.'

Long Back's club moved to under Marcus's chin. The prisoner looked at us, at the truncheon and at me, with his eyes very wide.

'The Tectons only used clubs,' he said.

And Long Back, incredibly, smiled. Well, the ends of his lips rose as if they were manipulated by a screwdriver. But in someone like Long Back that meant a hearty guffaw. I suppose that somewhere deep down he had a certain sporting nature. He went back to his chair and sat with the truncheon on his knees. It was a club covered with rubber. I wondered if that rubber had also come from the Congo.

'You don't understand,' said Marcus, relieved. 'The Tectons didn't have shotguns or pistols, or any special weapons.'

And after a very long pause he whispered, 'They were the weapons.'

FIFTEEN

THE TECTONS DIDN'T COME back for quite a while. They attacked with a new, but not very skilful, strategy in which a couple would appear from the anthill and, running in zigzag, try to reach the fence's door with the intention of smashing it down. They were suicide missions. The Tectons were shot down before they even touched the door.

They attacked sporadically. Sometimes one pair followed the other immediately, and other times they waited up to half an hour. The moon had already risen above the clearing and the Tectons, resolute, didn't give up. Now a solemn music came out of the depths of the mine. It was the coordinated sound of many horns.

'Do you hear that?' shouted Richard from his loophole. 'It reminds me of my regiment's anthem!'

And he laughed at his own sarcasm. William did too. Two more

Tectons came out of the anthill. William killed them with his repeating Winchester before Richard even had time to aim.

'William!' he objected. 'The next two are for me.'

Marcus had barely slept all night and he asked William for permission to rest. The danger seemed to have diminished and the Cravers were taking the incursions sportingly, so William let him have what he wanted.

Marcus took the chance to sneak closer to Amgam's tent. He found her tightly tied to the central pole of the tent. This time William had imprisoned her with the bearers' stocks. Had he discovered her previous escapes? They embraced. The only thing that Marcus could say was, 'Beloved, beloved, beloved . . .'

Her profusion of kisses and hugs, on the other hand, were of a different nature. She was glad that Marcus was alive, but at the same time she was a driven woman. She was trying to tell him something. He didn't realise, until Amgam grabbed him with both hands by the shirtfront. Amgam looked like a waiter throwing out a drunk. Marcus understood what she was saying to him: get out of here!

'You don't understand.' Marcus tried to calm her down. 'You don't know what is going on out there. It's the first vertical war in history. But the Cravers are winning.'

No, he was the one who didn't understand. Amgam tried to explain, drawing things on the sand with her sixth finger. But Marcus, clearly, didn't know the Tecton alphabet.

Outside the Tectons kept the skirmish alive. And the music. To the underground sound of horns there was now an added sound of stone against stone made by some sort of drums. All of the music, actually, sounded as if it was created by an orchestra of stone instruments. Through the clearing boomed a cold, military sound. William and Richard could also be heard encouraging each other. They even laughed, fired up by each good shot. Marcus caressed Amgam's cheeks with both hands.

'My dear, I only wanted you to know that I'm alive. I don't know how this will end. But remember that last night, even though it doesn't seem true, we were worse off.'

For a few seconds Marcus was unable to take his hands off Amgam's cheeks. He was even scared that his palms would get stuck to her. He had never felt them so hot.

Anyway, he had to leave the tent. He didn't even want to imagine William's reaction if he found them in there, together and embracing. As he was leaving she protested. She still hadn't made him understand what she wanted to tell him. Marcus was exhausted. Those twenty-four hours of tension had eaten away at his nerves. He needed to rest. He went into his tent and before his body hit the cot he was already asleep.

He was awoken by a hand shaking his shoulder. He ignored it, still half-asleep, until someone whispered his name in his ear. He would have recognised that voice anywhere.

'Pepe? Pepe!'

Pepe had to cover his mouth. 'Don't shout. The Cravers might hear you.'

'What are you doing here?' said Marcus, astonished. 'Why did you come back?'

'Why? For you, of course! I've been spying on you from the jungle for a while. I saw you come in, and when I was sure that the Cravers weren't paying attention, I slipped in here. They're keeping themselves entertained over there.'

Marcus's eyes were still red and puffy. He rubbed his face with his hands, while Pepe said, 'A miracle, Marcus, a miracle has happened to me!'

'A miracle . . .' repeated Marcus.

'Yes!' exclaimed Pepe. 'The men forgave me, that is the miracle. I thought they would kill me, of course. After I freed them we ran together one whole day and one night. And the next day I told them that if they wanted to kill me they should go ahead, my rifle wouldn't protect me. They didn't want to hurt me. They told me I had helped to take their lives from them, but I had also given them their lives back. So we were even.'

'That's good news, Pepe,' said Marcus, still half-asleep.

The Negro noticed the lack of feeling in his words and shook him by the shoulders. 'Don't you understand? That goes for you too! I asked them, and they told me they wouldn't do anything to you. The men know full well that the only evil souls in the clearing are the white ones, whether they come from above ground or below. You can escape!' said Pepe, pulling on his arm. 'Let's go!'

'Now you are the one who doesn't understand,' said Marcus, more alert and refusing to be pulled. 'I won't go anywhere without her. And she can't go anywhere.'

Pepe didn't say anything. From inside the tent they could make out the difference between the Cravers' weapons. William's rifle was heard more often. Richard's was louder and more powerful.

'Well then, stay in the Congo!' said Pepe finally. 'It's the only place where no one will do anything to you two. Live in the forest. Build yourselves a cabin, hidden but close to some village. When you need it, the people won't refuse you a bit of food, a kind word, or some help. Come on, hurry up!'

Yes, why not? Marcus felt euphoria spreading through his chest like a liquid. Just twenty-four hours ago everything seemed lost. And now he had the chance to win it all. Marcus reciprocated by hugging Pepe. He was a very lucky man. Life had brought him to the most ominous place, to a hole at the ends of the earth, and it was there that he had found Amgam and Pepe.

Now it was Marcus that was anxious to run away. Outside, for some reason, the Cravers had intensified the shooting. He asked Pepe to help him fill a haversack with equipment that would be useful for life in the wild. Their four hands packed tools and medicine quickly, and then Marcus said, 'Quickly, to William's tent. We have to get Amgam out of there.'

Marcus and Pepe left the tent crawling along on their elbows. They only had to cross the short distance to William's tent without the Cravers seeing them. Marcus only had eyes for the canvas of that tent. But behind him he heard Pepe let loose with an African expression. He looked behind him and realised there were Tectons everywhere.

It wasn't exactly a mass invasion. The Tectons ran alone or in pairs, avoiding the Cravers' rifles more than confronting them, without any apparent objective. William was more angry at his brother than at the Tectons.

'I leave you alone for one minute and you get distracted!' he said as he shot every which way. 'Instead of ten, a hundred could have come over!'

Marcus didn't have long to think about it: a Tecton jumped on him. Marcus made a mousy little squeal and defended himself by beating on him with his haversack. Pepe wasn't as lucky. The Negro was the target of two very tall muscular Tectons. My God, they were huge, those Tectons! Between the two of them they grabbed him like a river trout, they weren't afraid he could hurt them, just that he might slip through their fingers. With a desperate hand Pepe tore off one of the Tectons' helmets. He couldn't do anything else. When the Tectons had him well in hand they ran towards the fence. One had him by the neck and the other by the feet, carrying him in a horizontal position that impeded any resistance. Marcus no longer had any reason to hide and he shouted to the Cravers, pointing to the fugitives, 'Stop them!'

William eliminated the last few Tectons with a revolver in each hand. Richard was more focused on the inside of the fence, in case there were more invaders coming up. Neither one of them understood what Marcus was shouting about. And the two Tectons moved very quickly. Before they had time to realise one of the Tectons had already opened the floodgate. William killed him immediately, which didn't stop the second Tecton from jumping into the anthill. And taking Pepe with him.

'Don't let him get away!' shouted Marcus to William.

But Richard closed the door. The two brothers looked around them; all the Tectons that had managed to get over the fence were dead.

'That was Pepe!' Marcus got angry, moving his fists up and down. 'Pepe!'

'Pepe?' asked William, surprised. 'And what was he doing here, the filthy runaway?'

Marcus put his hands on his head. He fell to his knees. Pepe was inside the mine, the Tectons' prisoner!

'I don't understand,' said Richard, thinking aloud.

He examined one of the corpses, poking it with the barrel of his rifle. The Tecton's armour wasn't bullet-proof. With the butt of his rifle he banged on a helmet pierced by a bullet as if it were a cricket ball. He was disconcerted by the strategy they had chosen, sending up such a small but determined group.

'Ten Tectons can do nothing against two rifles,' he reflected. 'At this point they should know that. What did they want, then?'

'Prisoners, maybe,' suggested William.

From the depths of the mine came a howl.

'Oh God!' shouted Marcus. 'It's Pepe!'

The Tectons wanted them to hear him. Marcus covered his ears, but the screams went through the flesh of his hands. He didn't want to imagine the instruments of torture that could extract those sounds from a human being.

Suddenly, an invisible hand covered Pepe's mouth. And in its place spoke a Tecton voice. They heard it as if it came to them filtered through a stone loudspeaker. A brusque tone, with long pauses between each sentence. The speech stopped and started again.

Marcus jumped with a start. He put his hands on William's leather belt.

'What on earth . . .' he protested, but Marcus had already taken an iron ring with a bunch of keys hanging from it and was running towards his tent.

He returned with Amgam, freed from the stocks.

'Translate!' ordered Marcus. 'Translate!'

Amgam didn't need to be ordered. She listened attentively, and then she expressed herself in Tecton but with gestures added. She pointed to the inside of the mine, then to the wall of trunks and once again to the mine. It was simple blackmail, very easy to understand: if you want us to give you back Pepe, take down the wall.

There fell a silence that included the Tectons, Pepe and even Amgam. She was the first to react. Before the Cravers opened their mouths she moved close to Marcus. She grabbed his head and rested it against her chest.

First it was Richard. He let out a repressed gasp and then immediately after an irregular laugh. William joined in. His was a laugh that came from deep inside, dragging with it tar accumulated in his windpipe. One's laughter fed on the other's. They laughed and laughed, harder and harder. Rivers of sweat turned Richard's shirt into a dark stain, but he was so overtaken by laughter that he couldn't even wipe his forehead. William clapped like an epileptic trying to kill mosquitoes. It was really funny: the Tectons thought they would trade their defences for a Negro's life!

Marcus was like a child sobbing into his mother's chest. Predictably, Pepe's screams came from the mouth of the anthill again. The only thing the Tectons accomplished was to make the Cravers laugh even harder. None of them was expecting Marcus. He had left Amgam's breast and now ran with a lit stick of dynamite in his hand.

'No, not the dynamite!' shouted William. 'You'll make the beams collapse and we don't have miners to raise them again!'

Marcus had scaled the wall and was already jumping inside. The fuse let off sparks while he declared, 'I'm sorry, Pepe!' And he dropped the stick into the anthill.

I remember that when Marcus Garvey explained this episode to me he was crying. I hadn't yet seen him cry. He extended his right hand and wiped his reddened eyes.

'Who would have said it, Mr Thomson? That fate would punish this hand, which had killed so many Africans, by making it have to kill the only friend I had in the world.'

SIXTEEN

THE CRAVER BROTHERS WERE together, one at the five o'clock loophole and the other at seven. They had been talking about something for hours. Sometimes they shot into the enclosure created by the fence, at the helmets that occasionally appeared from the anthill, but it was clear that they were engrossed in a private conversation. Amgam was once again imprisoned and tied up in William's tent. Marcus had lost his courage. He sat beside the fire, feeding it now that dusk approached. Pepe was dead and he was a defeated man. He had been about to win it all and in the end he had only managed to lose a friend.

William took a few steps towards him. With his hand he made a gesture indicating that he come nearer to him.

'Come here,' ordered William curtly.

When all three of them were at the fence he said, 'Richard and I have been evaluating the situation. If we go on like this, it's never going to end. We have to switch strategies. This is the idea: tomorrow morning we'll throw a couple of sticks of dynamite into the mine. You got it started today. It doesn't matter now, we'll have to rebuild the interior,' said William without even mentioning Pepe. 'The explosions will kill many of them, but it won't be enough. It's possible that some of them will survive the dynamite, especially if they hide in some hole. Someone will have to go down there, immediately after, and throw another stick into the tunnel they came into the mine through, in case they're using it as a hideout. That way we'll be sure that none of them is still alive.'

Richard, who was keeping watch on the enclosure created by the fence, shot at something that was invisible to Marcus. Then he added, 'If one of them survives, even just one, we won't have won anything. The only possibility we have is that those in the place where they come from understand that the ones they sent here will never return. That way they'll forget about us.'

Marcus smiled enigmatically, 'And who volunteers to go down into the mine?'

'We had thought of drawing straws,' proposed Richard.

'No need,' offered Marcus. 'I'll go.'

William and Richard were shocked. Before they could speak, Marcus said the most intelligent thing that had been heard in that clearing.

'I was going to end up doing it anyway. Wasn't I?'

'I suppose the battles with the Tectons must have given you plenty of chances to get rid of William Craver,' I said at the end of that session.

'I don't quite understand,' he said.

'You were armed. You could have shot down your enemy in the clamour of the shooting.'

'But Mr Thomson,' declared Marcus with a thin voice, 'I couldn't shoot William.'

'No? Why not? He was watching you like a hawk?'

'No.'

'You were afraid of Richard's retaliation?'

'No.'

'Well then?'

Marcus glanced around, and then he clarified his statement with an extraordinarily kind voice.

'Mr Thomson, I couldn't shoot him because I'm not a murderer.'

I was quiet. There are silences and silences. Mine was the guilty kind.

I was becoming too absorbed in the book. I could recognise the symptoms: excessive sympathy towards Garvey, a shift in the narrative objectivity in favour of his interests. I thought it would do me good to have an injection of divergent opinions to counteract it.

The main originator of the accusations against Marcus was Roger Casement, the British Consul to the Congo at the time of the events. I had already spoken with the Duke of Craver, and I didn't see any reason why I shouldn't pay a visit to Casement.

At the offices of the diplomatic service they told me which hotel he was staying at. They also told me that he was heading to a new consular destination that very day. I was lucky to have caught him. At the hotel I asked for Mr Casement. The receptionist pointed me to the stairs.

'There he is. He was just leaving the hotel. All this luggage is his and they're taking it to the port,' she said, referring to the thirty or forty suitcases scattered on the ground around the reception desk.

But Casement was very understanding with me. He was so energetic that he instantly struck me as a pleasant man. He was one of those people that as soon as you meet them you think, 'I would pay to have him as my friend.'

'Marcus Garvey? The murderer of the Craver brothers? Of course I remember him,' he told me. 'I can only offer you five minutes. I'm on my way to Montevideo . . . if the U-boats allow it. Unfortunately, the boat won't wait for me. And there are no other boats to Uruguay today.'

He spoke with me right there, at one of the tables in the hotel lobby. His eyebrows were as thick as his beard and he looked as if he had practised ten different sports in his youth.

'Perhaps this will surprise you, but I work for Marcus Garvey's lawyer,' I began, deciding to be frank.

'Well, I think you've got the wrong man. What do you hope to get out of me?'

'Just the truth. Each day I have fewer doubts about Garvey's innocence.'

'Have no doubt. Garvey is guilty, guilty as sin.'

In other circumstances I would have beaten around the bush before getting to the heart of the matter. But as we were pressed for time I said, with a certain vehemence, 'Mr Casement, I admit that my feelings are not based entirely on rational evidence, but I find it hard to believe that Marcus Garvey killed the Craver brothers.'

Casement drew his body forward. He touched my knee with two fingers.

'Mr Thomson: there are places where God has written the word "no". And Marcus Garvey is not innocent. He simply isn't. No. Perhaps you would like him to be, but he's not. No, no and no. Have I repeated the word "no" enough times?'

A young man brought Casement an apple juice. He drank it in one gulp. Then he spoke: 'The autumn of 1912 was terribly muggy and more tiresome than ever. Nothing happened in Leopoldville, nothing new to inspire the labours of us withered Europeans. And all of a sudden Marcus Garvey appeared. He had returned from the jungle completely alone, without William or Richard Craver. The white community in Leopoldville is very small. It wasn't hard at all for me to find out what he was doing. He spent his nights in a horrible, seedy bar, drunk and surrounded by Negro prostitutes. When he met someone white willing to listen to him he didn't wait five minutes before he was declaring what he had done: he was boasting about having killed two Englishmen in cold blood, as boastful Irishmen often do at the pub.'

That same day, at the boarding house, Mr MacMahon had allied himself with Marie Antoinette in one of her usual tricks, and I murmured in solidarity, 'Those damn Irish . . .'

'Marcus wasn't Irish,' said Casement, interrupting me. 'I am.'

He smiled, I blushed. He continued.

'I couldn't ask the Belgian authorities to arrest him or even to interrogate him. I couldn't do anything. They were just rumours, the voice of a drunk in a bar. But, as I said, the white community in Leopoldville is very small. Everybody knows everything. Finally they told me the complete story: according to how Garvey himself had explained it, he had killed them for two diamonds. So we already had the crime and the motive.'

'So,' I replied, 'you weren't a direct witness to the events.'

Casement smiled.

'Allow me to take it one step at a time. If it were true, if Marcus had committed the crime, he would try to leave the country with his haul. And here his real problems would begin. The Congo is like a vice: going there is much easier than leaving. The traffic of precious stones and metals is severely punished. And you can't imagine how scrupulous the Belgian authorities are.'

'Were the diamonds that big? Would it be that difficult to hide them in a pocket or secret compartment and elude the customs officers?'

'I suppose that sooner or later he would have tried it. But I offered him a less risky alternative.'

'I don't understand.'

'I made friends with him. Or better put: I provoked a friendship. Sadly, going anywhere near that bar, and Marcus, sullied my reputation with a stain larger than the map of Australia.' Casement laughed and made a gesture of resignation. 'But what could I do? Setting a trap always has its risks. One day I mentioned to him casually what a diplomatic pouch is. Meaning that the customs officers never go through the luggage of the consular staff.'

'What you are telling me is that Marcus confessed to his crime the day he asked you to send the diamonds to England in your diplomatic pouch.'

'Exactly. He had trouble making up his mind. He didn't trust me. But I gave him enough rope and he hanged himself.'

'I can imagine how it all went. Marcus and the diamonds

travelled to Europe in separate compartments. One day Marcus showed up at some office of the Ministry of Foreign Affairs, asking for an envelope in his name and he was arrested immediately.'

'I sent the diamonds with an explanatory note, along with a sworn declaration made by some of the Europeans that had heard Marcus's story. Whoever claimed the package would be the guilty party. He did and he was arrested. The last news I had of the case was that Garvey had confessed and was awaiting trial. Are there any new developments?'

'Allow me one last question.'

'Go ahead,' said Casement, crossing his hands on top of his belly.

'Do you remember what colour Marcus Garvey's eyes are?'

Saints are possessed by the Holy Spirit in the same way that Casement was possessed by common sense. But for a few brief moments his conviction wavered. It made me think of a dog that had received a smack on the nose with a rolled-up newspaper. He spoke very slowly.

'Yes, his eyes. Don't think I don't understand you, Mr Thomson, I understand you better than you think. They weren't the eyes of a murderer.' He made a small pause. 'But a man consists of more than his eyes. And even though it's hard to believe, those two diamonds were bigger and shinier than Marcus's eyes.'

He recovered himself. His friendly fingers returned to my knee, and as he gave it a few little taps, he declared, 'Believe me, Mr Thomson, your efforts deserve a better cause.'

He patted my knee a little more, as if it were a cat's head. I didn't move it or get upset, and he left for Uruguay, U-boats permitting.

* * *

The next pair of Tectons that came out of the anthill launched themselves against the door with just as much force as the others had. But they found a surprise: the door opened just as they tried to knock it down. It fell like a drawbridge, and behind it appeared Marcus flanked by William and Richard. The two brothers shot the two Tectons point-blank. William shot his victim in the chest. The victim of Richard's rifle went flying, propelled by the powerful ammunition.

'Now!' shouted William.

They crossed the few feet that separated the door of the fence from the anthill. Marcus carried the ladder. William and Richard moved as if they were attacking with bayonets, with their rifles in front of them. Once they got to the anthill Marcus lit the dynamite's fuse. The day before, Marcus had only thrown a single stick, now he carried a whole bundle in his hand. Simultaneously, the face of a Tecton without a helmet appeared through the hole. He had chosen a bad moment to leave the mine. William shot him immediately, the rifle's barrel a hand's span from that face. The bullet entered the upper part of one cheek and made an eye go flying. The ocular sphere took off, upwards, until it reached the exact height of Marcus's nose. For an instant that ball of gelatine stayed there, hanging in the void, looking at a flabbergasted Marcus. And he had the sensation that, all of a sudden, the world had decided to turn with a cruel slowness. Meanwhile, William and Richard shot into the hole, without any concrete target. The fuse was burning down. But Marcus's fighting spirit had gone. He held a bundle of dynamite between his fingers the same way he might have held a cigarette.

'What the hell are you doing?' bellowed William. 'Throw the dynamite! Throw it or it'll blow us sky high!'

He didn't really throw them. Marcus got rid of the sticks of dynamite like someone shaking off filth stuck to their hand. William and Richard threw themselves to the ground. Marcus didn't. He looked at the black hole of the anthill, which now seemed bottomless. He had the feeling that the eye and the lit bundle were rational beings. The eye fell through a dark shaft, and the sticks followed it lovingly, with all the love that dynamite can feel for an eye. Marcus had a twisted, lucid thought, and he said to himself: she is the eye, I am the stick of dynamite.

'Come here, idiot!'

It was Richard. With one hand he grabbed hold of one of Marcus's ankles and pulled him to the ground, away from the mouth of the mine. Just in time. Down below, the dynamite blew up with a deafening, ugly sound. William, Richard and Marcus lay flattened on the ground, but the underground explosion made the three bodies rise slightly.

A few seconds later the anthill looked like the mouth of a giant coughing smokestack. A thick black cloud poured out and it was as if they were emptying sacks of soot above it.

'Now, now!' said Marcus, who had recovered his fierce spirit and was lowering the ladder. 'Cover me!'

'There's still too much smoke,' said Richard, his face blackened. 'You won't see them!'

'They won't see me either,' replied Marcus.

He went down with all the force his little legs allowed him. William and Richard's mission consisted of shooting those Tectons that tried to get near him. And they had to do it from a difficult position, since they were getting all the smoke still spitting out of the mine directly in the face. But they had few targets. In that enclosed space the expansive wave had reverberated against the wall, amplifying itself. The floor of the mine was a heap of writhing bodies and toppled beams. Most of the bodies were still moving, and Marcus thought of the worms in a fisherman's pot. The dying Tectons moaned, and their moans were very similar to horses neighing. The ones that were most burned gave off a horrible smell of vinegar. A whiff of that stench of detonated flesh entered his nostrils. He couldn't take it. He even wasted a few precious seconds covering his mouth and nose with a handkerchief, like a highwayman.

The mine was filled with a dense screen of smoke. The explosion had shook the red dirt walls, so that the black cloud caused by the dynamite had pomegranate tones. In addition, millions of tiny yellow dots like flying fleas floated in the air: powdered gold. And that wasn't all: from the knees down the surface shone with thousands of green sparks. He didn't understand it until he saw the stiff hands of some of the dead Tectons, which still held up tools in the shape of large pears. They were transparent bags, like sewn animal intestines. They were filled with extraordinarily luminescent green worms. 'The Tectons' lanterns,' he said to himself. Many of those lanterns had burst from the explosions, and had freed hordes of green worms that now slid free.

Marcus moved amongst those vivid colours, trying to contain his disgust. The contact with the dead Tectons frightened him. He moved forward by jumping, almost like a frog, but he couldn't avoid stepping on soft appendages, chests and stomachs. His feet touched flesh and armour, which crunched like glass underneath him. He kept sinking down and he finally fell on top of a heap of dead bodies. He dragged himself along the ground until he found Pepe, the remains of Pepe. All that was left of his friend was a torso and a disfigured head, a body that had all traces of human dignity torn from it. Marcus whimpered and raised his eyes to heaven in a gesture of piety. Up above, William and Richard continued to shoot every which way. The bullets whistled, grazing his ears with the sound of bumblebees. But no, at the moment, Marcus didn't fear for his life. William wouldn't kill him as long as he was useful. And he still needed him.

He arrived at the entrance to the tunnel that the Tectons had used to get into the mine. Marcus carried three bound sticks of dynamite and a long fuse. While he lit it he leaned against the wall, with the mouth of the tunnel above him. That way he could keep an eye on any wounded Tecton that still had the pluck to drag himself over towards him. It wasn't necessary, really. In that mine there were only two sorts of Tectons: dead ones and dying ones, and the Craver brothers' bullets were making sure to hasten that process.

The only thing that he hadn't foreseen, absurdly, was that they could attack him from the tunnel itself, where supposedly the surviving Tectons were hiding. Marcus didn't see the hand that came out of the hole and clamped his wrist. The Tecton stuck out half of his body, and with his free fist he beat furiously on Marcus's skull, once, twice, three times. They rolled around on the floor of the mine. Marcus lost the dynamite. Those three bound cylindrical units giving off sparks didn't mean anything to the Tecton.

'Help!' shouted Marcus. 'Help me!'

'If we shoot we could hit you!' said Richard from the entrance to the anthill. 'You're too close together. Get him off you!'

* * *

And now, a regrettable digression. We were all three at the prison, in the same cell as always. Marcus Garvey, me and Sergeant Long Back, sitting behind the bars. I remember that I had given up taking notes. I had my elbows firmly glued to the table, my two hands creating blinkers on either side of my eyes, to focus better on the story. I could see the landscape that Marcus described with hallucinogenic clarity. I saw the dying Tectons at the bottom of the mine, twisting like gutted octopi; I saw the torsos of William and Richard at the upper part of the anthill, shouting so that their vocal cords were about to burst. I could hear their voices, which reached Marcus's ear with the distortions a funnel would make. I could smell the corrupt oxygen of the mine, with some sort of metallic, yellowish dust floating in the air and the green sparks of the Tecton lanterns. I could feel the weight of the attacker with his dirty, silvery stone armour. I felt the touch of the Tecton, I hated his fists, fists that were the frontline of attack for an entire race. And, above all, I could feel Marcus's anguish as if it were my own, struggling hopelessly in the depths of a bewitched mine in the Congo. Marcus spoke and I was flooded with all those images. And what happened?

Well, at that moment in the story, at that precise moment, Tommy Thomson, your humble servant, the lily-livered Tommy Thomson, couldn't think of anything better to do than faint. And that's where the session ended.

SEVENTEEN

I HAD BECOME USED to working at night. Each evening I worked later and later. On one occasion, at half twelve in the morning, I went to the kitchen to make myself some tea. In the boarding house hallway it was very quiet. You could only hear, behind the doors, the muffled cough of some boarder. And, of course, Mr MacMahon's bowels.

I didn't find any tea in the kitchen. And I didn't dare take even a pinch from Mrs Pinkerton's tin. That crow in skirts was capable of mobilising all of Scotland Yard to find the thief. Mr MacMahon didn't have any tea either, just a giant carafe where he kept the poteen he got drunk on at the end of each month. After a few moments' hesitation I took the carafe to my room.

I don't know what was in that liquid, but before I realised it I was very drunk. And, the truth is I wasn't sorry. Since I hadn't had the intention of getting drunk it was like enjoying a surprise party.

Instead of continuing to write I decided to read what I had done up to that night. Actually, four-fifths of the novel was already written. 'Relax Tommy, just try to read the book like any other reader would,' I said to myself.

I was a fair reader, I think, even though MacMahon's alcohol ran through my veins. It wasn't all that bad, it wasn't bad at all for a lad who was just barely twenty years old. But what I wanted to know was if I had a superior piece of work before me. And I didn't. Not even close. How disappointing.

The more I read the more defeated I felt. Had I written that? The world came down around me. Where was Amgam's love? Where was the Tecton threat? Those pages were a landscape filled with fog; I, who knew them well, could guess at the outlines. But for an anonymous reader they would have been worthless.

I went to sleep with a knot in my stomach, as if I had swallowed a rock. The room spun. From the alcohol and from the disillusionment. Perhaps MacMahon's illicit whisky was one of those magic potions that made its victim smaller. Yes, I felt very small. The typewriter seemed larger than a piano, I was less than a molecule. What could I do? I drank more.

I had stretched out on the bed and was staring at the ceiling like a dead man. I said to myself: well then, so much anguish and so much discomfort, so much effort invested, and all for a mediocrity like that? One of the things that makes youth so painful is the belief that much struggling is enough to get what you want. It's not true. If it were, the world would belong to the just.

I left behind part of my youth that night. Or, at least, I had the impression that I matured more in that one night than I had in an entire year. I asked myself, 'Is it worth it to go on with this book?' I would rather have slept than answer. Even still, I forced myself to respond to that question, and an hour later I had arrived at a pact between my limitations and my aspirations: I decided that Marcus needed me to finish the book, whether it was good or bad, and that in our case that justified the author's suffering. Cold comfort.

And that's how, defenceless, with my conscience numbed by alcohol and resignation, I found myself in the midst of a catastrophe. It was a dry, hard detonation, followed by a crashing rain, like rubble falling. My God, what a shock! I leapt from the bed. The only familiar thing was Mr MacMahon's voice. I could hear it through the wall that separated our rooms. He was shouting out excuses, 'It wasn't me! I swear!'

I opened the door and I was immediately blinded by a cloud of grey dust. The other boarders had done the same and were gathered in the hallway. They were all in pyjamas or underwear and were more frightened than I was, because I, at least, had drunkenness to dampen my shock. The only one who was still lucid was MacMahon. While the others shrieked and asked stupid questions that no one could possibly answer, he trotted up and down the hallway like a buffalo, knocking on doors and ensuring everyone was out of their rooms. The scene was reminiscent of a shipwreck, all you had to do was substitute smoke for water. But it was all so unreal that I wasn't afraid, I couldn't be. And I don't really know how, separating myself from the hubbub, I ended up in the dining room.

It was right in the exact centre of the room, surrounded by rubble. On the floor you could see the enormous hole it had caused. It was like a small metal whale. Driven by the naïveté of the drunk

I approached it and placed my hand on its iron back. It was cold and touching it made me scared. It occurred to me that I could make use of that contact. Yes, I would make a metaphor between William Craver's skin and Amgam's. It wasn't until later that I thought: what on earth was a bomb doing in the dining room?

I looked up and, through the hole in the ceiling, in the sky, I saw some sort of gigantic flying sausage. It was fleeing from twenty or thirty thin, compact beams of light that crossed the air with frenetic strokes. Its objective, no doubt, had been Royal Steel. Either the zeppelin's gunner had a very bad aim or the spy had informed them that the factory's coordinates were Pinkerton's old boarding house.

'It's alive!' Mr MacMahon said suddenly from the threshold of the room.

I leapt, as if the bomb had bitten me. But Mr MacMahon was referring to some small columns of pressurised smoke coming out of the holes in the casing.

'Let's get out of here!' he bellowed, pulling me by the elbow. 'It's going to blow up any minute!'

In the hallway the whirlwind of dust raised by the bomb's impact wasn't dissipating. MacMahon shouted and everyone rushed down the stairs. I said before that I was drunk, much more drunk than I realised, because all of a sudden everything seemed hilarious to me: a bomb had fallen on our dining room. A bomb! MacMahon examined me with a quick once over. He saw how I was laughing, he smelled my breath, and he realised I was drunk.

'Oh, Lord . . .' he moaned.

While he held me with one arm, he used the other to shove the boarders in front of him. He turned his head and asked me, 'My God, where is Mrs Pinkerton?'

'A bomb!' I laughed hysterically. 'I can't believe it! A bomb fell on our dining room! It came in through the ceiling and flattened the table!'

'Mrs Pinkerton! Where is she?' shouted MacMahon, running through the hallway and dragging me with him.

'You don't know? I do! Where do you think she'd be?' I said.

MacMahon stopped for a second to listen to me. But I said, with a big guffaw, 'Negotiating the rent with the bomb!'

Pinkerton hadn't moved from her room. She was sitting on the bed, petrified. The chaos was too much for her organised little brain to take in. And a woman like her would never have come out of her room in a nightgown, in any case. Not under any circumstances. But Mr MacMahon wasn't going to waste time. He carried us, one on each shoulder, as if he were carrying two sacks at once, putting up no complaints, and he galloped through the hallway like a racehorse. Suddenly I saw myself hanging off MacMahon's back. If I looked down, I saw his heels, if I turned around, I saw Mrs Pinkerton's head, parallel to mine. She looked like a recently caught eel. I was about to burst with laughter.

'Hello, Mrs Pinkerton! Hello! Hello!' I said to her while I waved as if we were two acquaintances that happened to meet on a train. But when MacMahon started to go down the stairs things got more complicated. I had the impression that I had climbed up on a camel's hump. When we were on the street a safe distance away, MacMahon placed us on the ground. I couldn't get up. I was too dizzy. Some very civic-minded neighbours helped me to sit up. But nothing was wrong with me, I just wanted to throw up.

All of a sudden the bomb exploded with a black and bluish flare. From our position we could see perfectly the floor of the boarding house flying through the air. And that wasn't all. The force of the detonation and the weight of the rubble made the fourth storey collapse onto the third. The third onto the second and the second onto the first. The full effect was that the entire building folded like some sort of giant accordion.

Mrs Pinkerton cried inconsolably on Mr MacMahon's chest. He hugged her in solidarity while shaking his head sadly. I hadn't quite taken in the extent of the tragedy. I just laughed and laughed. I heard Mrs Pinkerton, as if she were very far away, lamenting the loss of everything she had in this life. I kept laughing. Lose it all? What could I lose, poor me, except an old gramophone and a typewriter? I abruptly stopped laughing. The book.

Everything I had written, including the four onion paper copies, was inside the house. Thinking of it sobered me up instantly, like a tap cutting off a stream of water. I leapt like a panther and grabbed Mr MacMahon by the shirt collar.

'Mr MacMahon! We've lost everything!'

'Everything, son, everything . . . But we're alive,' said MacMahon.

His arms held up both me and Mrs Pinkerton at the same time with tremendous ease. I freed myself.

'Mr MacMahon! The book is in the house!'

'Book? What book?'

'The book!' I was becoming distraught.

MacMahon was still consoling Mrs Pinkerton. With his free arm he gave me a manly pat on the back and said, 'Don't worry, son. It was just a book. You'll write another one.'

He didn't understand. I had to finish the book, good or bad. At that point it had become some sort of bank of the spirit where I deposited all my efforts as a human being. And now that bank had burned down and I could do nothing about it.

The neighbours looked on more out of curiosity than solidarity. It was one of the first air attacks and no one had been prepared. For them the bomb was more of a spectacle than a drama.

The firemen worked all night long. First thing in the morning, we were still there, sitting stoically on the pavement opposite. Some of the neighbours had brought us blankets, tea and biscuits. A kindly soul put a mug of warm milk in my hands. Wrapped in a blanket, sitting with my back against a wall, I simply couldn't believe I had lost the book, I just couldn't. But all of a sudden, hope. A fireman came towards us. Beneath one arm he an unidentifiable little bundle.

'We found this inside the house. Does it belong to anyone?'

The light of dawn was sluggish and we couldn't see very well. From the dimensions, the size, it looked like a packet of pages with singed edges. My heart leapt. Paper is much more fire-resistant than people think, at least when it's grouped together in a compact package. I launched myself up to grab the bundle with both hands. It wasn't paper, it was wood. Through a hole in the package appeared a head.

'Marie Antoinette!' exclaimed Mrs Pinkerton, bursting into tears again, this time from happiness.

There are cursed books just as there are cursed houses. Everything had conspired against me, so that I would never finish the book, from Marie Antoinette to the Kaiser of Germany. I threatened the heavens with a fist, bellowing, 'May God curse the German Empire! And its Kaiser! And its zeppelins!'

At that moment a postman appeared on a bicycle. He asked the neighbours some questions, until finally someone pointed at me. He approached me and said, 'Mr Thomas Thomson? Is that you? We've had quite a time finding you.'

I didn't pay any attention to him. I continued insulting all the powers that be. But the postman insisted that I sign a receipt.

'Now you can do something more than insult the Germans,' he said, amiably. 'Now you can kill as many as you like.'

'What are you talking about?' I growled. 'And what's this you want me to sign?'

'Your conscription papers.'

The next morning I had to go to the recruiting office. According to an old law, updated for the war, the beneficiaries of state poorhouses were obliged to serve in the armed forces in the case of war in return for services received from the state. They had been looking for me since the hostilities began. And I was lucky they hadn't declared me a deserter yet, with all the criminal consequences that that would imply. As wild as it seems, seventy-two hours after receiving the notice I was in uniform. I didn't even have time to see Norton. I wrote him a note, with great difficulty, explaining my transformation from civilian to soldier. As far as the book's destruction went, I didn't mention it. I wasn't even able to say goodbye to Garvey.

EIGHTEEN

MARCUS WAS STARTING TO lose consciousness from the Tecton's attack. Or to be more accurate, he was hallucinating from the toxic air he was inhaling and from the blows of the Tecton, who was intent on cracking his victim's skull. Guilt and memories mixed together, and the Tecton that was beating him, seated on top of him, holding down his chest with his legs, was no longer a Tecton. It was Pepe the bear, who had come from beyond the grave, furious because he had been turned over to the authorities of that Welsh town. Pepe the bear said, 'Do you know what they did to me, Marcus? Do know how the tools of an abattoir feel on a bear's body?' Pepe the bear turned into Godefroide Pepe, and said, 'Do you know what they did to me, Marcus? Do you want to know how the Tecton torturers treat their captives?'

'No!' shouted Marcus suddenly. 'I didn't turn you over to anyone,

Pepe! They took you away because Mum was dead! I was just a boy, I couldn't stop them from taking you away!'

The Tecton stopped hitting him. His curiosity was aroused by the tone of voice he had just heard, so despairing, so out of place. He contemplated his victim with the air of a hunter that couldn't quite identify what he had just caught. That gave Marcus a few precious seconds. Behind the Tecton, and up above, he saw the anxious faces of William and Richard. And while he spat blood, he cried out, 'Shoot! For the love of God, shoot!'

Richard decided to take the risk. And, by some miracle, the bullet lodged in the Tecton's back. He made a face that was more surprised than pained and he fell on top of Marcus like a felled tree.

He still wasn't free. With the Tecton's body and his stone armour on top of him, Marcus could barely breathe, much less get it off him. And far from his reach the last inches of the fuse were burning down. Marcus tried to push on the dead Tecton's chest. His hands felt richly embossed geometric forms. But the Tecton's body didn't budge an inch. A moan.

'You can do it, Marcus! Get him off you!'

It was William's voice.

'Stick your elbows in the dirt and push! Push!'

And, somehow, Marcus managed to get out of that spot. Not so much by the force of his pushing, but rather by sliding underneath the body. He looked for the fuse, a flaming spark. But he was half blind. Blood from his brow flowed into his eyes, covering them like a red liquid mask. The mine was one big crimson stain. From above William shouted, urging him to put out the fuse.

Guided only by the faint sound of the burning fuse, he looked for the dynamite. He dragged himself, feeling along the ground, until he felt sparks hitting his hand. He had never been so happy to burn himself.

What came next was more mechanical. Marcus wiped the blood from his eyes. Immediately after, more calmly, he pulled out the burning fuse and replaced it with another, longer one. He listened carefully: indeed, from the back of the tunnel he could hear the last voices. Some of the invaders were using it as a hideout, just as the Craver brothers had foreseen. Marcus lit the new fuse and threw the charge into the hole with all the strength he had left. The tunnel was L-shaped and the dynamite disappeared round the bend.

Marcus fled. As he climbed up the ladder Marcus could see in William's face the temptation to push it, to leave him in there forever. But there was also another hand that held the ladder with an unsuspected moral strength: Richard Craver's.

The dynamite took a surprisingly long time to explode. When it did, though, they had the sensation that it blew up very deep down. They heard a sharp rumble at first, then an opaque echo. For a few endless seconds the Englishmen's feet vibrated as if they had beehives in their shoes. Then they noticed the first sign that it was all over: from the jungle, surrounding them on all sides, the shrieks of the animal world awakening.

'Bravo!' said Richard enthusiastically, giving Marcus appreciative pats on the back. 'Bravo, lad! You were magnificent!'

Marcus's only response was to laugh like a maniac. The Cravers didn't understand until Marcus pointed to their faces: the smoke from the explosion had blackened all three of their faces. They looked like chimney sweeps. Or Zulus. Especially William, always so white and now so black.

When he stopped laughing Marcus felt exhausted. It had been twenty-four hours since he had slept. He lay down for a moment with his knees bent. William had already forgotten about him.

'Yes, it's a shame that the explosions destroyed the beams,' he said as he looked into the mine. 'The ceiling could fall in on us. We'll have to rebuild it all.'

But Richard replied with an icy voice, 'My God . . . Are you still thinking about gold? How is that possible, William?'

It drew Marcus's attention that Richard, someone like Richard, was able to express such a deep, lucid thought. But he was too worn out to be supportive. He needed to rest. He left a dreadful argument behind him. William and Richard were screaming at each other. This time Richard did not back down, as if everything he had been through had finally given him the strength to oppose his brother. Marcus could have taken advantage and, amid the confusion, moved closer to Amgam's tent. No, he didn't have the strength even for her. It had been hard enough for him to get to the campfire and drop down beside it.

He closed his eyes. One cheek rested on the red sand, that red African sand, as fine as if it had been through a sieve with a thousand holes. The contact was very pleasant. He could hear, at the fence, William and Richard's crossfire of expletives. Marcus discovered that being on the sidelines of a dispute could be a source of pleasure. And so, while he enjoyed that semi-unconsciousness that was so delightful, his thoughts turned, yet again, to her, to Amgam.

What had she wanted to tell him the day before, when she wrote those signs on the sand? Marcus didn't know how to read, much less in Tecton. Amgam was an intelligent woman, she knew her lover's limitations. Why had she been so stupid as to think he would understand?

A few minutes passed. No, he was the stupid one. Amgam would never have made such a mistake. Amgam hadn't written anything. She had drawn. He tried to remember. It was the shape of a spider web, with a centre and some points a distance away from the centre. What could she be trying to tell him?

Oh, my God, thought Marcus, what if Amgam was trying to depict the Tectons' excavations? And what if those drums that thundered, those attacks in pairs, were nothing more than a distraction tactic so they could drill somewhere else? And what if they wanted to hide the sound made by their digging other tunnels that would allow them to attack from behind?

He opened his eyes. The campfire filled his entire visual field. Suddenly the fire disappeared, sinking down as if it had been drawn in by a whirlwind of dirt. A growing hole appeared before him. Marcus had the impression that this part of the clearing was the surface of an hourglass, and the time had come for him to be sucked down into the lower half.

Everything happened very quickly. The Tectons appeared like white shadows, cleverly coordinated and with lightning speed. They looked like lizards the size of humans. One ran to the right, another to the left, alternately, keeping apart so they were harder to aim at. Marcus barely had time to shout at the top of his lungs, 'Tecton!' as he fled towards the fence.

'Let's go in!' improvised William. 'Barricade ourselves inside!'

It was a desperate defence. Marcus stopped abruptly. No, he couldn't face going back in there. Instead of obeying, he fled. He left them behind and ran towards the jungle.

He ran and ran. Fear had taken hold in his knees. But he ran and ran. As he arrived at the threshold of the jungle he tripped and fell. He looked back. What he saw terrified him.

William and Richard had hidden inside the fence, sticking the barrels of their rifles through the loopholes and shooting wildly, without even bothering to take aim. Marcus saw some Tectons scaling the trunks that made up the fence. One of the Tectons, very adept, slithered along the ground, beyond Richard's angle of sight. When he was underneath the shotgun, he grabbed the barrel with both hands. But after a few tugs Richard was able to recover the weapon. William and Richard fought back to back from the middle of the fence's enclosure, from the anthill itself, shooting any Tecton that dared to climb the defences. Richard was shouting wildly.

But Marcus didn't care about anything or anyone. He was no longer a man; he was a hare. Tectons! Run, run for your life, Marcus Garvey, run!

Thousands of branches whipped at his face and thighs. He only stopped when he was panting and completely out of breath. He hid himself at the foot of a tree, where he huddled in the angle created by the tree's trunk and a spur of wood, with his arms crossed over his knees. From far away, from the clearing, he could hear the sounds of battle. He could hear shots and shouts. William and Richard urged each other on. The Tectons' voices were spine chilling. He had never heard anything like it.

He didn't know what to do. His whole body was shaking, like a lunatic after a cold shower. He hid his head in his arms and closed his eyes. Sometimes, the shooting and the screams were more intense. Other times, the racket stopped as if it had ended, but soon after resurged with renewed energy. The Cravers must have been using the sticks of dynamite as hand grenades, because he could also hear explosions. At some point Marcus opened his eyes. And before him stood a man.

He was an incredibly small man, with skin that was black but with red tones. All he wore was a piece of tree bark covering his genitals. He carried a spear. But he didn't seem aggressive in the least. He wasn't a good man, he wasn't a bad man. He was some other sort of man. And he was a disconcerted man. He looked at Marcus and then towards the noises in the clearing. When he looked back at Marcus it was as if he were demanding explanations of him.

Marcus grasped that for him the Tectons and the Englishmen were one and the same thing. For him there was no difference between Marcus and the Cravers, between the Cravers and the Tectons. For that small man there was only an incomprehensible battle and unpleasant noises. He once again stared at Marcus with eyes that overflowed with contempt, and he asked him for the last time: what is all that?

Marcus didn't say anything. He didn't do anything. He only trembled, shrivelled at the base of the tree. The little man turned and left. He moved like a cat, noiselessly and without looking back.

The battle continued. Marcus thought it would never end. But all of a sudden the shots, screams and explosions could no longer be heard. First there was an almost complete silence, and then, once again, the syncopated rhythm of the jungle.

And what did Marcus do when he had caught his breath? He went back to the clearing. When I asked him what his motives were for such an incomprehensible act he didn't know what to say.

What nonsense. I would have understood if Marcus had stayed at the clearing to fight, and I also understood why he had fled. What I couldn't comprehend was his return to the horror. He knew the Craver brothers' position was untenable. He had seen the Tectons break through the enclosure of trunks, going beyond the last defences. And even so he went back.

I was insistent, I wanted to understand his reasoning. But there were many episodes that Marcus was unable to explain. He fell silent, overcome by the magnitude of the events he was relating. I never reproached him for his silences or his wavering: in fact, the opposite, I tried to get him unstuck. Often I had to reconstruct the narrative thread of the story by groping around. I could understand the pain, for him, in recalling these events. And, on top of that, he had to do so from a desperate personal situation, locked up in a prison and awaiting the gallows. Anyone may survive an avalanche, a war, a disillusionment. But not everyone is capable of explaining the experience. Even less so, a simple stableboy like Marcus Garvey. What's more, I was demanding that he make sense of a world that held no apparent logic.

So then, why did Marcus Garvey go back to the clearing? After my questioning I could only arrive at one conclusion.

Did Marcus know what awaited him? My conclusion was yes, he knew. That is as certain as the fact that he was inseparably tied to Amgam. In order to understand Marcus's reaction there was only one logical answer: that there are things, like love, that aren't. Love can't be measured with the rationality of a compass.

Marcus pulled back the last screen of vegetation that separated him from the clearing. The day was dying. The sun had become an orange ball that danced above the branches of the trees. William and Richard were sitting on the ground, surprisingly alive, back-to-back with their heads bowed, watched over by a single Tecton. Their faces were still blackened from the smoke and gunpowder of the battle. There was something unnatural in the image of the Craver brothers suffering a defeat. They were furious souls, they were destructive scourges. They had been raised to win, they were born to burn the world. And now they sat defenceless, beaten by the powers of an unforeseen element. Like torches in the rain.

He saw a few Tectons, five or six, resting by the tents. There was another Tecton, standing up, closer and with his back to Marcus. All of the Tectons had very oval skulls, but this one's was conical, like a bullet. He was incredibly tall, well over six feet. The light of dusk gave him a drawn-out shadow like a giraffe's. He held his helmet in the crook of his arm, his hand on his hip, and looked directly at the sun, his chin high. That way of holding the helmet gave him an aristocratic elegance. It was the seal of the perfect officer: lithe, straight-backed. He had just survived a terrible battle but his armour was already clean again. He even had time to take an interest in the sun. More than observing it, it was as if he wanted to suck it in.

For some reason the Tecton turned. He saw Marcus. He had a big horse's head, powerful and with long cheeks. Now, with his back to the sun, the pupils of the Tecton's enormous feline eyes contracted with frightening speed. But he didn't attack. Quite the opposite. He approached Marcus slowly and with his free hand grabbed him by the elbow. He took him to where William and Richard sat. He did it without any hostility, like someone helping a blind person across the street. Marcus didn't resist. Even he was surprised by his own docility. All he did was move his head to the left and right, looking for Amgam. He couldn't see her. The Tecton made him sit with the Craver brothers. He moved back a few steps and immersed himself again in his attentive contemplation of the sun.

'Where is she?' asked Marcus.

'And where were you?' replied William.

'If we are prisoners of war then you should respect our condition as such,' said Richard. 'There are international laws.'

Marcus heard the comment and for a long while couldn't think of anything else. How could someone like Richard Craver ask that they apply laws of war to him? Richard didn't understand anything. Maybe he didn't want to understand it.

Throughout the whole day the Tectons rested or looked over their spoils. Very few Tectons had survived the bullets and the dynamite. Marcus counted them: five, six, seven. Only seven.

When it got dark, though, all the Tectons came closer. The refined officer said something to his men, and they began to beat them with their feet and fists. At first, it was obviously revenge for their dead. The only thing that the Englishmen could do was protect their heads and genitals and wait for the beating to end. But it didn't end. William, Richard and Marcus found themselves in the middle of a circle, surrounded by Tectons that pounded on them furiously. The violence gradually took on a more calculated intensity. Marcus realised that the officer repeated some sounds. It was no longer punishment. The Tectons wanted to turn the blows into a message. The officer pointed to their bodies with a long thin finger. What was he trying to tell them?

Pain is an impatient teacher. Marcus took off his shirt. As a reward, the Tecton stopped the beating.

'Take off your clothes!' Marcus told them.

While they were removing an article of clothing they weren't beaten. But if they stopped, the blows continued. They didn't let them keep on even their underwear. Marcus had only ever seen Richard's arms and neck, which were browned by the sun. Now he discovered that the rest of his skin was as pink as a piglet's. The Tectons laughed.

A group of Tectons laughing was a frightening sight. All those faces encircling them, white as the moon, mortuary pale, their laughter sounding like crows. Their lips were much thinner than the Englishmen's, and their teeth had a yellow patina. They pointed between the three Englishmen's legs and laughed. The prisoners covered their genitals with their hands, but their captors moved them aside so the objects of their admiration could be easily seen.

'Why do we have to put up with this?' exclaimed Richard. 'We're British.'

'Don't do anything stupid,' warned William. 'Take off your clothes.'

By now Richard was completely nude except for some woollen socks held to his calves by silver garters. Those garters would cost him his life.

The garters became one of the Tectons' object of desire. He knelt down to snatch them from him. Infuriated, Richard responded with a kick to the thief's nose. The other Tectons fell on him. Richard struggled. His arms emerged every once in a while from within a *mêlée* of white appendages. A crunch was heard, a sound like nuts cracking. It was Richard's knee. That put an end to his resistance and the Tectons forgot about him. But neither William nor Marcus could come to his aid: the Tectons approached them and left some large objects shaped like half eggs at their feet. They were reminiscent of giant tortoiseshells, with cloth lining. Black straps hung from the sides. Marcus and William looked at the shells without knowing what to do. More blows. They tied the shells to their backs as if they were haversacks. The blows stopped.

The Tectons turned back to Richard. A couple of them looked at his wounded knee the same way a blacksmith might examine a horse's hoof.

'Stand up, Richard! Stand up!' shouted Marcus without taking his hands from the back of his neck.

'I can't,' he moaned. 'My knee is broken.'

'You can walk! You have to walk!' insisted Marcus.

William caught on, 'Come on, Richard! Strap a shell on your back and walk!'

A Tecton took out a knife with a wide, short blade. Richard saw it.

'I'm fine!' he shouted. 'You hear me? I've never felt better!'

What is the Congo? The Congo isn't a place. The Congo is the other side of the universe. And among all the possible Congos there is, without a doubt, a Congo in the service of atonement. Did Richard Craver understand that before dying? The Tecton stabbed him once in the back of the neck.

They must have hit a nerve, because Richard's legs and arms went rigid, as if they had been subjected to an intense electric current. But he didn't die. Not yet. The Tecton finished him off with clumsy stabs. A second Tecton reproached the executioner's ineptitude. Richard's contractions intensified, his eyes rolled back into his head. Two stabs more, three.

Then, Marcus and William were jostled to their feet. There was no doubt where the Tectons were taking them: the mine. Marcus and William went down the ladder, the Tectons slid down ropes that hung from the anthill. When they were all inside the mine, two Tectons entered one of the tunnels headfirst. Another Tecton stuck Marcus's shell into the same tunnel. With violent mimicry they indicated what they expected of him: that he advance into the hole with the shell in front of him, pushing it along. He resisted. He would never go in there, never. He felt hands all over his body, some held his arms, other grabbed him by the scruff of the neck, trying to get him to lower his head. Marcus struggled like a madman in a straitjacket. A club hit his lips. He spat pieces of teeth and blood into the faces of his attackers. He wouldn't go in there! As he was struggling, she appeared. Amgam.

The Tectons received her with a wordless clamour. She was wearing William's white trousers and white shirt. She approached Marcus. The Tectons stopped hitting him, observing the scene with feigned indifference. She was one of them yet radically different. The tall Tecton officer paid attention to her. He stopped her with his hand, delicately, and asked her questions as if he had known her for many years. His tone of voice was gentle, her answers weren't. Marcus had never thought that a Tecton man could speak with such delicacy. Two of his fingers kept Amgam from getting closer to him. Marcus held his tongue: not even his desperate situation got in the way of his realising that the officer and Amgam made a perfect couple. William hung his head. Before him was the woman that he had kept prisoner night after night. One word from her and the Tectons would rip out his arms and legs one by one, slowly. But she ignored him. All of her attention was for Marcus.

Amgam caressed one of Marcus's cheeks. He felt the comforting warmth of that hot hand. Because of Marcus Garvey's express wishes, I won't reproduce here the meaning of what she conveyed to him, and which he understood very well. (As ridiculous as it may appear, sixty years later and after everything that has happened, I still respect his wishes.) She kissed him on the lips. Him. And Amgam's public kiss was much more than a kiss.

The Tectons separated them. Marcus emboldened his resistance. He would never go into the tunnel! Never! The Tectons carried flexible black clubs and they beat him on the kidneys with powerful agonising blows. Marcus yelled. His shrill squeaks were like a badly oiled hinge.

Seconds later he complied.

NINETEEN

ONCE I WAS INTRODUCED to the ranks I had only one objective: to keep myself as far from the enemy as possible. My logic was very simple: if the Germans could drop a six-hundred pound bomb on the dining room of my house, in London, what would they be capable of if I got anywhere near them? Unfortunately, my intentions and my fate were not headed in the same direction.

And now someone might ask: must you interrupt the story right now, when Marcus is going through one of his most trying times, to explain your trivial little battles? Well, the answer is yes, that is what I intend to do. This isn't the story of Marcus Garvey. It's not even the story of the love between Amgam and Marcus. This is the story of the story. Which is to say, of Tommy Thomson's love for Amgam. And if I talk about my state in the trenches it's because it too relates to the book.

* * *

They sent me to an infantry regiment. When we were in France, waiting to be sent to the front, an officer showed up at our camp. He had us queue up in front of the khaki sea of tents and asked for volunteers for the artillery. I stepped forward. The idea I had was that artillery fought from a distance. With a bit of luck I wouldn't see a German in the entire war. Blessed innocence.

They turned me into an artillery observer. My job was to penetrate no-man's land, drag myself to some spot from which I could observe enemy lines and direct our cannons. In other words: three days after raising my hand I was crawling through the mud, in the rain and right under the Germans' noses.

I don't think that in the entire history of the British army there was ever a Tommy as useless as First Soldier Thomas Thomson. I had to drag myself and a portable telephone and unrolling telephone cable. It goes without saying that the German snipers' immediate priority was to shoot down the artillery observers. To top it all off, some administrative genius had given me a helmet three sizes bigger than my head. It danced like a spinning top, falling over one ear and then the other. Or, worse still, covered my eyes like a giant visor. At least it worked as an umbrella. For the seven days that I was on the front it practically never stopped raining. And what rain! How was I supposed to inform them on the movements in the German trenches when I could barely see the tips of my fingers when I extended my arm?

During the long empty hours in no-man's land I had time to think about my future. I decided that I would become a new Doctor Flag. Why not? I had been his ghost writer, so there was nothing standing in the way of my replacing him. I would explain my project to some bold editor. Any publisher in the world would sign me on. We could start a new collection to compete with old Flag. I would write all the books. Without ghost writers.

I recall that the morning of my sixth day on the front dawned cloudless. It wasn't raining and I found myself on top of a small hill. The relative height and the dry air allowed me to appreciate the region's landscape for the first time. I was able to see that the ocean of mud only extended between the British and the German positions. At the rearguard of the German line I could see a magnificent French plain, green, wet, dotted with church bell towers. They were all over, scattered throughout the entire area, here and there, silhouetted against the blue horizon. Those bell towers were uniquely beautiful, attracting one's gaze like magnets.

The last thing I was expecting was that someone would wish any harm on those jewels of medieval architecture. All of a sudden, though, one of the bell towers collapsed. At first I thought it was a misguided rocket from our artillery. But other bell towers started to fall in unison. What a scene! I scanned the horizon with my binoculars and, just as soon as I located a tower, it disappeared in a cloud of smoke and ash. They sank as if the earth had sucked them up, which made me realise that these were controlled explosions. The Germans were destroying any point that the enemy artillery observers could use as a reference. I felt vaguely guilty.

Don't ask me how, but somehow I established a relationship between my future as the new Doctor Flag and my role in this destruction. In theory I bore no responsibility for the Germans blowing up those stone works of art. But it was also undeniable that they were destroying those bell towers because someone, namely me, was looking at them.

I had let myself be led that war like a lamb to the slaughter.

And once I was wrapped in a sheep's uniform it was useless to try to get out of my responsibilities as a sheep. Sheep aren't innocent, they're idiotic. What had I said one day to Marcus Garvey? 'I never would have gone to the Congo.' A lie. It was impossible to imagine a larger massacre than that war, and in the heart of Europe itself. The Congo wasn't a place, the Congo was us. The day I consented to enlist I became the Marcus Garvey that held out his hand so that the Craver brothers could put lit sticks of dynamite in it. He threw the sticks one by one, I directed cannon fire to targets. Which was worse?

I should have understood it before. If I accepted my future as Doctor Flag, if I renounced literature in order to devote myself, simply, to writing pamphlets, what I was doing was enlisting in the ranks of human resignation. Every good book that I didn't write would be a bell tower destroyed. I said to myself, 'To hell with Flag! I'm not Flag's ghost writer, I don't want to be Flag. What I have to do is go home and write the book, and rewrite it a thousand times, and a thousand more, if necessary, until a great book comes out of it.'

And so I arrived at the sixth and last day of my stay on the front. I will never forget it. I found myself inside a hole that had been created by a large-calibre shell. It was shaped like a funnel and was larger than a circle of nursery schoolchildren. It began to rain again. I squeezed into the bottom of the crater as much as I could. At dusk there was a violent artillery battle. Since I was halfway between the British and the German positions, the projectiles from one side and the other made parabolas just above my head. There was an undeniable beauty in that pyrotechnic display. What a long night. I was beneath a cover of fire yet it was raining,

raining more than ever. From the brim of my helmet fell cascades of water. I have never again been as soaked as I was that day. The only thing I could do was curl up like a child, hugging my legs.

I couldn't move, I could only wait, so I entertained myself thinking about her, Amgam. At first I tried to mentally reconstruct her to the last detail of her hand. The matte whiteness of her skin, her six fingers, the extraordinary way her nails fitted into her flesh, up to the first joint on each finger. Then I thought about Amgam's vagina. Marcus hadn't mentioned it at all. What must it have been like? As white as the rest of her skin? Why couldn't it be black, as black as the pupils of her eyes? Red? Blue? Yellow? In the book, naturally, I didn't bring it up. Too obscene. However, as projectiles from the British German artilleries crossed over my head, I thought about the vagina of a Tecton woman.

The storm of bombs and the rainstorm stopped first thing in the morning. At the same moment, as if the artillery and the meteorology had signed an accord. My arms and legs were numb. There was a general silence, which was even more disquieting because it followed that monstrous racket. I started to worry. I had better get back to the trenches, and as quickly as possible. With all the caution in the world, I stuck out my nose. What I saw was an image of purgatory: an orange and violet-coloured fog coming towards me.

Never had three letters hidden such horror: gas! Future generations have had trouble understanding the fear that gas provoked as a military weapon. Gas! I put on my mask, but the bands didn't fit well round the back of my neck. I left the hole, pulling myself along on my knees and elbows. But I didn't get very far. About three hundred feet away, advancing behind the gas cloud, I saw thousands of figures coming towards me. Germans. They were advancing towards the English trenches. And me.

Even now, after so much time has passed, some nights I still dream of that French morning. The German officers used whistles to spur on their infantry. I remember that pointy, sharp language, packed with crackles and curses. They wore green uniforms, dirty with mud, and carried very long bayonets. Their helmets were much more compact than ours, which seemed more like toy chamber pots. Their masks had enormous round glass eyes. The helmets and the masks covered their heads and turned them into creatures closer to insects than to humans. They could have been Martians as easily as Germans.

The glass of my mask misted up. I was terrified. If I stayed there the Germans would kill me. If I went back it was most likely that, in the confusion, our men (in that sector a brigade of Irishmen) would shoot me. To top it all off, a few days earlier the Irish rebellion had broken out, and everyone doubted the brigade's loyalty. (Later I found out that they had maintained their positions with courage worthy of a higher cause.) Desperate, I opted to go back to the crater. I would hide there, I'd play dead. But I didn't foresee that gas has a tendency to collect in concave places in the terrain. Horrified, I saw that a large bubble of gas, half violet and half orange, had installed itself at the bottom of the hole. I was submerged in it. My ill-fitting mask danced over my face like the helmet did over my head. I looked up for a second, and I saw the surface of the world with the perspective of a fish. A wave of Germans was passing my position. I saw their boots and their legs. Some of them even stopped, using the upper part of the crater to hide themselves from the British fire, but the officers urged them to push on. More Germans came, then more and more. I didn't know there were so many Germans in the world. What could I do? If I stayed curled up down there, the gas would finish me off in only a few minutes. But if I moved the Germans would discover me. I didn't do anything, I buried my head underground like an ostrich. I felt my eyes swell to the size of potatoes. Red tears slid down the glass of the mask, and I realised I was crying blood. I dug with my hands. I burrowed a bit more into that soft humid earth. It was as if I were swimming, submerging myself. At first I told myself that I was digging to better camouflage myself from the Germans, but I think I was reacting that way simply because it was the only thing I could do.

And that was when the toxic mirages began. An instructor had warned us that gas absorption blocked the brain's access to oxygen and that brought on delirium. I knew that what I saw were hallucinations, but that didn't make them any less real.

The ground turned to liquid. At first it was an ocean of those horrible orange and violet colours, but the fusion of the two colours turned into a very dark, very sweet green. My gas mask allowed me to see in that underwater world, but I had no air. At least I would die enjoying all that beauty, I thought. And when I was suffocating, when my lungs were about to explode, a figure appeared before me. At first it was a white spark, very far below my body, which ascended from the blackness of unimaginable depths. It was her.

Our bodies came closer through that light, greenish, liquid world, exasperatingly slowly. Yes, it was her. But the gas I had inhaled made her shape more vivid than I had ever imagined it in any of my narrative efforts. I saw, for example, that she had a pear-shaped head, with an incredibly wide forehead. That forehead would normally have gone against my aesthetic criteria, as too exaggerated, but it didn't concern me. She smiled, and small waves of skin appeared on her cheeks.

I stretched out my hand as far as I could, towards her. She also moved a hand towards me, above me. That simple gesture made me immensely happy. Our fingers were very close to each other. We didn't quite touch. The only thing I can say is that if we had touched I wouldn't be writing all this now.

Imagine, now, some sort of reverse avalanche, a natural force that instead of pulling us, sucked us in. I felt as if iron pliers had grabbed my ankles and were pulling me, separating me from Amgam. I have to conclude that those pliers saved my life.

I had never been so close to the intangible. How can I justify, with any self-esteem, that one of the culminating moments of my existence was the product of a hallucination caused by military gas? Well, that's how it is.

The next memory I have is an infinitely more banal, and peculiar, feeling: waking up without being able to open my eyes. My face was covered with a big bandage. I inhaled deeply and my lungs filled with a mix of ether and mint. A hospital, I sensed. And if I was smelling such delicate odours, it must be a hospital quite far from the front. I must have been unconscious for days. I brought my hands to my face, reflexively. I was stopped by a woman's voice, who warned me with an urgent scream, 'Don't do that! Don't take the bandages off your eyes or you'll stay blind forever!'

I obeyed. Two more voices joined the conversation, the voices of two doctors very curious about my case.

'You should be dead,' explained one of them. 'That's why we're so interested.'

I was glad that my life had interested them enough to save it. From my wounds they only knew that they had been caused in a sector of the front that was affected by gas. Someone like me, located so far ahead, should have been more dead than a codfish in the desert. After an extensive interrogation they deduced that I had been saved thanks to my asthma. The asthma made me consume less air than is normal, and that's how I avoided certain death.

'Asthma!' concluded the second doctor. 'How can they send asthmatics to the front?'

'That's what I told them at the recruitment office but they didn't listen to me.'

'The war's over for you,' they announced.

And they left.

As for the circumstances surrounding my salvation, no one could give me any details. The medical staff only knew that I had arrived in their territory. While I was unconscious they had transferred me from some first aid post to a field hospital, and from there to that ward. It was impossible for me to follow the traces of my saviour.

Who had pulled me by the ankles? Who knows. I've always liked to believe that it was a German. That someone had saved my life so generously, going against the interests of their Fatherland, would be irrefutable proof of one thing, of only one thing, but an important one: that on that battlefield where millions of combatants faced each other there was, at least, one gentleman.

TWENTY

SOME MONTHS AFTER THAT postman on a bicycle had handed me the recruitment papers, I went back to the same place where I had received it: sitting in front of the ruins of the boarding house. As a whole, it looked just as I had left it, a collapsed stone accordion. The authorities had put a cordon around the entire perimeter to discourage looters. That was all.

Why go back to the ruins of the boarding house? Out of useless nostalgia, I believe, or to begin to orientate myself in my new life. I sat on top of a suitcase. I was there for a little while, looking at the house and playing with my fingers and my memories, until I noticed that someone had stuck a note on a pillar of debris. This is what it said:

Hello Tommy. If you are reading this its because your alive and we are all very very hapy that your alive and not dead.

Mareeantwonet is hapy to, I swear. Well, maybe your mutilated or missing an erm, or both. Or a leg, or both of them. Or both legs and both erms, because in war peple shoot and theres lots of splosions. We and Mareeantwonet dont care a lick about what your missing, just so you know. Maybe they sploded both your eyes and your blind. If you are, have someone reed you this note, because its from me.

We now live sumware else. You tell me in my letters your regiment but you don't answer and your regiment tell me that you are not in your regiment because youv volunteered for artilarry and that they cant tell me where artilarry is for security reasons. (our artilarry or the germans, that I don't understand)

If you read this note don't move. You sit and wait. You sit and wait. Sit, damn it.

Your good friend and fellow boarder:

MacMahon

I didn't have time to do anything else. Behind me I heard an all-too-familiar voice.

'Tommy!'

I'll spare you the description of our mutual joy. MacMahon was very sentimental and he started crying, and when he told me that since he had hung up the note he came punctually every day to see if I were there, I got weepy too and since we were both crying we hugged, and being together crying made us cry even more. I'll leave it at that.

He went to the trouble of carrying my suitcase, whether I liked it or not. While we made the trip to the new boarding house he told me everything that had happened in my absence.

For once Pinkerton's foresight had been of some use. The house insurance that she had acquired decades ago had covered all the losses. And much more: since it was one of the first English houses affected by a bombing, the company used the incident to create a publicity campaign showing off their patriotism. The president of the insurance company took a handful of photos with Mrs Pinkerton while he handed over a cheque. And it was a handsome amount. With the money, and taking advantage of the fact that the war had lowered property values, she was able to buy herself another boarding house.

'That's the good news,' said MacMahon.

'You mean to say there's bad news too?'

MacMahon went from euphoric to despondent in half a blink of the eye. With two fingers he pressed on the upper part of his nose in an attempt to hold back the tears. MacMahon had very fat fingers and thick wrists. Such virile hands weren't made for crying. And that made MacMahon's crying an even sadder phenomenon.

I guessed the reason.

'Mary? Your wife? She was that ill? It can't be!' I cried out.

MacMahon nodded, without looking at me, and said, 'The flu.'

I swallowed saliva. I didn't know what to say.

'It was sudden,' explained MacMahon. 'It all happened very quickly after the army took you away. Luckily Rose let me bring the children to the boarding house.'

'Who is Rose?'

We had arrived at the new boarding house. It was in the same district and, like the last building, was a giant among dwarves. While the old one had shone with the beauty of a crypt, the new one oozed a comforting peace, as if it were an immense farm transported to the city.

Once inside, the first person I came across was a woman about MacMahon's age. She wore a blue dress with a colourful floral print. A woman that dresses so elegantly, with such modesty and such good taste, always awakens some fondness. Even still, I only gave her a quick glance, because I was looking for Mrs Pinkerton. As much as I didn't want to, I had to thank her for opening up the doors of her boarding house to me. But MacMahon, who came in right behind me, warned me, 'Rose.'

And the woman said, 'Welcome home, Tommy.'

The collision between my memories and that voice made me very confused.

'Mrs Pinkerton!' I exclaimed.

'Mrs MacMahon,' she corrected me.

I didn't even remember that Mrs Pinkerton was named Rose. I looked at Mr MacMahon, who was proudly nodding to corroborate the extraordinary news. He moved close to her and gave her a kiss on the cheek. I had never seen a kiss that was so chaste and, at the same time, so passionate. I was standing there with my mouth hanging open. In that moment I wouldn't have been able to close it even with the help of a pair of pliers.

'Congratulations, Mrs MacMahon,' I finally stammered.

'Thank you, Tommy,' she said.

They looked at each other as only two lovers could look at each other. As only Mr MacMahon and Mrs MacMahon could look at each other.

Love had transformed Mrs Pinkerton. The change went beyond the wardrobe and hairstyle, far beyond. She was another person.

Only someone like Mr MacMahon could have managed that heroic deed. I was so stunned that I had to sit down. I sat and stared at them, my mouth hanging open. Mrs Pinkerton loved Mr MacMahon. Mr MacMahon loved Mrs Pinkerton.

I had the MacMahons in front of me, in profile, looking at each other like two dumbstruck lovebirds. I sensed, I suspected, that Tommy Thomson had lost direction some time ago, that he was being led by a misunderstanding, a misunderstanding so large that its proportions alone kept him from discovering it. It didn't take a genius to realise the basic contradiction between a Thomson and a MacMahon. Love had taken me to the centre of the Earth, while he had found it in the sitting room of the house where he lived.

In any case, I didn't allow myself much time for reflection, because a tribe of red dwarves appeared at the door. They were MacMahon's children, seven, eight, maybe nine, all of them exactly the same. The boys wore short trousers and the girls little skirts. They were all as redheaded as their father, all of them had hair as short as a brush, all of them boasted thousands of freckles on faces round as oranges. And all of them, boys and girls, had elbows and knees covered with scabs. They began to torture me with wooden sticks, which they used to poke me in the armpit and the ankles. My saviour (who would have guessed it) was Mrs MacMahon. They obeyed her like chicks do a mother hen. She had them queue up in my honour, by age. Each one was two inches taller than the next.

'This is Mr Thomson,' she announced. 'Say hello to him.'

'Hello, Mr Thomson!' they said with in unison.

'And from now on he will be living with us. Let's welcome him.'

'Welcome, Mr Thomson!'

Then Mrs MacMahon and the children went out into the garden. It really wasn't that strange at all, that this woman, who had wanted to be a governess all her life, was so happy in her new role as mother of a large family. Mr MacMahon took me with him.

'Tommy, lad, come with me,' he said. 'I want to show you the house. And I want you to meet someone.'

MacMahon showed me the whole house and finally took me to the boarders' parlour. Before opening the door he said, with the tone of a tourist guide, 'Now you'll meet Mr Modepà.'

'Modepà?'

Instead of answering, Mr MacMahon opened the door. It was a very large room, half library and half parlour. Sitting in an armchair, reading an illustrated magazine, there was a black man. When he saw us he stood up as if a devil had poked him in the arse. I was immediately suspicious of that reflexive act, and of the way he stood at attention like he was in the army. We shook hands. Yellow wormlike protuberances furrowed through the whites of his eyes. That spoke more clearly of his medical history than any clinical file. MacMahon said to me, 'He doesn't understand English.' And addressing Mr Modepà and pointing at me with his finger he shouted, 'Tommy! Tommy! Do you understand? He's named Tommy!'

MacMahon was one of those people who believe they can make up for the linguistic deficits of foreigners by shouting. The volume of his bellows was directly proportional to the lack of language skills the person he was talking to had, and hearing him I came to the conclusion that Mr Modepà didn't know one word of English. Mr Modepà smiled.

'The poor lad only speaks French,' said MacMahon, excusing him.

I pulled Mr MacMahon a few feet away to whisper confidentially into his ear, 'Where did you get him from?'

'From the same place I got you,' was his surprising reply. 'Like I told you, every day I went to the ruins of the boarding house to see if you were there. One day I saw him sitting right where I found you. I addressed him, but we didn't understand each other. He just kept repeating his name: Modepà, Modepà. The next day I went back to the ruins and he was still there. And the day after. And the next. And finally I felt so sorry for him that I couldn't help bringing him home.'

'Just like that. Without even knowing who he was?'

'Well, yes.'

Shortly after they demobilised me, a very sensational case occurred. A rumour went around that the German fleet had left their ports in battle formation and a convoy that carried a regiment of Senegalese had been forced to take refuge on the English coast. The Senegalese marksmen were confined to warehouses, waiting for the danger to pass so they could take them to the continent. Who knows how, but they found out that a few weeks earlier another African regiment had been annihilated. They deserted *en masse.* There were more than a thousand Senegalese fugitives, which started a large-scale hunt. Some of them made it to the streets of London in their wild flight. The newspapers published crazy photographs of English policemen chasing Senegalese marksmen. I reminded MacMahon of the case.

'Well, it's possible,' was his passive response.

'Don't you understand?' I said. 'In that case you're hiding a deserter. And that's a serious crime, very serious.'

But with a tired hand MacMahon waved at the air.

'It'll all work out, you'll see. This war will end one day, and on that day there won't be heroes or deserters, just the living and the dead. In this house Mr Modepà is not a deserter. He's the gardener.'

TWENTY-ONE

HE HAD NEVER IMAGINED that there could be such a dark, narrow, long place. He had been moving forward for hours and hours in a caravan of moles. At first he had moved through soft subsoil. The deepest tree roots still appeared at the ceiling of the tunnel, like hairy turnips that brushed his face. Then that earth was replaced by hard granite-like stone, too deep for any life to penetrate.

The corridor was horribly cramped. The walls clung to him like a second skin. His body often met with little splinters that scratched at his flesh like stone nails. He couldn't raise his head or turn his neck. The only thing he was able to do was push the shell with both hands. Forward, ever forward. Now he understood what those shells were used for. They fitted like projectiles into the bore of a cannon. And their oval shape was optimal for moving through the tunnel. He couldn't see anything, not a thing. Sometimes, when the corridor widened a few inches, the walls lit up with a gloomy green glow that came from the lanterns the Tectons carried.

He lost all sense of time. He had no idea how long he had been pushing the shell in front of him without pausing or resting. If his rhythm slowed, William's shell, behind him, threatened to break his feet. The tunnel led them downwards. For as much winding as they were doing, it was obvious that they were descending. Their wrists and ankles had been worked to the bone. Their elbows and knees were raw. And the heat. The air had become denser and the temperature had increased. It was a homogenous heat with no centre, that sucked the air out of them and melted their flesh.

More than the pain and the exhaustion, what really plagued him was the anxiety. He breathed like a fish out of water. He had the feeling that at any moment his heart would explode like a bomb. He couldn't take it anymore. He stopped.

'Go!' shouted William desperately from behind him. 'When you stop they hit my toes with their clubs!'

They continued. They were going down in a spiral. At a certain point he heard sobs. They came from William.

'Are you all right?' said Marcus.

'All right?' William's voice was the cry of a sheep. And he added, with trembling, broken vowels, 'Just months ago I was in my father's mansion. Now I'm in a crack where a lizard wouldn't even fit. I've lost a gold mine, Richard is dead and they are taking me to hell. How can I be all right?'

They had no way of knowing when that torture would end. Marcus noticed that, in front of him, a Tecton foot kicked at his shell to shut him up. He still said, in a whisper, 'They won't kill us. Before we went into the tunnel I saw them filling the shells with things from the camp and the clearing. They must be samples to take home. They need us to transport these things.' He let out an ironic groan. 'Who knows, maybe we're samples too.'

William was crying. He was crying so hard that Marcus wasn't at all sure that he had heard him. For a long time, hours and hours, he listened to William's childish tears. He also heard the Tectons swearing, as they pierced William's feet to spur him on. They continued their descent. Further and further in, deeper and deeper. Marcus fainted, or half fainted. But even after losing consciousness he still pushed the shell. He pushed and pushed. Then came an order to halt. Was it a moment's rest? The night's sleep? There was no way to know. He dozed off, with his arms still extended. He couldn't do it in any other position: the corridor was too narrow to allow him any movement.

Minutes later, or maybe hours, he was awakened by a shriek from William. The Tectons must have pricked him again, because Marcus felt William's shell pushing at his feet. And the journey resumed.

He was hungry. But the thirst was worse than the hunger, and the heat of the stones reinforced his suffering. He was dying of thirst. Marcus even went so far as to rip off the scabs from his forehead so blood would gush down onto his face and he could lick it. 'Think, Marcus, think,' he told himself, 'if you are so hungry and so thirsty, and we've stopped once, it must be more than a day.' He concluded that they couldn't continue that way forever. Even the Tectons, who weren't pushing shells and were protected by their armour, couldn't last much longer.

He heard a Tecton shout, and it seemed that the shout was directed at him. But it wasn't an order to stop – the caravan continued moving – or a threat, and it didn't seem like an insult either. What was he warning him about, then? He didn't understand until he realised that the green lantern was projecting a ray of light onto the ceiling. He looked up, without stopping his pushing, and saw some sort of bread, flat and round, hanging from the ceiling. The Tectons that preceded him had left it there. It was a thin enough slice so that the shell, even though it was fitted to the passageway, could get through without dragging it along.

There were two pieces, he grabbed one and shouted, 'William! The ceiling!'

He heard William's sobs, this time from happiness. Even more things began to appear on the ceiling. Some sort of lettuce leaves, two. The bread tasted of millet; the leaves had a high liquid content, sucking them calmed their thirst. They were so thirsty that William received the leaf with more joy than the bread. However, Marcus was smart enough to realise the downside: if they were being fed it was because they had a long journey planned. Very long.

They ate and drank without stopping. Maybe it had been two days that they had been slithering through the tunnel. Only two? More bread and leaves again. It didn't make for very solid nourishment. They grew weak. But all of a sudden, when their bodies were turning into snakes, they emptied out into an open space. A howl of happiness escaped from Marcus's lips. They had stopped in an air bubble. A place where they could change positions and relax their muscles! He laughed like a madman. And at the same time he realised that the reason for all that happiness, that euphoria, was a space that couldn't have been even six cubic feet.

Behind Marcus appeared William's shell, and behind the shell, William himself. The Tectons that had already entered threatened them with shouts and clubs. They made the Englishmen lie down with their hands on the backs of their necks. Soon the two Tectons that brought up the rear of the caravan entered.

They were inside a stone dome. A total of six bodies sharing a fox den, back to back. Marcus would never have thought that so many people could fit into so little space. He only had to stretch out his arm to touch the Tecton furthest from him. But now, after days of dragging himself through an underground chimney, he felt as if he had entered a dance hall. The Tectons knew the environment well. They were very skilled at stretching themselves in such a limited area. The silence of the stone was punctuated by a rustling of flesh that made one think of wet, taut nautical ropes. They rolled their necks and stretched their muscles, slowly, turning their appendages as if they were flowers opening. And, as a result shaking loose most of the crust of dirt stuck to their white armour, now covered with a layer of ochre.

The pause gave them a few minutes to reflect. There were two lanterns, each one stuffed with those luminescent little worms, which projected a weak green light onto the stone and the bodies. William looked downcast. A shark in a fishtank. Within him there still dwelled some sort of life, but in a state of suspension. Marcus tried to encourage him. Impossible. At the first word a Tecton hit him in the lips with one of those horrible clubs. William turned his neck, and looked him in the eyes. What Marcus saw scared him. Two cheeks like two funnels, sucked in; the unblinking eyes of a dried, stuffed animal. And lips with cracks that looked like slices from an axe.

William spoke with a voice that was not his own. As if he were already dead and he was communicating with the world through a spirit medium. Through those broken, cracked lips, a single word filtered out, whistled.

'Champagne.'

Three days later. (It's an estimate I made based on the caravan's pauses. Marcus assured me that during the entire trip he was absolutely incapable of calculating the passage of time.) The stone intestine that they hauled themselves through began to expand. The ceiling rose progressively, the sides of the corridor no longer scraped at their ribs. Yet the difficulties they had to face were no less. First of all, the geography. Now the passageway made a much steeper descent, with slopes of up to forty degrees. For long periods they advanced face down. Blood accumulated in their brains, causing fleeting hallucinations. Marcus saw some glowing green goblins passing through the rock, like small souls in the form of match flames. The goblins came through the rock like our ghosts go through walls and they happily greeted the underground travellers. The brain fever had another, more dangerous side effect. Preoccupied, his mind filled with blood, William's shell often slipped from his hands and crashed against Marcus's ankles. The shells were heavy, crammed with baggage. Marcus, in turn, would panic, thinking he might lose his grip on his shell too. He didn't want to even consider the retaliation of the Tecton who was ahead of him.

Then, the heat. It was enough to make one doubt whether they were travelling towards the centre of the Earth or towards the sun. Marcus felt he was breathing hot ash. He was sure his liver and his kidneys would melt. But all he could do was push the shell and keep quiet.

The ceiling rose a little higher each day. For the pauses, now, the

Tectons chose wider spots, cavities where they could at least sit. They watched the Englishmen. The Tectons slept in shifts. There was always someone awake acting as a guard. Marcus had noticed one of the Tectons in particular. He had the thick-lidded eyes of an idiot. He was also, by far, the fattest of the four, big as a gorilla. While they were in the narrowest part of the tunnel he had always been at the head of the caravan. His helmet and the reinforced shoulders of his armour made him scrape off all the things that stuck out, like a human drill. He often gave beatings in an erratic, unpredictable way, to show that he was in charge. While all the other Tectons slept, when he was left alone with the two humans, he was never quite sure that he was fully in control of the situation. Not even with a club in his hand. He looked at one, then the other, turning his head with the obsessive movements of a hen.

During his shift they took the opportunity to talk.

'I stuck my hand into my shell and all that's in there are worthless trifles,' whispered William. 'It's incredible. They're only interested in silly objects. Look at that bastard.'

He was referring to the gorilla Tecton, who wore a crucifix hanging from his waist.

'That iron cross was Richard's,' continued William. 'And he uses it as if it were a sword. They're a ghastly race.'

'Don't do it again,' said Marcus, interrupting him.

'Don't do what?'

'Go through the shells. Think about that Negro.'

'What Negro?' asked William.

'The one that looked at the bottle of formol with a beetle inside.' And he insisted, 'Don't rummage through the shell.'

The Tecton demanded silence with a threatening growl. They

were lucky that of those four there was one who was such an idiot, because for the last few days they had been watched more carefully. The vigilance increased in parallel to the possibilities of the terrain. Now, at times, they could even stand up. The next few days became a re-enactment of prehistoric man: each day they could rise up a bit more, like hominids advancing towards bipedalism. As for the cave that surrounded them, Marcus compared the landscape to the inside of a whale. Beneath their feet there even appeared steps, which were reminiscent of the ribs of a cetacean. They went down and down, now without spiral turns.

'Can't you feel it?' said Marcus.

'What do you mean?' said William irascibly.

'It's not as muggy.'

It was true. During the last twenty-four hours (another approximation of mine) the temperature had lowered a few degrees. That didn't make sense. According to William, who was better educated, the increase in depth should have been proportional to the heat. It frightened them to think of the thousands and thousands of tons of rock that there must have been over their heads. But the temperature, contrary to all logic, was decreasing.

Since the space allowed it, William and Marcus slept like polar dogs, with one's body curled round the other's. In that subterranean world where only night existed, the hours of sleep were the night, and William and Marcus held each other as if the other's body had become a child's blanket that protected them from all their fears. It was the fraternity of prisoners, for whom the closeness of death wiped clean memories and miseries. One night Marcus heard William talking. He wasn't at all sure whether he was trying to tell him something or if he was just talking in his sleep. 'And the Congo was my idea . . . mine . . . mine . . .' It was simply incredible to hear those words coming from William Craver's mouth. And Marcus thought that something good must come out of hell, or the road to hell, if it was capable of bringing someone like William Craver closer to being human.

The next day they were awakened with kicks. The Tectons ordered them to stop pushing the shells and to start carrying them on their backs. The space now permitted it. They had stood up, and Marcus thought that it was a good time to give his companion a gift.

While they were adjusting their enormous shells, Marcus diverted himself by studying the route they would follow. Now the worm lanterns became useful. The more space there was, the more light the walls reflected. Directly ahead, the stone tunnel stopped in front of a wall with five, six, maybe seven holes.

'Let's take note of the route they choose,' whispered Marcus.

William snorted. 'Why? We're never going back,' he moaned. 'My God, my God! Does your shell weigh as much as mine? How far do they expect us to get, with these on our backs?'

The Tectons interrupted the conversation with their clubs. The severity of those blows told them that from that day on it would be absolutely forbidden for them to open their mouths. Marcus shot a look at William, a look that said: look at my hand and don't take your eyes off of it.

Marcus was ahead of William. He was walking with his right fist closed. When he had the opportunity he opened it, a fleeing instant, just enough time for William to glimpse the five bullets. Marcus had removed them from inside his shell, going against his own advice. This act made William regain hope. It also had other consequences. William Craver couldn't stop being William Craver.

Actually, during that brief interlude, he hadn't been a better man. He simply hadn't been a man. But now an unforeseen element appeared: five revolver bullets.

Making up his mind with impressive speed, William banged his chest against the shell that Marcus carried on his back and set him off balance. He pretended it was an accident, but it was an excuse to discreetly get close to Marcus's hand. William forced Marcus's closed fingers open with his own. The Tectons shouted, angry with these clumsy creatures who tripped even when they could finally walk without difficulty. Marcus felt William's fingers jabbing at his hand. What could he do? The Tectons would take two seconds, three at most, to work out the real reason behind the stumble. They would see the stolen bullets, their last chance. It was suicidal blackmail. If they were discovered they would both suffer the retribution. But William didn't care about the consequences. He had employed a similar strategy with the bank's board of directors, but something had gone wrong. This time he pulled it off.

Marcus had no choice but to open his fingers. The bullets changed owners.

At bedtime William curled around him like the previous nights. But now he curled in even closer. Opening his lips inside Marcus's ear, he commanded him harshly, 'Now we need a revolver. Look for it!'

Marcus was horrified. William had not only appropriated the ammunition, he was now demanding that Marcus risk his life rummaging around inside the shells.

When the Tectons covered all the lanterns except one with rags William moved away from Marcus. One inch, two inches, three inches. And William fell asleep with his fist tightly closed.

TWENTY-TWO

THE UNDERGROUND LANDSCAPE APPEARED before them with a dead beauty. They no longer had any ceiling above them. The green light couldn't reach all the way up to that stone ceiling, further above their heads with each step. They went deep into a passageway that twisted and turned, always downward, and not even a palm's span wide.

The caravan came to a stop. A Tecton was adjusting one of the lanterns. Marcus had wondered how so many little worms could survive so long inside a bag. Now he had the answer: eating each other. There was only one worm left, longer and thicker than a sausage. The Tecton took it out of the bag. The worm wriggled and flapped. It let off a fantastic light: inside its body, the light of all its fellow worms gathered, amplified.

The Tecton dropped the fat worm down the deep black chasm to their right. Humans and Tectons queued up at the edge of the ravine.

That faint, live green light sank into the darkness, twisting in silence. It fell, and fell, and kept falling. The worm's form became smaller than a needle. Marcus couldn't believe it: almost a minute had passed and the worm's light hadn't gone out. The Tectons gave the order to move off again. Marcus gave it a last glance, and he could still see a miniscule green dot falling and falling.

After a few days the passageway emptied out into an unobstructed valley, a sea of solid magma. Marcus sensed a limitless flat plain where not even the green lights of the lanterns could be seen against the crimson of a severe, rippling sun, with capricious forms, as if waves of copper had covered a horde of crustaceans. All around them millions of shells, sharp as knives, emerged from the ground. In their bare feet they didn't dare stray from a thin flat tongue of land that traversed the horizon. 'Here the rocks bite,' said Marcus to himself.

The lanterns offered limited visibility. They couldn't see the immense spaces, but they could hear them. In that desert a mute and violent wind blew that smacked the intruders in the face as if it were led by personal animosity. There was also another unusual phenomenon: the temperature lowered so far that it was even cold. They slept in the middle of nothing, and when they woke up their tortured skin was covered with some sort of dense dew. They were so hungry that they licked it. It was gelatine and tasted of celery and sulphur. According to William, the ceiling must have been so high up that it allowed the condensation of clouds of putrid gases.

Marcus named that valley the Sea of Young Ladies, because here and there, along the road, appeared sinuous columns with thin waists, as if they had been compressed by a very tight corset. Some of the 'young ladies' were incommensurably large. They had a giant base that thinned as it went up, ten metres, fifty metres, a hundred metres, five hundred metres, and at that point got thicker again, more and more, until the form got lost up there, in a ceiling hidden by the most opaque darkness.

'My God!' said William, admiringly. 'The ancients said that the world rested on a tortoise's shell. But no one said what there was underneath the turtle. Now we know.' He pointed to a few of the young ladies, 'the pillars of the Earth.'

They were the first men to step foot in that world. They did so as two beasts of burden and, at that point in the voyage, Marcus couldn't take any more. That place made obvious to him the terrible injustice of only having five senses for pleasure and the entire surface of one's body for pain. Marcus discovered that hell wasn't a place, but a journey. He discovered that hell was coming to him as he went to it, and that the pain took the place of time.

The real nightmare began when they woke up. As he heaved the shell onto his back, Marcus's bones cracked like the walls of an old mansion. They had been eating no more than slices of bread and leaves. Their existence had been reduced to carrying that load, to putting one foot in front of the other. They didn't have wounds, they were wounds. And Marcus had an added torture to bear: William.

They had learned to speak without emitting hardly any sound. It was a language reminiscent of the one used by deaf-mutes, based more on the movements of their lips rather than sounds. It was no longer a dialogue, just a monologue from William: 'Revolver! Find it!'

At the end of each day, with all but one of the lanterns extinguished, William and Marcus pretended to sleep until the gorilla

Tecton's shift began. He soon started yawning. When those eyelids fell over his eyes like curtains, Marcus seized the moment. With all the strength of one hand, he raised up the shell an inch or two, imperceptibly, and with the other he felt around inside it. Nothing.

William was right. It seemed that the Tectons had only gathered trinkets and trifles. His fingers rummaged through minutiae. A comb. Cups. Pipes. Stones. Tree branches. An old brush, some keys. A broken piece of glass that cut his hand badly . . . He was getting desperate.

'Find it!'

Without the Tecton noticing, William and Marcus switched the shells they used as pillows so that Marcus could search inside both of them. Worst of all, they had no guarantee that the Tectons had even taken a revolver. Everything his fingers touched was a trinket. Once or twice, the gorilla Tecton's eyelids would move, opening rapidly, and he almost caught him with his hand in the shell.

'Find it!'

'I can't,' said Marcus, giving up on the third night. 'The shells are too deep. I don't have enough time to go through everything.'

'You have to find it!' insisted William.

'Then you'll have to keep him busy! I need time. I have to get my hand all the way inside. It's the last chance we have.'

'But if I distract him he'll use the club on me,' said William.

'Either keep him busy or forget about finding a gun.'

William grimaced.

'Maybe you want to stick your hand in there?' said Marcus. 'Would you rather they caught you red-handed?'

'Tonight,' said William.

* * *

'Now!' said Marcus, and William jumped.

The gorilla couldn't believe it. The human was coming towards him, gesticulating and addressing him with a voicc of authority.

'I am very sorry, Mr Smith!' shouted William. 'I have to tell you that the bank transfer is invalid, it didn't arrive at its destination!'

The other Tectons woke up. They brandished their clubs, but they didn't attack him. William's approach was so suicidal that they suspected some hidden trick. They surrounded him, watching suspiciously. Marcus took advantage of the opportunity to move his fingers frantically inside the shell.

'I swear to you that it's not my signature, Mr Smith!' continued William. 'I don't know who deposited a transfer of two hundred thousand pounds into a bank account in my name, Mr Smith!'

The revolver, the revolver, Marcus's fingers urged, moving quicker than a pickpocket's. Where is it, where is it? It wasn't there. The Tectons had decided that William's behaviour had no hidden dangers. They jumped on him from all sides, all four at once. Marcus cried tears of rage. Where is it, where is it?

'Don't get the police involved, Mr Smith!' screamed William as he received blows with clubs and kicks. 'My father will sort it all out, Mr Smith!'

The Tectons laughed. Beating up William had gone from being an act of repression to becoming a source of entertainment. Marcus's tears were so bitter they burned his face. His fingers now moved more out of nervous impulse than by his wilful control.

'My God!' he suddenly realised. 'It's the revolver, it's always been here.' All those nights he had been fumbling for the shape of a revolver. But the object that he now held didn't have the butt or the trigger protector. Marcus hadn't associated that mutilated weapon with the object he was looking for. But there it was: a revolver with the butt removed.

The Tectons threw William down beside Marcus like a sack of potatoes and forgot about him. He was a pitiful sight. His nose gushed blood and his right eye was swollen like a small tyre. But Marcus had the best medicine in the world. He turned his hand. And in the palm, with the barrel along his forearm, appeared the revolver he had wanted so badly. William whispered: 'Thank the good Lord. Give it to me!' he said, stretching out his hand. 'Those bastards . . . I'll kill them right now!'

Marcus was about to hand it over obediently. All of a sudden, though, an invisible light passed through his mind. In a particle of a second he vividly remembered Amgam's last kiss. And he knew that their public embrace had had a purpose beyond displaying her love: to distract the Tectons' attention while she hid the revolver and the bullets in the shell he had been carrying since the first day. It was quite possible, in fact, that Amgam herself had taken off the butt so that she could hide it in the shell.

The revolver belonged to him. It was his only hope.

William and Marcus were so close to one another that their noses touched. Marcus hid his arm. He wouldn't give him the revolver. Never. William opened his mouth, shocked. Marcus turned his back on him.

'The revolver, you idiot!' said William, lips clenched, pulling Marcus by the shoulder and then hitting him cruelly in the ribs.

But Marcus jammed an elbow behind him, violently, until he hit a soft stomach. The blow knocked the breath out of William. And after the beating he had received he was in no condition to argue.

William understood that he was up against a revolt. Because Amgam's gift began to achieve exactly what it set out to do: to liberate Marcus. It began to free him from chains that were much heavier than the Tecton enslavement. The submissive relationship that tied Marcus the stableboy to William the aristocrat no longer existed. If Marcus had only found a gun, nothing would have changed. But that weapon was much more. It was a fork in the road of destiny that forced him to choose between being stableboy Marcus or free Marcus. And Marcus knew one certain thing: that as long as he was breathing, as long as he was alive, he would never turn Amgam's love over to William Craver. Never.

The next day William began a new strategy. He knew that Marcus was stubborn. He also knew that he was more tired, so he opted to wear him down.

'The revolver! Give it to me!' he whispered into his ear the following night. 'You're a stableboy! The only thing you've done in this life is clean horse's arses and boil pots. How do you expect to challenge four Tectons?'

Marcus couldn't take refuge in sleep. It was highly likely that William would steal the gun from him as he slept. It seemed to him that William was sleeping, that he had taken a break from that peculiar conflict in order to recoup his strength. But how could he be sure? And, so, he had to stay up all night long.

They resumed their march. Marcus hadn't had a moment's rest. The shell weighed double on him. For a few days now the ceiling had begun to loom again, falling onto their heads. But it wasn't yet low enough that they had to crawl, pushing the shell, which would have made the load a little less heavy.

'The revolver!' insisted William at night. 'You don't know how to shoot! Your hand will shake! Give it to me! Don't you want to get out of here? Have you gone crazy, Marcus, completely crazy?'

But the only response he got from Marcus was that he pressed the weapon tighter against his stomach.

The next day they had to walk bent over. It was as if they were following the route of a funnel, the space that surrounded them narrowed in only one direction. Now they had to move forward with their bodies folded into an L-shape. William was losing hope. If they started to crawl again he wouldn't be able to steal the weapon. He couldn't believe it. He had five bullets in the palm of his hand, five. Enough ammunition to eliminate four Tectons. And that idiot Garvey was hiding a perfectly serviceable revolver from him. It got to the point where William could no longer control himself. He threw himself onto Marcus's back, making him fall. Marcus had the shell on top of him and on top of that an enraged William straddling the makeshift saddle, beating his fists furiously against his skull.

'The revolver! Give me the revolver, you bastard! Give it to me! They'll kill us!'

Marcus didn't even have the strength to get up, much less fight back. He could only cover his head with one arm, while with the other he hid the revolver against his belly button. He was saved, paradoxically, by the Tectons themselves. They attacked William with their clubs. They beat him on the head and ribs, and when he fell they continued hitting him for some time.

At night they lay down again together. William cried out of frustration, and he whispered, 'Gypsy bastard . . . you . . . you've taken us beyond death . . .'

Marcus just said, 'Sleep, William, sleep.'

And then, without warning, Marcus Garvey's last day underground arrived. And it was, according to Marcus, the closest to the end of the world that a human being can experience.

The stone funnel shrank more and more. Soon they were forced to slither like lizards, exactly like the first few days of their immersion into the underworld. And just as in those first days, the Englishmen advanced with escorts, two Tectons in front of Marcus and two behind William.

The Tectons were anxious to move faster now. But Marcus couldn't move, the shell itself had become a plug that stopped up the tunnel. He shouted. He needed the help of the Tectons in front of him, who eventually widened the cave with their clubs.

As a crack between the cave and the shell opened, a fierce wind attacked Marcus's face. Strong gusts, so strong they hurt his eyes. The wind was nothing like the air in the Sea of Young Ladies, silent and dry. This wind was cold, and was accompanied by a mechanical and furious whistle. And something more unusual: light. An unnatural light, orange in colour. The Tectons widened the breach, and through it filtered rays of light that pierced the eyes.

But what Marcus least expected was that, after going through that bottleneck, the cave would open out onto a landing, with open sky. The light bathing the landing was so intense that it burned his eyes. Marcus crawled on his knees and elbows, covering his eyes with his hands. He opened two fingers and saw William's head.

'Close your eyes!' he warned him.

The orange light dominated everything. The excess of light didn't bother the Tectons' cat eyes, but it was lethal to the eyes of men who had spent so much time being guided by lanterns made of green worms.

The two Tectons following William pushed him brutally. They were impatient to arrive at the landing. They jumped over the human and left him behind. For a few long seconds William and Marcus lay together on their sides, blinking in pain. Then Marcus slowly opened his eyes.

The landing was shaped like one of those mushrooms that grow on tree bark. The four Tectons were standing up on the edge of the landing, with their backs to the Englishmen. What were they looking at? Some hidden landscape? Beyond the stone mushroom there was nothing, nothing, just a void, a desert of air. He looked up. The ceiling must have been so, so far above that they only saw dark violet clouds. Inside the clouds, red lightning bolts chased each other furiously while thunderclaps rumbled like lions fighting. The Tectons were looking at something below them. He crawled to the edge of the mushroom keeping as far away from the boots of the Tectons as he could, and looked down. A hiccup emptied his lungs.

From that landing there was a magnificent view of the Tectons' city. The stone landing was so far up, or the city so far below, that Marcus felt like someone looking at the world from the moon. But the metropolis was so unbelievably huge that the height didn't lessen the visibility. Actually it was more the opposite, as if the city was proud of its vastness, of being visible from so far up.

Some of the avenues must have been a hundred miles long. Parts of the Tecton city followed a perfect geometric design. In other places the buildings were squeezed together any which way, and the tallest skyscrapers must have exceeded the highest peak on Earth. Marcus wasn't sure if the city was in the most utter chaos or the most perfect order. As far as his eyes could see there rose buildings of marble and coal, marble and coal, marble and coal, as if the two materials were engaged in an undecided, perpetual war. And he thought that the Congo could be bigger than God, yes, but that the Tecton metropolis would always be bigger than the Congo.

William imitated Marcus. And when he saw the city he wheezed like an overloaded donkey.

It was there, at the very gates of hell, where Marcus Garvey redeemed himself for all the impure acts he had committed in the Congo. The wind, with an incredibly violence, pushed the two Englishmen's eyes into their sockets. But while William's skin moved like the clothes on a scarecrow, the only thing that shifted on Marcus was his hair, wild from the slavery. The rest of his body was a human rock that stuck out its hand and demanded, in a tone that did not leave room for discussion, 'The bullets.'

That open hand was the exact opposite of the hand that had once accepted sticks of dynamite. It was another man's hand, because the Marcus Garvey that had arrived in the Congo no longer had anything to do with the Marcus Garvey that had arrived at the Tecton metropolis.

William yielded. He wanted to give him the ammunition, but he couldn't. He had crushed the bullets inside his closed fist for too many days, too tightly. Now his fingers refused to open, like the lid of a rusty chest.

'The bullets!' shouted Marcus, aware that the Tectons wouldn't stand there gaping much longer.

He forced open William's closed fingers, one by one. When he had opened his hand, Marcus couldn't help being shocked: the bullets had made wounds that were stigmata. He couldn't waste time. He had to load the five bullets into the chamber, and it was much more difficult than it seemed.

Marcus got onto his knees. He thought it would be easier to handle the revolver that way. No. His fingers shook so much that the bullets jumped like tiny live fish. And the wind. He couldn't get even one bullet into the chamber. Not even one. All five tumbled down onto the ground.

It was beyond him. He spent a second, an eternity, telling himself, 'For the love of God, breathe, think, get a hold of yourself!' But suddenly he changed his mind. He said to himself, 'Don't breathe, don't think, let your fingers do the work. They already know what they have to do.'

Somehow he managed to load a bullet. And the feeling of the projectile going into the chamber, the mechanical sliding of that small cylinder, encouraged his fingers, and they repeated the success with another bullet, and another, and another, and another, and finally he had the five bullets inside the chamber. He pulled back the hammer and took aim at the Tectons.

William was watching the scene with his hands on his head. The four Tectons still had their backs to them, absorbed in the landscape. Marcus was behind them, only a few feet away. And he wasn't shooting.

William couldn't take it anymore. He shouted, 'Shoot, you damn gypsy! Shoot!'

William's shouting alerted the four Tectons, who as one turned round.

Marcus pulled the trigger. But instead of a detonation, all he heard was an empty click. (Marcus would dream of that click on many nights.) William was the first to react. He fled back through the hole they had come from, on all fours and with the speed of a squirrel. Marcus pulled the trigger again.

The first bullet was lost above the Tecton city.

The second bullet killed a Tecton who was chasing after William.

The third bullet bounced off a rock, without hitting anyone.

The fourth bullet seriously wounded a Tecton in the neck.

The fifth entered another Tecton's stomach, who fell over the precipice from the impact.

There was one Tecton left, the gorilla, who fell on Marcus like an avalanche of flesh.

He was the biggest, strongest Tecton, but he surprised Marcus by shrieking like an enraged child. He dragged Marcus towards the precipice, throttling him and beating his head against a rock the way a gorilla would open a coconut. And now we might legitimately ask ourselves: how is it possible that a short-legged little man, with his body destroyed by slavery, starving, gaunt and exhausted, could beat a muscular Tecton warrior, protected by stone armour and an expert in man-to-man combat?

Marcus, naturally, was unable to offer me any rational explanation. He could only describe images, guttural sounds and a vertigo unimaginable to our senses. But I ventured an answer.

It was very simple. The Tecton couldn't kill Marcus because Marcus couldn't die. He lived because he had a reason to live: to be with her again. Marcus didn't die, in the end, because a man that has survived the Congo, the Craver brothers, the Tectons and that infernal underground journey cannot die when he is at the gates of salvation.

While the Tecton strangled him, Marcus kept his eyes fixed on those of his executioner. They fought at the edge of the landing. As the Tecton's hands pulled him back by his neck, Marcus saw the city below him upside down. At any moment he would push him over.

Here Marcus's memory suffered a lapse. He could only remember that, suddenly, the Tecton's hands stopped throttling him. His attacker had covered his face with his hands, like someone who wants to save himself from an unpleasant sight. And he remembered pushing his adversary with both feet. When the Tecton realised that he was falling it was already too late.

Marcus spent a few moments wheezing like a runaway horse. Because of the lack of oxygen, his brain created some very amusing hallucinations. Everything was twisting and turning. He would have been perfectly capable of throwing himself over the cliff. Only chance made his body fall in the right direction, towards the stone, and not towards the abyss.

He noticed that his hand was smeared with a greasy substance. His asphyxiated brain wanted to make him believe that it was banana marmalade. When he had licked off the last drop of jam he noticed the Tectons that had gone over the edge, who were still falling. He also realised that the gorilla was shrieking and had no eyes in his face. His body left a trail of two red liquid strings. They were the streams of blood that gushed from his eye sockets. Marcus had ripped out the creature's eyeballs with his desperate rat fingers and then he had devoured them. He stood up, very slowly. Only two bodies remained on the ledge. The Tecton he had wounded wasn't moving, so he wasn't certain if he was dead or alive. Just in case, he pushed him, as if he were rolling up a carpet, over the precipice. He was so exhausted, physically and mentally, that he didn't have the strength to repeat the operation with the dead Tecton. He turned around and headed towards the tunnel, shouting, 'William? William?'

He didn't get any response. Probably William was still fleeing, and would continue to flee for much longer without stopping or looking back. That created problems. But of another dimension. And in those moments he didn't want to think about them.

He glanced again at the void. The bodies were still falling through seemingly endless airspace, as if they were chasing each other in a deadly race. The city hadn't moved. He didn't have to worry about its inhabitants. Supposing that the three bodies didn't disintegrate on the fall, supposing that the Tectons sent out a patrol, they would still take days, entire weeks to get to the landing. Gradually, as if he didn't want to accept it, the vague idea that he could allow himself to rest began to take shape within him. He stretched out on the rock, nude, without taking his eyes off of the remaining Tecton. He was dead yet Marcus was still afraid of him.

He felt all the weight of the world on him; it was as if his shoulders were holding up all the stones that separated him from the surface. But he was a free man.

Sleep, Marcus Garvey, sleep.

TWENTY-THREE

MARCUS COULD BE COMPLETELY sure that he was the first human being that ever opened his eyes in a place like that one. The orange light of the Tecton world illuminated the landing with a stagnant peace. It was impossible to know how long he had been asleep, hours or just a few minutes.

It started to rain, as if the rain had been waiting for him to wake up. The clouds released some thick yellow drops that bombarded the landing furiously, like tiny watery meteorites. The raindrops soaked the stone of the landing and filled the open mouth of the rigid Tecton corpse. As they fell on the armour of the dead man, they bounced off with a metallic *plop-plop-plop*. In a few minutes Marcus was drenched, deliriously drenched. Suffering that extreme dehydration that affects men who have been fighting life-or-death battles, he knelt with his mouth open, drinking in all the water he could absorb through the pores of his body.

For a few seconds he felt as if the rain was washing his pain away like grime. He hadn't felt so fresh, so powerful in a long time. Even the numerous scratches etched on his skin seemed shorter and thinner, more closed.

Water? Marcus stuck out both his hands. He looked closely at the drops that fell on his palms. They didn't dilute and the yellow mineral reminded him of another, very familiar one: the gold that came out of the mine.

In the Tecton world it rained gold. When Marcus realised he spat it out. It was raining gold. But surprise gave way to pragmatism. Up until that moment he hadn't gained anything from the mine's gold. Why should he waste his time with this gold? He leapt over to the shells, and emptied the contents out onto the landing. The orange light illuminated everything, which he could finally look at without fear.

His fingers hadn't played tricks on him. What a load of rubbish, thought Marcus. One of the shells was practically filled by three large objects: the tusk of a small elephant, a whole rubber plant and a rock the size of a pirate cannonball, with encrusted shiny specks. He made a disgusted face. For this he had been about to die, for this the Tectons had attacked an entire world! To take some animal teeth, a plant and a stone with them!

He continued rifling through the things, and in the second shell, a treasure appeared in the form of tins of beef and peaches in heavy syrup. And, mixed in with some peanuts, he found more bullets. Then he approached the dead Tecton. He took off his armour to reveal the padded tunic. Underneath his armour, the Tecton wore some sort of padded pyjama that was all one piece. Marcus settled on the tunic. He tried the armour on, but the stone scales pierced his skin. It dawned on him why the Tectons must wear those pyjamas, and he stripped all the clothes off the corpse.

The pyjama covered him and protected him from the roughness of that mosaic of little stones that was the Tecton armour. That felt better. In the inner part of the tunic Marcus found some side pockets, like little leather bags, that fell parallel to his armpits. And inside one of them, with a big 'oh' of surprise, he found a second revolver. He guessed that the Tecton had taken it with him as a souvenir, without understanding the fatal possibilities it held.

He filled his pockets with the two revolvers, the bullets, the peanuts, and the tinned food. He took a few steps. At first he felt like a Catholic priest, or even like one of those young ladies from the eighteenth century who wore bell-shaped skirts. But if the Tectons went around in cassock-like clothing, he concluded, there must be a good reason for it. Then he stripped the dead Tecton of his footwear. He examined them and saw that the inner part of each boot was lined with a moss to muffle their steps. Carefully, he put on the left boot. Oh, Lord! What a pleasure to wear shoes again.

He went to the edge of the landing and gave the Tecton city one last glance. Nothing else in the world could be so sublime and so vile at the same time. Endless avenues. Perfect skyscrapers. And, what's more, it rained gold. But the golden rain, thought Marcus, hadn't made the Tectons any happier.

At first the armour was cumbersome, but he became accustomed to it very quickly. It was, more or less, like learning to ride a bicycle and row at the same time. He had to combine the momentum of his elbows and knees. And soon, his initial discomfort turned into enthusiasm.

The clothing was a miracle of rigidity and flexibility at the same time. It was infinitely lighter than iron armour, infinitely more resistant than any leather clothing. Moving through the cave with that armoured body was almost a pleasure. Marcus and the tunic strengthened their friendship as they advanced through the tunnel. *One*, *two*, *one*, *two*, he moved his elbows, *hip*, *hop*, *hip*, *hop*, he propelled himself with his knees. Since the inner pockets were below his armpits, what he carried there didn't constrain him. *One*, *two*, *one*, *two . . . hip*, *hop*, *hip*, *hop . . .* He had tied a lantern to his neck, there were only two live worms of similar size left in the bag, and since it was soft it fell to one side of his neck and then the other like a glowing yoke. Go on, Marcus Garvey, keep going! Go back to the world! Don't stop now!

Life moves at different speeds. And that trip back was a sigh. Thanks to the tunic and the strength that freedom brings, Marcus moved with prodigious drive. His one concern was William. When he got to the wall filled with holes, he shouted, 'William!'

He stuck his head into all the tunnels.

'William! William! William!'

Nothing.

He was glad William wasn't around. but not knowing his location did not make him happy in the least. What was he up to?

When he got to the Sea of Young Ladies he tried again.

'Wiilliiiiiaaam!'

There had never been such a solitary voice. A darkness without walls, a vast emptiness, inhabited by a compact mass of millions and millions of dead mussels.

His voice scattered through those desolate places, far, very far, dragged by an air so light it didn't offer resistance to the sound or dilute it. The shout surrounded the columns and extended above that carpet of petrified crustaceans.

'Wiilliiiiiaaam!'

Never had a voice produced so much solitude. Marcus knelt down. On the outward journey they had used the path. The trail that the caravan had left was still intact. In some spots, the softest ones, William and Marcus's bare footprints could still be made out. But only in one direction.

Marcus imposed on himself a very strict routine. Two morsels of tinned meat each day, half a peach and one sip of the nectar. To sleep he took shelter at the foot of one of the columns. The wind whipped him much less than on the journey out. The armoured tunic was expansive, and he drew his arms into the sleeves. He pulled on a string that ran along the edge of the skirt, closing it from below as if it were a sleeping bag, imitating what he had seen the Tectons do.

One night he was awakened by a noise that had no distinguishable form or content. He couldn't even say if it was the bellow of a hippopotamus or the bifid whisper of a snake. He heard a voice, a far off voice, saying, 'Maaar . . . cuuus . . .'

And then an echo, which sent his name back broken, '–us! . . . –us! . . . –us!'

The shout was repeated on other occasions. Always unexpectedly and when he had just closed his eyes. He would wake up soaked in sweat, grab the two revolvers and wave them wildly into the darkness.

'William?' he asked, without lowering his weapons.

But beyond the small circle of weak green light from the lanterns he couldn't see anything.

Did they really exist, those voices? Not even he himself was sure if he had really heard them, if he had dreamed them or just imagined them. In that mute underworld, where not even silence spoke, the border between dreams, delusions and reality blurred.

To free himself from these aural hallucinations, Marcus tried to think up a plan of action. But he was no strategist. He would get confused. He was alone and three Tectons remained on the surface. What could he do?

Manual work was the only activity that distracted him a little bit. During the rest periods, before sleeping, he looked for crustaceans to reconstruct the broken gun butt. He went off the narrow path and used the lantern to select the best shells. They were stuck into the earth as if covered by a layer of cement and he had to use a lot of force to extract them. On these excursions he acted like a caveman polishing flint arrowheads. It wasn't easy for him to find a piece that fitted. But finally he found the perfect one. It slotted in perfectly and he allowed his hand to close around it. He made violent gestures with the hand that held the revolver, like a real Wild West gunman.

The next day he began to ascend the passageway that twisted and turned. When he wanted to sleep he wedged himself into one of the cracks in the earth, beside the path. He hid the lantern between his feet, under his skirt, so that the light wouldn't give him away. He discovered that inside the lantern there was only one worm left. It had devoured the other one before they got to the surface. Marcus grew increasingly anxious, thinking about William.

That day Marcus looked back. From the heights of the passageway he seemed to see below, in the Sea of Young Ladies, there shone a little light. It was a small green bubble floating in the midst of the darkness. But it went out very quickly. Tectons following him? No, that was impossible. They would have taken weeks to organise an expedition, and even more to get from the city to the landing.

'William!' he shouted. No reply.

A mirage, then? His mind was divided. Until one fine day he said to himself: 'Don't be stupid, you needn't be afraid of what's around you, but rather of what awaits you.'

There were no more incidents. He entered the final crevasse, the one that led to the mine. He pushed along on his elbows and knees with the endurance of an athlete, and, even though it was very narrow, a few days later, before him, at the end of the tunnel, a weak white light appeared. He dragged himself towards the light slowly, making sure not to make any noise.

He put his face into one of the holes. A very small one. In fact, it was like sticking his head into the neck of a too-tight pullover. For a while Marcus just looked into the mine. Still, silent, attentive.

He reviewed his situation. Some place, very close by, there were three Tectons. But he had two pistols and the advantage of the element of surprise. There was nothing in the mine. The mine had been the scene of slave labour, of hate, of love. Of a battle. And now nothing could be seen there, nothing could be heard. The demolished wood beams were still there, where they had landed after the explosions. Someone had removed the corpses. And that was it. He could make out the remains of broken lamps, fragments of clothes, of useless things, as if the mine had turned into a rubbish dump.

Marcus hesitated. The Tectons were probably in the clearing. In order to attack them he would have to go inside the mine. While he was in there and as he climbed out of there – luckily the Tectons had left the ladder in place – he would be immensely vulnerable. The alternative was to look for some of the secondary offshoots that the Tectons had dug during their assault, which reached the surface in the area around the mine. That was how the Tectons had attacked them, from behind, and that would be a less risky manoeuvre.

But he soon he discovered that that possibility had its risks as well. On the way down to the mine an indeterminate number of small underground corridors came together. Each one of the holes in the mine walls was, in fact, a natural canal. The Tectons had done a lot of digging to find the paths that would take them to the surface, work that united those secondary tunnels to each other. At first Marcus opted for following one of the small tunnels, hoping to find one of the exits that would take him to the clearing unobserved. From there he could peek out and observe the scene before attacking. But he got lost. And he was losing hope. The outskirts of the mine were filled with tunnels that went up and down, that turned to the left and to the right. He didn't know if the underground labyrinth was leading him closer to the world or further from it. At one point he saw a small ray of light, in front of him, filtering through a stone pipe. Since that particular corridor headed upwards, Marcus thought that he would eventually emerge into the light of day. But he was wrong. He only managed to get to the mine through another tunnel.

Resigned, Marcus took a rest. He was watching the inside of the mine without thinking about anything in particular. Surprise: a bumblebee appeared who, bold or lost, had decided to investigate that uninhabited shaft. It was spinning around, then it got stirred up, and protested angrily with a buzz.

How lovely a bumblebee could be! Especially to someone who was returning from an underground experience that had taken him through extremes of pain and slavery. Marcus's heart beat as fast as a rabbit's. After sharing spaces with rocks and crustaceans that had been dead for millennia, that bumblebee brought him back in touch with the world.

He decided to take a risk. His body squeezed through the hole with short, decisive movements. And once he was in the mine, he went up the ladder as quickly and silently as he could.

When he got to the last few rungs he stuck his head out, up to the height of his eyes. At the southern end of the clearing, at the old camp, he saw a fire. One of the three Tectons, a very short individual, had the camp's enormous pot on the boil. He was stirring the contents with a large spatula. Tecton number two was a very fat creature who lay placidly on the grass, beside the same pot. He was looking at the clouds with his fingers intertwined over his round belly. The only visible activity from that individual was concentrated at his mouth, which chewed on a long piece of straw, like a cow. Where was the third Tecton? He was nowhere to be seen.

Marcus went closer. Out in the open, aiming at the two Tectons. He advanced step by step, without hiding himself. He was incredibly close to the two Tectons and they still hadn't seen him. The small one kept stirring the pot, engrossed in his task. The fat one daydreamed, watching the shapes of the clouds.

Both of Marcus's arms were rigid, a revolver in each hand. He was thirty paces from the pot. Twenty, ten. And the Tectons still didn't react. Not even in his wildest fantasies could he have foreseen something like that. He was convinced that as soon as he came out of the mine, they would attack him from three sides at once, that they would follow a perfectly coordinated military strategy. But no. A strange unease overtook Marcus. The Tecton cook was still focused on keeping the pot boiling; the other, spellbound by the clouds. In the end he was compelled to announce his presence. And the only thing he could think of was to say, 'Hello.'

The cook suffered a hand spasm. He dropped the spatula, his lower jaw opened as if it were thrown out of joint. He raised his arms in a sign of surrender. The other one acted with more composure. He sat up and, seeing the threat, slipped a discreet hands toward the club that hung from his belt. But Marcus aimed right at his face with one of the revolvers, as if to say, 'I wouldn't.'

The Tecton obeyed, against his will. And there was a strange pause. The one who's threatening always has to take the lead. But Marcus had no idea of how to proceed. He was incapable of killing them in cold blood. Time stood still. The Tecton cook's hands trembled. The fat one sensed Marcus's weakness, but wasn't able to act on it.

Marcus might not have shot, if it wasn't for the appearance, right at that moment, of the third. He was coming out of William's tent. It was the thin, tall officer that had captured him (that now seemed very, very long ago). Beneath his armour one could make out his long legs, with which he advanced decisively. He approached the pot, barking orders in a presumptuous and forceful tone, until he saw Marcus. He stopped shouting. He looked at Marcus with eyes closer to a rat's than to a cat's, small, black and hateful. When he had come out of the tent the Tecton had left the canvas door partly open. Through that crack Marcus could see Amgam inside, with her hands tied to one of the poles.

And now a short interlude to ask ourselves this question: were those three Tectons physically as Marcus described them to me? One as tall and thin as William? The other as fat and brawny as Richard? And the third, was he really a small cook who was subordinate to the other two? According to Marcus's words (my notes, very persistent in that aspect, didn't lie), that's exactly how they were. But I came to the conclusion that memory must be a very malleable thing, and that it had adapted itself around a core of truth: that Marcus Garvey's adventure was, in essence, a purifying epic journey, and that eliminating those three beings was the last step to becoming another man.

Seeing Amgam enraged Marcus. He aimed the two revolvers at the tall Tecton who, with impressively cold blood, shouted out an order. The other two jumped up. Marcus shot both of the revolvers into the chest of the leader. Even so, if the other two hadn't moved, perhaps nothing else would have happened. But movement incites shooters. The daydreamer attacked with his club, and the cook pulled the enormous spatula out of the pot to use it as a weapon.

Marcus shot wildly at the three bodies. At that distance it was impossible for him to miss. The Tectons fell, wounded, but they got back up and tried to attack again. Marcus shot and shot, until the revolvers just went *click*, *click*, *click*, and it wasn't until many clicks later that he realised that the three Tectons were dead.

It was all over. But he wasn't flooded with happiness. Quite the opposite. He sensed a vague fear, an uneasiness that moved within him like fog over a burnt forest. The leader had fallen dead with his face to the ground, as if he had wanted to go back to his world before dying. The cook looked like a dog run over by a car. And the fat one had fallen into the pot. Half of his body was inside, with his feet hanging out.

Marcus let his weapons fall. He couldn't take his eyes off the smoking barrels until he heard Amgam's voice. He ran to the tent, knelt down and freed her. Still on his knees, Marcus began to cry. It was more of a haemorrhaging of tears than a real cry.

I would have liked to be there to see that moment. Without envy, just for the pleasure of witnessing a joyous moment, a joyous moment *par excellence*. Amgam was still dressed in William's clothes, looking at him without quite believing it was him, that he had come back. Marcus was dressed in the filthy Tecton armour, covering his face with his hands to hide his tears. She moved closer to him, extended her hand and touched his cheek with one finger. He looked up, wiped his damp eyes with his dirty hands, looked at the clearing, looked at the dead bodies, looked at the mine, and when he looked at her it was as if he were awakening from a long nightmare, the longest of nightmares. You are you, and I am here, they said to each other, and it's all over.

There was no passionate kiss. Instead they embraced like two lost children that have found each other again. Marcus took off the tunic and the pyjama. She saw all his wounds and she also undressed, tearing away William's clothes.

Here Marcus had a wild impulse. Maybe he believed that the world owed him something, after having overcome such pain. And, carrying out poetic justice in the name of all the slaves in the world, he seized one of those odious bottles of champagne. One of the big bottles, five gallons of hot French champagne. Then she grabbed him by the hand and they ran. They reached the edge of the clearing and they kept running, into the jungle. Where was Amgam taking him? Nowhere. They were just running from the clearing with their fingers intertwined. The branches slashed their faces and bodies, but the pain didn't hurt them. Marcus even liked it. It was a sharp pain, not a pain that repressed life, a very different pain from the one he had experienced underground.

It's impossible to know how long they ran through the jungle. Finally Marcus stumbled on a wall of grass that blocked their way and he let himself fall. They rested right there, stretched out on the carpet of grass. They panted and laughed at the same time. They were in some remote, humid part of the jungle. The ceiling of green protected them from the tropical strength of the sun. After a little while Marcus realised that they had ended up in a very strange place.

The wall of grass that had stopped them was much more dense than it appeared. With both hands he removed the first layer of vegetation. He soon discovered that all that green was just a curtain. Behind it hid a wall of wood. He realised that the wall was the base of a tree, an immense tree. He tried to go around the perimeter, but he couldn't. Branches, thorns and thickets kept him from penetrating. The jungle, jealous, wanted to be the only one to shelter the feet of the giant in its arms. But more than actually seeing, he could sense that the wall of wood went on and on, and he couldn't even make out where its contours ended. If the tree's base was so vast, how high must it be? Marcus realised that he had stumbled upon a wonder of nature.

He began his ascent. Amgam didn't understand.

'Come on!' said Marcus, gesturing to her with his hand.

And she followed him. At first Marcus set the pace, clearing the way through the lattice of tropical creepers that, like them, climbed up the trunk. But Amgam soon overtook him. Cave dwelling and climbing must be similar arts. Perhaps it was that for that woman, who had gone beyond the heavens of the Tecton world, the top of a tree, no matter how big it was, was just a small step. Or perhaps it was, simply, that Amgam wasn't meant to have anyone setting the pace for her. Amgam's twelve fingers clung to the bark better than any ape's could, and, what's more, she had a special talent for finding places to shore herself up.

'Wait!' shouted Marcus, who was getting left behind.

And since she didn't pay him any attention he had to shout even louder.

'Wait!'

Amgam turned her head. Marcus raised the hand that held the bottle of champagne to make her understand that he was having trouble climbing with just one hand. She clicked her tongue, as if to say, 'Oh, that's it!' She came back, took the bottle from him and began climbing as fast, if not faster than before. She looked like a white spider.

The first part of the trajectory was relatively easy due to the vegetation that clung to the bark. An amalgam of tropical creepers, climbing plants and branches of nearby trees. Like the hands of a thousand religious faithfuls content to gaze toward the feet of their idol. But when they had gone beyond the jungle's ceiling of vegetation the ascent became more difficult. The trunk was solid, smooth, and very upright, rising with a pride more appropriate to a Babylonian tower than to a work of nature. Now they began to appreciate the size of the creature they had taken on. The exact dimensions? When I asked Marcus to compare it to Big Ben, he almost died laughing.

They stopped at the first branch. It was an enormous lateral projection, as firm as a ship's figurehead. Amgam was saying things. She expressed herself with joyful enthusiasm, speaking faster and more excitedly than ever. Most likely she had just grasped that the tree wasn't a mountain of dead wood, that it was a living being filled with living beings. Marcus had never seen Amgam's feline eyes so wide. But physically he was beaten. The underground adventures had consumed all his reserves. The momentum of willpower that had forced him through all the pain, all the endurance tests, had finally run out. His legs were shaking violently. She held him and whispered sweet nothings in her Tecton language. But Marcus freed himself from her embrace as if it were an insult.

'No, no,' he insisted. 'Higher, higher.'

And, so, the two naked bodies continued climbing the tree. He with every muscle in his arms and legs complaining with each movement he made, and she carrying the bottle of champagne. (It was useless for me to ask why they carried that damn bottle. They didn't know why they were carrying it just as they didn't know why they were climbing that tree.) Amgam knew how to find the smallest openings in the trunk. Frequently, she stopped to help Marcus with one hand, grabbing him under the arms. How many feet must they have climbed? Three hundred? Six hundred? Finally they arrived at the top, a small comfortable landing, a soft moss-covered hollow in the wood. Above them there was only a thin parasol of leaves. When Marcus had regained his breath he said only one word.

'Look.'

Tree, trees, and trees. Amgam inhaled. She filled her lungs with such force that Marcus got scared. All the oxygen in the Congo entered that body, which was created to breathe a very different type of air.

She said something.

'Yes, I know,' confirmed Marcus. 'No Pepe, no champagne. Congo.'

Marcus had already seen that immense jungle from a similar vantage point, on the expedition there. And he hadn't found it appealing at all. Quite the opposite. What was the difference? Marcus saw that Amgam moved her eyes upwards, fixing them on the tropical sun. He wanted to put a hand in front of her face to make her understand that the sun could hurt her. But at that moment he remembered the feline nature of Amgam's eyes. In the darkness her pupils dilated as wide as they could, filling her entire eye like an eclipsed sun, and now they shrank until they became a single vertical line.

Once again: what was it that made the Congo such a wonderful place? Marcus realised that the difference wasn't in the landscape, but rather in him. The beauty of the landscape, now, came from the fact that he was no longer the same.

Later, they lay on that wooden bed with its moss mattress. For a few seconds Marcus held up the bottle of champagne, looking at it fixedly, incredulous. He no longer remembered why he had brought it with him.

In the book I wrote that Marcus had offered the bottle to Amgam. Her curiosity aroused, she had taken the bottle, until she heard Marcus say 'champagne'. At that moment she had hurled it from the tree, angered by all the horrors that the word had conjured up. That's how I wrote the original version. But I admit that Marcus's account was quite different. In that particular passage I let myself get carried away, as much by hyperbole as by my passion for Amgam. Much later I realised the discord between the text and what I had written down at the prison. In order to free myself from my feelings and from the book, I decided to reproduce Marcus's exact words. So, in the third edition, I wanted to fix the paragraph. But the editor told me not to touch it, that turning Amgam into a champagne guzzler wasn't going to make the book any better. That was in the 1920s, in the midst of Prohibition, and the London publishing house had strong commercial ties with the United States, where they hoped to sell many copies. Later, in the fifth edition, I insisted on revising the error. But I had sold the rights to the book to another publishing house, which also begged me not to alter the passage. The new editor was a big advocate of symbolic literature and he alleged that we had to keep Amgam's gesture: the heroine rebelling against humans and Tectons, against corrupt civilisation as represented by a bottle of champagne. I settled. In the 1960s a new publisher rescued the book from the oblivion into which it had almost completely fallen. He also asked me not to touch that paragraph about the champagne. Environmentalism was in style, and Amgam's rejection of such a decadent drink as champagne was a representation of the couple's integration into a natural environment and blah, blah, blah. In the last edition that was published, finally, the editor was a woman. Her opinion was that a liberated woman had to break the champagne bottle into a million pieces, since in the narrative structure the word 'champagne' had become synonymous with the patriarchal order. In short, in sixty years I have been unable to change that fragment to match the notes dictated by Marcus Garvey. Now, finally, I will.

Marcus's version, Marcus Garvey's bloody version, was that the couple got drunk on the five-gallon bottle of champagne. That is what Garvey originally told me, damn it. And that's all.

TWENTY-FOUR

DO I HAVE TO say that I was the one who climbed to the top of that tree? At that point in the history I completely identified with Marcus Garvey.

Not even the best writer in the world could describe the force that united Marcus and Amgam. To say that they were happy would be stating the obvious. It would be like a naturalist informing us that butterflies and beetles are insects. Fabulous. But we'd continue to ignore the most marvellous secret in nature: the impulse that could turn a butterfly and a beetle into lovers.

Since I knew I was incapable of portraying Marcus and Amgam's inner life, in the book I decided to limit myself to recounting what they lived through up on the landing of that tree. Obviously, the moral censorship of the period only allowed me monstrous ellipses. Because, what is it that Amgam and Marcus were doing at the top of that tree? Making love, all day long, without pausing or resting. Now, six decades later, I find myself with an almost opposite problem: describing sexual acrobatics doesn't add any literary value and from my point of view literature has already covered, some time ago, the entire range of human emotions. Which is to say, that whatever I write I won't be original, so I'll just sum it up in three words and to hell with it: they were fucking.

Put two naked bodies up at the top of a tree, let them love each other, let them do things. While Marcus hugged her it seemed like Amgam had no bones, she was inhumanly lissom. And, yet, when that same body passed a certain limit of pleasure, it exploded like a wooden board breaking. In the surrounding trees, far below them, there was a horde of monkeys. The couple's moans excited them, or angered them, or both things at once, as happens with flocks of puritanical old ladies, and they replied with shrill squawks in a thousand different tones.

Even the rain adapted itself to the two lovers. If it rained while they were making love, the rain excited them even more. If it rained after they made love, the water washed them clean. Some drops had a prodigious size and density, and as they fell onto their bodies they were like thick lips sucking at their skin. When they were worn out they slept clutching each other, his chest against her back, or the other way around, joined together like two matching spoons.

The storms in Africa make the lightning in Europe seem like flickering, effeminate match flames. In the Congo not even the most timid bolts of lightning can be ignored. The emphatic outbursts demand your attention, be it day or night, eyes open or closed. When lightning struck and they had their eyes open, night became day. When they had them closed, behind their lids the blackness was assaulted by a yellow brightness, and that light reminded them that just closing your eyes wasn't enough to erase the world. They didn't sleep, in fact; a tenuous veil separated day from night. In the Congo Marcus learned a lesson that civilised life refuses to accept: that between sleep and wakefulness there isn't a clear border. If sleep were the sea and wakefulness terra firma, they lived on the beach. That, and the diet of fruits from the tree, altered their senses. Especially his. Sometimes it seemed that if he touched Amgam with one finger he would make her burst like a soap bubble. Other times, she was the only reality in the world, more tangible than the Congo, closer to him than his own body.

While he was up in the tree Marcus only managed to come up with one thought, just one: that all his life had had one purpose, one and only one: to get to the top of that tree, with her.

Either the world is imperfect or perfection is finite, because one day Marcus decided to destroy that paradise, by climbing down from the tree. Amgam didn't oppose him. She knew before Marcus what Marcus knew.

Can a single man save the world? I think, more likely, that it is the world that decides to save itself through a man. Until that moment the Tectons had only had fragmentary news from the surface. The Tecton command must have been awaiting the return of the military expedition. If they didn't return, sooner or later they would send another one. Between the humans' world and the Tectons' there was still an open channel. And Marcus was the only one that knew what that meant. Could he stay up there atop that tree forever while the Tecton army was preparing to invade the world? Marcus had seen the Tecton metropolis, more extensive and powerful than a thousand Londons. First they would take the Congo. And then? Where would their ambition stop? At the Great Wall of China? The Suez Canal, or the Panama Canal? Maybe the English Channel? No. The Tectons were like termites. Technologically, in some aspects perhaps they were behind them. But in others, certainly, they were more advanced. The Tectons had reached the Congo and humans didn't even suspect their existence. They would soon learn to copy humanity's most destructive instruments and would likely improve on them. How many soldiers could inundate the surface? A million? Ten million? One hundred million? Marcus had endured the Tecton regime. He didn't want to imagine what applying it on a universal scale would mean.

The idea had been formulating in Marcus's mind at the furthest margins, without him realising. Of the route he had travelled with William he especially remembered the Sea of Young Ladies, that immense expanse filled with stone columns. 'Look, the pillars of the Earth,' William had remarked.

If someone could blow up those columns the inner ceiling would collapse. The Sea of Young Ladies extended halfway between the two worlds, you couldn't get from one to the other without passing through it. And if the Tectons weren't discouraged by that unexpected obstacle, if they decided to excavate it stone by stone, it would take them a thousand years to get to the surface.

After their descent from the tree Marcus headed towards the clearing with Amgam. They began a march as resigned as it was determined. The jungle had never seen any living being face his destiny with so much energy and decisiveness. And his courage had better not abandon him, because the future of the world was in the hands of a short-legged, naked little gypsy. The days he had spent living up in the tree had regenerated his body to a miraculous degree. An invisible suture had closed all his wounds, which now seemed very old. The diet of rainwater, fruit and sex had slimmed him down. And it was as if that period filled with pleasure had sucked all the impurities out of his body.

The clearing was empty, exactly as they had left it. More desolate, perhaps. A languid tropical sadness floated in the air. The scattered remains made it look like a beach after a shipwreck. There was only one tent standing, but many of the pegs had loosened and the wind made the canvas tremble. The big pot where Marcus used to cook was knocked over like a defeated king in a game of chess. From inside it emerged a small anteater, hairy and tough, that ran away, shrieking indignantly, when it saw them. The dead Tectons were less than carrion. Besides that, the jungle had preferred to remain at the margins of that clearing, ignoring it. It seemed that all the trees had turned their backs on the mine.

Amgam got to work. From the remains of the Tectons' equipment she selected carefully the most useful pieces for the journey that lay ahead. Particularly a couple of very long sailors' haversacks. Once full they resembled sausages, which allowed them to be carried through even the narrowest corridors. Amgam made clear that they should be tied to one's ankles, so they could be dragged behind them. Marcus also packed dynamite, a lot of dynamite, as many sticks as they could find. Then they helped each other buckle up the clasps of the Tecton armour.

But when they were just about to go down into the mine, they were stopped by an authoritative voice: 'You see, Marcus? You see how we're all the same?'

It was William, of course. He was wearing Tecton armour and brandishing his Winchester. It didn't take Marcus long to reconstruct the events. William must have hidden shortly after abandoning Marcus to fight the four Tectons. He must have hidden himself in some corner, a bit further on, and realised that Marcus was returning to the surface. A Marcus that had won, that was armed and wore Tecton armour. In those conditions William must have decided not to attack him, and not to reveal himself. Returning to the lookout point where the battle had taken place, William would have gathered what provisions remained. He then followed Marcus at a safe distance, aware that there were still three Tectons alive in the camp and he was unarmed. When William finally decided to surface he found two very pleasant surprises: that Marcus had killed the Tectons and that the little packets of gold that he had buried under the tent were intact. For someone like William Craver that was incomprehensible. Why hadn't Marcus taken the gold, the poor devil? In any case, if Marcus were alive, surely sooner or later he'd come back to the camp to look for the gold. So he waited, and now Marcus's presence confirmed the criteria with which William judged the human soul.

Marcus quickly grasped William's reasoning and said, 'I'm not looking for the gold.' But he soon gave up. 'No, of course you can't understand what I'm doing here. You would never understand it.'

And he did the only thing that William wasn't expecting him to do: ignore him. He continued to pack the dynamite sticks as if William wasn't there. William triggered the Winchester's magazine with an abrupt noise, his way of attracting Marcus's attention.

'You're the one who doesn't understand. You don't understand that the only life you have left is the time my finger grants you,' he said.

In that moment Amgam said something. They couldn't understand her, but she seemed distressed. Any other person in Amgam's situation would have been rabid, indignant or frightened. She was just sad. No, it was more than that, it was as if Amgam's body was the vessel that all the sadness in the world had been emptied into. She took steps towards the two men. Her sadness was like a threat. Marcus realised that William's expression had changed. He didn't know who to aim at and even he looked inhibited. Marcus stood up.

'You haven't touched her, have you?' Marcus asked. 'That's what it is.'

Marcus and William were like a pair of duellists. They stood thirty feet apart. William was armed with a Winchester, Marcus with a truth revealed.

'All those nights with her, in your tent, you couldn't touch her,' he said. 'Not even *you* were able, you didn't dare. And all these days, here, hidden with a rifle in your hands . . . Be honest, you weren't waiting for me. You were waiting for her.'

Marcus looked at his rival as if he were a book, a book written in such tiny print that it was impossible to read.

'You love her?' he continued. 'No, I don't think so. You aren't capable of loving anyone. And yet you wanted her to love you. That's why you didn't kill me like a dog. You wanted it to be the Tectons, you wanted it to be them that eliminated me, so that she wouldn't accuse you of having killed me. But if that's the case, William Craver, what good does that rifle do you?' Marcus opened his arms. 'Will she love you more, when you've killed me? Do you think she doesn't know what you're like?'

Furious, William raised his rifle, ready to beat Marcus with it. But she didn't let him. Amgam held William by the wrists. She hung on to him with unshakable fingers and a disgusted expression. Everything happened quickly, so quickly that William didn't even have time to protest. Amgam made a sudden gesture with both hands. Through the clearing a sound like almonds cracking resounded: it was the bones in William's wrists, suddenly fracturing. William shrieked, more appalled than in pain. The rifle fell to the ground and he looked stupidly at his broken hands, which hung like those of a puppet. Amgam looked pensive; she hadn't wanted to hurt him, just prevent him hurting Marcus.

A concert of insects invaded the air of the clearing. Those happy songs couldn't have jarred more with William's stance.

'Now you can't use this,' said Marcus, putting the Winchester's strap over his shoulder. 'I may as well take it along with me, so you don't hurt yourself.'

Amgam went into the mine and Marcus followed her. With his body still visible above the ladder, he said farewell with the following words:

'You are a unique creature, William Craver. They should put you in some museum. Your existence proves the extent of inhumanity people can reach if they put their mind to it. That's why saving the world is worth it. Because the rest of the human race could have been like you, but they chose not to be.'

Marcus didn't want to tell me much about that second expedition to the depths of the Earth. The first days they advanced very quickly. Unlike before, Marcus wasn't exhausted and beaten and in pain, and Amgam was a master at moving underground. I said that Marcus didn't tell me much about that trip, but there was one scene that stayed etched in my mind.

They tumbled out into that small air bubble that was shaped like a stone intestine and which marked an obligatory stop in the route towards the underworld. What moved me was the image of Amgam and Marcus holding each other in that inhospitable space, without making a sound, together for the penultimate time. The two of them and nothing more, surrounded by all the stones in the world and the green half-light of a worm lantern. They were aware that soon they would have to say goodbye forever. Without them having to say so, they sensed it, knowing that once they had lit the fuse each of them would venture towards their own world. And, even still, they had made up their minds to save millions and millions of people they had never met in exchange for nothing. I couldn't imagine two more solitary lovers. All they had in that world was the will to save it and a handful of phosphorescent worms.

After some days walking they reached the Sea of Young Ladies. Soon everything was set. The dynamite was in place, carefully attached to the hourglass columns. Marcus slowed the preparations, aware that when the work was finished it would be time to say farewell. Amgam was the one who put the box of matches in his hands: he might never have made up his mind to do it. They had to go in opposite directions. Marcus came from one world and Amgam from another. Marcus could never live in hers, and it was impossible to imagine that she could have a remotely normal life in England. She'd be lucky if she ended up in a zoo. After meeting the Craver brothers, she knew that. What other options did they have? Live in the jungle like primordial man? No. With Pepe dead, without anyone to intercede on their behalf with the African population, Marcus didn't dare to risk Amgam's life. One can make love anywhere, even in a tree. But only monkeys live up in the trees.

Marcus lowered his head, shook those wooden matches that were as long as fingers and only said, 'Go, go, go.' He couldn't look her in the face. She didn't go. Marcus realised that Amgam was crying. A tear fell from each of her eyes, just one. A dense liquid turned slightly green by the lantern. The two tears slid down those long cheeks slowly. Amgam wanted to cut the agony short. She kissed her lover's lips and forehead, and when he moved to kiss her back he could only kiss the air. Amgam was already far away. She had fled into the darkness, back to the Tecton world. On the ground were the two tears, which had turned into diamonds the size of footballs. Marcus placed them in one of his deep pockets.

He waited another forty-eight hours before lighting the fuse. He had no idea of the magnitude of the destruction that he was about to cause, and he wanted to make sure that she had enough time to get far away.

At this point we could reflect on the philosophical meaning of that fuse. Lighting it meant separating two worlds forevermore, the two worlds that shared intelligent life on planet Earth. Did Marcus and Amgam do the right thing by blowing up the only bridge that connected them? I only can offer one response: that we will never know to what extent it was the right decision, but that it was unquestionable that they were the two beings best suited to make it, because no one knew the two worlds as well as they did and, above all, no one stood to lose as much as they did.

So two days later Marcus lit the long fuse and ran in the opposite direction of the flame. A few agonising seconds passed. Marcus ran, and behind him he soon heard some *pop*, *pop*, *pop*s, more languid than violent. Every *pop* was a column blowing up. The explosions echoed with a muffled sound, as if the dynamite didn't have the courage to detonate in such a spectral place. How many explosions had he heard? One hundred? Two hundred? Marcus ran and ran until he had to stop, gasping for breath.

After climbing through the canyon's passageway for an hour or two, he sat down, his tunic soaked with sweat. As light as it was, the stone armour was weighing him down. He could go no further.

He raised the lantern above his head, trusting that the elevation he had gained would allow him to see the destruction down below, in the Sea of Young Ladies. But what he saw froze his blood.

Yes, there was a vast area where many stone columns had been destroyed. He could tell by the immense carpet of red sparks and scorched rocks that were being consumed like coal. But it didn't look like the dynamite had achieved its goal: destroying the base so that the ceiling would collapse. If big boulders had fallen from that far up he would have heard them.

Marcus was devastated. He continued along the passageway whining like a puppy and fiercely biting his fist. According to William it was porous terrain, and he had referred to the columns as 'the pillars of the Earth'. But he was wrong. The columns must have been gigantic stalactites and stalagmites whose ends touched. They weren't the supports of that inner ceiling, just a simple product of the depths.

Had it all been a waste of time? The Marcus that had first set foot in the Congo had nothing in common with the one that had tried to save humanity. But what good had it done the world to save Marcus if the world didn't let Marcus save mankind?

He continued going up, listlessly. He lost all sense of time. Maybe he was already near the entrance to the cave. Maybe not. He didn't care. He lay down with the green lantern by his side, curled up like a dog and fell asleep. He dreamt that it was raining. In that dream Marcus was sleeping in some corner of the jungle until a clap of thunder woke him up. First it was a soft clap and then one a bit harder. But he wasn't in the jungle, he was still in one of the steps of the passageway. He heard another thunderclap, and he asked himself, 'Am I still dreaming?'

He was awake. And it wasn't exactly a thunderclap. It was a noise like paper being torn. A sheet of paper as large as the sky. He realised that up above, far above, the ceiling was cracking. He could hear stones crashing, all the stones in the world.

Run, Marcus Garvey, run! And, indeed, he now ran for his life. But he ran laughing, because only a little while earlier his life had been useless, and now even his death could not cancel out his victory.

It began to rain sand and rocks. At first they were just small rocks. Soon he was bombarded by increasingly large meteorites. Most of them he couldn't see. He could only hear them, falling very close to him, ringing against the ground and exploding like shrapnel. Some fell so close that his lantern illuminated them, as if they were green shooting stars.

The earth was crashing down onto his head. If he didn't manage to get into the cave ahead he would be crushed. He finally slid through the narrow opening that he and Amgam had left between the millstone and the wall of the cave.

He got there just in time, because immediately afterwards the world began to shake. Some people have been in the eye of a hurricane. Marcus could claim the bizarre honour of having been beneath an earthquake. Imagine a man that raises a box of matches to his ear and shakes it to see if any are left inside: Marcus was the match. As everything was shaking and jerking, deafened by a thousand drums beating at once, he was still heaving the millstone back into place. It had to fit perfectly into the cave's entrance. It was the only way he could block the tunnel from that solid flood. But he couldn't do it. The stone was too heavy. Amgam's more muscular arms had had no problem rolling it, but, by himself, he couldn't make it budge.

An ocean of grey ash and pulverised rock, a dense, dark wave, was coming up the passageway with terrifying speed. He had to move the stone or he would die. It was that simple.

And that puny, little, short-legged man did it. He fell back, exhausted. His arms felt as if they had been stretched on some medieval torture rack. Behind the stone floodgate he could hear the roar of the storm. He dipped his hand into a pocket and pulled out the two crystallised tears. He laughed. It was the most tortuous laugh in the world. He wasn't thinking about having saved mankind, he was only thinking about her. He was the happiest man in the world for having had her. And he was the unhappiest man in two worlds for having lost her.

We could say that Marcus Garvey's adventure in the Congo ended right there and that what happened after was just one long stroll leading him directly to prison.

Once he got to the surface he equipped himself as well as he could, with European clothing, his stableboy's hat and a Tecton haversack, and he set off through the jungle. In the end, the path that he took through the vegetation wasn't really that different from the underground tunnel. It rarely forked, so it was hard to get lost. He reached the clearing dominated by that large tree, the same one he had climbed up alone to look out over the vastness of the Congo.

William was there. He was hanging upside down from one of the lowest branches. The natives had left him that way to prolong his agony, with his head a few feet above the ground. William must have spent the last hours of his life twisting like a worm to protect himself from the scavengers' leaps. Marcus approached the naked body. The chest, arms and head were gnawed. Marcus wondered what kind of creatures had done that. It looked like they hadn't been large enough, or strong enough, to pull the body off the rope since they had only devoured the parts in their reach. Through the fleshless ribcage, he could see the other side as if he were looking through a window. From the elbows down, the arms had no skin or muscles, just bones. Both hands were missing. The savages had removed the upper part of his skull as if it were the lid on a small cooking pan. Marcus knelt to have a look. Animals had polished off the brain, every last morsel, but had left the shell. Marcus didn't have it in him to take the body down, and he left silently.

So that had been William Craver's end. A senseless ending? It depends. We might speculate that William's death indirectly saved Marcus's life: that William's murder served to mollify the local tribes' desire for revenge, thus allowing Marcus to cross that immense region safely.

Eventually, Marcus came upon a wood cabin beside a wide river. Scattered on the narrow pier lay dozens of Negroes. They must have been waiting for the arrival of a boat to load it with the rubber that was piled up on the bank.

The last thing they were expecting was a white man to come up from behind, from the forest. They saw him and all jumped up in surprise at the same time. One ran into the cabin to let someone know. A tall sweaty Belgian with red skin came out of the cabin armed with a shotgun.

'*Mon Dieu! C'est pas possible!*' shouted the Belgian, lowering his weapon. 'Where have you come from? I thought there was not a white man for five hundred miles!'

He invited Marcus into the cabin, and offered him a beer that he took out from the bottom of a box that no one had touched in quite some time. It was a dirty bottle, covered with dust and cobwebs. But it was a Belgian beer, it was civilisation, and before the first sip could reach his throat, Marcus was already back in Europe.

'And this is where it all ends?' I said.

'Yes,' said Marcus. 'This is where it all ends. Later, once I was in London, they accused me of killing the Cravers and stealing the diamonds.' He made a gesture that brought his shoulders closer to his ears. 'How could I explain that the diamonds were two tears from a Tecton woman?'

That time Marcus didn't look around agitatedly. His eyes were fixed on some distant point, a spot that the walls of the prison could never block. I didn't dare say anything more.

There are silences that announce to us that a terrible event is now history. The entire prison fell silent – the inmates must have been transferred elsewhere; perhaps it was meal time or exercise time. But I wanted to believe that the prison, the prison itself, was listening to us, that the end of the story forced it to hold its breath.

'Time's up!' said Sergeant Long Back, opening the iron door with a loud screech.

TWENTY-FIVE

THE YEARS FOLLOWING MY return from the front had little substance. I was writing and visiting Garvey, as much to polish the book as to boost his morale. The MacMahons' friendship and indulgence were endless. They asked nothing of me, and if I helped them with small tasks it was of my own volition. I didn't have to worry about money. I wrote and wrote, and my existence was as monotonous as a monk's, so there's not much to tell about that period. That the war with Marie Antoinette continued, perhaps.

I discovered that she liked to sniff shoe polish. If someone left a jar open she would spend hours with her beak inside it. The smell made her somewhat intoxicated, I think, because afterwards she moved in S shapes. I kindly offered to polish all the shoes in the house. My intention, it goes without saying, was not honourable. I sat on a stool surrounded by shoes and with a large jar of black polish open wide and in plain view.

I could see her peeking out from behind the door, observing me, her worst enemy, consumed by her vice. Finally the little beast could take it no longer and she approached, trusting that the task of shining shoes would absorb my attention.

As if it needs saying, that was exactly what I had been waiting for. I attacked her just as she plunged her beak into the polish. A good scrape of the brush along her bare back and Marie Antoinette turned into a Zulu turtle, blacker than coal. She fled with angry leaps.

Of course, in this campaign of guile and strategy, Marie Antoinette always counter-attacked. She decided to pee on my bed. For those who don't know, I should say that the stench emitted by turtle urine is only comparable to an omelette of rotten eggs sautéed with sea debris. When I least expected it I opened the door to my room and found the miniature deviant lying flat on the mattress, little tail erect and a stream of piss coming out from under her. I had taken a hundred precautions, locks and bolts included. All useless. Sooner or later Marie Antoinette took advantage of some distraction and managed to infiltrate, piss and run. If that sounds funny, I can only wish that one evening, after a long day of work, you get in bed and find your pillow sprayed with turtle urine. In short, once again the war against Marie Antoinette had arrived at a stalemate.

The only relevant aspect of that period was my relationship with Mr Modepà. It turned out that I knew more French than anyone else at the boarding house, so I became the official interpreter. From the very beginning, though, I kept our conversations to practical concerns. I told him the gardening tasks he had to perform and that was it. I didn't like him, no matter what Mr

MacMahon said. He was an efficient gardener, and a perfect toy for MacMahon's children, who adored him. He even got along with Marie Antoinette, but there were a few things about him that bothered me. For example, with the MacMahons and me he maintained an unnecessarily disciplined attitude. At first MacMahon tried to get him to relax the formalities. It was hopeless. His Irish cordiality came up against rigid habits that were too entrenched. Modepà was more like a sergeant than a simple colonial soldier. We all became resigned to it. After all, if someone is happier following orders than making friends, that's up to him. But, something inside me told me that I shouldn't trust him. One day in the garden, I confronted him.

'You must have noticed,' I began, 'that Mr and Mrs MacMahon are much fonder of you and more generous with you than I am.'

He didn't say anything. I continued.

'You're hiding out, aren't you? Who are you hiding from?'

'I'm not hiding,' was his response. 'I'm just waiting.'

'For what?'

'I am not authorised to talk about it.'

'You're waiting for the end of the war, aren't you? Well, you should know that war crimes have no statute of limitations,' I lied, to frighten him. And I shouted in my most melodramatic French, '*Jamais!*'

But my speech didn't affect him in the slightest, and he shut down like a deaf crab.

'Are you wanted?' I insisted. 'By whom? God or man?'

'No,' was his reply, as indignant as it was laconic. But all of a sudden, he corrected himself. 'Yes.'

'Explain yourself.'

'I can't.'

'You won't!' I accused him. And in the face of the silence that followed, I assured him, 'You should know that I don't believe a word you say.'

Subsequently, on a few occasions, I raised the topic again, or better put, the interrogation, and I always came up against that circumspect tone. From my point of view people who speak in spirals are either conmen or impostors. Most likely, Modepà was both. I was keeping a close eye on him.

As for the book, at the end of 1917 the second version was practically ready. Before writing the last chapter, though, I decided to subject the entire text to a careful, measured, critical reading. My conclusion? The book was worthless.

That same evening we had dinner in high spirits. There was no special reason for it. Life was good. The MacMahons were happy. And they had a gang of children. Why shouldn't we celebrate it? After dinner we shared a drink while MacMahon and Modepà competed at singing. (MacMahon sang Irish songs because that was what he wanted to sing, and Modepà sang African songs because MacMahon had ordered him to.) Mrs MacMahon stood by, lavishing attention on them. Every time she brought something to the table her husband gave her a 'thank you, my love' and ate her up with his eyes.

I still couldn't get over seeing them married. And watching them, witnessing that tranquil oasis they had created, I could only applaud them.

As I stood by the stove, MacMahon noticed that I was using a lot of paper to light it. He asked me what I was doing.

'Oh, nothing. I'm just burning something.'

That 'nothing' was an entire year's work. The failed second version of the book. But I did the right thing. I was no longer sorry about destroying what had to be destroyed. And now I was driven by fanatical willpower. I could have rewritten the book a thousand times, one after the other, without pausing or resting. I knew Marcus Garvey's story so well that I was guided by a sleepwalker's certainty. I could never hold Amgam in my arms. But I could write about how Marcus held her in his.

In the end, the question is how did I finally, almost a year later, finish the third and definitive version of the story of Amgam and Marcus Garvey.

I became very sentimental. And what was it exactly about that book that made me so emotional? It's beauty? No. Beauty is fickle: this book I am writing now is the same story that I wrote sixty years ago, and they couldn't be more different. Was it the truth? No, not that either. From the day I had jotted down the first note on Marcus's story in the Congo up until the day I sat looking at an enormous pack of bound pages, I had listened to millions of his words. We had gone over every scene until we were worn out. And in each version Marcus added or suppressed some detail. How could I know which of the versions was closest to the real truth of everything that had happened in the Congo? Marcus's memory wasn't infallible. It was a memory like any other, that modified the contours of the facts as time passed. My notes often contradicted themselves, and when I asked him to clarify he only added to the confusion. I couldn't criticise him. The same thing happened to me, because the book was now part of my memory and, as a result, I added and took things out with the same bastardising mechanisms. Besides the three definitive versions, I had rewritten each page dozens of times. If we were to compare the first page I wrote on an episode with the final, definitive one, I'm quite sure we'd find as many variations there as in Marcus's oral accounts. It wasn't out of a deliberate desire to alter the original. It was, simply, that the style became the interpreter of the contents.

What I was interested in assessing was not so much what Marcus had explained to me as what he had wanted to explain to me. The book elevated flesh and blood people to the category of literary characters. It was irrelevant whether they had said a specific phrase or not. Whether they had shot one bullet more or less. What mattered wasn't what the characters in that story did, but rather what history did with those characters. The trial could go badly and they could hang Garvey, or maybe a bomb from a zeppelin could turn Norton and me into ash. But while there were still readers, Amgam and Marcus would continue making love up there in that tree. All I could do was explain it, and that was exactly what I had done. The only thing I regret is that it was someone else's story. That I had had to turn myself into a parasite of someone else's experiences to write a good story. Still, nothing's perfect.

I wanted to have a smoke, but I had run out of cigarettes. I left my room. Mr MacMahon was still playing with three of his children, on top of and below an armchair in the dining room. I asked him to lend me a few shillings and I went out to buy some tobacco. It was night; it had rained. The streets were empty and they smelled of fresh stone. All the places where you could buy cigarettes were closed. Fortunately, I stumbled upon one of the children that sell them on the streets. He had fallen asleep on a corner with the box of cigarettes as a pillow. It gave him a good scare when I woke him up. I went back home, smoking. The street was incredibly silent. It was very pleasant filling my lungs with that mix of damp air and tobacco smoke. I felt empty and clean like a soap bubble.

What does it matter that I went out to buy tobacco that evening? I don't really know. But after so much time my memory floats like the ghost of a jellyfish and goes back to that sleeping boy. It's strange, I often wonder what must have become of him. Memory is a perpetually pregnant woman: it always has cravings. Or maybe not. Maybe it's that I've spent the last sixty years like that little boy. Sleeping on the corner of life, dreaming. That's why I think about that little boy so much.

Once I was back in my room I lit another cigarette. I wanted to stretch out on the bed. And who did I find? Marie Antoinette, of course, on top of the pillow and poised to urinate. I rolled up a newspaper into a paper truncheon. This time I had decided to make mashed turtle out of her.

As she ran away she jumped from the bed to my desk, and once there she began to walk on my typewriter. A fatal course: between the keys there was enough space to trap her. I raised the rolled newspaper, preparing to beat her cruelly, when I realised that there was a sheet of paper in the typewriter. By some bloody coincidence Marie Antoinette's little feet had written: VVvveryy well. I looked at poor Marie Antoinette, stuck in the keyboard, with more compassion. It was surprising, but I couldn't even remember how our battle had begun. Who knows? Maybe all that time we had just wanted to assert ourselves against the world, she as a turtle and me as a writer.

Marie Antoinette had written, 'Very well'. And she was right. What did it matter that my story was someone else's? Surely it was of as little importance as the fact that Marie Antoinette's shell was man-made. That didn't make me less of a writer, just as that wooden shell didn't make her less of a turtle.

Instead of tanning her with the newspaper, what I did was take her to the kitchen so we could share a moment. Whisky for me and shoe polish for her.

(You might be wondering what became of Marie Antoinette. That question is very easy to answer: she lives with me. I have shared my house with her since 1955, when Mrs MacMahon left her to me in her will. According to the vet she belongs to a race of turtles that can live up to three hundred years old, so when I'm dead she will have outlived all the characters in this story.)

I visited Norton's office to give him the definitive typescript. And I did it the same day that I sent a copy by certified mail to the Duke of Craver, respecting our gentlemen's pact. Norton and I agreed that we would meet up a week later to pay off the last of my fees. I took advantage of that time to pay a visit to the Duke of Craver.

The Duke had always had a very vague idea about how his sons had died. My sending him the typescript would force him to see Richard finished off like a beast in a bullring and William upside down with his brain devoured by African rats. I arrived at the Craver mansion with the excuse that I had gone to listen to the Duke's objections. But what really brought me there was the need for atonement.

'Oh, yes!' the butler greeted me. 'You should know that lately the mail has been slow and we did not receive your typescript until yesterday. The Duke has spent the day reading it.' And he added, in a sombre tone, 'He hasn't come out of his office yet.'

The butler made a couple of trips from the small waiting room where he had left me to the Duke's chambers. Finally he returned, ashen-faced, and said, 'The Duke will see you now.'

Instead of announcing me, the butler left me at the entrance to the office and departed nervously. I had to push the door myself. The office was still dark, like my first visit, with large curtains sealing off the windows. The only source of light was a blue-flamed lamp that let off gas with a dense hiss.

I was expecting the solid figure of the Duke fortified behind his large desk, poised to destroy me with his verbal artillery. Instead, I found a shrivelled man sitting in a chair, in the corner of the room. The Duke was one of those individuals that appeared to be much more strapping standing up than sitting down. Now that his bones had found a resting place, the spongy flesh expanded on both sides of his ribs. His chin touched his chest. That way he could distract himself watching the fingers of one hand play with those on the other.

'I can imagine how you feel. A little bit, at least,' I said. But the Duke didn't answer me. He didn't even raise his eyes from his fingers. In a very different tone of voice I said, 'I didn't want to turn either Richard or William, especially William, into one of the most evil characters of the twentieth century.'

The hissing of the gas was worse than the Duke's silence. I was grateful that my hands could keep themselves occupied holding my hat. Otherwise I don't know what I would have done.

'I am here to tell you something,' I went on. 'A father's criteria could never be replaced by a chronicler's. But it would be worth your while to listen to me, I think.'

I took a step forward, urging myself on, and, with a bit more of a decisive spirit, I said, 'It's quite curious, but if we analyse William as a character, objectively, we are faced with someone less guilty than the adjectives would suggest. It was even a surprise to me to discover that. In the end, William didn't commit any crime punishable by law. His attitude towards the Africans was in keeping with the colonial system. And for that, as Europeans, we are all responsible. As far as the Tectons, who wouldn't have shot them? So we are left with the girl and the ignominious kidnapping to which she was subjected. Kidnapping? We'll never know what happened between William and Amgam, inside that tent. The only thing that is certain is that at the end of the story we discover that William never laid a hand on her. He was incapable of it. And we cannot hate someone because they were unable to consummate a crime.' I shook my head sadly. 'Sir, perhaps I've been too cruel with William. Perhaps what ends up condemning a man is not so much his actions as the literary style of the one who transcribes them.'

The Duke said nothing. I wanted to respect his silence. I took two steps back without turning my back to him, like someone bidding farewell to a king. But just as I had grasped the doorknob, I heard a voice that said, 'William became something infinitely more odious than a rapist or a murderer.'

I stopped. Without every raising his eyes off of his fingers, the Duke added, 'William was an obstacle to love.'

I still waited seven days before going to see Norton again, as we had agreed. And so, after many difficult situations and many emotions, four years after our fateful meeting in the cemetery, we sat together in the same office. But with the definitive story between us.

I never thought I would see Norton excited, just as one doesn't expect to see a stone dancing. This time he didn't make that gesture so characteristic of him, ruminating with a pyramid of fingers touching his nose.

'It is a great book,' he began, tapping two fingers on top of the pack of bound pages, 'a fine book, Tommy. For its style, its plot, its characters. But above all for its perspective. You were able to find the core of the truth in that story, which was so difficult and twisted, so confused.'

He stopped. He lifted his eyes from the table, and his gaze paid me homage. He said, 'Some day, at some point in the future, critics will say of the authors that are now the stars in the British literary heavens: he was a contemporary of Thomas Thomson. And that's all they'll say.' He sat up straighter and concluded, 'You will make a career for yourself, I'm sure of it.'

Should I be apologetic when admitting that Norton's praise flattered my vanity?

'We will save Marcus from the pyre, won't we?' I asked, trying to create a distance between Norton's approbation and my work.

Norton said, 'With the blind help of justice, we shall.'

It was more of a slogan than a conviction. But that was where our meeting concluded. He had nothing more to say to me. He paid me, in cash, the fees he still owed me, and I put them in my pocket. I had done the job that Norton had assigned me, he had paid me what he owed me. We were even. Norton didn't ask questions or expect me to ask any of him. He remained stock-still. He didn't even blink. It was one way of telling me that he and I had finished. All of a sudden I felt uncomfortable, although I didn't know exactly why. But everything was as it should be. I left, of course. What could I do?

Once I was on the street, I was overtaken by a vague premonition that something wasn't right. I believe I was suffering from the symptoms of overwork. I had a hard time believing that it was all over, at least as far as I was concerned. I had been too involved in the Garvey case to purge it so quickly, so antiseptically. But that's how Norton was. And our relationship had always been defined by strictly professional parameters.

That day in the autumn of 1918, all of a sudden, I found myself on the street with my hands empty. I felt as if the prisoner we had been trying to get out of the cage was me, and not Marcus. I had been released with a small amount of money in my pocket and, just like a real inmate, I had little idea of what to do with my life. The book had absorbed me to such an extent that while I was writing it my future seemed to hold no importance.

As always, Mr MacMahon's help arrived before I even knew I needed it. A few days later he shouted to me, 'Tommy, lad! In the window of the *Times of Britain* there's an advert for a journalist's apprentice. Since you write those books I thought you might be interested.'

The *Times of Britain* was a small, sensationalistic weekly that eventually disappeared in the 1950s. I went there and they gave me an appointment for a test. A test of what? A writing test. I had to write a text of eighty lines on one theme. I could choose between 'The Epic Story of Aerial Machine-guns' and 'A Criticism of Darwin's Theories from a Christian Perspective'. At that point we were all sick of the war and I picked Darwin. I had only agreed to the test to make Mr MacMahon happy. Be that as it may, a few days later they had me enter the editor's office.

'Close the door, please,' he said to me.

Of that man I remember, above all, that he had lips that looked like red octopus flesh, specially designed to suck on cigars. And that he was an individual with very widely spaced eyes, enormous, fat and slow moving, like a toad without legs. It seemed as if they had used a crane to install him in his armchair and that he hadn't left it since.

'I found your essay against Darwin very original,' he began when I had sat down before him. 'It never would have occurred to me to have the narrative voice be that of a turtle without a shell. And it was right! If turtles are freer and happier without a shell, why the hell should they have to have them? That contradicts all of Darwin's principles.'

He leaned towards me.

'You are very young. How can the *Times of Britain* know if you've got what it takes to be a journalist?'

I shrugged my shoulders. Actually, I was more curious than he was to find out. The man had very thick fingers and held a cigar so long that it looked like a cane that expelled smoke from one end. He used the Havana as a pointer to show me the door that I had just closed.

'Try to make that door into a news headline.'

I turned my neck, following the direction that the cigar indicated. I turned back to my original position and said, 'The editor of the *Times of Britain*'s door is always open.'

I made him laugh and he hired me.

So the big change of those days was my work situation. I had finished the book and I had a new job. But that didn't help me get Amgam out of my mind.

I spent hours and hours thinking about her, as ridiculous as it was. I imagined us strolling together under the same umbrella. That we lived together and argued over trivial things. I experienced these fantasies in an intense, childish way. I could almost hear the banal reasons for a dispute, each of our arguments and counter-arguments, our making up. When I daydreamed that way, recreating time and again each and every one of the details of these fictions, I achieved some sort of pleasurable pain that is impossible to describe. Finally I would say to myself, 'Wake up, you'll never even see her face.'

Then, sadness.

TWENTY-SIX

WHEN I SAID THAT the *Times of Britain* was a sensationalistic weekly I was being very kind. According to today's standards it would be considered an authentic factory of the imagination. If, for example, a telegram arrived stating that there had been an overflowing of the Buenos Aires estuary, the headline became 'SERIOUS FLOODS SINK A THIRD OF THE ARGENTINE REPUBLIC'. If some Chinese bandits attacked a passenger train on the outskirts of Shanghai, the *Times of Britain*'s headline was 'YELLOW PERIL AT THE GATES OF EUROPE'. And if the eastern edge of the Crimean peninsula was suffering some flu strain, the news was, 'THE BOLSHEVIKS SPREAD AN ASIAN DISEASE THAT THREATENS THE HUMAN RACE WITH EXTINCTION'. It was the spirit of the times. The *Times of Britain* was not much different than other weeklies. Its strength lay in the photographs, engravings and tinted drawings, and the text was only expected to accompany the graphic display.

They assigned me some simple little tasks. As an aspiring staff writer I was not allowed to participate in the elaboration of copy, strictly speaking. I was an apprentice and I stuck to minor duties, like captions for the images. There was a printing requirement that stipulated the captions had to have an exact number of letters. There couldn't be one extra letter or one less, and that included the spaces between the words. Since then I have a gained a lot of respect for those invisible jobs, real literary sub-genres that are never recognised. And it wasn't easy at all!

I remember once, when I was sleepy, I accidentally switched an exclamation mark and the following capital letter. It was only an exclamation mark and a capital letter, but it had disastrous results. We were living in the culminating moments of the big German offensive of 1918. On the cover of the weekly there was an illustration of Paris being bombarded by the giant German Bertha cannons. In those days there was a controversy over whether it was a good idea to defend Paris. Some, the 'heroics', claimed that we had to defend the city to our last drop of blood. Others, the 'realists', believed that it was better to establish the defences in a more solid position, to the south, before counter-attacking. Naturally, those in favour of the defence at all costs accused the 'realists' of being defeatists.

All in all, it was just a polemic between café strategists, but it sold a lot of papers. The editors decided to align themselves with the 'heroics', of course. But instead of:

PARIS! NEVER ACCEPT DEFEAT!

I turned it into:

PARIS NEVER! ACCEPT DEFEAT!

It was a good excuse for Mr Hardlington to scream at me for the umpteenth time.

Mr Hardlington was my boss at the *Times of Britain*. For some reason I never worked out, he saw in me a human representation of all the defects of the journalistic profession. He was one of those people that need to show off their power, and since I was his only direct subordinate, my lot was doubled. Hardlington's image was extraordinarily reminiscent of that of the classic stylists, but with a more elaborate beard, groomed with a parting in the middle. He wore a monocle, those ridiculous artefacts which have thankfully fallen into disuse. In that period I knew a lot of people who wore monocles, and I have to say that all of them were rude and pedantic. Hardlington's eyes had that ill-directed fanaticism that usually exasperates anyone who speaks with them and consumes the prophet himself. He was a big fan of Zola. But comparing Hardlington with Zola would be like comparing a worm from an apple with an anaconda from Brazil.

All the English publishing houses, without exception, had rejected his novels. Often with verbal violence, because his unhealthy insistence tired the patience of even the most polite commissioning editors. But Hardlington, as is often the case with a certain type of failure, had only one talent: perseverance. And that he had in spades: he bombarded publishers in the United States, Canada, Australia and even New Zealand with his typescripts. As incredible as it may seem, some of these houses were so good as to return the originals to him with an attached note where they apologised for not being able to place him among the most powerful minds of world literature.

It was easy to guess when he had had a typescript returned by the expression on his face when he came through the door of the *Times of Britain* first thing in the morning. Imagine a man who looks up at the sky hoping it will be sunny and, just at that moment, gets slammed in the face by a meteorite the size of a tram. The whole staff knew that expression, and each passing staff writer would goad him.

'Dear Mr Hardlington, we are eager to read your work. Are your publishing contacts going as well as we all hope?'

His response was usually, 'You all live in the primordial muck of ignorance, but I have irrefutable proof that the Semitic tentacles have reached New Zealand.'

Or Tasmania, or Nigeria, or wherever he had sent his last book. It was great fun to see Mr Hardlington among the desks of the *Times of Britain*, piercing the air with his umbrella as if he were brandishing a rapier. What was the direct cause of his failures? A Jewish conspiracy, dead set on silencing human genius wherever it might manifest itself. He had an incredible ability to deflect his miseries onto a higher cause, as superior as it was intangible. The more the publishers ignored him, the more convinced he was that he was the victim of an intellectual plot. According to Hardlington, the German military staff was entirely made up of Jewish generals. All the rebellions against the empire, including the revolt of the Mahdists in Sudan, the Boer insurrection and the recent Irish uprising had been incited by Jews. The Jews were directly responsible for the winters being too cold and the summers too sticky, for the droughts and for the hail. They had invented syphilis, malaria, typhus, lice and plantar warts.

But while he was sometimes amusing, having him on my back all the time was real piece of bad luck. He was endowed with a very impertinent and unpleasant voice. Imagine someone that speaks as if they had their mouth full of broken glass. And now imagine that voice becoming the lord and master of your days.

Perhaps, one day, Tommy Thomson would be a journalist. But for the moment Tommy Thomson was nothing more than a receptacle for Mr Hardlington's frustrations. It would have made anyone depressed. In the mornings, when the Royal Steel whistle woke me up, the first thought that came into my head was of Hardlington, and all of a sudden the sheets became impregnated with synthetic glue.

I think that Hardlington, who was essentially rather insignificant, wasn't the real cause of my bitterness. More likely, I think that Hardlington was just sanding down my imperfections. Before the book I had been under Flag's orders. And now I was once again under the authority of another Flag. A miniature Flag, perhaps, but he closed the parenthesis of creative euphoria that writing the book had been for me.

I thought about Amgam, of course. More than ever. But without any real hope. What would I have done otherwise? Go to the Congo to look for her? Dig a deeper, larger hole than the one that day on the battlefield? No. I had accepted that love was a sad, desperate and cruel experience. My version of love was mist beneath the stones, and nothing more.

That's how sad and resigned my thoughts were when I finished the first month of my new job at the *Times of Britain*. They paid me my salary, my first salary, and it was some sort of balm.

Walking around with my pockets full! What a curious and pleasurable novelty! The summer had passed, but the weather still blessed us with some sunny mornings that were as cheerful as the war allowed. I headed to a bookshop. I wanted to buy a few books without thinking about the price. Before, when I was dependent on the ill-timed and poorly paid jobs from Doctor Flag, I always had to weigh up the purchase and ask myself: it is really worth the asking price? Does it offer me enough prospects to risk the fabulous sum it costs? And here I have to say that poverty is the keenest critic. But on that occasion, for once, I planned to buy myself all the books I wanted.

The bookshop I went to had always been my favourite. The walls were covered with book spines. Completely covered. Since the ceiling was very high, to get to the ones furthest up you needed a twenty-rung ladder. If I were a book, I would have liked to be displayed in that shop. You could almost hear the books talking amongst themselves.

I was thinking that and connecting it to the way Marcus felt about trees. Perhaps that was why I had emphasised Marcus's love for trees so much? It didn't matter. This was a real forest of a bookshop. The owner was up at the top of a ladder, working on a remote shelf. I made my presence known, saying, 'What do you recommend, sir?'

He was a man with saintly white hair who was a bit deaf. With one hand he cupped his ear and said, 'What's that you say, young man?'

I had to make a trumpet with both of my hands, and shout.

'What new book do you recommend?'

'Oh, yes! I agree!' was his response. And he continued with his job as a tree-dwelling intellectual. Since there was no point in trying to make myself understood, I ran my eyes along the books on display. I looked at one table, and another, and on the third there was a book that seemed to greet me. I had the sensation that all the blood circulating throughout my body had stopped and a second later reinitiated its course in the opposite direction.

On the book's cover there was a drawing of a couple; they held hands and ran desperately, through a jungle represented in black and white. He was a small man with olive-coloured skin. The illustrator hadn't shown the physical defects in Marcus's legs. She was much taller than Marcus, white, with pigtails. Marcus and Amgam were naked, but a strategically placed play of shadows and vegetation allowed the scene to respect the prevailing standards of decency. She was pretty. Stupidly pretty. A tender, weak damsel. The illustrator hadn't understood anything.

On the back cover the story was described as 'The extraordinary adventure of a young Englishman who faces the harshness of the tropics, the insanity of two corrupt brothers and the assault of an underground civilisation'. Norton had managed to get it published in a good house. Maybe not the best, but certainly not the worst.

I don't know how long I stood there with the book in my hands. My knees had become ice cubes. If I stayed standing up too long they would melt and I'd fall. Finally I heard a voice saying, 'It's an unusual book, don't you think?'

It was the bookseller, who had come down from the ladder. I opened my mouth, but I couldn't say a word.

'My friend!' laughed the bookseller, very amused. 'Are you all right? You're whiter than the girl on the cover!'

He came a bit closer and in a resigned and confidential tone of voice he said to me, 'I've always thought that the real danger would come from Mars. We were wrong, how do you like that? The great terror isn't beyond the stars, it's below our feet. And meanwhile we're wasting time fighting against these German cabbage heads!'

I then did the oddest thing: I bought my own book. The most

distressing aspect of the situation was that I couldn't complain about any of it. No one had done me any wrong. Norton had paid me religiously. What he did with the book later wasn't any of my business.

I reread my own story with the most conflicting feelings. From what I could tell, Norton hadn't changed a comma. He did, however, add a prologue. In it he explained that it was a real case, but that out of respect for the protagonists the real names had been suppressed. I presumed that his intention wasn't to hide the real identities, but just to get around the law if the Duke of Craver sued him. Marcus Garvey was referred to as Rufus Garvey, and William and Richard's surname was just never mentioned. (Although, he did state clearly that they were descendants of a 'distinguished gentleman that had taken an active part in the Sudanese campaign and its tragic ending'.) In its day the murder of the Craver brothers had received a lot of attention. Now everyone would associate the Garvey case with the book. As you already know, the story exonerates Marcus of any crime. It goes further: it elevates him to the category of hero. That could be beneficial for Marcus's interests. But Norton's sophistry seemed ignoble. For whatever reason, I didn't want to see him to argue about it. Knowing his rhetorical skills, he was capable of convincing me that England was allied with Germany and at war with France. Instead I decided to visit Marcus. It had been too long since I'd seen him. And it was even possible, I suspected, that he wasn't aware of the book's existence.

This time I wasn't going there as Norton's legal assistant. So, I didn't have access to the room we had always used. I would probably have to settle for seeing him in one of those small rooms where the prisoner and the visitor are separated by very thick bars. Once I was in the waiting room I realised that Long Back wasn't there. I saw one of the officials that was usually in charge of taking Marcus from his cell to the room where we did our session, and I asked him without thinking, 'Sergeant Long Back isn't here today?'

'Long Back?' he smiled. 'How did you know that we all call him that?'

'I didn't know. It's a coincidence. I gave him that nickname too,' I explained. 'In fact, he never bothered to tell me his name.'

The official laughed.

'Well, my name is John,' he said, 'so you don't need to make one up for me.'

John seemed much more human. I invited him to have a smoke, and he invited me, and I didn't even have to ask him for anything.

'On holidays, like today, there are a lot more visitors and Long Back usually "directs traffic" as he likes to say,' explained John.

I already knew that. I had always come in through the entrance for legal staff, but the day that Norton and I rescinded the contract that bound us I had had to give him back my pass. I had just entered through the same door I always used, and I shouldn't have been there. I should have waited in the queue with the other visitors, and John knew it.

'You don't work for Garvey's barrister anymore, do you?' he said to me questioningly; but then, waving one hand disdainfully, 'Oh, it doesn't matter.'

He stepped on his cigarette, looked from side to side with his hands in his pockets, and he said, 'Do you want me to bring Garvey to the room you always use? You'll be more comfortable.'

And he did. He took the chains off Marcus's wrists (but not off his ankles) and told us that he'd return when our time was up. We didn't have to be seated and we could even smoke. We had never had such freedom. But everything began badly. When he saw me, instead of being glad, Marcus just let out an 'Oh, it's you!' He smoked, expelling the tobacco from his lungs aggressively, as if he and the cigarette were personal enemies. Even with his ankles shackled, he shuffled incessantly from one side of the room to the other, with an unhealthy restlessness that reminded me of an animal that had just been locked up in a zoo. It was obvious that he wasn't interested in me. I had come on a bad day. But could there be good days, in a prison? For me it was a very uncomfortable situation. I had gone there to distract him a bit, and instead it seemed that my presence irritated him. But in the end, I couldn't recriminate an innocent man, whose life was hanging by a thread, for being in a bad mood.

I showed him the book. That stopped his pacing for a few moments. He weighed it in his hands. His lips, always so attractive, even cracked a smile. But all of a sudden he raised his head, his green eyes looked at me with almost a spark of hate, and he said curtly, 'What am I supposed to do?'

I couldn't answer him, I wasn't Norton. He himself mentioned the name. He put the book down, as it interested him less than the cigarette, and he shouted, 'What is Norton doing? Can you tell me that?'

I thought the only way to calm him down was to keep my composure and get him to reason it out. If I offered him convincing arguments it would force him to think of a way to answer me, and that would moderate his tone. I was scared that the guards might come and I wanted to avoid their intervention.

'Norton is working hard on the case,' I began, 'but you know it isn't an easy one. Remember, that there's a sworn declaration by none other than a British consul that condemns you. I don't think that will be easy testimony to refute.'

'Casement? Consul Casement?' he said, knitting his brows.

'Exactly. He and the page full of signatures he gathered from the British colony in Leopoldville. The profile that emerges isn't quite, how shall I put it, bathed in a favourable light.'

I was only managing to get him more worked up.

'Casement?' he repeated, raising his arms to the heavens. 'For the love of God, Casement is a sodomite! Ask any white person that has lived in Africa and they'll tell you! While I was in the Congo he was after me. Every day and every night that I was in Leopoldville I was subject to his attentions! Casement is bitter. He couldn't get what he wanted, his vile propositions, and he took his revenge.'

'So why didn't you turn yourself into the British authorities after what happened?'

'Why do you think? That the boat I boarded as a cook had any intention of changing its route just to take me to London? They were on a commercial route, and it took a whole year to touch English soil.'

'Yes, well,' I insisted, 'even though it was late, once you were in England why didn't you turn yourself in to the authorities?'

Marcus had never opened his eyes so wide. He lowered his voice, which up until that point had been an angry roar, and he said to me, 'How can you be such a complete fool, Thomson?'

I sat in my chair, defeated. I looked at the wall, avoiding his gaze. Marcus was right. It had taken me four years to write his story. How could I expect a man like him, without any credentials, without any friends, without a past and without a future, to walk into a London police station and boldly explain the whole story to them? I said, still without looking at him, 'There's still your statement. You confessed in writing to having killed William and Richard Craver. I've seen a copy of the confession in Norton's file with my own eyes.'

I shouldn't have said anything. It was a grave mistake. Marcus was now beside himself.

'Confess that I killed William and Richard?' he bellowed. 'Of course, I confessed to it! What do you think the police do with people like me? To get them to stop beating me, I would have confessed to killing Archduke Ferdinand of Austria!'

The only thing I could do was ask him to lower his voice. It was useless. Now he was shouting and jerking around like a madman.

'I suppose Norton must be very comfortable, in his office! He doesn't know how cold it can be in a cell.' He included me in his reproaches. 'And neither do you. No one can imagine how cold it is in a cell! It's a cold that lives in your bones like worms in wood. And this is happening to me, to me, who's lived in the Congo! The Congo! Why won't they let me go back there? I want to go back to the Congo!'

I heard the noise of gates opening, further down the hall, and I begged, 'Quiet down, please.'

But he was no longer listening to me. He was moving in circles like a spinning top and looking up at the ceiling.

'I've been in the Congo. The Congo! And now, while I wait for them to hang me, I sew sacks. That's all they let me do. Sew sacks in a prison workshop!'

John came to tell us something, maybe to ask me for another cigarette, because our time still wasn't up. But Marcus practically threw himself on him. He grabbed the bars and shouted, 'Sacks! Sacks! Sacks! Sacks!'

He looked insane. He was possibly insane. John ran off.

'Do you know what he's doing?' I shouted. 'He's going for backup! Calm down!'

Marcus's only response was to try to rip one of the legs off the table to use it as a club. He didn't have enough time. Long Back and a couple of guards showed up.

'Mr Thomson, what are you doing here?' said Long Back in a reproachful tone, more of a moral reproach than a legal one. 'You know this institution well enough, and you know that you're no longer authorised to access the inmates through this wing. You must enter as a normal visitor!'

Marcus shouted incessantly, wildly, 'I've been in the Congo, the Congo!' and continued to attack the table leg.

Long Back warned him three times, as the penal regulations stipulated. Then he immediately opened the door, the two other guards came in, and they beat Marcus with their cold rubber truncheons.

I never would have thought that force applied so brutally could, at the same time, be so strategic. Their truncheons hit his neck, kidneys and testicles, in that order, and started again. Marcus, on the ground, defended himself like a cat, scratching and biting at their ankles. I would almost have preferred to suffer that violence than to watch it.

I left before they finished. I walked out of the cell, turned two corners in the hall and I could still hear Marcus's shouts. 'I want to go back to the Congo, I want to go back to the Congo!' Somewhere I found a tap. I wet my face with the motions of a fly rubbing its head. Then, a bit calmer, I had an idea: it was very likely that at that moment, Marcus's friend that Norton had told me about was in the queue waiting to visit him. I knew that former African colonists were extraordinarily loyal to each other, to an extreme degree that the rest of the civilised world had a hard time comprehending. Since it was a holiday I wouldn't have been surprised at all to find he had come out to the prison. And completely sure that, whoever he was, he would appreciate someone letting him know what had just happened. So I went to the visitors' wing and I looked at the long queue of men and women. Two pairs of officials attended to them, filling out documents and checking them over before taking them inside. Four officials were not sufficient to take care of such a large crowd and the queue advanced extremely slowly.

Amongst the people in line there was an incredibly tall woman. She was very thin and must have been a good six feet tall. She was dressed in severe mourning attire, black from head to toe. Black skirts to her ankles, black calf-length boots, black hat and, sewn onto the hat, a very fine net veil, also black, which covered her face. At first I took very little notice of the woman. I was searching for someone that looked like a veteran Africanist, with a face marked by the pleasures and hardships of the tropics. But I ended up focusing on that tall, thin woman.

She must have been a special person, with her femininity hidden under so many layers of black clothing. And she seemed so downcast, she was so fixated on the queue, on moving even a step forward, that her entire world was reduced to the back of the person in front of her. She was like one of the spectres that live in Greek hells, for whom time and space don't exist. Seeing her filled me with depressing thoughts. In order to see her beloved she had to immerse herself in that dismal prison world. And, on top of it all, she was forced to suffer the added torture of a slow queue. As I headed towards the exit I shook my head sadly, saying to myself: here is a woman that is the complete antithesis of Amgam. I thought that then I stopped as if I had come up against a wall of air.

Could there be many women that were six feet tall, in London, in England, in the world? Who was that woman coming to visit? My eyes searched for her hands. She wore gloves, but they were of a strange design, like silk mittens, so I couldn't count her fingers.

Had Marcus changed parts of his story to protect Amgam? All of a sudden I opened my eyes to the truth: two lovers like Marcus and Amgam would never have separated. Ever. I said to myself, 'If it had been you that day at the Sea of Young Ladies, with the dynamite fuse in your hands, would you have let her go?'

I didn't even need to answer. The question wasn't what Marcus would have done. The question was that she, Amgam, would never have renounced love for something so trivial as saving the world. When she had to choose between the Tecton world and the human one, she had to have opted for love, wherever it might take her.

I felt my forehead to make sure I wasn't feverish. How could I have been so stupid? Marcus had tried to trick me about small details regarding Pepe, just to save his African friend's good name. What wouldn't he have said, or kept quiet, in order to safeguard Amgam?

I remember myself there, rooted to the spot, my eyes fixed on that woman. I couldn't move. It was as if my shoes had grown roots. While I stared at her without her realising, inside my head I constructed the entire story of Marcus and Amgam, the real story, at least that part that Marcus had hidden from me to protect his lover. I recreated it in a moment, like a spider web that's woven at lightning speed.

I saw Amgam taking the initiative. I saw her convincing Marcus to return to London, her beloved's home. I saw her superior intelligence being applied to understanding a new, unknown world. And to surviving in it. I saw her in front a mirror, learning the art of making herself up in order to hide her pale features. I saw her camouflaged in Victorian clothing, in the fashion of a period that actively constrained women's freedom, but which she used to her advantage. And then? Marcus arrested, her bewildered. Why? Why would men arrest the man that had saved humanity from the most destructive race in the universe?

I was ashamed to belong to the human race. Amgam had left everything to come to our world. She chose to live among us, an 'us' that Marcus embodied. And what was the first thing we did? Kidnap her lover, imprison him behind stone walls. Walls built with stones thicker and more indestructible than all those that separated the human world from the Tecton world, because between humans and Tectons there were only stones. But now, there were imperial laws that came between her and him.

I was struck by a cold sweat. Finding myself face to face with Amgam was what I had most wanted in the world. It was also the last thing that I had ever thought would happen. The place couldn't be more miserable. No one saw her. The visitors in the queue only cared about moving an inch or two forward. And the prison officials, with the intelligence of trained fleas, weren't prepared for Tecton women, just for metal files.

I approached her, determined to lift up her veil. But when the tips of my fingers were six inches from her face I stopped. What if I were wrong? What if she was just a very tall woman? In fact, what if I were right? That was an even more horrific possibility. If it was her, and I uncovered her in public, the consequences would be fatal.

She was so absorbed in the queue that it took her a few seconds to notice my fingers, so close to her veil. Finally she realised my intentions and she let out a startled shriek with a very masculine voice. I was more frightened than she was. She jumped back and fled. I chased after her, but before I had even left of the building I heard an authoritative voice.

'Mr Thomson! Do you mind telling me what you're doing?'

I tried to ignore him, but Long Back then bellowed a categorical 'Halt!' I couldn't disobey.

'I have always had a very good impression of you, Mr Thomson,' he said. 'Why are you trying so hard to change it? Do you know that you have committed a serious offence? Two offences? First, seeing a prison through a restricted channel, and then, harassing a visitor.'

Giving in seemed to be the best tactic, so I said, 'I'm a bit confused. Please accept my apologies.' And then immediately after, 'Can I go now?'

Long Back became more lenient. 'Mr Norton told me that you were in the trenches. You fought for our country and I respect that.'

I was like a child that can't hold his pee for even a second more. 'Yes, it's true. Artillery. Can I go now?'

Long Back, on the other hand, was talking while looking over my head and all around, as if I were the last thing in the world that interested him.

'Artillery is a great weapon. I suppose, as well, that it's the least risky of them all. Because of the distance from the enemy that it entails, I mean. Well, don't take that as a criticism. Did you come back wounded, in any case?'

'Oh, yes. My lungs are a bit less elastic, according to the doctors. But I consider myself very lucky.'

He detained me a little longer. He switched from ignoring me to scrutinising me with his characteristic gaze, like a lighthouse on full beam. Long Back looked at every human being as if he knew something bad about them. Then he gave me two affectionate taps on the chest with his truncheon.

'Just this once, we'll keep quiet about what we've seen. But don't push your luck.' He steered me to the exit with his rubber truncheon, while saying, 'On your way, Mr Thomson.'

When I got out it was already too late. On the street there was only the same old pavement, black and damp, with empty corners.

TWENTY-SEVEN

ALL OF A SUDDEN, my life did a double somersault. On one hand, the presence of Amgam. On the other, the book's success. The newspapers were talking about it, and the reviews were good. Now, with over a half century of distance, it is easy to understand the book's appeal. We were in the fourth year of war. Everyone wanted a change of climate. And Rufus Garvey, the character of Marcus Garvey, was ideal for asserting a different type of hero. People were sick of the war, which was becoming as absurd as it was interminable. Marcus's cause, on the other hand, was pure and simple. The Great War was a kind of worldwide civil war. But Marcus's odyssey reconciled humanity with itself.

The world seemed to be falling down around me. I was proud of being the writer that had given shape to the story. But, at the same time, I wasn't recognised as such and never would be. Can you imagine a more tragic situation for an author? And the book had even made it to the offices of the *Times of Britain*. By the hand, to be specific, of the ineffable Mr Hardlington.

One day he arrived and shouted with that ever so grating voice of his, like an asthmatic parrot, 'You should read this, Mr Thomson!'

He surprised me by dropping my book on the desk from a great height, as if it were a brick.

'A structure solid as steel and a style light as a feather.' Then he triumphantly announced, 'Goodbye romanticism! Goodbye social realism! This is real modern prose, Mr Thomson!'

I wish someone had taken a photograph right then. Of me and Hardlington. Especially Hardlington. He was enthused.

'I don't think you can appreciate this book's greatness, because you are a mere flea when it comes to literature. But try, Mr Thomson, at least try,' he said in a falsely paternal voice. 'You will never be able to thank me enough for lending you this literary gem.'

He sat down, paused and began with his usual mocking tone, 'By the way, how's the Western front today? Are our troops holding up? Or have we already lost Paris?'

Giving him back the copy, I said with a sarcastic voice, 'I've already read the book so there's no need for you to lend it to me.'

That only made him more predisposed against me.

'Really?' he said, genuinely surprised. 'So, tell me, Mr Thomson, what exegesis do you make of it?'

I didn't know what exegesis meant. Hardlington laughed.

'Which concept did you like best?' he said with an evil smile. 'The redemption of the two brothers? The sublimation of the cook, Garvey? Or perhaps the superiority of the English race over the Semitic threat?'

That threw me off. 'What redemption are you talking about? Both of the brothers were soulless degenerates! The book shows that well enough.'

'You see? You are incapable of understanding the internal keys hidden behind all great works. The two noble Englishmen, very possibly, had committed some social offence. Naturally, the battle in the Congo redeems them.'

I was getting worked up. 'But they were saboteurs! Garvey's the one who saves the world. Both the brothers, especially William, do everything possible to impede him!'

Hardlington had foreseen my response, because before I had even finished speaking he said, 'That is the sublimation I was referring to. Even a simple cook, if guided by the example of two English noblemen, ends up acquiring the English race's nobility of spirit.'

'But Garvey is half gypsy!' I said. 'What racial spirit are you talking about?'

Hardlington struck a pose of feigned resignation. 'Oh, my little friend. I see you haven't understood a word. It's clear that this book was written in symbolic code and has to be interpreted. Do you really not see that the depths from which the Tectons come are a metaphor for the great threat that hangs over our times?' Hardlington crossed his arms on his chest ceremoniously and asked me, 'Let's see, Mr Thomson, what race hides in the sewers, waiting for the opportunity to attack humanity's collective interests?'

'But the Tectons aren't a symbol of international Judaism!' I replied. For a few moments I felt like the book's author again. With a rigid finger I tapped on the book's cover as if I were trying to perforate it, while saying, 'The book says what it says and that's all.'

'Bravo!' said Hardlington, applauding me sarcastically.

But I paid him no mind and continued, "The Tectons are the Tectons. And the two English noblemen are an exact copy of the Tectons. Or vice versa. That is the problem!' I pointed to my chest with both thumbs, 'We are the Tectons.'

Hardlington clicked his tongue in a particularly annoying way. It made him seem like a kangaroo trainer. He refused my interpretative pretensions, waving his finger like a pendulum.

'No, my little friend, no. Your naïveté stuns me.' He paused and asked, 'According to aspiring staff writer Thomas Thomson, what is the fundamental core of this masterpiece?'

I had never challenged Hardlington so decidedly. Maybe that was why I now had the attention of all my colleagues, who had stopped working to follow the controversy as spectators. Ten typewriters that stop at once create a very loud silence. Hardlington was waiting for my reply. My colleagues were waiting for my reply. I was waiting for my reply. After interminable reflection I said, 'That Garvey and Amgam love each other. And that love, as an indirect consequence, saves the world.'

Hardlington's eyes swelled like two billiard balls. They grew so big that for a moment I thought they would fall to the ground, like ripe fruit falls from the trees.

'Are you trying to tell me that such a sophisticated narrative structure's only objective is to tell the story of the flirtation between a half-lame gypsy and an ugly, milky woman?'

I hesitated. 'Actually, yes.'

My response made him laugh so hard that all the other employees were astonished that Mr Hardlington, usually so serious, would devote his lung strength to such a gratuitous activity as laughing.

Then he came even closer to me, he gave me three pats on the back with his palm, apparently friendly, although the real intent was to use my jacket to wipe his dirty hands, and he said, 'You are reducing a cosmic conflict into a wild love affair. No, my little friend, no. High literature is not the patrimony of the simple.'

The most unpardonable thing about Hardlington was that he really enjoyed mocking me. I was just a lad, and Hardlington's systematic pressure made me begin to have doubts. About what? About everything?

I wasn't even sure what my true contribution to the book had been. The real protagonist of the story was Marcus Garvey. And his guardian angel, Edward Norton. Without them there would have been no story. They, both of them, had been indispensable to the book. I wasn't. There were plenty of writers capable of writing Marcus Garvey's story. But there was only one Marcus Garvey. There were plenty of barristers. But barristers that would have handled the Garvey case as Norton did, only one. Everything was becoming confused, dry and grey.

As far as Hardlington was concerned, I didn't yet know that mediocre souls like to surround themselves with even more mediocre people. That way it was easier to blame their failures on cosmic injustice. It was as if they were saying: compare my intelligence with that of the person next to me, isn't it obvious that I deserve a situation more worthy of my character? The most curious thing was that I was affected by almost the opposite limitation: I could never prove the truth to Hardlington, so I didn't even bother to state it. Besides, Hardlington's presence filled me with as much grief as Amgam's absence.

The mere possibility that in those same moments she was

somewhere in London tormented me. I couldn't get the image out of my head of that back, so tall and thin, so black and so fleeting. My fingers had been about to touch her, and this time it hadn't been a hallucination induced by military gas. Why had she run from me? Most offended women, in those circumstances, would have reproached me for having brought two insolent fingers so close to their face. But she had chosen to run.

This war on two fronts was too much for Tommy Thomson. The following days a strange apathy took hold of me. Outside office hours I lay in my bedroom, or in some corner of the boarding house, and I did nothing unless I was directly asked to by someone. It was the stupefaction of someone who comes up against a wall at the end of a dead-end street. Everything in the world provoked tremendous indifference in me. I soon became a kind of discoloured imitation of Mr Modepà, with the difference that he, at least, smiled all day. Often Mr Modepà and I would meet in the small dining room of the boarding house. He would smile, that stupid happy smile that was so characteristic of him, and I couldn't do anything but smile back in mute dialogue. Every once in a while Mr MacMahon took us out of the house. We all three went to an Irish pub two blocks away from the boarding house and we drank beer with MacMahon's gang of Irish friends that frequented the place. Modepà was as passive as ever, with that silent smile on his lips. What a contrast we two made, amongst all those Irishmen, cordially shouting insults at each other behind a cloud of smoke.

Well, at that point I was filled with a new drive by the person I least expected to do so. The ineffable Mr Hardlington.

I don't know why I speak so ill of Hardlington. In his own way, he occupies quite a relevant place in our story. The book's fame grew, and the torture it inflicted on me eventually made me react. In the end what did it was Hardlington's adoration of the book. At first he praised its contents. Then he pontificated daily on its literary virtues, claiming to be the only man on earth capable of correctly interpreting the work's meaning. 'The word 'reader' has no plural form,' he declared. In fact, the text's faults ended up making him change his attitude: 'Well, we have to recognise that I would have polished up some of the paragraphs,' he said. And he proceeded to add and subtract paragraphs in a copy with his caustic pen. I could no longer contain myself and I attacked him.

'If it's so easy for you to correct the mistakes of a masterpiece why don't you write one yourself?'

He answered me without lifting his eyes from the book and with an exquisite self-sufficiency.

'I am in no hurry to expend my work. These days usury dominates everything. The Jews have made themselves the heads of the publishing world and have excluded anything that isn't profitable. But I do not aspire to make myself rich, only to make myself immortal. I do not mix art with financial interests.' He moved an instructive finger in the air and said, 'The difference between literature and the literary industry, Mr Thomson, is that the first one moves among letters and the second among numbers.'

That gave me a lot to mull over. Quite a lot. I had never stopped to think that a successful book could make so much money. But someone like Norton had. That idea shattered the image I had of Norton and the Garvey case. It was like seeing a familiar landscape from a different angle. The more I thought about it, the more wounded, angry and exploited I felt, and on the third day I headed off towards his office. I went there in the evening, I had left the *Times of Britain* very late. It had been a particularly hard day. Hardlington had been on top of me the whole time, castigating me every time I made a typographical error. It was better that way. That way he was activating a bomb. The bomb was me.

Norton wasn't expecting me, of course. He was wearing house slippers and a silk dressing gown. But he had me go into his office. I didn't give him time to sit down. I still had my last visit to the prison, which had been very recent, in my head, and I began like this: 'You have to do something for Marcus. That boy can't take much more. He's becoming a lunatic.'

Norton was a very intelligent man. I hated that intelligence. I had meticulously prepared my speech, but as soon as I opened my mouth he had all the fuel he needed to frustrate my plans.

'You didn't come here to talk about Garvey.'

After a few flustered seconds I reacted, raising my head to the ceiling with my fists tightly closed. I had never imagined myself that way, with my fists above my head.

'Yes and no!' I shouted. 'You tricked me!'

He made a strange face with the help of his eyebrows and his little moustache. That made me even more furious. A man with both fists in the air is demonstrating that he is at war with the world, but when he only has one, tightly closed, and at nose height, he is demonstrating that he is at war with the person in front of him. I said, 'Don't pretend you don't know what I'm talking about! If there is one sharp-witted person in this office, I am quite sure it is not me. And if there is some fool here, we can be sure it's not you!'

Norton didn't lose his calm. He just redirected the situation. 'Would you like a glass of cognac?'

And with one hand he pointed me towards the door that led to his private chambers.

We entered an inviting little room. There he had two armchairs and a small fireplace. It felt very strange to me to have a man like him pouring me a brandy. And the change of scenery definitely had its desired effect. We sat on either side of the fireplace and I was more calm, although not less angry. But Norton didn't want me to shut up; with the glass of cognac at his lips he made an indulgent gesture with his free hand that said: explain yourself, please.

'I believe you have betrayed us,' I began. 'Marcus and me! I believe that you never thought of me as an assistant in your legal task. I think that you never thought that my efforts would help Marcus.' As I spoke I got more worked up. I pointed at him with an accusatory finger. 'I believe that your actions, from the very first moment, were driven by an opportunistic and corporate mentality, and that Marcus and I were stuck in the role of exploited proletariats. Proletariats of the pen and of the shackles, but proletariats, when all is said and done!'

'Is that what you think?'

'What else could I think? You realised Garvey's story was very promising, but you're not a writer. That's why you hired me, a poor devil, only nineteen years old. If the book hadn't been bought by any publisher, you wouldn't have lost anything. But if it ended up becoming a bestseller, and all signs pointed to that, you would stand to make a lot of money!'

I snorted and took a very large sip. I did it more to rein myself in than for the pleasure of drinking. But I continued.

'You got me out of the way with an insignificant compensation. Since we never signed any contract, who could I complain to about it? If I did object, who would believe that a young, inexperienced author had written such a book? Ever since we met that day in the cemetery, you knew that Doctor Flag would never give me his support. So there was only one other witness: Marcus. And Marcus will be eliminated by the gallows. A perfect crime!'

Norton followed my logic, making slight affirmative movements with his head.

'Yes, of course, I've always thought that perfect crimes are committed within the law,' he joked. But he soon added, in an iron tone that I had never heard from him and which left me speechless, 'Do you really have such a low opinion of me, Mr Thomson?'

Norton was much more of a man than I was at that point. More mature, more self-assured, quicker. I had trouble holding my ground. I didn't speak, but I didn't move either. He relaxed. It was as if the spongy armchair had sucked him in a bit.

'You've put me in a difficult situation, Mr Thomson. Whatever I tell you, you won't believe me. As they say in court, I have the burden of proof. Which is to say, that I am the one who has to prove my innocence.'

I couldn't help admiring the way the man bound his personality and his character. I had made an effort to show up at his house dressed as elegantly as I could afford. Even so, my outbursts had already dishevelled my clothes. He, on the other hand, even though he wasn't expecting my visit, looked like a dandy: black silk socks, immaculately pressed trousers, his dressing gown also silk. And his baldness, which was always magnificent, was now powerful. That bald head proclaimed to the world that between its clean, convex walls there hid an intelligence it was best not to challenge.

Norton was deep in thought, and I knew that he enjoyed ignoring me, showing that in order to put a stop to my wild impulses all he had to do was begin meditating with a cognac in his hands. While he reflected, Norton swirled his glass, holding it with his thumb and index finger like an expert. Was he thinking about the Garvey case or the cognac? I was sure that Norton knew as much about cognac as the Tectons did about astronomy. All of a sudden he looked up from those liquid depths and he exclaimed in an almost high-flown voice, 'Very well, Mr Thomson, this is what we'll do. You have arrived at just the right moment. You should know that because of its success the publisher is about to print a second edition. But before they do it I will send them a note to be added to the first page. I'll write it right now.'

He left me in my armchair, alone with the cognac. The walls of Norton's house were also painted the colour of cognac.

Norton returned and put a page in my hands. I read it. It was impeccable. In less than forty lines it explained my relationship with Norton and with the book, without alteration or distortion. Norton apologised for having taken my name. At first he hadn't given it much thought, the use of a 'ghost writer', but once the book had gone beyond the legal realm it seemed only fair to make public the name of its real author: Thomas Thomson. He had only served as the liaison between Garvey and Thomas Thomson, a fact that filled him with extreme pride. Starting with that edition he would remove his name and request that young Thomas Thomson be considered forevermore as the real and only author. Norton ended by asking for justice for Garvey.

The critics won't approve of these lines, because books are immortal and men merely have one life to live. And legal cases have an even more limited time period. But I am not the author of this book and I never should have been listed as such. Therefore, now I can resume my private function and judge it with foreign eyes. That allows me to state an obvious fact: that the artistic heights that this book reaches are directly proportional to the underground depths that Garvey arrived at, and that both voyages have a noble purpose. One, to elevate British literature to heights previously unattained; the other, to save all humanity. And here is where I implore the reader to ask himself the following question: wouldn't it be incredibly lovely if our reading contributed to making the world a little bit more just? When an innocent is condemned, part of our innocence as a people dies with him. Let's prevent that from happening.

I was left with my mouth agape. Norton declared, 'To literature what belongs to literature, and to law what belongs to law.' And he added, 'From this moment, and retrospectively, all rights derived from the book will belong to you, Mr Thomson. That includes the artistic glory and the economic benefits.' He smiled and added slightly contentiously, 'Have I changed your opinion of me in any way?'

What could I say? A simple 'yes' would have been grossly insufficient. Norton had not only dissipated my suspicions, he had even satisfied pretensions I hadn't yet formulated. I was very young. I still didn't know that calculating men are often generous.

'In effect, my strategy in regards to the Garvey case is extralegal, Mr Thomson. But not in the sense that you believe,' he said when we parted.

In the following days that strategy became clear. The book leapt from the literary critics' pages to the general press. Garvey was here, there and everywhere. One day, at the newspaper, I was carrying a pile of papers in my arms, a pile so large it reached up to my chin. I was chasing Hardlington's back, who had me loaded down with files that he was selecting from some old bookshelves. I was carrying so much weight that I began to identify with the bearers in the Congo. We were halfway to our desks when a voice demanded that Hardlington go to the editor's office. I followed him, borne by that mule instinct.

'Hardlington!' shouted the editor before we had even crossed the threshold. His head vacillated between two papers, to which he alternately directed his attention.

'What should we devote the cover of the next issue to? The Bergström case or the Garvey case? By the way, does anyone know exactly what it's about, this Garvey thing?'

The Bergström case needed no introduction. Bergström was a Swedish businessman who had been accused of selling war munitions to the Germans. It would have been perfectly admissible for a businessman from a neutral country, but since Bergström had business dealings with England he had always denied dealing with the Central Powers. Bergström was a very well known man in the more frivolous parts of London, rich, young, attractive and famous for his private parties. That such a man could fall into disgrace was a scandal that went from espionage to high politics, and all wrapped up with a patina of glamour. Which is to say, the *Times of Britain*'s speciality. As for Marcus, Hardlington summed it up somewhat laconically.

'Mr Garvey is a secondary character in a strange story set in the Congo.'

'No, no!' I protested, from behind my load.

No one had given me permission to sit, and my arms began to tire under the weight of the files. But I had to defend Marcus.

'Garvey is the main character of a universal epic! His story deserves an entire issue of the *Times of Britain*!'

'Which of the two stories has more human interest?' the editor asked.

'Both,' said Hardlington, 'but Bergström's is more patriotic. It's a financial scandal with military implications. Thanks to the intervention of the Home Office it has been discovered that the Swede had double-dealings. And I'm quite sure he's a Jew . . .' He very enthusiastically raised his fist and stated, 'The boys in the Home Office are true heroes!'

'But, Mr Editor, sir!' I permitted myself to intervene. 'Heroism isn't a question of numbers, it's a question of generosity. And Marcus is a unique hero.'

'A hero,' said the editor, intrigued. 'I like heroes.'

'Yes!' I said. 'Garvey saved all of humanity!'

'Humanity all over the world? He's saved the lives of every person in this world?' He shifted his cigar with an ironic look at Hardlington and asked, 'My mother-in-law's as well?'

Hardlington didn't get the joke. And I couldn't laugh, because I was on the point of collapse. But while Hardlington pondered whether or not Marcus had saved the editor's mother-in-law or not, I took advantage of the pause to say, 'Bergström is just a Swedish millionaire who is a victim of circumstances.' Speaking required superhuman effort. 'But Garvey is an anonymous hero. Unlike today's heroes he didn't become one by eliminating a nest of machine-guns. He's a hero because he sacrificed his happiness in exchange for the world's freedom.'

'That's good, that's good,' said the editor, shaking one hand impatiently. 'But which story has more sex? Bergström's or Garvey's?'

'Both of them!' I shouted. I was folding like a human leaning Tower of Pisa but I managed to declare, 'But in Marcus's story, there is love too.'

'Love!' exclaimed the editor. 'I like it. Love sells a lot of papers. Make it Garvey.'

I heard him and I collapsed. The muscles in my arms slackened like springs. All the files scattered on the ground, and I fell on top of them like onto a mattress of paper. The pile was so big that the editor hadn't even seen my face. He didn't recognise me until that moment.

'Oh, Thomson, it's you, the shell-less turtle lad,' he said bending down a little. 'How's the work suiting you?'

The *Times of Britain* wasn't the first newspaper to cover the Garvey case, not even the first weekly. But it was one of the first that took a position that was devoid of all nuance. The *Times of Britain*'s business consisted in offering straightforward stories of good guys and bad guys. It wasn't about generating debate, just about provoking emotion. And in that case the victim, naturally, was Marcus. For once sensationalism allied itself with the truth. Well, that's not entirely true either. When the *Times of Britain* published headlines announcing that 'The British people clamour desperately for Marcus Garvey's freedom' what it meant was that the *Times of Britain* clamoured desperately for Garvey's freedom. Or more accurately, that the *Times of Britain* hoped to sell many copies clamouring desperately for Marcus Garvey's freedom.

A self-perpetuating circuit was soon established: the book sold copies of newspapers and magazines like the *Times of Britain*, and reading the *Times of Britain* sold more books. Working in a newspaper room allowed me to gauge the direction of changing public opinion. On one hand, the *Times of Britain* wanted to know which way public opinion was leaning (in order to sell more copies). On the other hand, it was clear that the *Times of Britain* collaborated in creating that very same public opinion (due to the fact that people read the *Times of Britain*).

One day two letters arrived from readers interested in Garvey. Another day three more. On another not a single one, but on the day after five very indignant ones. The following week, a journalist who worked for the competition showed up, a friend of mine and of the other writers at the paper, and told us that they too were going to do a special issue dedicated to the Garvey case. And on another day one of the most prestigious columnists of one of the most prestigious papers in the country dedicated his space to the Garvey case.

All of that made me happy. But if that was the case, if the echo was extending and as a result many copies of the book were being sold, what was the publishing house waiting for? Why hadn't they brought out the second edition with Norton's note? Two more weeks passed without any news, and I could only say to myself, 'Norton has tricked me again.' Because it was clear that the Garvey story exceeded the limits of our modest editorial staff. Those days I was able to get away from Hardlington, at least for brief periods, attending the Army's press conferences as a *Times of Britain* journalist, which were so tedious that no one ever wanted to go to them. Until one day, when I came back to the newsroom after attending one of those informative meetings, and found myself in an unusual situation.

The editor was running crazily through the newsroom with one hand raised showing a book's spine.

'Listen up!' he said, his favourite war cry. And then, 'We have to change the headline!'

I had never seen the editor out of his seat. I've already mentioned that he resembled a giant toad, always embedded in his chair, but once out of it he moved with the agility of a hippopotamus out of water: as quickly as possible so that he could get back to his natural element. The comings and goings of that man had turned the newsroom into a henhouse. Without taking the cigar out of his mouth he bellowed, 'The second edition has appeared of that book about the gypsy who gets it on with the albino girl!'

'I completely agree, Mr Editor, sir!' Hardlington hastened to second, trotting behind him. He was a man who was ill accustomed to physical exercise and he ran raising his knees very high. 'That book is a very, very important work of British literature and it deserves a thousand editorials in the *Times of Britain*!'

'Idiot! Who cares about literature?' shouted the editor without stopping. His gaze found me, and he came closer. 'It turns out that the author is an employee of the *Times of Britain*! Did you hear me?' and rotating his neck on its axis, accusing everyone and no one, 'Why didn't anyone tell me? I had to find out from my wife, who wastes her time going to coffee mornings.' And pointing with his cigar towards the machines: 'Write this down. Headline with lettering in Imperial font: THE AUTHOR OF THE STORY OF MARCUS GARVEY IS AN EMPLOYEE OF THE *TIMES OF BRITAIN*. Smaller line below: THE *TIMES OF BRITAIN* CONTINUES TO DEMAND MARCUS GARVEY'S IMMEDIATE RELEASE.'

Then he turned to me and said, 'Thomson, my boy, why didn't you tell us?'

The editor handed the book over to me as everyone watched expectantly. It was the second edition. The author's name read Thomas Thomson. And on the first page Norton had added the note we had agreed on. He'd had been true to his word.

After me, the person most affected by the news was, naturally, Mr Hardlington. If someone had touched him with a finger in that instant he would have collapsed like a statue made of sand. I had never seen anyone so stunned. His lower lip hung down to his chin. That shred of shiny red flesh was the most repugnant and obscene thing I had ever seen. It is the only time in my life that I wanted to laugh and throw up at the same time.

The editor put an arm over my shoulder and introduced me to the entire staff, as if we had never met. When we got to Hardlington, who was frozen to the spot, I was afraid he might have a heart attack right there. But I was too worried to think about revenge. The very next day Marcus's trial was set to begin, and I took advantage of the editor's public euphoria to ask him for a few days off.

'Of course!' he conceded. 'Well, before you go someone will have to interview you. But what the hell! Why should we waste our time? Truth is, since I founded the *Times of Britain* we haven't published a single interview without rewriting it from top to bottom. You go ahead and come back when you feel like it. I'll do the interview myself.'

I went to the prison as fast as I could, with the intention of giving Marcus support, even though I was convinced they wouldn't let me see him, especially without my legal pass. Luckily that day Long Back was in a good mood and he was very genial with me.

'Ah, Mr Thomson!' he said. 'That's strange. You and Mr Norton don't usually coincide. Well, I'm sure Garvey can handle two visitors at once.'

It was weird seeing them together. The truth is neither of them paid much attention to me. They were busy preparing for the trial. They looked like a theatre director and a lead actor during a dress rehearsal. Norton, who had taken off his jacket, was standing beside Garvey and pointing his finger at his nose vigorously.

'If someone in court says something funny, don't be the first one to laugh. Wait until laughter breaks out in general, just in case. Do you understand?'

'Yes, yes,' said Marcus submissively.

'Don't lower your gaze, they'll think you are hiding something. Don't ever look at the ceiling, they'll think you're lying. When in doubt, buy time. How? With some candid, sad gesture. The judge must think that he has someone in front of him who's incapable of insulting a dog. Do you think you can give that image?'

'Well . . . no . . . I . . . never . . .' faltered Marcus.

'Perfect!' said Norton. 'Like that, just like that! Rehearse that gesture as much as you can.'

TWENTY-EIGHT

GARVEY'S TRIAL HAD CREATED a buzz of anticipation. Perhaps because it was one of the first cases of the twentieth century where justice and heroism intersected. The journalist the *Times of Britain* had sent, a real veteran, was astonished by the crowd of his colleagues. He told me that in the military press conference where the Somme offensive had been announced there were thirty-eight journalists. And there were already almost fifty covering the Garvey case. It's difficult to know whether that audience was drawn by the literary Marcus or the martyr Marcus. In any case, the room was filled to overflowing. Luckily I had had the foresight to show up an hour early. Even still, and although the room held about five hundred people, I was among the last few to be admitted and I had to sit at the back, very close to the door. At least that allowed me a small pleasure: when they brought Marcus into the courtroom, shackled and escorted by two guards, I was able to greet him briefly.

'Don't worry, Marcus!' I said, grasping his hand in mine. 'Everything will work out fine, have faith in Norton!'

The guards didn't let me retain him much longer. Maybe it was better that way. I am one of those men whose voices catch when they get emotional, and my words convey more concern than hope.

Now I understood the scope of the strategy that Norton had explained to me. The public wanted Marcus's freedom. And popular indignation was not a force to be trifled with. But in that first session it was also made clear that we had to fight against immensely powerful forces.

In the first place, the setting itself. The judge, the wigs, the red and black gowns, the ornate mahogany furniture. It was all done on a scale designed to reduce human beings to insects. And when the prosecutor stood up, when he pointed at Marcus Garvey with his finger and accused him of murder in the name of the British Crown, at that moment my heart shrank to the size of a little cherry. And if I was so affected, imagine poor Marcus. He seemed smaller than ever. From where I was sitting I could only see the nape of his neck. It was as if he had been plugged into an electrical current: his hairs were standing on end so that they looked like the spines of a sea urchin. The entire weight of the British Empire was falling onto one man.

At the beginning of his speech the prosecutor was restrained. But his tone rose progressively. And through it he expressed a righteous fury. He described Marcus as a vile creature, a treacherous snake, a monster unworthy of belonging to the human race. When he asked for the gallows there was silence throughout the courtroom. The five hundred people present all inhaled at the same time.

But while Marcus and I were being exposed to the legal universe for the first time, it was Edward Norton's preferred territory. I can still see him now, erect, calm and resolute, his bald head hidden underneath the white wig. The prosecutor's speech had been firm and ponderous. Norton, on the other hand, limited himself to the following words. I remember each and every one.

'Mr Garvey is innocent. And at the end of this trial we will have destroyed all the rational elements that could lead one to think the contrary. Mr Garvey is innocent. And he is a hero. At the end of this trial we will have shown all the evidence necessary to prove that.'

I think with that brief statement Norton won half of the trial. His tone was so deliberate, so sure of the truth that it pronounced, and so detached from the prosecutor's emotional incitement, that any neutral spectator would have tended to lean towards Garvey.

They took many days to call Marcus to the stand. When he finally moved, he dragged his legs exaggeratedly, making his defect seem worse. I knew that those little legs were short and that the knees didn't work well. I knew that when Marcus walked, his body moved as if his kneecaps were defective pistons. But I also knew that he was exaggerating. And it was a good thing he did.

The prosecutor began his interrogation. I don't remember the question. I remember Marcus looking from one side to the other, as if he was searching for protection, and that little gypsy, who was accused of two heinous murders, surprised everyone with an incredibly polite tone of voice, saying, 'Pardon. Would you be so kind as to repeat the question?'

And I, who knew from personal experience the effect of that hesitant gaze, could only think: 'Bravo!'

The prosecutor hadn't gauged well enough the magnitude of the opposition he was up against. In the first stage of the trial Norton kept himself to a strategy of containment. It was as if all the efforts of the prosecution came up against an unexpected wall that diluted any incriminating argument. That human breakwater was Edward Norton. During the first days he demolished each and every piece of evidence against Marcus. He did it methodically, with a premeditated slowness, as if he enjoyed murdering the hopes of his adversary. Then he entered into a more languid phase.

It is remarkable the amount of insignificant things involved in a trial. Trials, even the most spectacular, are essentially mind-numbing. Most of the sessions are devoted to completely dull procedural minutiae, at least for those of us who aren't versed in legal matters. During the second week the room emptied. All those who had no direct relationship with the cause stopped coming, waiting for the most decisive days. On the eighth day, there was almost no one left in the room. I only stuck it out in solidarity with Marcus. I remember that one day the prosecutor referred to the Duke of Craver. I felt a lump in my throat, as if I had swallowed a piece of meat the wrong way. I thought of him and his robust stature. He had been a great man and had died a year ago. In that endurance test that the Garvey case had become, he was one of the victims that fell by the wayside. Maybe it was better that way. Whatever the results of the trial, the book's success had condemned his sons in a parallel trial that he could never win.

On the eighth day I was sitting in one of the front rows, closer than ever. Since I was very close to the bench, I made sure to cover my mouth with my hand. But I only managed to draw more attention to my yawns that way. At one point I turned half my body to hide from the judge's condemning gaze.

The rows of wooden benches behind me were practically empty. There must have been, at most, ten people. Some of them were completely uninterested in the trial, like the fifty-year-old woman who brazenly crocheted. The light in the room was reduced to a sad penumbra. On the ceiling, high above, there were large glass skylights designed to allow in natural light. A very praiseworthy intention on the architect's part, but he hadn't taken British clouds into account. There I was, trying to stifle a yawn while mulling over the architecture and flagging attendance, when I saw her.

It was her. In the last row, very close to the exit. Even seated, her body rose practically to the height of the porter who was standing next to her. She was severely dressed as before, with that thick black veil over her face.

I was frozen in shock. But that was to my benefit, since my immobility gave me a few extra seconds to think. Instead of rushing to her wildly, this time, I decided to move slowly to the side aisle, where the darkness was even denser. Once I was there I stayed tight against the wall and moved discreetly among the shadows. But I realised that the veiled face was turning a few degrees. She had located me. I was sure that behind the black cloth two eyes scrutinised each and every one of my movements. I decided to stop. 'It's impossible that she's seen me,' I said to myself. 'Not for someone with the pupils of a cat,' I replied to myself. I took a step forward. In response, she stood up, but didn't move. I understood that she had established a safe distance. If I didn't respect it, she would disappear. What could I do? Not much. I put my hands together as if praying, begging her with that silent gesture not to run from me, that I didn't want to harm her. With one hand I wrote in the air with an invisible pencil. I was trying to tell her: I am the author of the book, I understand it better than anyone else. Behind me Norton was speaking to the court. I don't know what he was saying, I didn't care either. I made a small bow with my head, and then took a step. She remained immobile. I took two steps. She turned and left the room.

My God, what frustration. I was overcome with a horrible desire to scream and run, two of the things prohibited to me in this courtroom. She knew that I would have to travel the length of the aisle that separated me from the door more slowly. She took advantage of that time to create an insurmountable distance between us. I followed her out of the courtroom. But outside there was only an old porter. The man was between the massive stone columns that supported the building's archway. He was sitting in a small wooden chair that contrasted strongly with that gigantic frame of marble columns and stairs. I asked him if he had seen a tall women dressed in black. He told me that he had. I asked him what direction she had gone in. The man made a tired gesture with one arm, as if he was tossing down a card, and he said lethargically, 'That way.'

'That way' was all of London.

I tried to review the events that evening. I had plenty of reasons to feel guilty. Sooner or later Amgam had to appear at the trial, to offer support to Marcus. Why had I not realised before? Surely things are much easier to understand than to predict. It was also obvious that what I had done would keep her away from Marcus for the rest of the trial. I was even less proud of that. And there was an even more depressing aspect that had to be added to all that: it didn't take a genius to know that in those moments when she had stood by the door she was sending me a message. It would have been very easy for her to run away as soon as she had seen me approach. She hadn't. She had chosen to establish a dialogue. She wanted to show me her refusal. I had presented her with my credentials. And I had requested a hearing, and she had denied me one: 'Please, I don't want you to come near me.' That was her sovereign opinion and who was I to question it.

I spent the night sitting on the bed, my elbows on my knees and my head in my hands. And now a painful and honest confession: sometimes, as strange as it may seem, love and altruism move in totally opposite directions. In my case, at least. Or is there someone who thinks that my love for Amgam didn't rival Marcus's? Who ever said that love is pretty? Love is, above all, powerful. Love can distort our ethics just as an iron beam, so solid and hard, bends in a furnace. Rationally I wanted Marcus to be declared innocent. Of course I did. But a part of me was crying out for him to be executed. No one knew her as well as I did, no one else could get close to her with more knowledge of her situation.

Amgam was an extraordinarily intelligent creature. She had surely learned English by now. To speak it and read it. There could be no one more interested in reading the book than her. So, then, what was the exact reason for her categorical refusal? Had she not understood that I was offering her the kindest, warmest hand?

Maybe she had understood it, in the end. Maybe she was the only being on the planet that understood the feelings that moved the keys of my typewriter. And maybe precisely because of that, she refused to speak to me. Beyond security measures, perhaps there was an added reason for which she kept that distance: to show me that she was Marcus Garvey's woman, not mine.

Imagine that the love of your life is hiding under a billion stones. There's nothing worse. Or there is: that she lives around the corner and doesn't want to have anything to do with you.

A fortnight after it began, the trial against Marcus Garvey started to heat up again. There were more exciting witnesses called and, most importantly, we were getting close to the end. On the last day the crowd was so packed together it was as if we made up one impatient body; a pinch on one arm was felt by all the other arms. Unlike the first day, I had come very early and I sat on the first bench, right in front of the railing that separated the public from the court proceedings.

It was written in the stars that this would be Edward Norton's great day. I still admire the way he had manoeuvred to ensure that, on that day, all the mirrors were in position to reflect it. The press was there, the public was spirited, and the prosecutor was long defeated. He wasn't incompetent, not by any means, but from the first session he made me think of a boxer who had been promised that he would fight against a midget and finds himself in the ring with a titan. In one of his desperate attempts, he had been forced to resort to Casement's statement. My God, what a lame ploy. Casement had indeed been a brilliant diplomat. But here fortune played on Marcus's side. Casement was Irish, and two years earlier, in 1916, he had been one of the leaders of the Dublin revolt. Once he was arrested, to destroy him definitively, they had discovered irrefutable proof of his homosexuality. No one wept at his execution. With that record, and in 1918, what English court would have taken Casement's opinion into account? The war had reach its climax and the patriotic atmosphere was so fervent the colours of the Union Jack could be seen everywhere, even in restaurant butter.

Norton was waiting to bring Marcus to the stand. He condensed it all into a single question.

'Mr Garvey, what estimation does Mr Roger Casement deserve?'

Marcus was melodramatic enough to hold himself back for a few seconds, containing a broadside, and then he exclaimed, 'The same that any traitor to the Empire deserves. He should rot in hell until the end of time.'

Hats flew through the air. And in the midst of the euphoria, Norton moved towards the judge, with a hand raised holding up the thirty-seven ('Yes, indeed, Your Honour, thirty-seven') petitions for voluntary conscription that Marcus had presented since the war had broken out, all systematically refused by the military administration. Of course, Norton had advised Marcus to present all those petitions because he knew the army would never accept the petition of someone awaiting trial for murder. But it was very impressive seeing Norton handing those papers over to the judge in a masterstroke as excessive as it was unnecessary. In theory he should have handed them over to a porter, who in turn would have placed them in the hands of a secretary, who would have made sure the papers got to the judge. But it was Norton's triumphal march. Who could deny him that? Anyway, even if only to keep up appearances of convention, the judge banged and banged with his gavel, on the verge of losing his patience.

And now I need to interject. I still didn't know it, but the trial was won before it began. How? Norton was a member of one of the most exclusive clubs in London. Even though he was a man without great fortune or influence, it wasn't hard to understand why they would admit him. Someone like him had it written all over his face that sooner or later he would become a part of the patricians' circle. In the same way that a letter can be addressed incorrectly, sometimes fate makes mistakes too, and an individual is born in the wrong house. But letters eventually arrive at their destination, and men to their destiny.

In that club the most affluent society members established relationships and did business with the excuse of playing billiards or enjoying a glass of malt whisky. Norton was a member, and so was the judge assigned to the Garvey case. I am not alleging, not in the least, corruption. That wasn't Norton's style. On the other hand, the club was governed by unwritten rules that no one wanted to break. Since it was such a private place, where only the elite were admitted, the barristers from the large firms and the judges in charge of their cases often crossed paths there. In those cases they would politely avoid each other until the end of the trial.

One day Norton ordered one of his cognacs. He felt the need to sit at a round table with a four-hundred pound chandelier hanging over it. But when he noticed that the judge of the Garvey case was sitting in one of the chairs, he turned tail immediately. He didn't have time to get very far.

'Ah, Norton!' said the judge. 'Sit with us, please. I understand that professional discretion distances us. But I am told that beyond law you also write books. And since our companions at the table won't stand to hear us talking about legal rubbish, I don't think anyone will reproach us for talking about literature, which is the highest written art humanity can devote itself to, after jurisprudence.'

All those present, including two lords and a Member of

Parliament, applauded by clapping two fingers together, which was how the members of that select club applauded.

'I imagine that everyone has had the pleasure of reading our Mr Edward Norton's excellent work,' said the judge.

And during almost twenty minutes he devoted himself to sustained praise of the book. Norton understood it as a coded message that Marcus would be absolved. The judge was even more explicit; when it seemed that he was finished, he continued to expound on a case of legal philosophy.

'Dear sirs, are you familiar with the case of the Greek plank?' There was general negative murmuring among those present and the judge continued. 'It is an old dilemma faced by the Greek courts. Imagine a shipwreck on the high seas. Only two sailors survive, floating helplessly on the waves. They find a wooden plank. Unfortunately the plank can only take the weight of one of the two men. The shipwrecked sailors fight and finally the stronger overpowers the other and kills him. What sentence should that sailor receive?'

Norton knew the answer. But he stayed silent. The judge was in no hurry to make it public, and he sipped his whisky, very slowly.

'The are places, sirs, where the law has no place. There are acts that are beyond human jurisdiction,' the judge continued. 'Our laws can ask that men be honourable. But no law can demand that a man be a hero.'

He paused again. He took in a breath and said, indignantly, 'And now let us imagine the case of a man who has to struggle in coordinates beyond morality, beyond geography. And let us imagine, in addition, that his acts save the human race from a threat more serious than smallpox or German artillery. Should we condemn him for the fact that in that conflict two comrades were lost?'

The judge settled back into his armchair. According to Norton, he looked up at the club's ceiling the same way Moses might have looked up at the clouds when Yahweh gave him the tablets. And he said, 'I can tell you, and I don't mind saying it publicly, that while I'm judge no man will be condemned for an act of that nature.'

And those seated at that round table applauded enthusiastically. Could there be any doubt as to what the judge was referring? Since that day Norton only had one goal: to shine in the public sessions, so that Marcus's absolution would be a huge professional success.

Norton explained all that to me shortly after, as we were leaving the courtroom. But at that moment, while the judge pronounced the famous phrase, 'And the accused is free to leave this instant,' our joy could have resulted in a catastrophe. The book had cost me so much effort, Marcus being freed had seemed so improbable, that I couldn't help jumping over the railing that separated me from the dock.

'Oh, Marcus, my boy!' I said, taking his tiny body in my arms.

I hugged him, and in doing so I realised that I had never before hugged him, that it was the first time I had had any physical contact with him. My leap had taken the two policemen guarding him by surprise. But they didn't stop me. They couldn't, in fact. Marcus was a free man and whoever wanted to hug him could.

Many feelings, many of them contradictory, came together in that embrace. What are we men? A point in time and space. And in that point of time and space, so small and so twisted, in that point named Marcus Garvey, many things that affected me came together.

I wanted to believe that my inner struggle with the writing of the book had had a purpose that went beyond the literary: obtaining Marcus Garvey's freedom. But, objectively, that success distanced me from Amgam. It didn't take a genius to imagine what the couple would do next. If I were in his place I would flee to some tranquil island, where contact with other people was sporadic enough that no one would ask too many questions about Amgam's skin and eyes. Yet I wasn't upset. While I hugged Marcus I realised that the happiness I felt at having contributed to freeing him was greater than the sadness I felt at losing Amgam. And I said to myself that perhaps, in the end, the book had another objective besides freeing Marcus: making its author into something better than he was before writing it.

But that's enough about what I was feeling. When the judge declared Marcus's innocence a clamour of joy spread throughout the room. And since I had jumped over the railing that separated me from Marcus, the crowd didn't think twice and they followed me. My exuberance was interpreted as a licence to imitate me, and everyone wanted to touch the hero of the day. The problem was that the enthusiasm provoked a human avalanche. Remember that the room was packed, so packed that hundreds of people had followed the last session from outside. The trial had ended and the doors were opened. But instead of the people inside leaving, the ones outside rushed in.

All that enthusiasm had created a perilous situation. It was like a landslide, all the people in the room were leaning on us, the ones furthest in. There were only four porters in the room and a couple of policemen protecting Marcus. What could they do against a tide of bodies? The judge banged and banged his gavel. What an absurdity! The gavel was a perfect representation of judicial power.

Now that no one was willing, or able, to obey it, it was utterly insignificant. What was, after all, a judge's great sign of authority? A wooden implement that couldn't even crack nuts.

We were becoming more and more crushed against the wall. If someone didn't intervene, we would die suffocated by the pressure. Even the large desk the judge sat behind while presiding over the sessions overturned under the advancing human tide. Marcus, the judge and I ended up on top of that massive overturned piece of mahogany furniture. It sank among the bodies like a deflated lifeboat in the middle of a shipwreck, and we were fortunate to be able to clamber up on top. All around us were drowning bodies shouting for our help, too tightly pressed together to even move an arm. I realised that the people at the rear of the courtroom didn't fully understand the risk. They kept pushing with the blind obstinacy of sheep. We were all acting like irrational beasts. All of us? No.

When a hecatomb seemed inevitable, a voice was heard above the others. It was Norton. He wasn't talking, he was singing. I couldn't believe that someone as sober as him would do such a thing as sing in the middle of a crisis. He was reciting the national anthem and my astonishment grew even more. Norton was singing 'God Save the Queen' in the midst of an ocean of bodies!

He knew what he was doing. The first one to join him was a large woman, the one who usually crocheted. Then a young man, who had surely learned the words during military service. Norton moved one arm as if he were rowing, encouraging everyone to join in. It worked. Slowly the furious throng stopped, and the agitated crowd turned into a choir. The danger wasn't so much the crowd itself as the crowd's movement. The singing forced us to stop. Everyone was singing. Including me! To my surprise, my throat swelled and I sang 'God Save the Queen' with a passion I had never before felt for God or the monarchy.

Marcus was standing on the tipped-over table, higher than everyone and in full view. He was the point of reference for every eye. The muscles in his face were squeezed tightly and he was crying his eyes out. The danger vanished like an exorcised demon leaves a body, evaporating completely. I admit that tears fell from my eyes. Because at that moment, that packed room was much more than a room for the administration of justice. It was the place where a thousand people had poured out their most noble sentiments. There were men, women, children, young and old. There were the curious who had come to kill some time. And among the curious, there were rich people and poor people, saints and drunks. There may even have been bored German spies. We were all united by a song that represented something more than British monarchism, much more. We were all singing, and our singing declared that man's most honourable instinct is his protection of the weak. That day, the weak had won an unforeseen victory over the biggest forces in the universe. I became so emotional that I almost wiped my runny nose with the wig of the judge, who was sitting by my side.

Once the last note was heard, Norton raised one hand. He clambered upright on the table, hugged Marcus, and I think he was reading everyone's thoughts when he said in his brilliant and concise style, 'Now we must leave here peacefully. And once we get home, when we close the door behind us, we will rejoice in having come back better citizens that we were when we went out.'

And, thus, everyone left the room with the same serenity they might have felt leaving a cathedral after services. Norton, Marcus and I waited a little while longer for the room to empty. Then we left together. When we were at the door of the building, before walking down the enormous marble steps, we said farewell to Marcus. I couldn't help asking him what he planned to do with his life.

'The world is very big and I am very small. And now that I'm free I would like to travel around it a bit,' he said. And he added candidly, 'After all, it's the world I saved, isn't that right?'

Norton and I laughed. Marcus waved and went down the immense steps on his little wiry legs. I knew that those little legs were taking him to her. No one had ever been more envious. I turned my head.

I remained at the top of the stairs for a few minutes more. Norton told me the story of the club and the judge. Then we said goodbye. While he was putting on his hat, I heard Edward Norton at his coldest and most rational. The idea of singing the anthem had been his, so I congratulated him for having saved us.

'It's all a question of style,' he said. 'And that is the useful part of anthems: they are magnificent tools of group cohesion. In the case of an emergency they can turn urban beasts into docile flocks.' With that comment he pulled on his hat and walked down the stairs. 'See you later, Mr Thomson.'

As I headed home I couldn't get the image of Marcus and Amgam setting off for some remote country out of my head. A lifelong honeymoon awaited them. I thought of a story in which the protagonist was the mysterious Mrs Garvey. On the voyage she never comes out of their cabin and ends up arousing the suspicions of the other passengers, who insist on knowing who is hiding in there.

Unfortunately, Poe had already written a story that was very similar, I discovered later. I would never been able to convince the critics that my story wasn't plagiarised. In fact, the two stories were completely antithetical. In Poe's story the husband is transporting the body of his dead wife: death. In mine, Garvey is travelling with Amgam: life. When the passengers burst into the cabin of the man transporting a body, they are horrified. When they burst in on Marcus, they discover a woman born under a stone sky. But Amgam is Amgam. And the crowd, instead of lynching her, transform into more worthy, more tolerant, better people. Well, it doesn't matter. No one would have believed that it was an original idea and I ended up tossing it in the bin. But my story was better than Poe's. I wanted to at least mention that here.

TWENTY-NINE

ONCE, DURING ONE OF our sessions, Marcus told me about a scientific argument the Craver brothers had had. It happened during one of the more uneventful periods in the clearing, before the Tectons came. I don't remember the exact terms of the debate. I think it had something to do with the rotation of the planet. According to Richard, a marksman that shoots a bullet vertically into the air will never run the risk of being wounded by that bullet. In the brief lapse that the projectile would take to ascend and descend, the earth would have moved, and the projectile would fall at a certain angle with respect to the gun's barrel. To prove his point, Richard ended up shooting into the sky, in the position of someone starting a sprint.

That bullet went up, very high up. That solitary bullet went even further up than Marcus and Amgam when they climbed up into the great tree of their love. At some point the force of the ascent and the force of gravity must have equalised. In that precise moment, if the bullet had had eyes, it would have seen the Congo with more perspective than any of the characters involved in the drama in the clearing. Its fall would have also been more painful: he who has seen more loses more, and the more astounding the thing he's seen, the harder it is to give it up.

In a way I was that bullet. My instant of balance between the force of ascent and descent was right there at the courtroom exit. Like that bullet, I couldn't fall in the exact place I had come from, but the fall would leave me wounded.

In any case, in the days following the verdict, the only thing I thought about was setting my life on some constructive path. Thanks to that chain of events, the editor of the *Times of Britain* had promoted me. My new position wasn't up to much, but I let myself get absorbed in my work, devoting myself to it with the unrestrained energy of someone who had been promoted prematurely. The first problem that I had to face had a proper name: Hardlington.

The years have only confirmed for me an idea that the Hardlington case brought to light: that odious situations are more common than odious men, and that being around humiliated people ends up humiliating us. Once the hierarchical relationship between Hardlington and me was reversed, he went from being a despot to being a ghost. I couldn't take his perpetually contrite face, I found it morally intolerable, so one day I decided to deal with the situation. I could have called him into my office, but I chose to approach his desk, so that everyone could witness it.

'Mr Hardlington,' I said, 'I think we should have a brief conversation on the fundamental literary principles.'

When every typewriter in the room had stopped, I continued,

'I have read your complete works.' It was a lie, of course, but it sounded really good. 'And I think that you are making one mistake, only one but it is a decisive one. You are a great reader of the classics, but only of the classics. Think about this, none of the authors who have become classics wanted to be like the classic authors read in their day. They admired them, yes, but they didn't imitate them. On the other hand, Mr Hardlington, it is obvious that the greats cannot compare themselves to one another. To truly measure the value of a good author, what we need to do is compare him to bad authors.'

I held up a book with both hands; I extended my arms towards Hardlington as if I was making him an offering. It was an old one of mine and the worst of them all: *Pandora in the Congo*, the first assignment from Doctor Luther Flag.

'I am of the opinion, Mr Hardlington, that a good author has to follow his own path, far from the one forged by the classics. An author should never focus on the books he wants to imitate, but rather on the ones he doesn't want his to be like.'

And I finished by saying, 'The way I see it, Mr Hardlington, a good writer should only have one goal in his life as a narrator, only one: to never write this book.'

Things got better. Since I had written *Pandora in the Congo*, and I had publicly given Hardlington permission to criticise me, his humiliation was mitigated. He even regained some of his old petulance. But since he no longer had any power it wasn't hateful, just quaint, and our day-to-day relations improved immeasurably.

And that's how it was for a few more days. My increased salary allowed me the luxury of making plans for a future beyond the boarding house. I didn't know how to thank the MacMahons for their hospitality. Meanwhile Mr MacMahon took up reading the story of Garvey. He had never read a book, so I considered it an honour. Would he read it from start to finish or would he end up using it to steady the kitchen table?

My answer came soon. Two nights later MacMahon had reached the climax. I was asleep when I felt a hand shaking my shoulders.

'Tommy, Tommy! Wake up, son!'

I jumped, convinced that we were being bombed again, but before I could get out of bed MacMahon asked me, 'Who are these people?'

'What people? What are you talking about?' I said.

'The Tectons! What will we do if they decide to invade us? The Tectons are worse than the war, Tommy!'

The way he said it, it sounded like he had a Tecton under his bed.

'Mr MacMahon,' I informed him, rubbing my eyes, 'a book isn't finished until the last page.'

And I must say that when MacMahon had finished reading the book, he was more pleased than I was when I finished writing it. It was a Sunday morning.

'I finished a book! I finished a book!' he said, brandishing the copy like a trophy.

He was bounding about the dining room and his tribe of children danced around him delightedly without quite understanding why.

That same day, after lunch, we were still at the table when MacMahon said to me, 'Can I ask you a question about the book, Tommy? I'm very curious.'

'Ask away, Mr MacMahon,' I said.

He brought his head close to mine and asked me in a confidential tone, 'Remember the chapter where Garvey and Amgam are up in a tree?' He lowered his voice with a complicit smile on his lips, 'You know, when they're up in that giant tree touching each other and doing dirty stuff.'

'I remember perfectly, Mr MacMahon,' I informed him. 'I wrote the book.'

'Where was their toilet?' MacMahon asked me.

After a pause, I said disappointedly: 'This is your big question?'

'Well, I have a lot more, but that one's important, don't you think? Look, Tommy, I've made some calculations.' He showed me a sheet of paper filled with simple arithmetic. 'I multiplied the approximate daily amount of human excrement produced by two people over seven days, the approximate period that according to the book Garvey and Amgam were up in the tree together. And I got a lot! The question is: how could they stand the smell? If the tree were that big and dense, it would have landed in the branches below them. The heat must have made a horrible stench! How could they stand it?'

'I don't know!' I protested. 'The Congo is an immense humid place, the rains are torrential. Maybe they washed away all the filth!'

'No, no, no,' insisted Mr MacMahon with the perseverance of a termite. 'I consulted the *Encyclopaedia Britannica*, and when Marcus was in the forests of the Congo it was the dry season. It didn't rain or hardly at all! And it was frightfully hot! All that shite must have got in the way of any amorous stuff!'

I became a little annoyed. 'Please, Mr MacMahon! What do we stand to gain by destroying such a lovely scene?'

Mr MacMahon gave in. Or to put it a better way, he let it go. Since he looked disappointed, I suggested that he ask me some more questions. Maybe my answers would satisfy him more and that would put an end to the debate. Here MacMahon exposed an incredible quantity of formal defects. For example: on such and such a page Richard complained that he had no more tobacco, and then later on he smoked a cigar. Things like that.

'Yes, I know,' I said in my defence. 'Marcus's experiences in the Congo caused him to have an emotional collapse. I think that we have to be a bit indulgent with the minor details of the story. Anyone who had been fighting for his life, for his beloved and for the freedom of all humanity, would have been unable to retain such insignificant minutiae as the ones you are mentioning.'

I convinced MacMahon. But I hadn't convinced myself. I began to feel as if I was being interrogated by a prosecutor, a prosecutor a thousand times more sharp than the one Norton had had to go up against. MacMahon turned a few pages. Then he filled his lungs, large as barrels, with a whale's sigh, and he said to me with genuine candour, 'Tommy, why didn't the Negroes just run away? Do you understand it?'

'But, Mr MacMahon!' I put forward with a triumphant smile. 'They were shackled at the neck with iron stocks. Don't you remember?'

'No, no,' he corrected me. 'I'm talking about in the second phase, when they were turned into miners.'

That worried me. I was afraid that my description of the mine hadn't been clear enough. I explained to MacMahon that the inside of the mine was a spherical space with a hole above that was the only exit.

'Imagine some sort of skylight,' I said pointing to the centre of the ceiling with my finger. 'As much as we might try to scale the walls it would be impossible for us to get to the top, because we would have nothing to grab on to.'

'That's perfectly clear,' said MacMahon, 'but in the book it says that at night no one watched over that exit, or the anthill.'

'That's right. It wasn't necessary. It was enough to just take away the ladder. A solution as simple as it is ingenious! Don't you think?'

But MacMahon flipped through the book and shook his head. Finally he said, 'No.'

'No?' I said.

'No,' he insisted.

He continued flipping through the book with a grimace, as if it were the book and not me that had to resolve his questions. Finally he raised his head, looked at me with his little pug dog eyes and said, 'Look, Tommy, how hard would it be for those boys to climb up on each other? With a simple human tower they would have managed to get to the anthill. Don't you think?'

I didn't know what to say. All of a sudden I found myself making a gesture I knew all too well: I looked from one side of the table to the other. And I wasn't making that gesture because I was actually hesitating over something, but because I needed to buy time while I made up something to get out of the situation. I sensed some sort of indecent horror floating in the air.

'You know why that didn't occur to the two brothers?' And he himself replied, 'Because they were English. I know because I'm Irish. The English think that they rule Ireland because they are cleverer than the Irish. It's not true. They rule only because they are stronger. That's why they didn't think that a handful of

Negroes could conceive of such a simple escape plan. Because they thought that the Negroes were idiots. But they weren't idiots. Just slaves.'

MacMahon went back to examining the book, looking at it against the light as if he was going to find the solution somewhere, written in invisible ink. And he concluded, without looking at me, 'But why didn't the Negroes escape from the mine?'

I had no answer. In fact, I didn't have an answer to any of the questions that MacMahon had asked me that morning.

'Well,' I said, my mouth dry as I swallowed saliva, 'I am English too, Mr MacMahon, and I don't have anything against the intelligence of the Irish. Or the African's.'

'Oh, of course not, Tommy!' apologised MacMahon. 'You can be English and a good person! I'm only saying that the English, the good and the bad, think like the English. They never think like the oppressed because they've never suffered the oppression they impose on others.'

MacMahon turned a couple of pages and it was if a little light suddenly switched on. He looked at me with his eyes opened very wide and said, 'Now that I think about it, you interviewed Marcus Garvey.'

'Yes. Many times.'

'Then you, a good English person with great consideration for the African intelligence, surely must have asked him that question many times. What did Mr Garvey say about that?'

I couldn't stand being compared to the Craver brothers. Or maybe what I couldn't stand was not having the answers to such simple questions. Or the fact that I'd never thought to ask Marcus Garvey such an obvious question. I left the boarding house with the excuse of taking a walk, furious, after replying curtly and rudely. Poor Mr MacMahon. He still resents me for that.

I took a walk through the neighbourhood, smoking constantly. I was so upset that I lit one cigarette with the butt of the previous one. I wanted to get MacMahon's question out of my head but I couldn't. Why hadn't the Negroes escaped from the mine?

Before going back home I couldn't help stopping in front of the old boarding house, still in ruins. The building looked like a poorly made cake, and I could still make out the window of my room, now a rhombus. I was thinking about insignificant things when I felt a finger tapping on my right shoulder.

'Excuse me, is your name Thomson? Thomas Thomson?'

It was the local postman, accompanied by his pouch, his peaked cap and his inseparable bicycle. I confirmed his suspicion, and the man explained himself with a wide smile.

'I remember you very well, yes. You were the young man that cursed the Kaiser the day the zeppelins bombed that building.' He pointed to the boarding house in ruins. 'I arrived right at that moment to give you a notice. You were really angry! It's hard to forget such a young man.'

'Well, yes, it was me,' I remembered, smiling back at him.

Seen with the distance of survivors, the anecdote became funnier than it had been before.

'Pardon the interruption,' continued the postman, 'but shortly after I had to deliver another letter that was also addressed to you, Mr Thomas Thomson. Unfortunately, I didn't know what to do with it. They had evacuated the building and I had no idea where you'd been posted. I thought to myself that such an outspoken and decisive boy as yourself, if he ever found out that someone had written him a letter, he might come to look for it. Some day.'

I shrugged my shoulders.

'Thank you for your concern. But I have no family and few friends,' I said, 'so I doubt it was important.'

'It was,' insisted the postman. 'It came from a prison and the sender was awaiting execution. I know because it was a very famous name.'

The man got back on his bicycle. As he headed off down the street, he said, 'Well, as you wish. If you are interested, the letter is still waiting at the main post office. Do you know what? There are letters that have waited entire decades to arrive in the right hands.'

Why had I happened upon that kindly postman? When the German bomb destroyed the book it was inevitable that someone like Tommy Thomson would rage in the middle of the street. And my display had made the postman remember me, which made it practically inevitable that soon or later I would meet up with him again.

Why had that German zeppelin bombed us? Because we were at war with Germany. And why were we at war with Germany? For the colonies. Why the colonies? Because the colonies made countries and men rich. That's why the Craver brothers had gone there: to get rich. And if they hadn't gone I would never have written anything. It's all very simple and at the same time it's all very complicated.

From the postman's description I assumed he was talking about a letter from Marcus. 'Perhaps,' I said to myself, 'Marcus wrote me something after I went into the ranks.' I hadn't been able to say goodbye to him then.

I was wrong. The letter wasn't from Garvey. It was from Casement.

Casement couldn't have known that as he wrote me those lines I was sheathed in the uniform that he had fought so hard against and that, as a result, the letter would be stored away for two years. Remember that the letter made it to my hands in the autumn of 1918, and that Casement had been executed in 1916, when I was at the front. My God, that letter! I didn't open it in the post office. I remember that I went back to the boarding house, headed to the dining room and sat in an armchair with its back to the window. In the armchair facing mine sat Modepà, as usual. He was flipping through the latest issue of the *Times of Britain*, to which we had a free subscription thanks to my job.

No other letter, or anything else I have ever read, has moved me so much. Sixty years have passed and I can still recite it from memory.

This is what it said:

> Dear Mr Thomas Thomson,
> When you read these lines my body will have already served to stop twenty-four bullets. So I have little time left, and I don't want to waste it on laments. During the short time you and I spent together you seemed to be a young man whose virtue stood out above all the others: a love for the truth shone inside you. In any case these lines are not meant to convince Mr Thomson to try to change the sentence that weighs on me – an impossible task – but that of another legal case in which we have common interests.
>
> The Garvey case, which began before mine, will also end

later. Remember that I was one of the instigators for the collection of signatures within the European community in Leopoldville. All those good citizens, Belgians and British, signed a document remarking on Marcus Garvey's criminal nature. I know what you are thinking: that Garvey's defence will have a very easy time, now, destroying my credibility. It makes no difference. If my calculations are correct, Marcus will not escape justice that easily.

You must have already imagined – and if you haven't, I'm deeply sorry that you hold me in such low esteem – that a man such as myself would never be content to hand over to a court a simple list of signatures. I also have a witness to use against Garvey. But during the meeting that you and I had, the Irish Revolution had already begun. And my fate, triumph or defeat, was also written. It was defeat.

Now it is impossible for me to personally take care of that witness. Can I trust anyone but you? In my circumstances I have no other options. You should know that this witness has received my instructions to go to the address that you gave me. I hope you can offer him the protection that I am unable to give him. Make him take the stand, have him speak. I ask nothing more of you. I know that you are paid by Garvey's barrister. But I also believe that in this struggle of interests between your superior and justice you will choose justice.

One last thing: the man I am sending to you is a faithful, reliable and disciplined soul. I told him to go to your boarding house and not to move from there until someone attended him Christianly. And believe me, I ordered him not to move and so he will not move. Whether it rains or it's sunny, or if a thousand years pass. (So I ask you to keep a close eye out for his arrival.) Another thing: this man of ours has been given the strict order not to identify himself or speak about the Garvey case except in front of the right person. And how will this person (that is to say, you) identify himself? With a password. This one:

The Congo is the Congo is the Congo is the Congo.

Repeat this formula three times, for a total of the word Congo twelve times. Sorry, I'm not very original with passwords. But if any word can identify my witness it's that one. And common sense tells me to keep it simple as to avoid postal censorship; soon I will be a cadaver like any other, but in the meantime I am not a man like any other.

P.S. After reading this letter the authorities whose custody I am in have, very indulgently, determined that it doesn't contain political information and they have agreed to let it through. So they won't censure it and it will be sent to the address I have indicated.

May you live for many years and may justice grow up around you like a luxuriant leafy forest.

I had finished reading but the letter continued, in human form, in the seat in front of me. Mr Modepà.

'Your name isn't Modepà, is it?' I said.

Before I finished the sentence, while I was speaking, I realised that 'Modepà' was the phonetic translation of the French expression *mot de pas,* or 'password'. When he heard me, Modepà moved the *Times of Britain* from in front of his eyes with the same brusque gesture I had used when lowering the letter to my lap.

'You are Pepe.' He looked at me attentively and I said, 'You should be dead.'

He analysed my statement slowly, and finally said, 'No. I am alive.'

I stood up, offered him my hand and, with a shiver I was unable to hide, said, 'Mr Godefroide: I would be immensely honoured if you would allow me to buy you a drink.'

I took him away from the house. Why did I take him away? Surely because, deep down, I knew the truth and I was looking for a way to put off hearing it. We went to MacMahon's Irish pub, which had a private booth.

The scene that followed showed that the most dramatic moments of our lives could also be the most ridiculous. I knew Godefroide's real name, and therefore his identity. So, my saying the password was irrelevant. But he insisted on it with fanatical perseverance. He had orders not to tell his story to anyone until the person in question had said it, and he had been waiting for two years and he could wait for two more.

So I had to recite the entire password, but that repetition of the word 'Congo' seemed absurd. If Casement, wherever he was, was watching us, he would have killed himself laughing. Godefroide was doing all he could to help. 'That's it, you can do it,' said his face each time I said a 'Congo'. It became too much when, after that string of 'Congos', Godefroide looked up at the ceiling pensively and said, 'Sorry, could you repeat it? I've lost count . . .'

Somehow we worked it out. And when we had it all in order Godefroide revealed himself to be a real chatterbox.

'Mr Casement told me to go to the address of the old boarding house. According to Mr Casement sooner or later someone would show up and offer me lodging, and sooner or later someone would ask me about the password. And that's how it was.' He drank some whisky and continued. 'But instead of a building I found a pile a rubble, so I sat down and when someone showed up I repeated, *'Mot de pas? Mot de pas?'* But no one said the password. Until now. What took you so long?'

I wasn't at all sure I wanted to ask him the crucial question. But I didn't really have any other option. It was a miracle that we were there. Godefroide was seated before me and willing to speak. I had spent four years writing a book, always basing it on invisible characters, and now one had appeared. I only had to ask him one question, just one.

'Godefroide, what happened in the jungle?'

At first Godefroide's story was very similar to Marcus's. Godefroide had been hired by some white men, the Craver brothers, as their assistant on a mining expedition. They left Leopoldville with one hundred bearers. They went deep into the jungle through a tunnel hacked into the most aggressive vegetation in the world.

'One day,' continued Godefroide, 'when we were very, very deep into the jungle, the caravan stopped in a clearing. Young Master Richard was convinced that there was a large diamond mine there.'

'Diamonds? Are you sure?' I stopped him. 'They found a diamond mine or a gold mine?'

'Diamonds. Young Master Richard said that one could see gold and one could smell diamonds. And he smelled diamonds,' said Godefroide unwaveringly. 'We set up camp at the clearing. The Craver brothers slept in one tent, Marcus and I in another. The truth is that they only found two diamonds. But what diamonds they were! Each one was as big as a baby's fist. The night they were found Marcus was so nervous that he couldn't sleep. He kept turning on his cot, muttering, "Bloody hell, why do those two get to keep the two diamonds and I don't get any?" And I said to him, "I'm tired, Young Master Garvey, let's go to sleep." But he went on and on, "Bloody hell, why do those two get to keep the two diamonds and I don't get any? And I politely repeated, "I'm tired, Young Master Garvey, let's go to sleep."'

Godefroide's reiterations were starting to irritate me. I grabbed his forearm and said, 'Godefroide! What else happened?'

He opened his eyes extraordinarily wide. In that face so black, and with his retinas so yellow, his eyes looked like two fried eggs. 'Well, then Young Master Garvey said to me, "Shut up, you bloody nigger," and he left the tent with a lamp and a revolver and he headed towards the tent of the Young Masters Craver. He threw the lamp inside, any which way, to see them better, and I heard him fire six shots from his gun. I'd left the tent. I could see the two silhouettes of the Young Masters Craver outlined against the canvas. William was thinner and Richard was fatter. I could also hear them. They were wounded. They were crying and begging Young Master Garvey not to kill them. But Young Master Garvey, who was standing outside the tent calm as could be, reloaded the weapon with six more bullets. He shot the Young Masters Craver again, this time at closer range. All six bullets. But he still hadn't killed them. Young Master Garvey loaded again and shot six more bullets. First William, then Richard, then William, then Richard, then William, then Richard. When he was sure they were quite dead, Young Master Garvey turned round. He saw that I was behind him and he said, "And what the hell are you looking at, coon?"

But then he changed his attitude and said, "Wait a minute, Pepe, I want to talk to you about something." Young Master Garvey, when he was in a good mood, didn't call me a coon, he called me Pepe. But the truth is he was almost never in a good mood. I realised that he was pretending to be nice, but that meanwhile he was reloading the revolver. Why would he need to load it when the Young Masters William and Richard were already dead? That could only mean that he wanted to kill me as well, and since I didn't want him to kill me I ran into the forest as fast as my legs could carry me. Young Master Thomas!'

Godefroide had noticed that my palm was bleeding. My nails had punctured the flesh and it was bleeding. I was so absorbed in the story that I hadn't realised. I poured whisky on the wound and wrapped it up with a handkerchief.

'Godefroide,' I said. 'Why don't you explain it all to me?'

'All of it? What do you mean, Young Master Thomas?'

'All means all,' I said.

'Well, all it is,' obeyed Godefroide. 'I managed to get back to Leopoldville, but I didn't know what to do. I was terrified at the thought of seeing Young Master Garvey again in Leopoldville, and I was afraid he would accuse me of the murders. Since I am black and he is brown, the whites would believe him before me. One day I did see him walking along the streets of Leopoldville! I was very frightened, so frightened that I gave confession to a Belgian missionary. I confessed my sins, but above all those of Young Master Marcus Garvey. The missionary had known me for many years, and he also knew Mr Casement. The missionary urged me to speak to Mr Casement, and Mr Casement believed me. He told me to keep quiet, that if we wanted justice we had to be very crafty. Mr

Casement didn't trust the Belgian courts. But when he found out that Young Master Garvey had been arrested in England, he sent me money for a boat passage. I had to go there to testify in a trial. But that trial never took place. Then the war broke out and my trip was postponed many times. The rest of the story you already know. When I was able to leave, Mr Casement sent me a message. I had an address to go to where they would take me in. But I shouldn't give my statement until I heard the word "Congo" twelve times in a row from the mouth of the same person. Mr Casement did it that way so I could remember it more easily: the word "Congo", where I was born, and twelve times, like the twelve apostles of the Good Lord.'

'And what else? Where is the rest of the story?'

Godefroide didn't understand my impatience. He looked up at the ceiling, then turned to me and said concisely, 'That is all. Is there something else I should know?'

'And the white men?'

'All the white men of the expedition are dead, except for Young Master Garvey, who is brown and who killed them.' Godefroide was sincerely hurt when he asked me, 'Maybe I didn't explain it clearly enough? Young Master Garvey is a murderer and justice must be done. Young Master Thomson, your hand is still bleeding.'

I hated being called 'Young Master Thomson.' And he knew it. But insisting was futile. Godefroide was one of those men willing to offer his life for his superiors, but incapable of changing a habit even if the good Lord Jesus himself commanded him to.

The music passed through the wooden walls and reached our ears clearly. I didn't know that Irish music could be so sad. Godefroide had taken my hand. He undid the handkerchief and poured whisky on it from his glass. While he redid the bandaging he continued.

'I was very frightened, and when I ran away I didn't look back. I returned alone, through the jungle, and it's a miracle I survived. I ate mushrooms off tree bark, fruits that hung from branches, and I gobbled down grasshoppers as they jumped. I had to hide from the savages, because on the way to the clearing we had done ghastly things to them. Ghastly, Young Master Thomson, you can't even imagine! And I survived like that for a month! Young Master Garvey was a bad sort. On the trip out he liked to throw bombs of dynamite at the villages, just for fun. The Young Masters Craver, who wanted healthy bearers, would often scold him because he went too far and threw many more bombs than was necessary. He also made the trip back alone, like I did, but armed with rifles and sticks of dynamite, and no one would have dared go near him. He would have bombed even the lizards he came across!'

'So William wasn't killed by your fellow countrymen? They didn't hang him upside down so the rats would eat his brain?'

'Master William hung upside down?' Godefroide laughed. 'No, of course not! I can't even imagine anyone doing that to Young Master William. That was the punishment the Craver brothers applied to lazy bearers. Although the original idea for that punishment was Young Master Garvey's.'

'And what happened to the white woman?' I tried again.

'Oh, please, Young Master Thomson!' he said. 'What white woman are you referring to? On the expedition there were no women, much less white ones.'

'Go home, Godefroide,' I said abruptly.

At that moment the musicians paused. My change of tone and the musical silence disconcerted Godefroide.

'Did I say something wrong, Young Master Thomson? Are you angry with me?'

'Go back to the boarding house.'

He left. I ordered another double whisky, then another, and another. At first I said to myself that I was drinking because the whisky helped me to think. It was a lie. I was drinking because drinking helped me not to think.

Fear and phlegm accumulated in my chest in equal parts. My brain wanted to discredit Godefroide, or Modepà, or whoever he really was. I said to myself: he's an impostor; he's a deserter; it's a trick by Casement, a resentful sodomite; he's an uneducated Negro, don't trust him. But as I downed the last of the whisky, I realised that without fuel those ideas had no substance. I decided, 'I need to find more fuel.'

I left the pub. But instead of going back home I went to another drinking place. And when they closed it, another. Each place was worse than the one before. Finally I couldn't find anywhere else open. But I persevered in that dumb heroic way drunks have. In the docks I found an open pub, the worst of them all. It wasn't a pub so much as a hideout. All the women were prostitutes and all the men were thieves, or vice versa. I didn't care. I could get drinks in exchange for money.

The place was shaped like a laboratory tube, with a very narrow neck cut by a bar and a wider expansion at the end. It was packed with people, and the noise was so loud everyone shouted instead of spoke. I had to bawl into the waiter's ear to make myself understood. I asked myself why they would have such uncomfortable architecture. Even with the all the alcohol fumes fogging my brain I got it and I laughed.

It was the most abject, perverse and degenerate den in London. The regulars had to be always on alert for police raids. The tube shape allowed you to see the police enter from far away. The density of bodies would make it hard for the officers to move too quickly. Meanwhile, those being chased had time to jump through one of the windows that opened out on the other end of the tube, where the widened space seemed designed for people to be able to dance.

I had drank far too much. I had a spiralling thought. I thought that England had the largest empire in the world, which made my country the most evil in the world. I thought that London was its capital, which made it the most perverse city in the world. And since I was in the worst bar in the worst city in the worst country in the entire world, its regulars must be, logically, the worst specimens of the human race. Following this reasoning, then, the worst of the worst of the worst had to congregate at the bottom of the tube, far from the entrance and close to the window. I stretched out my neck from where I was, at the middle of the bar, to observe those representatives of the dregs of humanity and, naturally, there was Marcus Garvey.

He was dancing with an old prostitute painted like a tropical cockatoo. The music was created by a violin, heels that tapped against the wooden floor, hands that clapped without rhythm, and many voices tortured by tobacco. Marcus and the woman laughed. She laughed like a madwoman and Marcus laughed at her. The woman's dress was covered with stains, small and large, old and recent. I couldn't even imagine the variety of human liquids that must have come together to create that archipelago. Among the dancing men was one who was so drunk he couldn't stand up. But the throng didn't let him fall. He swayed from back to back, resting his head on some shoulder until two arms pushed him a bit further on, towards another body.

Marcus grew tired of the old woman and traded her in for a tankard of beer. The woman protested, so Marcus broke the tankard over her head. The people that noticed laughed. A mixture of blood, beer and pink dye trickled down the woman's head. She had been knocked unconscious but, like the drunk man, she didn't fall to the ground. Their heads hypnotised me. They both floated among a sea of shoulders, unconscious, moving like two spinning tops. Sooner or later they would meet up on some shoulder and kiss in oblivion. Then I said to myself, 'Wake up.'

I headed towards Marcus. But moving in that forest of chests and backs was impossible. I pushed without thinking, using my arms as crowbars and poking ribs with my elbows. Marcus saw me when I was only a few feet away. But in that place a few feet was an unattainable distance. He remained motionless like a lizard in the sun. Now he could see no one but me. And he was a different man: all of a sudden I saw his famous green eyes as pools of rotting seaweed. I had never seen him with that expression. It was an insolent hate, a hate as hard, concentrated and dense as a bullet. That expression was nothing like the sad, helpless face I had witnessed in our sessions. The racket made it impossible for us to hear each other, even though we were so close, so Marcus moved his lips very slowly, mouthing, 'You fucking bastard.' And he leapt through a side window.

I lunged after him. I could see his silhouette running into the docks, and before the fog swallowed him up I gave chase. The piles of unloaded goods created labyrinth-like passageways. Bundles, bales and containers of different shapes and sizes were heaped around us forming random circuits. Marcus tried to lose me in one of those cargo corners. His little legs ran at a surprising speed, as if impelled by an engine that was independent from the rest of his body. I had drunk too much. All I could do was run and yell, 'Come here, you bastard!'

I chased him for quite a while. Marcus was just a fleeting black form, some kind of human beetle. I was grateful for the black trousers and pullover that he wore, because otherwise it would have been impossible for me to see him through that fog, thicker than butter. Even so, he got further and further away from me. Those passageways were truly diabolical. I turned a corner and just had time to see him before he was lost again around the next corner. Sometimes the path forked and I couldn't find him on either side. In those cases I chose the route with less rats, supposing that Marcus must have scared them off on his way through. I didn't want to give in. But my nature made the decision for me.

All of a sudden I felt something breaking in my ribcage. I didn't know what had happened but I knew it was something very serious. I could barely breathe. The slightest movement was unbearably painful, as if my ribs were boring into my chest like red-hot irons. I slumped right there, leaning back against a container as large as a train carriage. (The next day the doctors told me that my lungs had collapsed. I needed an entire month of rest for them to weld together again.)

I don't know how long I sat there, hopelessly. If it hadn't been for the whisky, I would have howled in pain. The cold that November was particularly pernicious. And Marcus had escaped.

I looked up and noticed it was raining. But it was too narrow a stream to be rainwater. It took me a few seconds to realise that the liquid falling into my eyes was Marcus's urine.

He was on top of the container. He pissed for a very long time, calmly emptying his bladder. I didn't have the strength to stand up. I just moved my head so that the liquid fell onto the nape of my neck instead of my face. Then, as he buttoned up his fly, he asked me, 'Do you mind telling me why you are following me? Do you want me to kill you?'

The vapour from his mouth mixed with the fog. But his breath was shinier and greyer. And I could smell it. Each one of his words had a different smell. That voice was nothing like the one I knew. It had the tone of a criminal who knows he is invincible as long as he stays in his world of degradation.

'I talked to Godefroide,' I said. 'I'll make them reopen the case!'

Marcus didn't seem very impressed. 'My only crime was treating Englishmen like Negroes.' He spat with the wind and said, 'And you won't reopen anything, you idiot.'

'Yes I will,' I said defiantly. 'They'll hang you!'

He opened his eyes wide and laughed loudly.

'Me? But I saved the world! Don't you remember?'

He laughed like a hyena. Then he fell silent. When he opened his mouth an icy voice came out, 'If you come back around here, I'll eat your kidneys. And then I'll kill you. You don't know what the Congo is like.'

He jumped into mid-air and disappeared. I was still saying something, I don't remember exactly what. His acid voice replied. Through the night fog I heard him say, 'Norton, idiot! Norton!'

THIRTY

THE STORY OF THE death of Stanley, the great explorer of Africa, has always provoked contradictory feelings in me. Stanley was in his deathbed, from which he could hear the bells of a clock tolling. And one evening, after the last stroke of midnight, he mumbled, 'And that's time . . . it's so strange . . .'

Those were his last words.

Sometimes I can understand Stanley's insight: the most important thing about time is that time can decide not to be time. Sixty years ago I sat on the ground in the docks, humiliated, surrounded by fog and rats, with my lungs detached. It was sixty years ago and only a paragraph ago.

For an interminable hour I was unable to move my back from the wall of the container. I couldn't and I didn't want to. I didn't care about anything. The cold, Marcus's urine that ran down from my ears, even the rats, who had grown used to my presence and scampered around my feet. I thought about everything and I thought about nothing. It was as if my mind was a desert: I could have walked for entire days inside my head and the landscape would have always been the same.

But if at any point Thomas Thomson did anything that could be considered brave, it was that night when he stood up and headed towards Edward Norton's house. I could have gone back to the boarding house, but I chose to go to Norton's house. I couldn't get Marcus's last words out of my mind. 'Norton, idiot! Norton!' Now I wasn't sure if it had been Marcus or the wind. Whatever it was, Norton had some explaining to do.

I brushed back my hair with my hands and wiped away the yellow drops that fell from my nose with my sleeve. I moved mechanically. I had to stay straight and stiff, as if I had swallowed a broom, with one hand supporting my chest and the other supporting my back. Otherwise the pain was unbearable. Imagine that your thorax had become a bag of keys. It was a miracle I made it to Norton's office.

The sun hadn't yet come up, but a tenuous light began to overtake the city. If he was keeping his usual hours, Norton should be up.

He opened the door and said calmly, 'Do you know what time it is?'

I replied, 'Do you know who I just spoke with?'

He looked at me and knew immediately what had happened.

'Come in, Mr Thomson,' he said with textbook courteousness. 'After all, we haven't celebrated the success of our enterprise.'

When Norton closed the door behind me, I said, 'I would like to kill you.'

'Don't do it,' Norton replied, cool-headed. 'They'd hang you. And do you know why? Because the only barrister that could save you would be dead.'

He looked me over without speaking, and he concluded, 'No, you don't want to kill anyone. What you want is an explanation.'

He extended his arm towards the sitting room door and I went in. I sank into a wing-backed armchair. I was a wreck. Norton, on the other hand, had been interrupted in the middle of getting spruced up for the day. He turned his back on me for a moment in order to adjust his tie in front of the mirror. I took a good look at him and saw a more smartly dressed Norton than usual. His sock garters were silver, and his tie-pin was gold. Norton always wore an elegant waistcoat over his shirt, but I saw that this one was more expensive-looking.

'How do I look?' he asked, opening his arms. He must have read my face because Norton hastened to say, 'Have patience. You wanted an explanation of everything. Well, you're about to get it.'

I interrupted him. 'Why did you do it, Norton? What exactly did you get out of it? That's all I want to know.'

But Norton didn't want to listen to me. He was paying much more attention to the door and to the clock that sat on the mantelpiece. Without looking at me he said, 'Now I will ask you a question. What moves the world, Mr Thomson?'

I didn't say anything. Norton approached my armchair from behind. With all my weight still in it, he moved it a little, until it faced the door. He was standing beside one of the wings. He knelt down until his mouth was at the height of my head and he whispered, 'This race is extremely punctual.'

The clock marked seven in the morning. And the last stroke, in effect, coincided with the doorbell. As if in a dream, I heard Norton say, 'Come on in, my darling, the door is open.'

I had never stopped to think of something so basic: that besides Marcus Garvey and me, a third person knew the whole story, Edward Norton himself. Why couldn't he have fallen in love with Amgam as much or more than I had?

A thin black tower advanced towards us. Its hat looked like a gateau from which hung a black veil like a miniature theatre curtain. When the woman saw me she stopped cold. But Norton's gallant arm pointed to the armchair opposite mine while saying, 'Sit, my darling, he is a friend.'

I wanted to die. If Garvey had explained the story to Norton, his barrister, it was also logical that he would have put him in contact with her. While I dreamt of her, smoking on my bed in the boarding house, Amgam was sharing office hours with Norton. At night, while I suffered for the sentence that had not yet been handed down, Norton was sleeping with her.

Norton left his position beside my armchair and took an equivalent one beside hers. He raised the veil with four delicate fingers, slowly. The world stopped. The only thing that moved was the veil. And when it was raised, Norton asked me, 'You know her, don't you?'

I curled up a bit more inside my seat. Of course I knew her. At the *Times of Britain* I had written the caption to many photographs where that woman appeared, accompanied by her husband or alone. It was Berit Bergström, the wife of the Swedish businessman imprisoned for his treachery. It wasn't Amgam.

'Now you have your answer,' said Norton. 'Prestige moves the world. And now I'm the barrister of the Garvey case. The Garvey case has turned this practice into the one with the best reputation in London. My clients are the *crème de la crème* of the country. Mrs Bergström is an example of the new clients I now attend to. She even went to the trial one day to be sure she had hired a good barrister. By the way, did you know that Mrs Bergström's husband is awaiting trial in the same prison as Garvey?'

There was a long satisfied pause until he resumed, 'Prestige, Thomas, prestige. Barristers want prestige to be successful. In a certain way they complement each other, don't you think?'

I couldn't take my eyes away from Mrs Bergström, I was transfixed. Without looking at Norton, I said, 'I thought that you were only moved by money.'

'It is prestige that moves money. If you were a multimillionaire with serious legal problems what practice would you turn to? And how much would you be willing to pay to be freed from prison?'

He sighed happily. 'If one wants to get rich one should never go after money, one has to get money to go after him. And do you know something, Mr Thomson? Renown is the shepherd of capital.'

A vestige of professional curiosity led me to ask him, 'Marcus didn't make up the story about the Tectons all by himself, did he?'

'No,' confessed Norton. 'Garvey was an incredibly limited person. He followed my instructions.'

He was talking about Garvey as if he didn't exist, as if he had vanished from the world long ago. For Norton, for whom reality was confined to legal files, perhaps that was the case. Norton looked out the window. A ray of sunlight entered the office, announcing the new day. He sat in a third armchair, alongside Mrs Bergström. He threw his head back and stared at the ceiling. Now he spoke with his eyes closed.

'We had no chance of winning the case. So I thought of an extralegal strategy. It occurred to me to raise public opinion in our favour. A remote possibility, but the only one within our reach. In that sense the book was the last recourse that came to me. I explained the story to Marcus in chapters. He rehearsed them in his cell. He rehearsed over and over again, until he was convincing. When you think about it, he didn't have much else to do. When he was younger he had been an actor and I convinced him to act well. His life was at stake. I made it very clear that we had no other possibility besides the book to get out of this one.'

Norton opened his eyes and, without blinking, told me in the most inhuman voice I had ever heard, 'If the book wasn't successful enough and didn't stir public opinion, they would just hang Marcus. But if it was successful, I would win the case and legal glory.'

I didn't have the energy to say anything. I felt like an oil stain in the middle of an ocean. And oil stains don't speak, they just float. I looked at our companion. The woman had gone to prison to visit her husband. She hid under mourning clothes, simply, because people don't like to be recognised when they are in a queue at a prison. Especially the rich. The mysterious friend that visited Marcus wasn't Amgam, it was Norton, who dictated chapters to Marcus. The woman wasn't Amgam. Marcus Garvey was a murderer. Norton was an ambitious barrister, so ambitious that the financial gain from the book wasn't enough for him. With the fame he had acquired from the Garvey case, rich clients would make him richer. Nothing more.

Norton made his familiar finger pyramid. And he said to me, with sincerity, 'I felt great literary admiration for the chapters you gave me. The story that I explained to Marcus was very thin. But you had an immense capacity to endow it with force. You raised it to its natural ceiling. The human soul is extraordinarily subjective. That's literature, I suppose: turning the dregs of humanity into gold. This case deserves an essay.'

I should have said that the essay was our book. I didn't. I didn't feel anything. Maybe I hadn't had enough time to hate him. Or maybe, I was simply exhausted and hung over. Norton took a step forward, trying to defend himself from an accusation I didn't make.

'You should know that I am protected by many arguments. On one hand, I am genuinely against the death penalty. A British court would never have done justice in a case like this. And I believe that any European should be exonerated for what he has done in exotic latitudes, just as the judge said. As for the rest, I'm sorry to have involved you, I couldn't explain all this to you until you had finished the book. You had to be excited about the story, otherwise you wouldn't have been able to make it credible. And the only weapon I had to assure me that you would give it your all was elevating the book to a just cause.'

Mrs Bergström coughed slightly. Besides that, it was as if she weren't there. I asked, 'And the woman?'

But Norton was too engrossed in his world of arguments. He continued explaining and reflecting, avoiding me, looking at the wall as if he were defending himself from a vague accusation, without any real substance, and thus impossible to refute.

'You left me no choice but to redo Marcus's story,' he asserted. 'That day, when you told me that you had given a copy to the Duke of Craver, I was forced to change my strategy. Until Mr Tecton appeared it was all more or less true.'

We had reached a point where principles such as justice, truth and liberty mattered very little to me. I insisted, 'Yes, but what about the woman?'

He wasn't listening to me. He was contemplating, rubbing his chin with one hand.

'That doesn't change the fact that we have freed a murderer, obviously . . . On the other hand it was a murderer of murderers in a time of murders . . .'

Norton had lowered his voice so much that his last words were practically inaudible. Suddenly he turned to me, as if he had just woken up, 'The woman? Pardon, what woman?'

And I, with a patience, kindness and delicacy that left my own mouth hanging open, insisted, 'The woman in the book. The protagonist. Where did she come from?'

'Oh, yes. The woman,' said Norton, as if he were recovering a lost thread, running two fingers over an eyebrow. 'I stuck her in as I went along.'

I remember that I stammered a bit. I wanted to say something, but it seemed as if my mouth had been injected with poison. Miraculously I was able to articulate, 'Some day everyone will know that it was all a lie.'

Norton shook his head.

'People aren't interested in the facts fitting perfectly to the truth,' he said. 'What they want is to be moved.'

'But they'll know it was all a lie,' I insisted. 'Before or after.'

'After what?' said Norton, surprised. 'There is no after. The case is closed.'

But I didn't give up. 'Some day,' I said, 'they will fully explore the centre of Africa. And they won't find any trace of the Tectons.'

'Yes, Tommy, someday,' said Norton. Now he spoke with grave

compassion. 'And that day they will continue congratulating you for the book's literary merits, not me. And if some day, although I doubt it, they decide to accuse someone of false testimony or falsified documentation, it will be Thomas Thomson, not me. Because you are the author.'

Norton looked at me in a new way. It made me think of an eagle that has eaten too much, looking down from his perch on a rabbit far below. He flattened his thin moustache with a finger and said, 'I remember that the objective of your last visit was to demand your legitimate rights as the author. Isn't that so?'

Even when he said that, I couldn't hate him. I felt a strange moral apathy. As if the truth had the virtue of liberating me from any passion. What's more, I understood that for someone like Norton disloyalty was just one of the forms his deviousness assumed. He had nothing against me, of course.

I could only look at Mrs Bergström. She was a tall Nordic woman, nothing more. While I observed her I asked myself if my lack of response was due to something more than fatigue and pain.

'But you are a man without imagination,' I said. 'How could you think up such an elaborate story?'

'Who? Me?' asked Norton, sincerely surprised. 'I didn't think up anything. I am a man without imagination, as you say. Besides legal documents I am uninspired.'

'And so?'

'Well, you, one day, told me about the primordial function of the literary outline. So I used a book by Doctor Luther Flag as a literary outline. And I did it as faithfully as I could.'

'Doctor Flag?'

'Yes. *Pandora in the Congo.*'

When I remember that moment, sometimes, I hear the bells of Big Ben tolling. Was it that way or do I just remember it that way? Did the clock strike just as Norton revealed that he had followed a secret outline, an outline called *Pandora in the Congo*? I don't know. It's been a lifetime since that encounter, and I am no longer certain of the details.

'The day we set up our contract I showed it to you, don't you remember?' continued Norton. 'You were the author. It seemed adequate as a manual. I only had to retouch the characters. I adapted Marcus to the missionary who suffered a spiritual crisis. Simba the lion, the main character's friend, turned into Pepe. The Cravers are the two legionnaires that defend the camp to the death. In *Pandora in the Congo* the pygmies were tree dwellers. In the book I changed them into Tectons because I don't know anything about African tribes, and I was afraid that Garvey would make too many ethnographic mistakes. But what African race could I choose? None!' protested Norton, suddenly indignant. 'Any tribe that he could mention would surely be the specialty of some anthropologist. I consulted the encyclopaedias, and even the most remote tribes in central Congo were well researched. I couldn't take the risk that Marcus would say something stupid that could be refuted in the trial by some suspicious Africanist. And I thought, "Where can I hide a tribe that no one, not even the anthropologists know about?" I could only come up with one solution: if the pygmies were tree dwellers, the Tectons would live below ground. I have interrogated too many witnesses not to have learned a singular lesson: that the most credible lie is always the biggest one . . . Why are you looking at me like that?'

Norton had become animated. He was standing up straight and

gesturing energetically. He looked like someone explaining to a friend what good times he had devoted to his hobby.

'You asked me before about the woman. In *Pandora in the Congo* there's a princess. I talked it over with Marcus, because I wasn't sure what to do. On one hand we needed a female protagonist, in order to follow Flag's outline. But incorporating a love story seemed overly melodramatic. I hesitated, as you say I am not a novelist. The only thing that we wanted was an alibi that would acquit Marcus. I didn't know what to do. And finally I said to Garvey, "Look, Marcus, have a girl come out of the mine. If Thomson likes her, let her live. And if you see that he doesn't like her, have the Craver brothers kill her, for whatever reason. Improvise." And he said to me, "Oh, don't worry, Mr Norton. I've got this poor devil's number. The secret is telling him what he wants to hear. Every day, when we start our session, I just encourage him a little bit so that he himself tells me where the story should go. I tell him what he wants to hear, and that's it."'

'And that's it,' I said.

Norton stopped dead. As incredible as it may seem, he still hadn't realised that I could find his words offensive. His body suddenly jerked, aware that he was acting cruelly. But he couldn't help a timid smile, like someone remembering some insignificant, pleasant detail. He said, 'Garvey often rebelled. One day I showed up with a pile of pages that you had written and I said to him, "Garvey, there's an inconsistency here. In all these pages, and there are many, you never mention any cannibals' pot. I want one of those pots, round and big enough to boil up two men in there." Garvey replied that in Africa he had never seen one of those pots. That at the camp they used quite large aluminium military pots, but nothing as big as what I was describing. "I don't care," I said. "In Doctor Flag's book there is a pot, do me the bloody favour of telling Thomson there was one at the camp." But Garvey refused, had one of his tantrums, like a spoiled child. He said that they would never have been able to transport such an enormous oval pot, that they were already very loaded down. He said that in our story Africans barely appeared. And that in the Congo he hadn't met any African cannibals. So, why on earth would they cook at the camp with a bloody cannibal pot? "How can you write an African novel without a cannibal pot?" I had to threaten him. "Either tell Thomson about a big pot that you had at the camp or you can find yourself another barrister!"'

I didn't respond. He felt obliged to add something else. His gaze turned me into a transparent object. 'You didn't know it, but we were a good team. For example: one of the literary problems was the character of Pepe. In *Pandora in the Congo* Simba the lion returned and saved the main character *in extremis*. Fine, so I had Pepe return to the clearing to rescue Marcus. But as you probably remember, in *Pandora in the Congo* Simba ends up in London Zoo. For obvious reasons we couldn't allow Pepe to end up in England. I didn't know what to do. Marcus took responsibility of finding an end for the character. Torturing and killing him, of course.'

Norton paused. Since I remained mute, he commented, 'Garvey was a cruel creature. We can put hyenas in cages, but we can never domesticate them. I often butted heads with him. He wasted three entire sessions, for example, talking exclusively about his supposed sexual exploits with the female protagonist. I shouted at him,' and here Norton pointed into thin air as if Marcus was still in front of him, '"Behave yourself, Garvey! Don't stray from the script! Doctor

Flag ties up his protagonists on separate stakes to avoid the temptations of the flesh. And look what you're doing!" But he laughed, and he said, "Oh, shut up, you don't know how boring it is in here. Let me have a little fun with that poor devil Thomson."'

'Before, you said that barristers and novelists complement each other well,' I cut him off suddenly. 'There is a difference. Novelists' lies don't hurt anyone.'

Norton opened his arms and counter-attacked, 'But, don't you understand, for God's sake? That turns your book into a real literary work. Until now you were just a chronicler from a distance, a journalist of secondary sources. When it's consecrated as a work of fiction it will be a novel in every sense of the word.'

Here I wanted to respond, but every time I tried to say anything I stopped myself just as the words were about to cross my lips. Norton respected my silences. Since I was still half drunk and my lungs had collapsed, it became more and more evident that I wasn't going to manage to express myself with the plenitude the situation demanded. Norton smiled. His speciality was leaving his dialectical opponents speechless. I had to struggle to hold myself up, even seated in the armchair. How could I talk? But Norton was wrong. Finally I was able to concentrate the entire matter into three words. And, like a child that spits out a poorly chewed mouthful of food about to choke him, I vomited out, 'You tricked me.'

Norton's face contracted like a sponge. Why did he place so much importance on my accusations? I don't really know. Maybe it ruined the resolution of the Garvey case for him, which was masterful, a perfect legal conspiracy. Or maybe he didn't want to hear any voice that reminded him of the ultimate essence of his profession.

He sat down again. Beneath that apparent calm hid a barely contained displeasure. I had truly offended him. I had never noticed, but he was a man with very long extremities. His arms extended beyond the arms of the chair. The tips of his fingers grabbed the velvet. In that position he looked like a pharaoh about to pronounce a sentence. Finally he spoke.

'Love stories, as enchanting as they may be, always create problems, a multitude of problems. On the other hand, when a love story is perfect it has one problem, just one: that it's a lie.'

Possibly Norton wanted me to interrupt him, that we talk about something, anything else. But I didn't. I didn't want to spare him the sentence.

'You are an intelligent, talented and well brought-up person,' he continued. 'Now answer a question frankly, just one. Tell me something, Mr Thomson: did you not doubt Garvey's credibility at any moment? Did you really believe that entire story of underground races and ladies the colour of cheese with hot skin?' Norton made, for the last time, the pyramid of fingers that ended at his nose. 'Did you believe Garvey's story because you wanted to save him or because you had to write a novel? The heroine: did you love her because of what we can read about her in the book? Or is she so seductive in the book because you wanted to love a woman like her?'

I didn't answer. I didn't want to answer. I can only say that more than sixty years have passed and I still haven't been able to answer. The answer to that question is, in fact, this book.

I wanted to leave. I had trouble keeping my balance, as I got up from the armchair, like a boxer that doesn't want to admit he's been knocked out. Norton also stood up. He reverted to the kind host that accompanies guests to the door. And he said, with his hands in his pockets, relaxed and calm, 'Tommy, can I ask you one last thing?'

I didn't have the energy to refuse. I could barely locate the door, which spun in front of me like a top.

'In *Pandora in the Congo* there is a concept that I don't understand,' he said. 'I never dared to ask you about it because I was afraid that you would then make the link between the two stories. Well, I suppose that doesn't matter now.' He wrinkled his brows, seriously absorbed, and asked me, 'What on earth is the Spore Theory?'

I don't recall any more of that dreadful conversation. I can't even remember how I got out of the house. I only remember that as I crossed the threshold it occurred to me to think out loud, 'Can you imagine the laws of the universe having been written like this? The declarations of independence, King's wills, our holy books. Imagine they were all the work of a ghost writer, and that behind the ghost writer lay nothing? Or at most, a writer of bad outlines.'

Norton passed a very long arm over my shoulder. He was trying to be affectionate, but had the mechanical compassion of a doctor administering chloroform. That arm comforted me and pushed me out of his house.

'Trust me,' said Norton, 'don't think about things like that.'

Once I was out on the street he added, 'Everything is a question of style.' And before he closed the door, 'Farewell.'

The light of the new day hurt my eyes. I took stock of myself: I was a wreck, dirty, drunk and my lungs ached. My cheeks felt like used sandpaper. My tobacco breath disgusted me. I only thought of her, her, her. Do we stop loving a person when we realise that they are dead? Why should we stop loving them when we realise they were never born?

I stumbled through the streets and they all seemed the same to me. At first it was a distant buzz. Then a shouting framed by drums and trumpets that became clearer and clearer. Without wanting to, attracted by the sound, I approached the source of the music. I arrived at a large avenue. Before I realised it I was immersed in a joyful crowd. The Great War had ended. Everyone was celebrating. The Great War had ended, and the world's pain had vanished along with it. The crowd trapped me like an octopus. They didn't let me past.

The people were happy. Norton was happy. Garvey was happy. Everyone was happy. I wanted to go home. What could be lonelier than a sad man in a crowd celebrating victory?

The Congo. A green ocean. And, below the trees, nothing.